PRAISE FOR *THE LITERARY UNDOING* OF *VICTORIA SWANN*

"Virginia Pye's novel invites us into a distant era that—in its depiction of the challenges faced by women of letters —seems hauntingly familiar. But Victoria Swann persists—and prevails! The story of her undoing is generous, fierce, and inspiring."

—Jennifer Finney Boylan, co-author (with Jodi Picoult) of *Mad Money*

"How could I not fall in love with Victoria Swann, the wildly successful lady author who is determined to escape her best sellers? Although she never leaves Boston, Victoria's story is as full of dangers and dragons as one of her novels. Surely all readers will want to find the bookshop where she works and join the Swann bookclub? *The Literary Undoing of Victoria Swann* is a captivating and delicious novel."

—Margot Livesey, author of *The Boy in the Field*

"*The Literary Undoing of Victoria Swann* is a book lover's delight—by turns hilarious and scathing in its cultural critique, this meticulously researched novel exposes the unseen and sometimes unsavory under-belly of Boston society and literary publishing. The adventures and dreams of Victoria, a brilliant and irreverent romance novelist from more than a century ago, will resonate with readers today."

—Kerri Maher, author of *The Paris Bookseller*

"Virginia Pye has written a novel as full of vital ideas about truth, progress and how to live with intention as it is with wild romps and charming encounters. *The Literary Undoing of Victoria*

Swann may be set in Gilded Age Boston, but it's a celebration of readers, writers and bookstores everywhere."

—Elizabeth Graver, author of *Kantika*

"*The Bostonians* meets *Writers & Lovers* in Virginia Pye's gossipy and substantive historical novel about women authors and book publishing. Compelling, fierce, and utterly charming, Victoria Swann is a literary heroine for the ages."

—Laura Zigman, author of *Small World*

"Boston on the cusp of the twentieth century and its vibrant literary world are rendered in evocative detail in this entrancing ode to how books can save us. As Victoria navigates her place in society, she learns to live and write her truth at a time when women are mostly unseen and unheard. Filled with grace, charm, and an acute sense of place, *The Literary Undoing of Victoria Swann* shows us the power of stories to connect, heal, and reveal our hearts."

—Marjan Kamali, author of *The Stationary Shop*

"Witty, intelligent, and exuberant, *The Literary Undoing of Victoria Swann* is a love letter to all of us who cherish books, writing, and writers themselves. It's also an engrossing and empowering historical novel of liberation that reminds us, with deep resonance, of the many ways in which we are still not free."

—Christopher Castellani, author of *Leading Men*

"At the heart of this insightful novel lives Victoria Swann, a wildly popular author who yearns to jettison the unrealistic romance and adventure of her nineteenth century novels in favor of depicting the struggles of ordinary women, a topic not discussed in high society let alone portrayed in literature. As the scaffolding of her comfortable life begins to crumble, Victoria discovers the power of authentic relationships and the strength of her own convictions. At once an historic time capsule and an entirely modern tale, *The Literary Undoing of Victoria Swann* had me cheering for its heroine straight through to the final page. You'll love it!"

—Katherine A. Sherbrooke, author of *Leaving Coy's Hill* and *The Hidden Life of Aster Kelly*

"From the first page of this delicious, fizzy novel, I was totally immersed in the adventures of lady author Victoria Swann, a heroine with wit and grit who is determined to follow her artistic passions and live her life with intention. Delightful, fresh, and surprising, *The Literary Undoing of Victoria Swann* is a rollicking feminist tale that brings the Gilded Age vividly to life while exploring themes that are still strikingly relevant to women today."

—Whitney Scharer, author of *The Age of Light*

THE LITERARY UNDOING
OF VICTORIA SWANN

Virginia Pye

Regal House Publishing

Published by
Regal House Publishing, LLC
Raleigh, NC 27605
All rights reserved

ISBN -13 (paperback): 9781646033973
ISBN -13 (epub): 9781646033980
Library of Congress Control Number: 2022949420

Cover images and design by © C. B. Royal
Author photo by Margaret Lampert

Regal House Publishing, LLC
https://regalhousepublishing.com

Printed in the United States of America

For my mother, Mary,
my sister, Lyndy, and my daughter, Eva,
each a heroine of her own story

Lovely weather so far. I don't know how long it will last,
but I'm not afraid of storms,
for I'm learning how to sail my ship.

— Louisa May Alcott, *Little Women*

PART ONE

ONE

On an overcast afternoon in April, Victoria Swann stepped from a carriage onto a brick sidewalk in Beacon Hill. Under her boots coursed rivulets of slush and mud, evidence that Boston had survived yet another winter. She gripped the iron handrail and climbed the steps to her publisher's door. Lifting her face into tepid sunlight, she felt the early spring air brush her cheeks. She was a mountaineer, high at the peak and flush with accomplishment. In her carpetbag lay the start of an altogether new sort of novel, unlike any of her previous ones. She lifted the knocker and struck it against the brass plate. Her writing had gotten her into this mess, and it would have to get her back out.

The door swung open, and her editor's gangly clerk bowed and moved out of the way.

"Welcome, Mrs. Swann, welcome."

Victoria prepared for the fanfare that greeted her at Thames, Royall & Quincy. Her editor would serve her favorite pastries, and as she sipped tea, the young clerks would circle around as if she were that rare snow leopard Mr. Barnum paraded about the country. But who were these young men who liked to toss furtive glances her way? Aspiring editors, they were never the best-looking specimens, their posture weakened from hours bent over manuscripts. But at least a husband of this sort wouldn't go missing for days. These fellows were decent. They were, after all, book lovers.

Victoria craned to search for them now but sensed something amiss. She stood alone in the Spanish-tiled vestibule with the brass hat stand and chinoiserie umbrella holder. Not a soul in sight, she deposited her parasol with a disappointing *thunk*. Down the hall, she spotted the bustle of a ruby-colored dress and an equally startling mane of flowing red hair. A handsome gentleman with his own abundant silver mane followed. Victoria watched them disappear into an office while her bald-headed editor, Frederick Gaustad, waddled after them, cigar smoke in his wake.

A moment later, several stray assistants passed close by and Victoria caught the eye of the gangly one who had let her in. She asked him what was going on.

"It's terribly exciting," he said, coming to take her things. "Miss Pennypacker is paying us a visit."

"The dance hall singer?"

He bobbed on the balls of his feet. "Yes, she's writing an advice book for young ladies and we're to publish it."

He invited Victoria to take a seat in the front parlor and said that Mr. Gaustad would be with her shortly. She strode onto the Persian carpet but didn't know which way to turn. She couldn't possibly wait contentedly on the deep leather sofa. Was it true that Thames, Royall & Quincy planned to put out an advice book by someone other than Mrs. Swann? And why was she being corralled into the waiting room like a traveling salesman or, God forbid, an aspiring author?

In the gold-framed mirror above the mantelpiece, Victoria caught a glimpse of herself. It took only a fraction of a second to spot the frown lines at the corners of her mouth and the pinched redness around her eyes from too much reading and writing. She tried to recall the girl she had been a dozen years before when, unable to resist her own pretty reflection, she had stood on tiptoes to see herself in the glass. Full of gumption and more excited than nervous, she had been sure that good things were about to come her way. And they did. A robust Frederick Gaustad had made a quick assessment of her first romance and adventure novel and promptly decided to publish it. Victoria's life had changed that day and was never the same.

A much-changed Gaustad appeared in the doorway now. More rotund than ever, he limped to greet her and emitted a slight groan as he bent to kiss her hand. How astoundingly delicate oversized men could be.

"Lovely to see you, my dear."

"Good to see you, too, Frederick."

"I only wish it were more often." He waggled a finger at her. "Your readers are always eager to hear from you."

"My readers hear from me as often as humanly possible." Victoria forced a smile. "Any more frequently and my hand would drop to the page, pen fallen from a lifeless grip. You wouldn't want that, now, would you?"

"Ever so dramatic! But I don't see how you manage without the use of a typewriter. You know how it slows you down."

"I'm anything but slow. It's the constant deadlines you set. My poor assistant, Dottie, pounds away to do her part. I can't imagine the chaos of two machines clacking at once. But come now, Frederick," Victoria said and held out her elbow for him to take. "Don't we have other things to discuss? I'm here for my final edits."

"Yes, of course. And whatever your methods, we're grateful for the outcome." With a feeble hand, he steered her toward his office door. "We're counting on you. You're my special girl."

He squeezed tighter and Victoria was glad that his vigor had returned, though then he began to cough and pulled a handkerchief from his pocket.

"Your illness is back. You should see a doctor."

"Doctors!" Gaustad said, putting away the cloth. "The only one I've ever liked was the fellow who saved the day in one of our early Mrs. Swann's. Remember how splendidly we did on that one?"

Victoria did remember. The doctor who had saved the day had used indigenous medicines concocted by female spirit healers of the jungle. She had learned all about those remarkable women and their magical substances at Harvard's Peabody Natural History Museum. Sadly, the skills of those Amazonian women had been lost not only on her editor but her readers as well. According to Gaustad, the interior plate depicting the heroic doctor in an open-necked shirt had been the cause of the stampede at the booksellers.

But Victoria didn't remind him of any of that now for she had started to sense that her editor was losing his grip and not only on her elbow. As they entered his office, he babbled apologies about the state of his headquarters, which was, as ever, a bookish mess. Muscular, glass-fronted cases with scrolled pediments loomed from floor to ceiling, the shelves several deep in leather-bound books. Papers and thick portfolios lay strewn across the massive desk and matching credenza. Heaps of other manuscripts pooled in the corners. A potted palm, added for civilizing effect, drooped over its parched soil.

Gaustad called out and a young lady with impeccably coiffed hair and a trimly tailored jacket hurried in. She snatched up full ashtrays and kicked crumpled balls of discarded paper under the desk. Victoria observed that girls these days had to perform a vast array of duties while bone stays poked their flesh, stiff material squeezed their midsections, or cumbersome bolts of fabric tripped them up. She would encourage Dottie to dedicate one of Mrs. Swann's upcoming advice columns to the absurd challenges faced by corseted and constrained women trying to compete in the work force.

But for now, Victoria took a seat in the cracked leather armchair the young lady had liberated from a stack of books. "Won't you sit, too, as you usually do?" she asked her editor. "Everything's a little off-kilter here today."

Gaustad shifted from foot to foot, his paunch swaying his watch fob. "Mr. Russell has asked me to extend his apologies as he's been unexpectedly detained by one of our new authors."

"I see. I noticed that the note summoning me here today was signed by someone of that name. But who exactly *is* Mr. Louis Russell?"

Gaustad leaned closer. "It's the damnedest thing, but he appears to be our new publisher. We're in the midst of being acquired, my dear. Thames, Royall & Quincy as we've known it will be no more."

"That sounds ominous. Should I be alarmed?"

Gaustad gave an exaggerated shrug. "It's difficult to say, but changes are most certainly afoot. I'm afraid I won't be overseeing your copy edits today or perhaps ever again."

"But I've only ever worked with you. I'm not interested in working with anyone else."

"Russell insists on breathing new life into our enterprise, starting with new blood. He himself is of quite new blood, too, if you know what I mean." A rumble came from deep within Gaustad's chest and he began to cough again. When the spell subsided, he carried on. "You've been assigned a new sub-editor. A Mr. Cartwright. He comes with the highest of recommendations. Everyone says he's most sincere, no doubt because he had the misfortune of being raised the son of a minister."

Gaustad grimaced, making clear his distaste for anything connected to the cloth. In his student days he'd rubbed elbows with the elderly Transcendentalists and preferred a walk in the woods to hours spent in a pew ever since. As an editor, Frederick Gaustad benefitted from those early connections, and over the years had come to be much respected. Once, he'd held open the door to the literary establishment, though lately he'd stumbled backward with it swinging shut before him. For years, Victoria felt she had no choice but to do as he asked, but as she'd garnered more readers with each new novel in her series her confidence had grown. The moment had finally arrived. She reached for her carpetbag and lifted it onto her lap.

"Dear old Frederick, I'm willing to do my edits today with whomever you prefer, but I'm also eager to discuss something else with you." Victoria gave the bag a friendly pat. "I've started writing a new, rather different sort of story."

Gaustad blew his nose loudly and carried on as if he hadn't heard. "Everyone agrees Cartwright's top notch. He's been across the river engaged in scholarly work, though I gather he's no moldering classicist. He's up on the latest literary trends, about which I confess I know little."

Victoria undid the clasp and pressed on. "Should I speak with *him* about my future plans?"

Gaustad paused and seemed to take her in. "Future plans? Why, your plan is to carry on as Mrs. Swann. There's no deviation from that path, regardless of who oversees your efforts."

"*Or*," Victoria shifted in her seat, "I might care to write something more interesting. I think my readers would appreciate it."

"Oh no," he said, shaking that finger at her again. "Now is not the time for a change. We have enough of that going on around here already. You must stick to your usual high standards, as Russell intends to publish supremely unqualified writers. Certain people should *not* be encouraged to pick up a pen."

Victoria sat back. "And what people might that be?"

"The clouds of perfume billowing through these halls should make the answer abundantly clear."

"But I gather Miss Pennypacker intends to offer her hard-won wisdom to young women. Is that so objectionable?" Victoria found herself a little surprised to be defending someone whom she'd never met and had only moments before thought of as a rival.

"Encouraging girls to pursue fanciful ambitions and aim for the highest of aspirations? I'd call that the opposite of wisdom."

"Frederick, you've become appallingly old-fashioned."

"So I have!" He let out a guffaw. "Like Mrs. Swann. Old-fashioned all the way to the bank." He pushed off from the desk and made his way around it. "Miss Pennypacker's advice is suited to high-born ladies, like her, not someone like you, though you've done exceedingly well for a farm girl. But we all know that the vast majority must be content where they are. They do better to stick with Mrs. Swann. Straighten up! No complaints! Girls entering the work force need the guidance they receive from Mrs. Swann." He fell into his desk chair, and it groaned under his weight.

"I hope that's not all Mrs. Swann offers them. I must see that

Dottie is keeping her up to date. I wouldn't want to discourage the young ladies."

"Did you notice we hired one for our ranks, by the way?" Gaustad reached for a half-smoked cigar from the heavy pewter ashtray on his desk. "Only gentlemen have ever worked here before, but not anymore. I assume she won't last long, as a woman's natural vocation is marriage."

"I gather several Boston publishing houses have women in respected positions, all the way up to managing editor, not to mention what goes on in New York. Your new assistant may rise to that level someday."

"No need to mention New York," Gaustad said as he struck a match, puffed hard several times to get the cigar going, and let out a pained sigh.

"You must take care of yourself. Gout's a serious illness," she said.

"The only thing that will keep me well is if Mrs. Swann stays exactly as she is." He tipped back and sent a stream of smoke into the air.

Victoria opened her carpetbag all the way. "Frederick," she began again as sweetly as she could, "as you know, I've become bored with the terrain of hapless women and heroic men in distant lands, yet I've carried on as you've asked. But now, I want to write what I please."

To Victoria's ears this request sounded eminently reasonable and long overdue, though she was aware it wasn't much of a literary creed and thin on the particulars. But to Gaustad, her words appeared to strike with the force of a blow. He sucked in his gut as if he'd taken a load of buckshot.

"I'm surprised at you, Victoria. No one does as they please in life. Certainly not ladies who've been given the rare opportunity to publish at all. You're usually most agreeable."

She had known this wasn't going to be easy and did her best to ignore the tears of frustration building behind her eyes.

"All I'm saying," she tried, "is I'd like the chance to explore new subjects, new landscapes."

"Every one of your stories is set in a new and different land. I don't see why that doesn't satisfy this sudden craving for novelty. Why must you make yourself unpleasant?"

"But those settings aren't *real*. I want to write about women who are made of flesh and bones, with the kinds of problems that my readers might have experienced themselves. I'm sure they would like that."

"That is where you're mistaken." He caressed the tip of his cigar against the side of the ashtray and brought it close to his face, but didn't smoke, just admired it. "When a lady picks up a book, she does so to escape her life, not to be sucked down into its misery and awfulness. And you, Victoria, have everything a writer could want. Fame, wealth, and I'm proud to say, a supportive publisher. With Mrs. Swann's novels, and the thin dime story pamphlets that you pen, plus the advice column that your assistant oversees, you already have a great deal of variety in your output. I've never heard of such selfishness. You have no reason to complain, none at all." He waved the cigar in a conclusive arc and placed it back in the ashtray.

"But that's the thing, though I love my novels, I've grown restless with their sameness. I don't like to think of what I write as *output*. I've become a sausage factory, or a brick works. I've lost all originality."

Gaustad gripped the desk and pulled himself closer to it, the brass wheels squeaking. He leaned across the surface crowded with splayed books and stacks of manuscripts.

"My dear," he said, the red rising on his cheeks as he poked a stiff finger at a nearby manuscript for emphasis. "Mrs. Swann is nothing if not an original. I created her myself, right here in this room out of whole cloth."

They glared at one another, the last of the cigar smoke creating a veil between them. Gaustad did not flinch, and Victoria was forced to do what she always did when feeling trapped and alone. She sought the refuge of books. Noticing the towering piles of manuscripts on the floor, she began to grow calmer, her heart racing less, and her agitated mind becoming soothed by the thought of all those words on all those pages. She sought out the titles and author's names of the published books too. Each and every book, she reassured herself, was evidence of someone's supreme effort. Each and every one was filled with promise and a good heart. Even those that might never see the ink of a printing press gave her hope. The mere existence of these human efforts meant that someone had believed in him or herself enough to set pen to page. Someone had tried to speak his or her mind, as she, too, was trying to do now.

Reaching into her bag, she brought out the thin folder that held the first chapter of her new, and different, novel. It felt light and inconsequential in her hands yet was anything but. With a great flourish, and a similar feeling of profound appreciation that she held for the works of others, she presented it to her editor.

Gaustad pointed at it. "What's this?"

Victoria thrust the folder forward. It hovered in her hand over his untidy desk until he had no choice but to take it.

"I've begun a new novel," she said. "One based on my own life's experiences. It isn't set in a foreign land and the heroine, well, I'm not sure if she will be a heroine in Mrs. Swann's usual sense of the word. You see, I find that I'm compelled to write about that most difficult chapter of my life when I first came to the city as a young woman."

Gaustad placed the folder gingerly onto the desk and spread his hand over it, as if trying to trap it in place. "I remember," he said, his eyes narrowing. "I never asked you to explain your erratic behavior, and I don't see why you would want to revisit that time now. I never knew what took place, though I could have demanded to know. I respected your privacy and did not pry."

"That was good of you," she said, lowering her eyes.

"You must be careful, Victoria. You must not, indeed you *cannot*, under any circumstances invite scrutiny of your personal life. That would be an unmitigated disaster."

"I understand," she said and folded her hands in her lap. "But will you at least give it a read?"

Years before, when she had presented him with her first novel, he said he would be in touch if he liked it. Young and confident, Victoria had spoken up and announced that she would wait right there while he read it. In the front parlor of Thames, Royall & Quincy, she had sat with her father and her beloved childhood librarian, Ruthann Sullivan, while Frederick Gaustad determined the course of her life. She wanted to ask him to do the same now, but after a dozen years as a team, she knew she must trust him with her pages.

"My eyes aren't what they used to be, but I'll get to it as soon as I'm able. I will let you know my opinion."

"Thank you," Victoria said.

She then watched as Gaustad opened his desk drawer and dropped the manuscript into it like a dead body in a shallow grave.

With some effort, he rose. "Now, time to address the final edits on your latest Mrs. Swann. Afterwards, you can take tea at the Parker House or enjoy a trip to the milliner. I know how you like that. But don't rest for long. Russell intends to increase you to three novels annually and is upping the number of penny dreadfuls too."

The air went out of Victoria's lungs, and she let out a muffled cry.

"Oh, now, so dramatic." Gaustad stepped around the desk and took her by the arm more firmly. "You have it in you. I know you do. Let's go meet this Cartwright fellow and hurry the next Mrs. Swann into the hands of her faithful readers."

While much about Boston tried its best to remain unchangeable, the weather tended toward the mercurial. On this afternoon, the temperate skies grew dark as wind picked up from the east. Out the windows over the trees of the Public Garden, a rain squall appeared imminent. The polished mahogany table reflected no light but became a stormy pool into which a visitor might fall and disappear without a trace. The young lady who had tidied

Gaustad's office turned on the gas sconces and the shiny brass chandelier. While other offices in the city were becoming lit by electrical current, Thames, Royall & Quincy flickered still with the unsteady illumination of the past.

From the threshold, Gaustad announced Victoria's name as if this were a ballroom in one of Mrs. Swann's tales. For an instant, she was that eye-catching beauty, hair cascading down her back, skin burnished and alive. Though she'd come to feel stifled by her romance and adventure narratives, they could still envelop her imagination in their gauzy, shimmering layers. She could so easily transform herself into the wayward, desperate heroine of *Damsel of the Deep Sea* or *Fair Lady of Forgotten Shores*.

But the new young editor seated at the far end of the table didn't seem to notice one way or the other. He leaned over the manuscript before him, blue pencil pressing down. Even from a distance, she could see his fingers whiten with the effort.

"Cartwright! Look lively," Gaustad said.

The young man continued scribbling, though he held out a pinkie finger to indicate he would be available shortly.

"Maddening," Gaustad said sotto voce. "Do they no longer learn manners inside the ivy-covered halls?"

"Apparently, the gentleman's occupied," Victoria said.

Jonathan Cartwright slapped down his pencil and rose from his seat. Buttoning his coat as he came forward, he bowed before her. "Sorry to keep you waiting. I was finishing my comments on your manuscript. Such a pleasure to meet you, Mrs. Swann."

Victoria greeted him and waited for a customary compliment, an appreciative word or two about his reading experience, but none came. Who was this Cartwright fellow? She took in the classical Roman nose, the sharp slope of his smooth cheeks, and the fine cleft at the center of his chin. Handsome, though of slight stature, in his late twenties, not much younger than her thirty-three years. A surprising shock of wheat blond hair fell carelessly over his brow. Gaustad introduced him as Jonathan Cartwright, PhD in Letters, a new field that Victoria wasn't familiar with, but which clearly indicated something impressive.

"Ready to steer the ship, my boy?"

The young editor pulled back his shoulders like a captain heading into stormy waters. "I'm sure we'll manage, won't we, Mrs. Swann?"

A little surprised by the question, she nodded gamely. Gaustad had always acted as if the steering of the ship was a task for the gentlemen publishers alone, while she was but a deckhand, churning out the words and pouring them like soapy water to be swabbed across the boards with a mop.

"We have your favorite pastry, Victoria," Gaustad said before turning to leave. "Strawberry tarts!"

Victoria experienced yet another wave of disappointment. Her long-time editor had once known her fondness for profiteroles, but apparently not anymore. She seated herself in the chair that Mr. Cartwright pulled out for her, and they exchanged pleasantries. Gaustad's gangly assistant soon brought in their tea. Victoria couldn't for the life of her recall the tall clerk's name. He needed a name that suited his awkward outline and stride, perhaps Mr. Achingly or Mr. Lankington. He would never be mistaken for a leading man, but a lesser character, not deserving of a full name.

But the real question in her mind was whether her new sub-editor was leading man material or not. He had the looks, though not the bearing. He was too thin and refined. His nervous fingers patted her manuscript pages as he chattered on and she noticed that the fingernails were chewed, a sign of inner turmoil and self-doubt, though often intelligence too. With his long lashes fluttering and bright blue eyes, Victoria came to the conclusion that Jonathan Cartwright was unsettlingly pretty.

While he brought out his notes and offered a preamble to their conversation, she nibbled away at the pastry, and the storm began to unleash itself outside. Rain pelted the blown glass windowpanes. The faintly green and reddish tops of the early spring trees swayed in the Public Garden below. Victoria followed the frantic waving of the limbs, and though she wanted to pay attention to her new editor, she was soon thoroughly distracted. Beneath the waves, the stormy tides rocked the sunken ship where a mermaid heroine remained mired in sea wrack and the tangle of a fisherman's net. Who would rescue her, poor dear, poor dear? Yes, who would rescue her, indeed. That was always the question.

"I'll be honest with you, Mrs. Swann, I'd never read this sort of popular thing before. I was pleasantly surprised."

Victoria snapped out of her reverie by the backhanded compliment. "What types of books are you familiar with, Mr. Cartwright?"

"Oh, I've been holed up in the academy for years, reading heavy tomes. You know, *serious* work."

He rolled his eyes in an effort to be amusing. Victoria didn't care to be talked down to. She had no illusions that her books would ever be taught at Harvard, but out of reflex and what remained of her pride, she felt protective of them. It was one thing for her to question the value of her Mrs. Swann novels, but quite another for someone else to do so, especially someone interested in being her editor.

"I'm only saying I now understand why you have so many devoted readers," Jonathan Cartwright tried again.

Victoria gave a slight smile and he let out a relieved breath, blue eyes sparkling gratefully. She might enjoy working with this fellow after all. At least with him, she could have the upper hand and he might be amenable to her new plans. She rose and went to the windows that faced the tumultuous trees. The willows by the pond resembled ladies whipping back their wet hair on the rocks. Victoria did her best to ignore them. Putting her fingers to the glass, she followed a single droplet as it made a long, lonely path downward.

"Mr. Cartwright, I should inform you that I've begun working on something altogether different from my other books."

He hopped up and came to stand beside her. "How interesting, Mrs. Swann."

"Call me Victoria." She turned to him. "Did you know that Swann isn't my name? Or my husband's name, either?"

"Why no. No one explained that to me. I've been here only a few weeks, and so much has happened."

"Mr. Gaustad re-christened me before publishing my first book. He thought my maiden name, Victoria Meeks, was too, well, meek, and lacking in sophistication. He wanted to create a romantic image of a lady author to appeal to lady readers."

"How clever of him."

Victoria hummed in reply and turned back to the soggy view.

"He also pressed me to marry someone, anyone actually, so I'd have more authority when replying to the lovelorn or when offering marital advice in Mrs. Swann's columns. Though, as it turns out, I know little about such things. The truth is my marriage is as abysmal as this rainy afternoon."

Jonathan gazed down at his shoes, apparently embarrassed by her sudden confidence. He was an anxious man, wringing his hands and shifting his weight.

"I gather that your readers consider you an exemplary role model," he offered. "And of course, everyone adores your adventures set in exotic lands."

"Predictably exotic." Victoria began to pace before the windows. "I place my heroines on tropical shores, in Russian palaces, or deep in the jeweled bowels of Nefertiti's tomb. The sorts of places where my readers have never been, and, Mr. Cartwright," she stopped in her tracks and faced him, "neither have I."

She watched closely for his reaction to this revelation.

"Please, call me Jonathan. But how remarkable," he said cheerfully.

"*Why* is it remarkable?"

"Because apparently people think you've traveled widely. Isn't that a topic in the society pages? Where has she gone and what has she done? That sort of thing." He brushed back the blond locks that had fallen across his brow.

Victoria leaned against the windowsill. "I was hoping you'd say it was remarkable because I've made my settings *believable*, when clearly, I haven't. I've created useless fantasies, pleasant confections spun like sugar."

"Everyone loves spun sugar."

"My point is, I've become a cottage industry in predictable, frivolous words."

"Oh dear. That *is* troubling."

"I want to write something *meaningful*."

"A noble goal, and one I assume we can achieve together. But perhaps first we should press on as Mr. Gaustad has instructed?" He gestured to the manuscript that lay abandoned on the table.

Victoria let him lead her back to her seat where he opened the folder and placed his index finger on the title page. She could hardly recall ever having seen such a gentle and loving gesture. He was quite appealing, but since her arrival, he had given her only cursory looks, her fine clothing and jewels lost on the man. It was disappointing to be ignored as a woman, but possibly far better to have his interest in her as a writer—an altogether new sensation.

His pencil made a big blue circle around a passage. "Now here's an example of superior expression."

Victoria shoulders relaxed as she took in the compliment. Her attention zeroed in on the fine square tip of his nose. It was as pink as an azalea in bloom, either from exertion or from being in the great out-of-doors. Had he been in sunlight earlier that morning? Did he walk to work, or row on the Charles River? That would be a marvelous practice, and feasible, because although he was a bit too thin overall, his torso seemed capable. She could picture her new editor as he pulled his oars through choppy waters, back straining against a herringbone vest, scarf loose at his open collar.

"And this shows your keen imagination." He pointed out another passage.

Victoria bent her head closer and noticed his scent. Could it be pine needles? Had he rowed to the office after pulling his boat out of a stand of evergreens? Oh, how romantic! It made little sense, but she loved the image. Taking another bite of pastry, she didn't mind the strawberry filling. How admirable he was as he commented on the dramatic climax of her story in which a white dove settles on the sleeve of a girl at the same moment a gentleman steps forward to ask for her hand in marriage—a moment of elation in which good wins out over evil, purity is upheld, innocence rewarded, et cetera, et cetera, with love rising to the top.

"Remarkable confluence of good luck." He gave a slight smile.

Or was it a smirk? Or perhaps a sneer? Victoria jolted free from her reverie, recognizing that her ego had succumbed to easy flattery. Far too often she gave in to self-delusions. It was more important than ever that she learn to judge her own efforts with a level head, but hubris had a way of sneaking up on her, ensnaring her in its conniving trap.

"Please, Mr. Cartwright."

"Jonathan," he insisted.

"All right, Jonathan, let's be honest." She set down her pen. "I'm sure my readers have become tired of my shopworn plots. I know I've become sick to death of them. And I assume they're as annoyed as I am by the patronizing voice woven into my tales, instructing women on how to behave and what to believe. Mr. Gaustad has demanded it."

"I don't want to be disrespectful, but I wouldn't worry too much about his wishes any longer."

"Why, what do you mean?"

"That times are changing. But I do agree that your readers wouldn't recognize Mrs. Swann without those instructive elements."

"My guess is that they skip right over those passages in order to get to the fun parts."

"I wonder if that's true." He leaned back in his seat and tapped the end of his pencil against his thin pink lips. "You know, several of my sisters have read your books over the years. If you think it at all helpful, I could take an informal polling."

"How many sisters do you have, Mr. Cartwright?"

"Five."

"Five!"

"Yes," he said, as if it was the most natural thing in the world. "Do you have siblings, Mrs. Swann?"

"Victoria," she insisted. "No, I was an only child. I grew up alone."

"Oh, I'm sorry."

"I shouldn't say alone. I had my father and our mule, Oscar, and the library nearby. I petitioned the Town of Lincoln's school board to study at home so that I might read and write according to my own interests. My father, poor man, was mystified by me, but honored my wishes. And my local librarian became my most important teacher, supplying me with the volumes that gave me all I needed to know. Books were everything to me."

"As they were for me." Jonathan gave an easy laugh. "Growing up with five sisters, you can imagine how essential it was to escape into stories."

"How nice that your sisters have enjoyed mine. Where do they prefer to read them? I like picturing my readers with my books."

Jonathan's gaze fell to the manuscript that lay between them. "We should get back to our deadline."

Victoria tapped the table. "Are they no longer interested in my novels?"

"Truthfully, my middle sisters have moved on in their tastes." His head bobbed, clearly not wanting to offend. "And I'm sorry to say that the two youngest hardly read anything at all. They only care for famous persons and spend hours poring over illustrated magazines that feature them. They'll hound me to death when they learn I've been assigned Miss Pennypacker."

"Aren't you the lucky editor. That must be a gentleman's dream."

"I can't imagine she writes well. She's a singer after all."

"You're as much of a snob as Gaustad. But won't it be fun to work with such a flamboyant and attractive author?"

"Honestly, she's not my cup of tea."

Victoria placed her elbows on the table and leaned closer. "What is your cup of tea, Jonathan?"

A delightful blush rose from below his collar as he aligned the edges of the manuscript. "I'm afraid we're getting way off track."

"But don't you have one more sister to tell me about? You didn't mention her tastes. What does she like to read?"

"You don't miss a trick, do you, Victoria? My oldest sister Clara and I admire the same writers. We've shared books all our lives. In recent years, we've come to prefer literature in the modern realist vein."

Victoria jotted down *modern* and *realist* in a little notebook she kept in her pocket for this purpose. Beside the words, she drew repeated question marks, having only a vague sense of what he might mean. She wanted to ask her well-educated editor to explain the terms more fully, but she would have had to admit she had hardly had time to open a book since writing on deadline as Mrs. Swann.

As a girl Victoria had read constantly. With a book in hand, she would tuck herself into the branches of a budding cherry in springtime or sprawl on a flat rock beside a babbling brook in summer. She read while strolling between tendrils of pumpkins in an autumn field and lay curled with a volume before the hearth in winter. But her favorite reading spot by far had been the window seat in her garret bedroom overlooking her father's apple orchard. Now, she wondered, what had she been searching for so desperately in those volumes? What did a girl want from the written word that she could not find in life?

"I gather you know a great deal about current literature. I wonder, what do you think a reader *wants* in a story today?"

Jonathan paused and considered the question. "I suspect they want a story that reflects the changing world around them."

"Exactly! Young ladies in particular must be hungry for a

new voice to capture their new reality. Doesn't that seem so?"

"I suppose that sounds right. But," he hesitated, "I don't believe Mrs. Swann offers that and we can't forget that the company is counting on us. Which is to say, we must stick to our deadline."

Victoria was no longer listening. She stood and wavered over the table, not fully sure of her intentions. "Sometimes," she announced, "a woman must take matters into her own hands." She reached across the table for the folder that held her latest Mrs. Swann with his comments in the margins.

Jonathan clamped his fingers over it. "What do you mean?"

"I mean that I'm taking this back." Victoria wrenched the folder from him.

"I wish you wouldn't do that. If you leave the manuscript here with me, I can push it forward."

"I don't care to be pushed forward any longer." She tied the string around the binder and returned it to her carpetbag.

"I didn't mean you, Victoria, just your work."

"There shouldn't be a difference. I wish for my stories to be my own."

She turned and headed toward the door.

Jonathan scrambled after her, his reflection rippling frantically across the dark pool of the table. "But we haven't got a finished book yet."

"Revision applies not only to books, Jonathan. Sometimes a woman must take a blue pencil to her life." She liked the sound of that, though wasn't one bit sure what it meant.

"I shall be in touch!" She waved a hand over her head.

"Please don't go," he blurted out. "They'll fire me, if you do."

Victoria stopped on the threshold. "They wouldn't dare. I'll refuse to work with anyone else but you."

"You want me as your editor?"

"Of course, I do. Gaustad's ship may have run aground on the shoals, but we will steer ours to safety, won't we?" Victoria let out a laugh. "And by the way, do you own a boat?"

"*A boat?*" Jonathan blinked several times. "I had thought you were speaking metaphorically. No, I don't have a boat."

"That's too bad. Where do you live?"

"Across the river."

"In Old Cambridge, where I am?"

"I'm afraid not. I've moved recently into a boarding house in Cambridgeport, a different sort of neighborhood."

"I'm on Brattle Street," Victoria said, chin up. "I purchased my home with the proceeds from my Mrs. Swann novels."

"How impressive. I thought those houses were kept in the old families and out of reach of everyone else. Good for you, though I don't know if I could ever feel at home in that part of town myself."

Victoria swallowed, for the same was true of her. "I don't really know my neighbors, though everyone agrees they're the best of Cambridge society."

"Perhaps you'll get to know them someday, and meanwhile, there's no denying the beauty of the trees. Some of our great literary figures of the past have staked their claim on Old Tory Row."

Victoria frowned. "Not entirely past, I hope."

The son of a minister, Jonathan couldn't help his honesty. "That is my hope as well."

He bowed his farewell and though his words had not meant to goad Victoria, they did. As she made her way out, several assistants scattered, and one presented her with her linen duster and parasol. Gaustad called out for someone to procure the company carriage for Mrs. Swann. On tedious afternoons such as this one, her old editor enjoyed a snooze in one of his comfortable chairs. He suggested she might want to wait out the rain squall in his office, too, as if she, like him, was a moldering antique. *Literary figure of the past!* Not on your life, Jonathan Cartwright, Victoria thought as she headed straight into the storm.

Two

J onathan waved his arm and accidentally jostled the ink pot as he leaned on his colleague's sloped desk. "She left with it. She took back her manuscript."

The other young man pushed his printer's visor up from his forehead. "Calm yourself, Jon. It'll be all right."

Perry Bliss, the lanky assistant whose name Victoria hadn't been able to recall, often offered Jonathan a sanguine perspective. He and Jon had been classmates at Harvard since their first semester. After graduation, Perry found immediate employment at Thames, Royall & Quincy while Jonathan remained engaged in graduate work on campus. Jonathan had Perry to thank for his new job and this exciting chapter of his life just beginning. He wanted to buy his old friend a bottle of fine Spanish port, but only after he'd paid off his debts.

Jonathan owed the landlady at his new boarding house, the tailor for the suit he had purchased before joining the firm, and the hatmaker for the top hat he had foolishly deemed necessary too. There were also dinners taken at Perry's club to position himself for the job, and drinks bought all around once he got it. There were so many ways the City of Boston had filched from him since he'd left behind the confines of the college. Jonathan looked forward to the day when his fingers didn't come upon promissory notes in the pockets of his overcoat, and he could eat more than salt cod and beans for dinner.

He crossed to his own desk in the windowless office. "She's going to ruin everything, and I have my sisters to consider. Why on my watch would Mrs. Swann decide she wants to pen something better?" He hurried back to Perry. "Do you think she's capable of it? *Could* she write something better?"

"Have you *read* any of her books?" Perry asked, his pencil copying the sums.

"Only the current manuscript, but I must study them all in order to assess her talent."

Perry paused to twirl the ends of his moustache. "Maybe you don't need to take her quite so seriously."

"But I must. I'm her editor. And besides, my sisters are relying on me." Jonathan began to pace the small office.

"From what you've told me, your sisters are managing as best as they can after your family's tragedy. As are you. You'll come into your own as an editor soon enough. Have patience, Jon."

Perry somehow knew how to buck Jonathan up. In his unobtrusive way, he had been a great comfort in the difficult months since Jonathan's parents had died. Jonathan felt increasingly lucky to have such a solid, considerate friend.

"You'll work it out with Mrs. Swann. You often found promise in writers when none of the rest of us could spot it. Remember that dreadful British poet who visited campus and smelled of vinegar and sardines? You picked him for the big poetry prize. I lost good money on that one."

He called Jonathan over with a bent finger. "Speaking of money," Perry said and dipped his head closer to the ledger, "we seem to have gobs of it all of a sudden. Gaustad never looked at the figures, but that's the only thing Russell cares about, and I can see why. He's rolling in dough." His eyes grew larger behind his round spectacles.

"Wonderful. He can raise our salaries and pay our authors more."

Perry let out a laugh. "You *are* new to publishing, aren't you?" He put down his pencil. "You know, when I recommended you, I told them that you're not only an academic, but a man of the world, savvy about current trends and the marketplace."

"I am, more or less."

"This isn't a colloquium, Jonathan. It isn't a seminar."

"I know."

"This is *business*." Perry lowered his voice again. "And a damn serious one. Russell instructed me to balance evenly our income and expenses at the end of each month. He's not investing the extra funds back into the house. The money is in our accounts for a short time, but then he dispenses with it elsewhere, if you know what I mean."

"I don't, actually."

"I'm not completely sure either, but I have my guesses, and it isn't good. Which is all the more reason we must do our jobs."

"I suppose I can grasp that part of the equation, though the problem is, I'm not entirely sure what my job is. Being an editor is an amorphous position, as far as I can tell."

"You'll get the hang of it."

"But you don't think we could be held responsible if Russell gets caught at something, do you? I have my sisters to consider. We'll all be carted off to the poorhouse."

"You've been reading too much Dickens, Jon. Relax. Your sisters will manage. Women today have far more options than our mothers did."

Jonathan let out a long breath. "Thank you, Perry. You always know the right thing to say."

"Everything's going to be all right. But I better get back to it. Russell's waiting for this week's numbers."

"Should I speak with the gentleman myself? We can discuss the correct editorial approach to Mrs. Swann."

"Not a good idea. He's made it clear he doesn't want to be bothered with the details."

"Meaning?"

"Meaning, books."

Jonathan rested back on his heels. "What about Gaustad?"

"You won't find much satisfaction, but he's in his office. Give a hard rap to the doorframe to wake him. The man snores louder than a steam engine."

Jonathan adjusted the handkerchief in his pocket at precisely the right angle. He'd observed that gentlemen of business aligned their cravats with their kerchiefs, nothing like the more haphazard habits he'd grown accustomed to as a graduate student. Upon arriving at the editor-in-chief's office down the hall, he did as Perry suggested, and knocked several times and stepped inside. Gaustad's eyes flew open and for a moment the old editor appeared panicked, his bushy eyebrows shooting up and his dome quivering.

"I must have been daydreaming." He straightened himself in the leather reading chair. "The Huns were taking Bunker Hill. You don't resemble their leader, but I couldn't be certain."

"One can never be too sure," Jonathan said as he stepped around stacks of manuscripts and crumpled-up wads of paper. He didn't know precisely what he wanted to say to his boss, but it seemed best to set an amiable tone.

"Sit, sit." Gaustad gestured to the other armchair. "You seem like a fine young fellow. You remind me of myself when I first came across the river and into the world of publishing. May I offer you a brandy, my boy?"

Jonathan was not accustomed to drinking in the middle of the day but didn't want to offend. Perhaps gentlemen editors enjoyed a nip as they verbally sparred with one another. He and his classmates had done the same over whiskeys in the sitting rooms of Harvard houses, bandying about ideas while lounging in worn leather chairs similar to one he settled into now.

"You'll see that publishing agrees with you."

"It already does, sir."

"Call me Gaustad. As you may have noticed, we go by surnames here, as in the military." He let out a broad yawn, rubbed sleep from his eyes, and went to the cabinet where he lifted a crystal decanter with an unsteady hand. "Now tell me, how did you like Mrs. Swann? A delightful lady, isn't she?"

"I was saying as much to Mr. Bliss."

"You won't have any trouble with her. She gets her books in on time and never puts up a fuss." Gaustad shuffled back and handed Jonathan a glass. "But best to protect her from the business side of things. Keep the focus on her charming tales." He took his seat and pensively swirled the amber liquid. "And make no mistake, it's crucial she meets her deadlines."

The whiskey burned the back of Jonathan's throat.

"I was reminded today of a short period of time when she didn't. Years ago, the lady ran amok."

"Really? How so?" Jonathan could feel the liquor already at work.

"It may be hard to imagine, as she's one of our most prolific and agreeable authors, and also our best bargain, too, I might add. But once, she got caught up in sordid goings on."

"Yes, that is hard to imagine."

"She's clever at creating the ne'er-do-wells in her tales because she plucks them from right here in Boston and sets them down in foreign lands." Gaustad leaned over the arm of his chair. "Somehow, the lady knows her way around a bordello!" He let out a blast of laughter.

Jonathan's pulse increased at the thought of his author's mysterious past. He wasn't sure why it made him uncomfortable, but he had already taken a liking to Victoria and didn't want to think of her mixed up in anything unpleasant. "I suppose she must do her research in inventive ways, since she hasn't traveled to the countries where her stories take place."

Gaustad set down his glass with a splash on the table between them. "That is top secret information, young man. She never shares that with anyone. At least, she isn't supposed to."

"I assumed it was in my capacity as her new editor that she told me, sir. So that I might better grasp her books."

Gaustad gave a reluctant grunt and picked up his glass.

Jonathan took his own fortifying sip. "It *is* a little surprising that no reporter or curious inquirer has unmasked the deception."

"People believe what they want to believe. And *everyone* loves Mrs. Swann. But under no circumstances are you to breathe a word about her private life to anyone. Her marriage is strictly off limits. Is that clear, Cartwright?"

"Absolutely."

He was aware of his head bobbing too much. Gaustad's scowl frightened him, as had his father's. Jonathan searched his thoughts for what might make the older gentleman less agitated.

"I wonder how you managed her during that rocky period? You have so much valuable experience to impart to a young editor like myself."

He was certain he was going overboard, but Gaustad soaked it up. Men of his type, Jonathan knew from his father, found purpose and resolve in the sound of their own voices.

"She came back around eventually. Tail between her legs. A little defeated by life, but that worked in our favor. She's never been late with a manuscript since. But she mustn't write about that lost chapter of her life." Gaustad eyes darted to his desk drawer and he gave a shudder. "If the pages she gave me this morning are what I think they are, it would ruin Mrs. Swann. I took them from her and will make certain they never see the light of day."

"She gave you a new manuscript today? How exciting. Have you read it?"

"I don't need to. As an editor, you must save your authors from themselves. A squalid, true-to-life tale from Victoria could sink our whole operation. We have our positions to consider."

Jonathan set down his own empty glass. It was time for him to leave, but he couldn't let it go. "I'd be interested in taking a look at it, if you don't mind. As her new editor, it seems prudent for me to know her full range of talent."

"No one wants to read that thing. And you, my boy," Gaustad said and pointed a thick finger, "stick to the straight and narrow. You hear me?"

"That's my intention."

Gaustad stood unsteadily and made his way to his desk. "But you must look forward to working with that other fine creature?"

"Miss Pennypacker?" Jonathan stood, too, his head a little woozy.

"A barmaid."

"Have you heard her sing? She has a heavenly voice."

"I thought all the fuss was about her looks and her pedigree. Born high and winding up low, and all that."

"I did a little research in the broadsides and learned that she was forced to renounce her upbringing in order to achieve her accomplishments."

"A predictable path."

"But an artistic odyssey, nonetheless, showing the sacrifices one must make for a higher calling in life." Having skipped lunch, the alcohol had loosened his tongue.

"The woman can't write."

"Do we know that?"

"The minute Russell grows tired of her, we'll let the project die. It used to be we had a reputation to uphold here at Thames, Royall & Quincy. Too bad you weren't with us back in the day, Cartwright."

"I'm honored to work here now."

Gaustad dropped into his desk chair, reached for his pince nez, and placed it on his nose. "An Oxford scholar is penning a biography of Tennyson and has asked for my recollections." He gazed into the middle distance over the rim of his frames. "Our evenings together hover in memory like a glowing orb."

Jonathan found himself flat-footed before this great man. Imagine that: dining with Tennyson. But *was* Gaustad great? Had he ever been great? Or was it merely a matter of being in the right place at the right time, especially, Jonathan noted, if you were a scion of one of Boston's oldest families. Men like Gaustad had been given extraordinary opportunities and needed only to remain upright and behave not too foolishly, though great latitude was given for their eccentricities. But what did it mean to be an editor? Should one simply get out of the way of an author whose genius you happened to help bring to light? Or must one use alchemical skills to help bring forth the golden ore in an author's mishmash of words?

Gaustad lifted a sheet of cream-colored stationery before his eyes. Jonathan had been dismissed, but he needed more.

"Pardon me, sir."

Gaustad eyed him over the rim of the page.

"I'm interested to learn more about our domain as editors. What, exactly, is our mission?"

"Cartwright?"

"Are we to mold our authors? Is it our task to chisel and shape them? Or instead to erect the pedestals on which to place their finished masterpieces?"

Gaustad slapped the letter onto his desk. "Young man, Mrs. Swann's formula appeals to the vast majority of those buying books for the first time. Your job is to see that we stick to it. *That* is your singular task. Now, off you go! I'm not paying you to idle away the day, gabbing like a scullery maid."

Jonathan bowed and hurried from the room.

THREE

The rain stopped as quickly as it had started. Dusk hung in golden circles of mist around the gas lamps in the Public Garden. Victoria stood under the awning of the St. Jerome's Club and took in the salty air wafting up from the seaport. Her latest Mrs. Swann manuscript weighed like ballast in her carpetbag. The gentlemen inside the club didn't care about her success as an author, and she wasn't as proud of her books as she had once been, but she had at least accomplished *something* in her life. She was more than simply the wife of Raymond Byrne.

After she rang the bell an elderly attendant in a brass-buttoned uniform ushered her into a chilly vestibule. He took her things and guided her toward a low-ceilinged closet that served as a waiting room for ladies—only recently added, he wanted her to know, as women had never been allowed inside the club before. Victoria avoided the overstuffed chintz floral sofa and settled on a backless settee. The excessive rose-patterned wallpaper pressed in around her as she waited for her husband.

But here was Raymond already. "Sorry to keep you waiting, darling." He came at her with puckered lips, purely for show. They hadn't kissed in years.

Victoria shot up from the pouffe to avoid him. One look and she knew. "You're pickled," she whispered.

He did a sloppy little shuffle on the rose carpet. "I think better this way, more in the moment, quick on my feet."

A lick of black hair rose in a pompadour like an ocean wave above his brow. Victoria thought he might as well have been wearing a buccaneer's sash, high boots, and plumed hat in place of his ill-fitting frock coat, wrinkled tie, and two-toned spats. Raymond Byrne had long been the prototype for the ne'er-do-wells in Mrs. Swann's novels. It made her cringe with the obviousness of it.

"Where have you been?" she asked as he shifted unsteadily in the narrow room. "I haven't heard from you in days. For all I knew you were at the bottom of Boston Harbor."

"Don't worry about me, Victoria. I'm perfectly all right. Now, hurry up. They're waiting for Mrs. Swann." He strode off through the tiled lobby and up some low carpeted steps.

Victoria followed, whispering, "But am I permitted to enter? Have you arranged for me to be here?"

"I've taken care of everything." Raymond waved her on with a bony wrist.

She couldn't help noticing how skeletal he had become, his suit hanging from his frame, with the cuffs of his pants frayed and skimming the carpet. His beard had lost its clean line and a ducktail poked over his collar. Put in another setting, he might have been mistaken for a shady character whom society people avoided on the street. On the landing, he leaned against the crimson-striped wallpaper and caught his breath.

"You don't look well, Raymond." She pushed his fallen lick of hair back into place and used her linen handkerchief to wipe hair oil from her gloves.

"Focus on entertaining them with your charming anecdotes and bookish chatter. Nothing too heady. These are important men of business, not useless intellectual types from over in Cambridge. I need my colleagues to be impressed, not intimidated."

"You don't have any colleagues, because you don't have a job."

"That's why you're here. The owner of an import firm has a sideline in books and is hiring an assistant. I want to get in his good graces."

Victoria whisked what appeared to be ashes off her husband's shoulders. "Has he got an opening for you to run a bookshop?"

"Nothing like that."

"What sorts of imports does he deal in? Will you sell Asian urns and jade gewgaws?"

He pushed her hand away, his eyes darting. "Don't ask so many questions."

"Raymond, look at me."

But he wouldn't. He squirmed away.

"You're not getting caught up in that world again, are you? You'd be a fool."

He turned on his heels and took the crimson-carpeted stairs. Victoria rose after him and paused at the entrance to a Moorish-inspired lounge. Scattered about before a roaring fire in an impressive stone hearth were deep leather armchairs and ponderous rough-hewn furniture that belonged in the Alhambra. A gentleman in a houndstooth topcoat gazed down, a monocle at his eye, from a gilt-framed painting, a poorly rendered hunting dog at his side. The pompous figure might have made Victoria laugh, if it weren't for the steely expressions of the real gentlemen eyeing her over the tops of their newspapers. She sensed they perceived her as a threat to everything they held dear, though she was the one with the fast-beating heart and damp palms. She would have liked to remind them that she was the prey and not the other way around.

Raymond returned and took her by the elbow. "Come along," he hissed. "Don't dawdle or draw attention to yourself. You'll get me kicked out. They've already cut me off at billiards and cards, I can't risk having my wife cause a ruckus."

Victoria yanked free and trailed him down a hallway that ended in a set of back stairs. "Where are you taking me?"

"Where ladies are allowed."

"The cellar?"

"We can't have women in the dining room." Raymond glared at her, as if he'd instituted the rule himself. "The gentlemen ate there earlier but were game to take their brandies down below. I framed it as a daring ramble."

"How very brave of them." Victoria gave her husband a

steely look. But then she noticed his hands' tremor and softened. "Raymond, I don't see how I can help you when you're
in this state."

He slumped. "Is it that obvious? I'll clean up when I get this
position. I promise. Please, do your best for me, will you?"

Victoria let him escort her to the basement. But on reaching
the dirt floor, he cornered her on the bottom step, reached for
her sleeve, and wrinkled the linen between anxious fingers.

"You know, you and I can still make a winning team, if only
you'd relent."

She brushed past him. "That makes no sense. You can't take
care of yourself, let alone a child."

"But a baby would turn me around, I know it would. Yet you
deny me that right. Don't forget, at any moment I could share
with the world how the great upholder of marriage defied her
husband's wishes by refusing her natural role in life."

"You've been threatening to reveal it for years, but a scandal
of that sort would get you thrown out of all your clubs for
good. You would suffer more than I would."

"I doubt that. You'd be in jail."

A door swung open at the far end of the corridor and a wait-
er came careening toward the stairs, a crowded tray balanced on
his shoulder. The smell of rare roast beef and buttery potatoes
taunted Victoria and made her stomach rumble. At this hour,
wives sat down at well-laid tables with respectable husbands,
yet here she was in this depressing place with her unworthy
one. The only thing more wearying than being Mrs. Swann was
being Mrs. Byrne.

The afternoon's hard rain had leaked down the crumbling
brick walls and created runnels along the hallway. Mud stained
the lace hem of her cream-colored dress, and the soles of
her boots quickly became wet. Victoria could sense Raymond
watching her, deciding which strategy to use in their ongoing
battle. But he didn't say anything. Could he tell she was changing and that there was little point in bickering anymore?

She pushed away from the damp wall. "I'll do this for you one last time. But I won't tolerate threats any longer. I refuse to be bullied. I'm done with all that."

Before he could ask what exactly she meant, Victoria strode off along the basement hall. She paused at the threshold to a low-ceilinged, smoke-filled room where a dozen gentlemen sat, sated and flushed and ready to be entertained. She patted her bun in place and straightened her fine shirtwaist. Victoria had dressed as Mrs. Swann, ever elegant and composed, and entered the room with her arms upraised, as if in praise of their presence and her great good fortune at having them as her audience. She thanked them for indulging their wives' reading habits and for being patient with the young ladies whom they employed and who enjoyed her stories to the detriment of their work practices. Though Victoria preferred to keep a low profile and had performed as rarely as possible over the course of her career, and even less often with the years, she had, nonetheless, become accustomed to appealing to those who did not appeal to her. She spoke not as the famous Mrs. Swann, but as *their* famous Mrs. Swann.

All the while in the back of her mind as she spoke, the truth of her situation was becoming clearer. But what had changed? Certainly not Gaustad. Nor Raymond. No, it was the start of her new, different novel and her new editor who seemed hopeful about her as a writer. Victoria glowed with the promise of that thought. As she finished up, she realized that this event would be Mrs. Swann's last hurrah.

An older gentleman asked the first question, chomping on the end of his cigar so the words slipped out sideways. "My wife is mad for your inventions, Mrs. Swann. If she's any indication, I'd say you have an almost religious following."

Though he frowned, Victoria took it as a compliment and thanked him.

He craned around to address the other gentleman. "But do we think it wise for our wives to be so admiring of one of their own sex? In my day, ladies turned to the pulpit for instruction. Ministers kept them appropriate, unlike today's outrageous specimens of womanhood."

General acknowledgement of this truth rippled through the crowd. The heat in the room couldn't be blamed for the prickling on the back of Victoria's neck. She took a sip of water and tried to form a quip, a bon mot, the right words to slap him down while seeming to appease.

"I can't imagine that your wife needs much instruction, sir. She must be a clever woman. She married you, after all."

This got more than one chuckle. At that moment, a gentleman with silver hair rose at the back of the room. Impressively attired in a mulberry tailcoat and white tie, he raised a snifter of brandy in her direction, a diamond ring flashing on his finger.

"Gentlemen," he said, and the others craned their necks to see him. "Mrs. Swann is a fine raconteur, and I gather, an even better writer. It seems to me that she's a superior example for our ladies. I can only say that I'd want any future bride of mine to exhibit as much class as she does."

Victoria spoke to him across the smoky room. "How gallant of you to come to my rescue, sir. You must be a white knight from one of my tales."

"Hardly, but we do need stylish, intelligent women if Boston is to be a first-class city. We must keep up with the times, or at least with Gotham."

Several gentlemen mumbled in disagreement, grateful that Boston would never be New York, while others snapped their fingers in approval, though secretly knowing the same.

"Mrs. Swann speaks to the New Women who've come in from the farms to flood our cities," he continued. "These ladies need guidance in order fill their roles and stay out of trouble."

"Though of course," Victoria interjected, "I'm not a New Woman myself. I'm not single. I'm contentedly married."

The gentlemen peered over at Raymond and he gave a little bow. He would owe her for that.

"In any case, I say bravo to Mrs. Swann." The silver-haired

gentleman lifted his drink. "And now let's all buy many copies of her clever books for our ladies."

The men clapped politely, though several groused about women today as they puffed on their cigars. As the gathering disbanded, the gent with the silver hair tipped his top hat in Victoria's direction and exited without a word.

Raymond came to her side, his face slick with sweat, as if he had given the talk himself. "Isn't Russell marvelous? He's a powerful man, everyone says so."

"The same Mr. Russell who now runs my publishing house?"

"It's a side business for him, a dalliance."

"He certainly is a salesman."

"In any case, he's the one I needed to impress, so well done, darling. Our ship is coming in. Just you wait, Mrs. Byrne."

Raymond veered off to join the others. He liked to refer to her by his surname, though she never used it. Victoria supposed it made him feel better about himself, more in charge of something or someone. But she didn't care about that any longer. For now, all she wanted was some supper.

Head low and steps swift, she crossed the reading room of the St. Jerome's Club. The gentlemen didn't peek out from behind their broadsides, having decided she wasn't in fact a threat to their peaceful evening. In the lobby, the elderly attendant retrieved her coat, parasol, and carpetbag and offered to hail her a cab. Victoria prepared to follow him to the sidewalk when the front door swung open and two gentlemen entered, one familiar to her.

"Why heavens, if it isn't Mrs. Swann," he said, leaning on an ivory cane and bowing stiffly.

"Theodore Upchurch." Victoria gave a respectful curtsy.

The long-time editor of the oldest literary journal in the country, *The North American Scribe*, was an astoundingly short grey-haired gentleman who rarely smiled.

"What a surprise to find you here of all places." The timbre

of his Brahmin accent was at such a low volume that the words
slipped out and expired on the marble floor. "Mrs. Swann, you
should know my colleague, the brilliant young author, Buckley
Johnson."

The other man wore a thick canvas coat with leather cuffs
and offered a cheerful hello, his lack of reserve the opposite
of his colleague. "Pleased to meet you, ma'am. I've heard your
name for years."

Upchurch's already drawn lips curled downward, but the
younger writer's acknowledgment of her fame gave Victoria
renewed energy. The day had taken a great deal out of her, but
she could feel the balloon of her ego filling out again.

"Thank you, Mr. Johnson."

"Call me Buck. Everyone does."

"I wrote of a grizzled prospector by that name once. He
lived out on the gold dust trail in one of my early novels."

Buck leaned closer as if taking her into his confidence. "You
sure write them aplenty, while I eke out mine only every five
years. I bleed with each word and sweat like a wrangler throwing down a bull. It nearly kills me every time."

What a character this young writer was. His fictional heroes
must really be something.

"Is that your subject then?" Victoria asked. "I'm afraid I
haven't read your work."

"Buckley Johnson is the voice of America today," Upchurch
interjected. "He writes of war. War against our fellow man and
war within our consciences. As we all know, there is no more
essential subject."

"Why yes, war," Victoria said.

Buck took off his ten-gallon hat and held it between his
hands, leaving his hair to need some wrangling. "But I mean
it, how *do* you do it? How do you manage to put out so many
books and have so many readers?"

With this question, Victoria's confidence billowed back full
blown. "I do it, Mr. Johnson, by writing what they want to read."

Buck slapped his hat against his thigh, as if she'd told a good one, but Upchurch beat him to a reply.

"You're not saying you'd want *her* readers?" he asked the younger writer.

Victoria tapped the marble tile with her parasol. "And why wouldn't he?" she demanded. "What's wrong with my readers?"

"Shopgirls and widows, seamstresses and the occasional curious male accountant or underling?" Upchurch said. "Who knew they'd want to buy books in such numbers? Young lads have saved up their pennies for weekly Westerns and frontier tales in the thin dime-novel format, but Gaustad managed to harness the craze for lurid and sentimental stories for young ladies. Forward thinking of him, though a little shocking."

"More people are reading all the time," Buck said, stealing a line of argument Victoria had been poised to make too.

"That may be true, but we've lowered our national standards. Never before has there been so much frivolous writing and so many uneducated readers."

"*Frivolous writing?*" Victoria's voice bounced off the tile lobby. "*Uneducated readers?* My readers may not have fancy degrees, but they're hard-working and decent. They deserve the distraction they find in the pages of my books."

Buck Johnson placed his hat back on his head. "I imagine this lady here has had more success at getting people to read than Mother Goose herself."

Victoria wasn't sure she cared for the comparison to the insignificant children's rhymer but could see the young man was trying.

"Also, I'm personally indebted to you, Mrs. Swann."

Victoria turned to Buck. "Really, why is that?"

"Thames, Royall & Quincy can't pay me without you, ma'am. Your efforts keep the whole operation afloat."

"That has to be an exaggeration." Upchurch leaned on his ivory cane, as if the idea exhausted him.

"The latest from Steven Crane couldn't be in print without

Mrs. Swann. Old Gaustad said so himself after several glasses of schnapps."

"By the way," Upchurch said, turning to him, "I hope you realize you're every bit as good as Crane. Don't ever let anyone tell you otherwise."

"Thanks, Teddy."

The men exchanged further compliments, but Victoria had heard enough. She interrupted them to bid farewell.

"Can't you stay?" Buck asked. "I'd love to raise a glass to you, Mrs. Swann."

"I'm afraid club rules are club rules," Upchurch said. "No ladies in the dining room or bar."

The younger writer tipped his hat to her. "If ever a woman was admitted to St. Jerome's, I'd vote for you, ma'am."

She thanked him, though that was the last thing she might want.

"Out west, gentlemen throw back whiskies with ladies all the time," Buck said, "even fine ones like yourself."

Upchurch smoothed his mustache over his thin lips. "The country is changing in ways that would have shocked my father and grandfather before me."

"You need to get out of Boston more, Teddy." Buck slapped his colleague on the back. "Doesn't he, Mrs. Swann? He should travel more like you."

Victoria's head wavered noncommittally, as she did whenever people assumed things about her that were untrue. She was thirsty and hungry and needed to go home. As she waited for a cab, she realized that Upchurch was right. When the literary canon of their time was written, Buckley Johnson's name would be written in black ink, while hers would only be jotted in faint pencil and easily smudged off. Though wildly popular in her day, Mrs. Swann would soon be forgotten. But what about Victoria Meeks?

FOUR

Through the front door of his family's home, Jonathan listened to his sister Philomena as she pounded out the latest dance hall ditty. From the second floor came the vocal scales of his other middle sister, Tessa, the notes cascading down the steep steps faster than water. Playful chatter from the young twins circled around the side of the clapboard house, high voices slicing the dusk in two. Though pleased to hear these familiar sounds, Jonathan waited for what he longed most to hear: his mother's tread as she stepped to welcome him, eyes bright at the sight of her only son. But she would not open this door or any other. Nine months before she had passed away from whooping cough. One month later, his father had followed, succumbing to an intestinal tumor.

On the darkening lane, ribbons of smoke spun upward from the chimneys of the narrow houses and the brick sidewalks grew slick and black as oil. Caught in that lonely quiet, it was hard to recall this had once been a magical kingdom. As children, Jonathan and his sisters used to dash past the teetering slate grave markers in their father's churchyard as they set off to explore the neighborhood. Back gardens and alleyways became tropical coves, quicksand marshes, and Venetian causeways. Jonathan and Philomena would dress as pirates, complete with eye patches, while Clara and Tessa became lady adventurers with plumed hats when navigating a land of their own making. Their mother twisted old rags into turbans, used oil sticks as war paint on their cheeks, and made crowns of vines to halo their disheveled hair. On early spring evenings like this one, Evalina Cartwright stood on the stoop and called out their names, her voice echoing off the homes of her husband's parishioners. She wanted all the world to know that Mrs. Cartwright's children, as they were called—never the reverend's—were the prince and princesses of Boston's South End.

Jonathan pressed gloved fingertips to closed eyelids. As soon as the congregation engaged a new minister, his sisters would be forced to vacate the parish house. Each day he searched the broadsides for new arrangements for them, but with the city's growth, prices had shot up, making it nearly impossible. And now, he had his own boarding house rent each month as well. With this and other burdens on his shoulders, he inserted the key in the lock and stepped inside his family home. As he took off his plaid McIntosh, his little twin sisters came charging from the back of the house and placed themselves directly before him, their hands on narrow hips.

"Did you meet Miss Pennypacker today?" Rosalyn asked.

"Was she beautiful?" Rosemond asked.

"I did. And she was."

Jonathan reached to pat them on their heads, as their father used to, but they leapt at his touch. He didn't blame them. He wasn't their parent; they had none. His dark mood wanted to evaporate in their sudden sunshine but didn't dare. The twins were often rosy, but like the plant, could prick you unexpectedly with sharp thorns. So far this evening, they seemed agreeable enough, though in general his youngest sisters mystified him.

"Roses, why are you wearing those big boots?"

They glanced down at the waders on their feet.

"It was raining today, silly," Rosalyn said. "Didn't you notice?"

"He never notices anything. His head's always in a book," Rosemond said.

They took his bowler and umbrella and hooked them onto the arms of the brass coat tree.

"Did you bring us something of hers?" Rosalyn asked.

"Who, Miss Pennypacker?" He set his satchel on a high shelf where they couldn't reach it. You never knew what they might get up to. "Why would I do that?"

The twins turned to one another, and Jonathan receded from their sphere of interest.

"He could have stolen her pen for us."

"Or a hair pin."

"She'd never miss a hairpin."

"She must have oodles of them."

"Girls," he interrupted. "We do not steal from other people."

They squealed and dissolved into giggles. "We do not steal from other people!" They raced off down the hall, their thick boots clomping. Clods of mud trailed them on the carpet.

He must speak to Clara about how wild the Roses had become, though his mother whispered in his ear to hold off. Steeped in Transcendentalism with a dabbling in Theosophy, and despite her orthodox husband, Evalina believed that children deserved freedom to release their truest selves and inherent divine spirits. Jonathan was only beginning to grasp the ways he had benefited from that bit of wisdom. But how had his mother managed with six children? Granted, she'd had help in the kitchen. The family cook still insisted on preparing their dinners, albeit for half her former salary, which wasn't right and couldn't be justified much longer. Jonathan leaned against the tin wainscoting and let out a worried sigh.

With a crescendo from the parlor, Philomena put a showy finish on a piece and swooped into the front hall. He was taken aback by the sight of her in a dressing gown at six p.m.

"Why didn't you put on proper clothing today, Phil?"

"Good evening to you, too, brother." She leaned to let him kiss the air near her cheek, which he did distractedly.

Jonathan felt faint from lack of food and the weight of his responsibilities. "That's not a good habit to get into."

Philomena swirled away, billows of lace flowing after her. "Have no fear, I'm getting dressed now. We're performing this evening."

"Performing?" He followed her back into the parlor as she gathered up her sheet music. "Where are you going exactly?"

"I told you about our new jobs. We're employed at the Music Hall four nights a week now, Tessa joining me in song."

He vaguely remembered them saying they were off to an

audition, but he had been too preoccupied with his own new position to pay attention. "Is it wise to be out and unaccompanied at night? Shouldn't I go with you for protection?"

"You, protect us? With your fear of spiders and unwillingness to swim the Charles because of snapping turtles? I think not." She closed the lid on the piano keys. "And who says we're unaccompanied? Tessa always has a young gent willing to walk her home. I manage an escort of my own from time to time."

Jonathan tried to think what their father might say. "Won't that type of work spoil your chances?"

Philomena scowled at him. "Chances for what?"

"I don't know," he said, his voice rising in exasperation. "Joining society and getting married, I suppose. Shouldn't you be thinking about that?"

She reached across to pat his flushed cheek. "You worry too much, Jonathan. You should come hear us. It would do you good to have some fun."

He followed her into the front hall. "Father would have put his foot down."

"Yes, he would have, but he isn't here, is he? We need food on the table, and not to rub it in, but I suspect with tips we make more than you do."

Jonathan looked down at his scuffed boots and knew she was right. "I had hoped you girls wouldn't have to work. You each deserve the life of a lady."

Philomena wasn't the prettiest of his sisters—Tessa took that prize—but her round, freckled face was open and her prominent teeth made her smile more appealing.

"I enjoy what I do, Jon, and so does Tessa, at least for now. She'll make a good catch someday but being a kept wife would never suit me."

She gave an innocent shrug, then dodged past him to stomp up the steps. Jonathan knew her tread so well and the sway of her thick braid like a metronome down her back. Thanks to their mother's benign and encouraging influence, each of his sisters seemed confident she could find her own way. About himself, Jonathan wasn't as sure.

Back in the parlor, his gaze settled on the reverend's spindly rocker with its faded scene of willows by a stream painted on the back. A threadbare, flattened cushion was all that his father had ever permitted to soften his seat. Jonathan's sisters had offered plumper pillows, but like many Bostonians of Puritan stock, the reverend was made comfortable by less comfort.

As a boy, Jonathan had sat in a hard pew every Sunday, not daring to move as his father loomed over the congregation from his unadorned pulpit. The long white beard thrashed when he railed against sin and issued the stern warnings of an Old Testament prophet. Having seen a reproduction of Michelangelo's magnificent figure with the outstretched finger and head of flowing white hair, young Jonathan had conflated his father with that God. Both had spoken in irrefutable voices in his head ever since.

He avoided the rocker in favor of the sagging sofa, book satchel at his feet, and his mother's crocheted blanket enfolding him, less for warmth than familiarity. His father had stopped eating soon after her death, though Jonathan and his sisters had tried to ply him with soup and porridge. The young Roses offered up their favorite sugar sticks to no avail.

The growth that had knotted the reverend's intestines, and the anger he had held inside himself all his life, only made worse by doctors who had failed his wife, stole what was left of his appetite. The children sat by his bed for five days and five nights as he withered away. The old man's eyes didn't open once, which to Jonathan seemed entirely in character, as their father had never taken much notice of them during his lifetime.

But in the wee hours of the vigil, after his sisters had given in to exhaustion and gone to bed, Jonathan pulled his chair closer. Through a fog of sorrow and all that remained unspoken between them, he released a soft wail into his folded hands. "Oh, Father, I've been such a disappointment to you."

The reverend, mistaking Jonathan's plaintive cry for that

of a parishioner asking to take the Lord into his flawed and
paltry heart, opened one eye. Jonathan let out a quiet gasp at
the miracle of being heard and seen by his father. He slipped
down from the chair and knelt on the bare floorboards beside
the bed.

"What can I do to please you, Father?" he asked.

The reverend kept the one eye trained on the bowed head
prostrate before him and extended the same bony digit as the
figure in the Sistine Chapel. Jonathan, who as a boy had rarely
been offered his father's hand and had never been invited onto
his lap, eagerly took hold. He squeezed the finger, but not too
hard, as it was no thicker than a twig. He ignored the pain in his
knees, his aching back, and his tired, stinging eyes. The white
beard wafted, the breath rattled inside, and the chest heaved.
More than wisdom, Jonathan hoped for, if not love, at least
acknowledgment. From deep within his father's chest came
muffled words propelled by a gasping exhalation, more air than
sound falling from the trembling lips.

"Give yourself over to Jesus, my son."

The reverend shut his eyes for the last time. Jonathan let
go of the finger and fell back onto the cold floorboards. He
wrapped his arms around his legs and tucked his forehead to
his knees. In the fetal position, he missed his father's final exhalation and the harsh, shuddering finale. The old man had lived
alone, though in a family of eight, and had died alone, though
in the company of his only son. A zealot to the end.

Jonathan heaved his book satchel onto his lap. If only his father
had lasted long enough to see him become a sub-editor at one
of Boston's oldest firms. His thoughts were interrupted by his
oldest sister at the parlor threshold. Clara came swiftly across
the carpet and leaned down to kiss him lightly on the cheek as
their mother used to.

She settled beside him on the faded cushions and asked, "Are
you all right, Jon? You look a little peaked."

He took her hand and clasped it in his own, their skin tones and bone structure so alike.

"I'm all right. How was your day, sister?"

"Well, let's see, we went to the Italian market, the Roses and I, so you know how that went. It took forever but was much more lively than if I'd gone alone."

Clara's name suited her so well, with her soft brown curls tidily grazing her shoulders and her grey eyes plain yet lucid. She had put off marrying Timothy Maverick, a neighbor boy who had once punched Jonathan over some squabble, but who more recently had been named a junior partner at the Federal Savings Bank of Boston. The long-time match was forged in childhood love. But after their parents' passing, Clara had made the decision to care for her younger sisters instead of leaving home, though Jonathan had tried to insist it was his obligation, not hers. He was the man of the house now, though for some reason whenever he used that phrase, Clara just smiled.

"Would you care for a glass of sherry?" she asked.

Though their parents were teetotalers, they kept a few dusty bottles tucked away in a cabinet for when company came.

"I'm ashamed to admit, but I imbibed earlier, so I'd better skip it."

"I hope you won't get into the habit of stopping off on your way home for a nip, like so many men."

"No, you see, I had the drink with my boss right there in the office. That's how it's done."

"What fun!" Clara's eyes lit up. "Though Father would have called your workplace a den of iniquity."

"I suppose he would have." Jonathan pulled from his bag a stack of papers and a folder tied off with a string.

"He wanted you to take up the cloth like Grandfather and his father and all the Cartwright men going back for generations."

"Don't remind me. He thought it would straighten me out, whatever that meant." Jonathan gave a worried sigh, as if his father were with them in the parlor.

Clara reached to brush back the stray blond lock that flitted over his brow, as his mother used to do. In moments such as this one, his favorite sister wouldn't let him forget that she was older by two years. Her eyes fell to his ratty fingernails, which he tucked under his thighs to keep her from scolding him.

"So, tell me, what else happened today at your new job?" she asked.

"Let's see, I met with several authors, including the famous Mrs. Swann. I had that man-to-man conversation with the editor-in-chief, Mr. Gaustad himself. He's the one who served me the drink."

"Is he very good at what he does?"

Jonathan's head wavered from side to side. "He's been at it a long time."

"Wonderful!" She patted down her skirt and started to stand, but Jonathan caught her elbow.

"But, you see, I stole something from him."

"What?" She sat again. "Why would you do that?"

Jonathan's fingers grazed the file on his lap. "Mr. Gaustad told me that Mrs. Swann had given him the start of a new novel. I helped myself and brought it home to read."

"Helped yourself? What does that mean?"

Jonathan explained that before leaving Thames, Royall & Quincy at the end of the day, he had walked past Gaustad's open office door and, seeing no one inside and no one in the hallway, he had slipped undetected into the room. He wasn't sure what had gotten into him, but something compelled him to make this secret foray on Victoria's behalf. At least that's what he told his sister, because he couldn't admit that he'd done it for himself—for his rising, though as yet unarticulated, ambition as an editor. On his way home he had composed his explanation in his mind, but now that Clara had asked, all he could say was how he had accomplished it, and not why.

"I searched the papers on his desk and the manuscripts on the floor. Then I remembered that when he was telling me about it, he had looked down at his drawer."

"Tell me you didn't go into his desk?"

Jonathan brought a fingernail to his lips.

"You were possessed. That's the only explanation for it."

"In a manner of speaking, I was."

Clara's usual optimism rose to the surface, and she stood. "It's too late to worry about it now. You may discover something exciting, like one of our treasure hunts. You were the best at finding the prize."

"I'm going to read it tonight and return it to the drawer before Gaustad gets in tomorrow morning. He'll never know."

"Wonderful! Now, I better go see that the Roses aren't getting into mischief."

"I wonder," Jonathan said, standing, too, "would you have time to read it this evening? I'd love to know what you think."

Clara wiped her hands on her linen apron. "Why not hand it over now? I'll dive in while you see to the girls."

"But I haven't read it myself yet." He clutched the folder to his chest. "As her editor, shouldn't I read it first?"

"Are you worried I'll get to the buried treasure before you?"

He saw how silly he was being and gave it to her.

"Tonight's your favorite. Cook made corned beef hash. Go help yourself." She settled into the window seat. "The twins were hungry, so we ate earlier."

Jonathan's shoulders drooped. He had hoped they might wait for him and all have supper together. Father had dined alone or with their mother at the big table. But Evalina Cartwright had made a practice of sitting with the children while they ate in the kitchen, inquiring about their adventures each day. His sisters were finding a new rhythm to their lives now, and Jonathan didn't live here anymore. Everything had changed.

"I'll see to the Roses. You go ahead and read."

Clara didn't reply. With Victoria's manuscript open on her lap, she was already eager for the promise of reading.

FIVE

Victoria's *cheveret* was of burled walnut, accented by rosewood inlay on the bowed front, with curved cubbyholes and brass-knobbed drawers. The elegantly tapered legs stood on tiptoes, as if eager to assist with her writing. Yet on this morning, even her charming desk couldn't help with the task of final edits. Her eyes drifted to the empty notebooks waiting to be filled with her new project. Gaustad should have read her first chapter by now. Why hadn't she heard from him? And why did Mr. Cartwright—Jonathan, as he had invited her to call him—write his comments on her current galley in such a cramped hand, as if eking out his thoughts through a narrow funnel?

She pushed her chair away from the desk and paced a worn path across the room, pink slippers skimming the Turkish carpet and kimono fluttering at her ankles. Past her four-poster bed, the washstand, and the lady's dress form in the corner, Victoria paused at her bookshelves and ran a hand over the leather-backed volumes, many written by authors of the day—that is to say, mostly men. Had they been instructed to write only what their publishers demanded and not what they themselves wanted in their hearts to write? Somehow, she doubted it.

Retreating to her rose-colored chaise, she reclined and brought to her chest a decorative pillow embroidered with Mrs. Browning's words: *Art is Much, but Love is More.* As a girl, she had believed such oozing sentiments, and in Mrs. Swann's tales it went without saying that the heart was a simple, predictable organ. But by now Victoria had come to realize the sad truth that she knew little about either art or love.

Jonathan had sat with his head bowed over her manuscript, the dreamy strand of flaxen hair falling across his brow. Mrs. Swann's characters surreptitiously swooned over one another all the time. A lady's cascading curls, dainty shoes, and low-cut bodice, or a gentleman's broad shoulders, manly stance, and clenched jaw prompted similar sighs to the one she released now. Hearing herself, she felt foolish and tossed the pillow to the carpet. She could routinely create a leading man but had no idea how to obtain one for herself.

The first time she had laid eyes on Raymond Byrne, he had been leaning against a tent pole at the county fair, the picture of nonchalance and savoir faire in his colorful plaid suit and rakish cap cocked over one eye. From the podium, Victoria read the opening of her first novel to a sparse audience who had wandered in, listened for a bit, and wandered back out, eager to ride the whirlygig and see that year's blue-ribbon livestock. As one or two ladies waited for her to sign copies of her book, Raymond had moved stealthily forward, a cat closing in on its prey. His shadow crossed the page, and she took in his sideways grin that seemed to suggest she might want his autograph instead of the other way around. Lean and handsome, with a debonair mustache, Raymond Byrne could have been a star of the stage for all she knew. From the start, they spoke in hushed tones, as if they had something to hide, which soon they did.

Taken with her gingham dress and the ribbons in her hair, he seemed momentarily boyish and hopeful, though in fact he was world-weary. She mistook his longing for sophistication. She didn't realize that all he was craving was a smoke and a drink and for someone to come along and save him. When he opened his silver cigarette case to her, she shook her head and he tucked it away.

"I didn't know girls like you existed in real life. You're a good one, aren't you?"

She wanted to refute him, but what was the point. He was right. She was unbearably good. With confidence he actually lacked and a meanness he later showed, he did something surprising. Raymond reached across for her braid and tugged it, mischievous as a bad boy in class, and hard enough to make her heart jolt and her insides leap. At that moment, her father had stepped back into the tent. Charles Meeks took one glance at the stranger who had a fist around his daughter's lovely hair and, though a man of few words, made his opinion clear. On the way to their wagon, he told his daughter in no uncertain terms that she was forbidden from seeing someone of that sort ever again.

But flying high from her first public appearance as an author and determined to leave her father's provincial ways behind her, Victoria announced she would do as she pleased and refused to sit beside him on the way home. Instead, she swayed and sang with her boots dangling down from the back of the buckboard while old Oscar the mule carried them along the familiar, rutted road. She had secretly agreed to let Raymond pay her a call the following Saturday when she knew her father would be out.

As if she'd written it herself, romance was rising off the page and into her life. But one week later when Raymond arrived in a borrowed buggy and offered flowers swiped from a neighbor's yard, she could hardly remember him. It was as if he'd stepped out of a distant dream, an apparition from a forgotten, better time. Her father was gone by then and the innocent girl who Raymond had hoped to find at home was gone too.

Victoria rose from the chaise, more tired than ever, and wasn't sure what to do. Her empty notebooks called to her, but she couldn't bring herself to create a new invented world if it meant remembering an old sorrowful one. She might as well stick to Mrs. Swann if she wasn't brave enough to look back. But then Victoria remembered her memory chest and went to take it down. Whenever she felt most unsettled and stirred up inside, she retrieved it.

Moving the vanity pouffe over to her wardrobe, she kicked off her slippers and stepped up, holding out her arms for balance. Reaching past the silk and satin dresses and around the stacks of hatboxes, she found a wooden crate made by her father for her twelfth birthday. As Victoria lifted the heavy thing down, she almost lost her footing but managed to carry to her desk the rough box that held what was left of her childhood.

Removing the lid, she lifted out a yellowed ivory comb that had belonged to her mother. Priscilla Meeks had died when Victoria was only four, not long after her father had returned with the Massachusetts Ninth Regiment, a bullet wound to his left thigh. Victoria set down the comb and took from the crate the offending bullet. It seemed unlikely that such a small thing could have started a series of events that created such havoc and pain.

With Charles laid up from his injury, his sister Edwina had come to help with the farm and with young Vicky, as she was called then. A few days into Edwina's stay, Priscilla went to collect eggs from the coop, but a hen got underfoot and tangled in her skirts. Victoria's mother tripped and scraped her elbow on a rusty nail. Later that week, she was overtaken by lockjaw. With Charles infirm and too distraught to take care of his wife, it fell to Edwina to tend to her sister-in-law. Being only twenty-three and lacking any medical knowledge, she turned to *The Frugal Housewife* for trusted advice.

Victoria lifted the tattered book from the crate and thumbed through it, amazed that no one had thrown it into the fire for all the harm it had done them. Edwina had followed the book's instructions carefully, placing a rind of pork on the wound. When that didn't work, she stirred pulverized chalk into a thick batter, poured it into a cheesecloth sack and treated the site. Priscilla's cries of pain struck terror into her family. But as Victoria thought of it now, she felt most sorry for Edwina, who had tried her best. Frightened and unsure what to do next, her aunt had used turpentine as suggested in the helpful guide, though she wasn't sure if she was supposed to douse the wound or pour it down her sister-in-law's throat. In the end, she did both.

Victoria put aside the disastrous book. As the story went, after a long night during which Priscilla's other-worldly howls forged deep grooves into the cerebral hemispheres of Charles, Edwina's, and young Vicky's brains, sunrise arrived, and with it one of the most famous doctors and authors in all of Boston. Dr. Oliver Wendell Holmes had been visiting his good friend

Ralph Waldo Emerson and, getting wind of the tragedy taking place in the next town over, appeared at the Meeks' farm. After consoling Edwina and giving no clarification on the correct uses of turpentine, he took the patient's pulse and pronounced her dead.

Victoria was ashamed to admit that the unexpected arrival of the great literary figure into her life had come to feel almost as significant to her as the loss of her mother. Surely it must have meant something that he had patted her on the head and given her a barley sweet from his vest pocket. But nothing more had come of it, and, the truth was, she could barely remember that day. But the aftermath of that time was inescapable. Victoria could feel the ache of the solitary days and weeks and years following her mother's passing.

As a girl on her father's farm, she had endured a winter's worth of grey skies, an endless ocean of dull hours, a tsunami of loneliness. Charles turned his grief into labor, staying in the fields from dawn until after dusk. Edwina, whom Victoria had come to count on, departed not long after the tragedy, leaving the girl in the care of a series of local women whose attentions made little impression on her. As soon as she was old enough to read, she turned to books for companionship.

Books still provided the same consolation in her room on the second floor of the house on Brattle Street, the shelves crammed with volumes that made her feel too much for them. They had saved her as a child and offered her a direction in life. But the truth was, when the last page was read and the last page written, the sorrowful grey fog that had been with her all along remained. Not even Mrs. Swann's success had rescued Victoria from it. If anything, the isolation required to keep up her false identity had made matters worse. With each book written and each passing year, she knew less than ever about Mrs. Swann's purported expertise: love.

Victoria sank into her desk chair and pushed aside the galley. She could hear her assistant tapping away in the next room, busy corresponding with Mrs. Swann's readers and conducting research for the next Mrs. Swann tale. She hated to interrupt her, but if anyone could help get her back on track, it was Dottie Windsor. Victoria called for her and she came, tucking a pencil behind her ear and placing an envelope into the pocket of the apron she wore to protect her dress from ink stains, purposeful as ever. They wished each other good morning, and Victoria asked what Dottie had been working on.

"The usual. Replies to the *Letters of the Lovelorn*. But I see you're not dressed yet. Don't forget you have the Ladies Book and Travel Club this afternoon. Best to get a move on."

Victoria gazed down hopelessly at her desk.

"Making any progress?" Dottie asked.

Victoria gave a faint sigh. "I don't seem to know what I'm doing anymore."

"You have a deadline. That's what you're doing."

Though they were the same age, they both thought of Dottie as an older, more mature sister to her employer. Seventh of eleven children raised in a Catholic household, Dottie and her siblings had slept four to a bed and spent their days navigating the crowds in Dudley Square. Her early years had been as overpopulated as Victoria's were solitary. She often counted on her assistant to know what she did not: how to grapple with people, including herself.

Dottie began to collect the dirty dishes scattered around the room. She couldn't stop from being helpful, although Victoria reminded her often that she wasn't the maid. Victoria returned the items to the memory box and stowed it back on the top shelf.

"I have a new editor, Dottie. Did I tell you? His name is Jonathan Cartwright, and he was at Harvard until recently. I wonder if your Fletcher knows him."

"Jonathan? Why of course we know him." Dottie gathered up the clothes strewn across the back of the chaise and headed to the armoire. "He and Fletch were undergraduates together. They got their higher degrees at the same time too. Everyone listens to what Jonathan has to say about books."

"That's reassuring." Victoria tied a stray scarf around the tailor dummy's headless neck. "But I wonder why a person would want to study a book and not simply read it?"

Dottie laughed. "I'd say that's a question for the gentlemen."

"No, it's my ignorance. I should have attended school and not read in a hodgepodge fashion at home. I was in such a hurry to become a writer."

"And a fine one you are!" Dottie hung up the last piece of clothing and banged shut the wardrobe doors. Brusque and efficient, but not unkind, she offered an encouraging nod to the desk. "Shall we get back to it?"

Victoria's assistant was a writer, a poet, and a top-notch researcher. She had been the one to suggest malachite for the hilt of the pharaoh's sword in Mrs. Swann's popular Egyptian tale, *Sunstruck on Desert Sands*. Dottie had also insisted on a shaggy Mongolian pony to carry the hero across the steppes of Central Asia in *A Lady Lost in the Orient*. Without Dottie's clever additions, the adventure tales would have been far less convincing. Also, without her, there'd be no advice column in the back of the monthly dime stories. As the years had worn on, it wasn't lost on Victoria that her assistant had become more Mrs. Swann than Victoria herself. But what, Victoria wondered for the first time, did Dottie herself choose to write?

Victoria drifted to the windows and brushed aside the lace curtains. "Dottie, are your poems set in made-up lands like Mrs. Swann's tales? Are they about fairies and nymphs and mermaids and such? I know that sort of thing is popular."

"I don't write nonsense verse or children's rhymes, if that's what you mean."

"But as a poet, I imagine you express yourself in a heartfelt manner that suits your subject and pleases your readers?"

"I haven't any readers. Though my husband enjoys my poems."

"Raymond used to read my novels but now he only cares about getting his hands on the royalty checks."

Dottie continued to busy herself by collecting dirty teacups and the Cantonware teapot from where they had been left around the room. She muttered a reminder to herself to instruct the maid to tidy up twice a day not once. Victoria continued to gaze out the window where spring had begun its quiet fanfare. Twin cherry trees burst with pink flowers, and a pair of goldfinches streaked by with surprising dashes of color.

"Are your poems grounded in nature?" she asked. "Daffodils recollected in tranquility, that sort of thing?"

"I write about nothing fancy, just everyday life. I might do a poem about this teapot here." Victoria turned to see Dottie place the pretty blue and white ceramic on a lacquered tray.

"That teapot there?"

"Yes, why not?"

Victoria came closer. "The point being that a writer can find inspiration anywhere, if willing to see things as they *truly* are?"

"You are in a strange mood today."

"No, I'm fine. I'm just tired of my fantasy tales. I want to write about life as we know it."

Dottie crossed her arms over her sturdy chest. "What does Mr. Gaustad have to say about that?"

Victoria touched the teapot with the tip of her finger, a little afraid to tell the truth. "He wasn't enthusiastic."

"I should think not."

The violet-covered wallpaper—nosegays all the same, one after the next—offered no escape. Victoria had found refuge in this sunny corner of the house in which she slept and wrote and read and roamed in her thoughts, but there was little to it.

"I'm tired of exotic locales, but I can't set a story here where nothing ever happens. There's only the sloshing of the Charles River and the call of the tinsmith as he roams Brattle Street. There's no story in the sound of coal falling through the shoot and into the basement. It's all so dull."

"Maybe, but I much prefer Brattle Street to my neighborhood."

"There's nothing of interest in my life since becoming Mrs. Swann. I've done nothing but write. I must try to imagine what it's like to be a young woman new to the city as I once was. It's too bad I don't know any young women anymore. I could ask them about their experiences today."

"You may think you don't know any, but they think they know you." Dottie went to the four-poster bed and vigorously smoothed the chenille covers. "We get dozens of letters a day," she continued, "from girls sharing their most intimate concerns with you."

"Ah, of course! What a good idea, Dottie. I must read their letters." Victoria joined her at the bed and plumped the pillows with renewed energy. "I imagine they can teach me a great deal at this juncture."

"I doubt they can teach you anything. They're silly girls who get themselves into one mess after the next."

"What sort of messes?"

Dottie took a pillow from Victoria and set it down properly. "Well, this morning, for example, there was a letter from a young lady whose boss keeps her late at the office after everyone else has gone home so he can make advances on her."

"How monstrous. The man should be stopped. And what did you advise her?"

"I told her she must take the situation in hand and get a new job right away."

"But what if she were to take a stand against him and put up a fight? Her difficulty isn't altogether different from being kidnapped by pirates or held in the chamber of an Incan king. She must use her wiles, mustn't she?" Victoria was enjoying herself now and flopped down on the made bed. "Come on, wouldn't you love to put a cutlass into that young lady's hands? That would show the gentleman."

Dottie stood over her and scowled. "In case you haven't noticed, we're not afloat on the Indian Ocean. We must remember that a young woman's reputation is more important than her wages, especially since her ultimate goal is marriage." Dottie smoothed her apron and returned to the door.

Victoria sat up. "But *is* that the goal for every young lady? Must it be?"

"Their letters express as much. Marriage remains the best way out."

Victoria ran her fingertips over the bedspread. "But out of what, I wonder?"

Dottie gave no reply.

"Out of this world, I suppose," Victoria answered herself, "which explains why my romance adventures are so popular."

Dottie lifted the tea tray. "Is that all this morning? I need to get back to work."

Victoria stood. "I'm sorry to have kept you, but I really would love to hear how you solve at least one of these young ladies' problems."

"Mrs. Swann doesn't solve anyone's problems. That's up to them."

"But you do offer them some hope?"

Dottie set down the tray. "Have you ever read Mrs. Swann's advice columns?"

"I'm afraid I've been too swamped with my novels and writing the penny dreadfuls."

"Let me put it this way, Mrs. Swann is known for her forthrightness. She doesn't sugarcoat."

"She does in her fiction. I mean, I do, in my fiction. It's *all* sugarcoating."

"There's a world of difference between your fantasies and my column. Here," Dottie said and pulled an envelope from her pocket and unfolded it. "This letter will give you a sense of the tangles these girls find themselves in and how we advise them."

"We, meaning you. You've done such a fine job, Dottie."

Slight pink colored Dottie's cheeks, but she cleared her throat and began to read.

Please allow me to tell you my tale of woe. I am sixteen, and I work in a store, but there is a rich man in town who says he wants to marry me. This man has bachelor apartments, and he has taken me to them twice. His rooms are beautiful and I would dearly love to live there. When I was there, he gave me some wine, and he says if I will

come again and be his wife, I can have everything lovely.
I'm feeling poorly now and am worried what might be the
cause. I want him to hurry up and say when he will marry
me. Do you think I can trust him to marry me? Why, I
wonder, doesn't he set the wedding day and make us man
and wife?

"We receive at least one like this a week. I respond directly,
lest we be too late."

Victoria went to the window. "We must assume her circumstances are as bad as she fears."

"The number of unwed women in a compromised state is
astounding. I'll send her information about adoption centers
through the church. What I *should* do is contact the Gerry Society to go after the man for taking advantage of an underage
girl."

Victoria put her fingers to the pane. "But if the young lady's
situation is truly urgent, she must be informed of a more expe-
dited way to manage it. There is another choice." She could feel
her assistant's eyes on her back.

"Irregular doctors who prescribe poisons and conduct illegal procedures? Back alleys and wads of cash handed over with
no questions asked? Is that what you're suggesting?"

Victoria's fingers grew white where she pressed against the
glass. "I know it's not a desired option, but sometimes it's the
only one a woman has."

Dottie folded the letter and returned it to her pocket. "Good
thing I'm the one writing these replies and not you. The hint of
such a suggestion would lose us not only our readers, but our
publisher as well. Have you forgotten that Mrs. Swann has a
reputation to uphold?"

Victoria had never known Dottie to sound angry before.
Stern often, but never angry.

"But the girl mustn't throw away her life. We need to *help*
young ladies like her. She has no one to turn to."

"She has Mrs. Swann," Dottie said firmly. "Which is why
we cannot allow soft sentiments to guide us when dealing with

her and others like her. It's fine for your fictions, but these are *real* people with *real* problems. You must stick to Mrs. Swann's tales while I focus on the harsh world in which we live."

Victoria bowed her head. "I'm sorry, Dottie, I didn't mean to question your judgment. Of course, you're right. I just wish it wasn't so."

Victoria thanked her, but her mind was spinning with what she would have wanted to say to the young lady who wrote that letter. Like her, she had been trapped once and had believed there was no way out. Indeed, she still felt that way, but there was no time to dwell on it now. She was due at the Ladies Book and Travel Club at noon.

SIX

When they first learned to read as young children, Jonathan and Clara would sit huddled over the same book, taking turns flipping the pages. They recited Robert Louis Stevenson's *Child's Garden of Verses* in unison and debated their favorite illustrations—Jonathan preferring the toy soldiers on the counterpane, while Clara loved the daffodils blown by the wind on the hill. About the many books that had entered their lives since, they had had only occasional disagreements. While Clara was buoyant in appearance and outlook, she preferred serious literary texts, rich with complex sentiments. Difficult characters, ones who were not entirely evil but not altogether good, helped Jonathan to grapple with his simultaneous reverence for, and fear of, his father. And the sudden loss of both parents, one so soon after the other, proved that changes could occur as precipitously as in the arc of a written story. At any moment, a page of life could turn, revealing an altogether different, and far less rosy, chapter.

Jonathan hovered over Clara as she sat curled up in his favorite reading spot, the parlor window seat overlooking the street. He yanked the damask curtain tighter behind her and adjusted the lamp on the shelf to cast a better glow on the manuscript that lay open on her lap. Despite his fussing, she remained absorbed in Victoria's prose.

"So?" he interrupted. "What do you think?"

Without lifting her eyes, she made a soft, indecisive sound. "You'll have to see for yourself."

"Oh dear, that doesn't sound good." He held out a hand for the folder.

Clara gave it to him and stretched her arms over her head. "It's the start of a realistic story about a poor, uneducated country girl who comes to the city where she encounters difficulties right away—untrustworthy people and harsh conditions, that sort of thing. Her downfall seems inevitable given the foreshadowing. Rather predictable, I'm afraid."

"You're a tough critic."

Clara stood and tipped her head from side to side to release a crick in her neck. "Your Mrs. Swann swings from one extreme to another. If I remember right, the heroines of her romance adventures strain credulity with their happy endings, while a tragic downfall appears inevitable for this one."

Jonathan flopped onto the cushions that she had warmed. "I suppose we'll never know, since Gaustad is determined to discourage her from completing it. It's terribly sad."

"It would be sadder if you were to lose your job over it. You should go along with whatever Gaustad says. He knows more than either of us about what ladies like to read."

"You're a lady."

"Yes, I am, but not a typical reader. You should know that by now. I should have gotten a higher degree like you, only I couldn't bear being in class with you pretentious fellows. Anyway, I encourage you to make up your own mind. Don't listen to me or to Gaustad."

Jonathan made a worried little grumble.

"Trust yourself, Jon. Really, it's high time you did," she said, and left.

First thing the following morning, Jonathan slipped into Gaustad's empty office and returned the opening chapter of the manuscript to his desk drawer. He had read it the night before and would have liked to have kept it but worried about the consequences should Gaustad find it missing. Perry had been sent out to purchase pastries for Miss Pennypacker's upcoming visit, so Jonathan alone welcomed the entertainer into the offices of Thames, Royall & Quincy. As he lifted his head from a low bow, he tried not to stare, but, my goodness, that face! How had the Lord—whom he rarely called upon, but in this instance was much needed—deemed it wise to put such ideal features together in one person? The lips curved lusciously, the cheeks angled sharply, the chin arrived at a cherubic point, but mostly, those smoky green eyes.

Jonathan knew that most men would have been enthralled by the singer's curvaceous outline, but he was more drawn to her spectacular ensemble. She wore a dress of shimmering peacock-blue silk with an extravagant feather boa in a matching hue. High on her head of red hair sat a crowned hat overflowing with flowers and birds as abundant as a summer garden, surrounded by chiffon net and lace, all of it buzzing with razzmatazz. He felt a little faint but cleared his throat and got hold of himself.

"The directors of the company are meeting down the hall, so we'll take tea and get acquainted in Mr. Gaustad's office."

"Yes, let's get acquainted."

A sly expression crossed Miss Pennypacker's perfect features and Jonathan's cheeks turned beet red. The lady seemed more than accustomed to men fumbling in her presence. She waved a gloved hand in the air, multiple diamond and emerald rings flashing from her black-laced fingers. He could already picture his youngest sisters imitating Miss Pennypacker with cigar bands rings.

"So long as I can rest my feet. These new button-ups are the worst."

She lifted the frills at the hem of her skirts to expose white leather boots with pointed toes and substantial heels. Her layers of petticoats, some black and some royal blue, were edged in turquoise and mauve stitching. Jonathan had only ever seen such iridescent shades on the wings of the stuffed tropical birds at the Peabody Natural History Museum. There couldn't be a more exquisitely attired lady in all of Boston. Jonathan felt frantic to memorize every detail for the sake of his sisters.

"Come along, dear boy. We have things to discuss."

Though striking, Miss Pennypacker's voice was the only thing that wasn't beautiful about her—grating couldn't quite capture it. She spoke loudly, as if to an assembled crowd, which she must be accustomed to doing. It made little sense that a woman with the singing voice of an angel had the speaking voice of a harpy, but there it was. The Lord worked in mysterious ways, his father often said.

In Gaustad's office, Jonathan pointed Miss Pennypacker toward one of the leather chairs and prepared to take the seat opposite. Instead, she roamed the perimeter, her ample silk and satin skirts swishing provocatively with every movement. She paused before the wilted palm. "Blazes, I hope you treat your authors better than your plants."

Jonathan started to apologize for its poor care when shouting erupted from the hallway, followed by a crashing sound and angry accusations from gentlemen whose words were far from gentlemanly.

"Sounds like McDuffy's after hours," Miss Pennypacker said, referring to a Boston drinking establishment Jonathan had yet to visit.

While his instincts told him to stay put in Gaustad's office, and quietly shut the door, Miss Pennypacker went straightaway to the threshold. She craned her head out, the silk flowers and birds bobbing. Her abundant red hair and the swan's-down boa on her shoulders also shook, though not out of fear or anxiety, but from an unmistakable delight. She clapped her gloved hands and the rings dinged together.

"A brawl at a publishing house of all places. How exciting!"

Jonathan edged closer—standing near enough to catch her rose perfume, which almost made him swoon—and peered out into the hallway. No, not rose perfume, he reconsidered, gardenia. Tessa would want the same once he told her.

"Shall we shut the door and discuss your book project?" he tried.

But at that moment, Gaustad stormed from the meeting room into the hallway, huffing and puffing, his paunch protruding and his face aflame. "You have no business running a gentleman's business, as you are no gentleman!" he shouted.

Behind Gaustad, the stylishly dressed Louis Russell leaned

against the doorframe, his spats crossed at the ankles. "Sorry to say, old man, this isn't your place anymore. Might not be your town. I might have purchased your home too." He raised his palms, as if to say it was all beyond his control. He turned to one of his henchmen. "See Mr. Gaustad out, will you, Byrne?"

"Yes, Mr. Russell," said a tall, lean man in an ill-fitting suit.

Russell's lackey followed on Gaustad's heels, his black pompadour bobbing with each swift, loose stride. He didn't acknowledge Jonathan, but eyed Miss Pennypacker in a way that Jonathan didn't care for, but which she seemed to take in stride.

Gaustad arrived at his office door, greeted the lady, and muttered, "Out of my way, Cartwright. I must collect my things."

From his desk, the old editor began to gather stacks of papers and notebooks, his pen, several antique leather-bound tomes, and more. He placed them all on the worn leather seat of his desk chair and frowned down at the sad mess.

"What are you going to do, sir?" Jonathan asked him.

"I'm going to take half a century's worth of publishing know-how and walk out that door. God help you if you choose to stay working for that cussed, uneducated heathen. Pardon my language, Miss Pennypacker."

"Not at all."

The unpleasant man with the slick black hair stepped into the office. "I'm here to escort you out, Frederick."

"What are you doing here anyway, Byrne? Does Victoria know you're here?"

Jonathan couldn't fathom how Gaustad might know this fellow or how Mrs. Swann could possibly be involved.

"It doesn't matter what she knows," the unpleasant man said. "I work for Mr. Russell now. I'm part of the *new* Thames, Royall & Quincy. We're going to liven up the place. Isn't that right, Miss Pennypacker?" He winked at the lady, but she brushed him off with a cool gaze.

"I don't know what's happening here, but I love Mrs. Swann's books. I've read every single one and decided on this publishing establishment because of them."

Gaustad puffed up noticeably.

Jonathan summoned his courage to say, "Have no fear, Miss Pennypacker, I'm committed to seeing that Thames, Royall & Quincy continues to publish Mrs. Swann."

He hoped the long-time editor-in-chief would be pleased that he had taken up the mantle with gusto, but Gaustad remained preoccupied with adding items to his chair. A stack of manuscript folders teetered there now, and Jonathan feared Victoria's chapter was in amongst them.

"I'll be the one to tell Victoria what to do," Russell's lackey said.

"Excuse me?" Jonathan asked with a nervous laugh. "But who, in fact, are you?"

"I'm her husband, Raymond Byrne."

Jonathan tried to control his shock. This unsavory character was married to Victoria?

"You must be Cartwright." Byrne looked Jonathan up and down. "You should know that Russell says it's time to pick up the pace. She's gotten a little lazy working with Gaustad here."

"Victoria and I worked tirelessly together for years," the old editor said. "We were highly successful at our current rate of output." Gaustad pressed his fists decisively onto the desktop, but then let his head droop between his shoulders and shook it slowly from side to side. "Oh, forget it. I refuse to share any further publishing insights with the new owner. I'm sad to say, I leave Mrs. Swann and all my authors to the dogs."

Jonathan prepared to counter that, but Russell came into the office with several businessmen trailing behind, their cigar smoke swirling and the whiskey and ice in their glasses rattling. They peered from the threshold, as if witnessing one of Mr. Barnum's freak shows.

"Byrne, I see you've fallen down on your first assignment," Russell said, seemingly ready to blast Victoria's husband, but then he noticed Miss Pennypacker. He strode over, took her gloved hand, and kissed it, pausing to admire the many rings.

As Russell and Miss Pennypacker engaged in flirtatious banter, Jonathan studied Mr. Byrne. With a poorly groomed beard and an oversized suit, his eyes beady and darting, the man was downright disreputable. He was jittery all over, as if invisible ants crawled up his legs, and far too gaunt to be an effective henchman. Jonathan himself was slight and of medium height at best, but if forced, he could take on Mr. Byrne with a swift punch to the ribs. He wasn't in the habit of concocting pugilist strategies, but something about the man brought it to mind.

Gaustad shrugged away the sweaty grasp of Raymond Byrne, placed his hands on the back of his chair, and began to push it forward.

"Should I stop him, sir?" Byrne asked.

"No." Russell waved a hand. "Let him go. It can't be that difficult doing whatever it is he did all these years. What does an editor do, anyway?"

No one answered and the brass wheels squeaked and complained with each rotation. The old editor moved slowly across the threadbare, stained carpet. The books and the papers on the seat quaked with each bump as he made his way over the threshold and out the office door.

It was a shocking sight—one that seemed to capture so much: Boston's past being escorted out by a ruffian and overseen by a rogue. A grander, more genteel world had been kicked to the curb. As the young editor Perry Bliss came hurrying up the sidewalk, bakery box in hand, he froze in alarm. Several other young men of publishing followed at Gaustad's heels, forming an impromptu funeral procession. Miss Pennypacker trailed behind as well, adding to the spectacle.

Only Jonathan stayed in the editor-in-chief's office, admiring the crowded shelves and the surfaces burdened with important projects. He was tempted to pull up a chair—except that Gaustad had taken it. Someday, he might put his feet up on the desk that, if all went well, could be his, especially if he succeeded in retrieving the promising opening chapter of Victoria's new novel. Clara hadn't been captivated by it, but he had. After turning the last page, he had longed to read more. He could imagine how this new book by Victoria could change the course of not only her career, but of his as well. So it was with a great flourish that he flung open the desk drawer, looked down, and let out a gasp. It was empty. Not only was Gaustad gone, but the start of Victoria's new book was gone too.

SEVEN

The Ladies Book and Travel Club met quarterly in the chilly basement of Memorial Hall. The fathers and husbands of the members had built the impressive structure in honor of the sons of Harvard sacrificed over a quarter century before. Visitors whispered the names of the dead etched in marble accompanied by the names of haunted places—Antietam, Gettysburg, Manassas. With its two-toned brick colonnade, massive stained-glass rose window, and high-arched ceiling of ribbed mahogany, Memorial Hall housed a vast dining room, a bell tower protected by gargoyles, and, best of all, a concert hall that boasted the finest acoustics in the nation after Mr. Carnegie's own.

Each opulent detail stood in marked contrast to the women who stepped from their carriages and marched up the brick paths, chins thrust forward in steely determination. They wore thick overcoats with old-fashioned bonnets or unadorned woolen caps. The more distinguished the family, the less the appearance of wealth or ease. Elder matrons ran the club with iron efficiency. Meetings began at noon and ended at one. Social hour took place afterward, though was sparsely attended. What was the point of standing around chatting while the day slipped away?

As a younger and newer member, Victoria might have liked to get to know some of the more approachable dames but had her own reasons for avoiding social interaction. She tried not to draw attention to herself and came and went without a word, yet never missed a meeting. These gatherings provided invaluable details of cuisine, costume, and culture from distant lands which she used in her novels. Speakers shared not only personal anecdotes of their travels, but research gleaned from authorities on each destination under discussion. Their presentations weren't frivolous travel logs, but scholarly reports, complete with bibliographies.

Unlike other ladies' clubs across the country, where the participants gossiped and tippled sherry while playing whist or canasta, the Cambridge women took their task seriously, as they did most things. The suffragette cause and the plight of the poor were never far from their minds. Their gaze remained focused beyond their cohort, which was why none had ever asked Victoria anything personal or surmised her identity. Known only as Mrs. Byrne, they took her for a nicely dressed, unassuming lady who never added to discussions, so didn't warrant their attention. They never pieced together that her pleasant enough countenance was, in fact, that of the elegant and much-admired Mrs. Swann, as depicted in silhouette portraits on her books' frontispieces. When first put up for membership by a neighbor on Brattle Street, the only question posed by the admissions committee concerned her husband. Victoria let fall from her lips the name of his club on Beacon Hill and that was that. In Boston, it took little to join society, but to belong was another thing entirely. That took generations, if ever.

Had they known who she was, the Cambridge women might have approved of Mrs. Swann's stern replies to the *Letters of the Lovelorn*. But they would have peered down their noses at the penny dreadfuls—the thin, pamphlet-length stories with enticing etchings on the covers of leading ladies in distress and titles surrounded by Art Nouveau floral designs or other decorative embellishments. Young women rushed to purchase these morsels from the newsstand each month. At this moment, as Victoria made her way up the brick walkway toward Memorial Hall, shopgirls on their lunch breaks perched on park benches, faces hidden behind Mrs. Swann's latest dime novel. Hours of filing and copying dull paperwork, days of selling clothing they couldn't afford, weeks of scrubbing floors and polishing silver, or years of servitude to deafening machines would drift away as they read of heroines strolling barefoot on tropical shores or striding up boulevards in a sun-blanched city. Who could blame her readers for longing to be elsewhere when their lives were filled with such drudgery? At least Victoria assumed that was the case. She hadn't actually met any of them.

She often tried to imagine her readers, not only the common girls who devoured her stories and wrote their lovelorn letters, but the more prosperous married women who purchased her full-length novels. Upper-class ladies sought refuge from the strains of their complicated, acquisitive lives by enjoying the nineteen hardbacks of Mrs. Swann. This thought usually brought a smile to Victoria's face, but today it only caused her to let out a stuttering breath. If she didn't give them what they had come to expect, would they abandon her altogether? They could so easily turn their striving eyes elsewhere.

She knew all about their fickle tastes from the ladies' magazines, which she studied with the care of an anthropologist. Thanks to rising industrialization and booming commerce, husbands toiled longer at their desks and their well-off wives grew restless and in need of greater diversion. They painted at easels or spent hours over intricate needlework at country homes. They adventured along dirt lanes, lace parasols protecting them from the sun as their voluminous skirts brushed aside wildflowers. They took up backgammon and croquet, and rode railway cars to the end of the line, only to turn around and ride them back.

Though never asked to join them, Victoria tried to keep up. From advertisements in the glossies, she learned that sophisticated ladies had a fan to match every outfit, kid gloves in a rainbow of colors worn at the wrist or to the elbow, and multiple styles of hats, piled with ruffles, bunches of lace, artificial or real flowers, fruits and vegetables, not to mention copious feathers that were quietly decimating America's bird population.

She adjusted the tulle that encircled her French chapeau and smoothed the pearl buttons on the cuffs of her linen duster. The exquisite cream-colored hand stitching on her chestnut brown Italian leather gloves took her breath away. If only she could write a novel, or a story, or a single sentence, as honest and true as those perfect stitches, then she might be satisfied. The longing in Victoria to be a fine writer outweighed the hope of ever being befriended by fine ladies.

With some effort, she pulled open the door to Memorial Hall and headed down to the basement. The scheduled speaker was the newest recruit, a young Mrs. Harrison Sturgis, recently moved from the wilds of Texas. Apparently, the Sturgises had traveled to Egypt and she would share a description of that experience. Victoria had set at least one novel there—*Trapped in a Pharoah's Tomb*, a high seller if she recalled, though the details were hazy to her now. A final sword fight in a cool, hidden chamber of a pyramid, the heroine holding her own with a saber, though it was the hero who plunged the decisive blade into the black-robed villain. Trunks of gold and an elaborate mask, unless she was getting the story confused with one on a sultry isle involving pirate treasure. She offered a tight-lipped greeting to mirror that of the Cambridge ladies and joined them in an actual cool, hidden chamber—a music practice room with bare walls and folding wooden chairs.

After Mrs. Robert Bigelow read aloud the minutes from the previous meeting and they were approved, all craned around to locate today's speaker, though there was little doubt she must be the bright blond in the back row. Mrs. Sturgis was awfully pretty but badly overdressed in a deep salmon-colored silk extravaganza, stunning pink bolero jacket, and large toque, ruched with tulle and feathers at her neck—far too much frippery for this crowd.

She came up the aisle, beaming at first and shuffling note cards in her small gloved hands until they accidentally fell to the floor. As she crouched to collect them, she sputtered apologies in a light accent. Victoria knelt and helped her pick them up. The young lady thanked her, lovely head bobbing and eyes moist with fright.

"It's all right," Victoria whispered. "They don't bite."

Mrs. Sturgis let out nervous giggle and held out her hand. "I'm Missy."

"Victoria Byrne. Good luck, Missy."

To her credit, Missy gave a perfectly acceptable travel talk. She wasn't eloquent but didn't need to be. The photos did all the work. The ladies passed around the stack of brown-tinged images and, when they reached Victoria, she became lost in them. The pyramids at Giza rose from an ocean of desert and she could see a heroine, brave and true, arriving on horseback, wind tossing her scarf and tangling in her hair. A woman could so easily lose her bearings and drown in all that sand. But what a glorious submersion it would be!

Missy caught Victoria's attention as she described a danger-ous-sounding incident. Her party had returned at dusk to their Bedouin tents after a long ride. The wind whipped up and the desert sands swirled around them. Suddenly, her camel brayed, spat, and reared back. Victoria leaned forward in her folding chair as Missy described the moment she feared for her life. But luckily, a native guide, a man named Mohammed, had handled the situation with aplomb. He spoke to the animal in the correct way and helped Mrs. Sturgis find her footing on solid ground. Mr. Sturgis had merely chuckled and captured his wife's fright-ened expression on his box camera.

Missy gamely shared the photo now. She was a fine girl, but clearly her husband was a lout. What if she'd been knocked unconscious to the hard dirt? Would he have laughed had the camel stomped and broken her every rib? Before ever meeting this Harrison Sturgis, Victoria had cast him as the rogue in one of Mrs. Swann's tales.

Missy's adventure differed, though, from one by Mrs. Swann in one essential way. Mohammed was no stagy, handsome prince, but an actual man with common sense. He didn't per-form a daring rescue, but simply offered Missy a hand up so she could dust herself off. Standing at her side, he had asked her a simple question that would reverberate throughout any woman's story: *"Are you all right, miss?"* It was all a real woman ever needed to be asked.

Missy's voice cut into Victoria's thoughts, and, to her surprise, she saw that Missy was holding up a copy of Mrs. Swann's Egyptian novel. The cover was unmistakable. The printer had pulled out all the stops with the swooning pink and orange sky. From beneath the heroine's jaunty pith helmet flowed abundant locks and a flimsy shirtwaist opened at the neck to suggest a shapely bosom. The ladies of the Book and Travel Club released audible gasps and grumbles and Victoria's cheeks grew instantly warm.

"Mrs. Swann is terribly clever," Missy was saying. "She tells the most wonderful tales. Once you start one you can't put it down. They're as good to sink your teeth into as a Tootsie Roll."

General tutting bounced off the thick plaster walls and several of the women turned to one another for an explanation of the latest candy bar that hadn't yet made it into the more austere Cambridge households.

Mrs. Bigelow spoke up on behalf of the others. "Mrs. Sturgis, we use only *legitimate* sources in our reports. Based on the cover alone, it's clear that the author you have chosen lacks quality. You really shouldn't waste your time on such rubbish."

Victoria's pulse throbbed loudly in her ears, as if she'd been swept into a dangerous undertow of ocean waves. Once, she might have fought her way back to the surface and spoken up on behalf of Mrs. Swann, but she felt too weary for that now. She let herself drown in the ladies' collective disdain.

"In the future," the matron continued, "I'll ask you to submit a bibliography in advance for approval."

"If you say so," Missy said cheerfully, and continued to cradle the book. "But honestly, it must count for something that so many people like Mrs. Swann's stories."

"We don't concern ourselves here with what 'so many people' like. In fact, it takes the better few to recognize what will withstand the literary test of time."

"All right, but I think you'd like her advice column. The replies to the lovelorn are exceedingly strict."

Victoria gazed fondly at her faithful reader. Missy didn't deserve such punishment for her devotion.

Mrs. Bigelow pulled out her ladies' pocket watch on a gold chain, glanced at the time, and snapped it shut. "That will be all for today, ladies. Thank you, Mrs. Sturgis, for your presentation."

Intellectual snobbery could cut to the quick in Cambridge, but Missy appeared either blissfully unaware or exceptionally resilient. If only the other women would make an exception and applaud, though that simply wasn't done. They rose and began to shuffle out, mumbling their opinions to one another while donning their dreary outerwear. Missy came straight over, and Victoria was glad to see that she was all right. Apparently, Texas toughened a person.

"Thank goodness that's over," she said.

Victoria handed her the photos that had been making their way around. "These are marvelous, by the way, and you did well in your talk. I wish they had treated you better."

Missy leaned closer and whispered, "They're as chilly as this basement, aren't they?"

They made their way out of the room and up the stairs.

"I must have missed why you were in Egypt, Mrs. Sturgis. What was the purpose of your visit?"

"My husband is in oil and the Middle East is the place to be these days."

"Is that so?"

"Harrison says everyone is going to be as rich as Rockefeller."

"Won't that be good for the people."

"Oh, I don't think he means the people who live there."

They burst through the heavy doors of Memorial Hall and stepped into daylight.

"What's *your* husband's line of business, Mrs. Byrne?" Missy asked.

"My husband does any number of things. At the moment, I gather he's trying to land a position with an import-export firm, China trade."

"Doesn't that make you nervous? I had butterflies when

Harrison was waiting to hear where he would be sent next. But it all worked out, though Boston wasn't our first choice, or our fifth."

"I do my work and we putter along."

Missy stopped on the walkway. "You *work*? I don't know any women who work. I mean, ladies like us. Lovely hat you're wearing, by the way. I adore ostrich feathers. So, *au courant!*"

With her good-natured effusiveness, Missy appeared terribly young. For someone who'd seen something of the world, she was quite green, although, come to think of it, Victoria didn't know any society women who worked either.

"What sort of work do you do?" Missy asked.

The girl's genuineness encouraged Victoria to let down her guard. Perhaps this was a person to trust—not to reveal all to, of course, but to share with selectively. Mrs. Sturgis was as out of place in Cambridge as Victoria had felt when she had first arrived. If she had had a friend back then, who knew how differently things might have turned out. Or a friend now.

"I'm an author," Victoria said as they started to stroll.

"How exciting! I wonder if I know your books."

"I write under a pseudonym."

"Do you publish as a man? Treatises and philosophical tracks that gentlemen like to read?" Missy stopped. "Oh, heavens, you're not Margaret Fuller, are you?"

"What?" Victoria asked. "No. Definitely not."

"I assume everything Cambridge ladies do is way over my head."

"What I write isn't over your head, Mrs. Sturgis. In fact, I happen to know that you like what I write a great deal."

"You do?" Missy's face went still. "How do you know that?"

Victoria's half veil did little to hide her expression.

"*No!*" Missy exclaimed, with a great intake of air. She found Victoria's wrist with her salmon-hued gloves and squeezed. "You're *not* Mrs. Swann?" Her eyes bulged under her extravagant hat. "But you *are!*"

Victoria gently shushed her. "No need to make a fuss."

They made their way to the curb and Missy continued to emit little shocked sounds.

"I can't believe it. You know, until this moment, I had thought Mrs. Swann was too good to be real."

"You're right about that."

"Wait until I tell Harrison. He said we'd meet interesting people in this dull city, and I doubted him, but it's finally happened."

"I'd rather you didn't mention it to him, if you don't mind. Let's keep this our little secret."

"Whatever you say, *Mrs. Swann.*" Missy clapped her gloved hands together with a soft patter. "I won't tell a soul. I don't actually know a soul, not around here anyway. Why didn't you speak up and explain yourself to those snooty ladies? You could have told them all about Egypt. That would have impressed them."

"I'm sorry I didn't rise to your defense, Mrs. Sturgis, but it's important that I stay incognito."

"Oh?"

"It's a long story. Perhaps I'll tell it to you sometime. I'm just grateful that you enjoy my books."

That seemed to appease her for the moment, and now it was Victoria who let out a breath.

"I more than enjoy your stories. I positively live for them. One of the reasons I felt bold enough to go to Egypt was because of you. I thought, if Mrs. Swann can do it, so can I!"

"I'm glad."

"You travel so widely. How do you manage to visit all those exotic places that you write about?"

At the edge of the campus and with her carriage waiting, Victoria became Pandora with the untamed spirits straining to break free and rise around her. She had lifted the lock and was dizzy at the thought of opening the lid the rest of the way and telling all—how she had been hiding for years, holed up in her bookish tower with a hook on her bedroom door to keep her husband from intruding on mind and body; how she had gotten herself into an arrangement with her publisher she could not sustain; how she had made a decision she would forever mourn, yet could not have chosen otherwise; and how she was every bit as friendless as her newly arrived acquaintance. She felt like a foreigner here on her own soil and, truth be told, had never ventured farther than Greater Boston. But, of course, she said none of that.

Missy spoke again. "Would you mind if I asked you about your novel set in Giza?"

"Certainly, though I wrote it years ago and have forgotten much of it."

The girl expanded her plush, fur-lined cape and secured her footing. "Why, I wonder, did you say that there's a side entrance to the pyramid, when there isn't one? I know your characters had to escape, but why that way?"

The concerned expression on her young reader's face helped bring Victoria back from the fantasy of revealing the whole sorry truth. It would break Missy's heart to know it and, more importantly, create a bigger tangle than the one Victoria was already in.

She pulled back her shoulders and spoke with practiced confidence. "And escape they did! Wasn't that marvelous?"

"But it wasn't exactly accurate, was it? Unless you saw something that I didn't when you were there?"

"No, I saw precisely what you saw."

"But why—?" Missy pressed.

"Because it is *fiction*, Mrs. Sturgis. My story is *made up*."

A little flame ignited behind Missy's powder-blue eyes. "Ah," she said, her voice following Victoria as she climbed into the carriage. "Still, it makes me wonder if other details are wholly accurate. Which leads to a larger conundrum of what is real and what is imagined in your tales."

"Excellent questions, Mrs. Sturgis. I can only tell you that it's all a swirl of invention."

Victoria waved her beautifully gloved hands in the air, hoping that their artistry might dispel the young lady's concerns.

True art could do that, remake the world in its own image. Or at least hoodwink some into thinking so, but by the skeptical look on her face, not Missy.

"I suppose the sad truth is that brave women like your heroines don't really exist."

Missy appeared crestfallen. A young woman finding her bearings in a new city was both the most difficult and the most hopeful thing Victoria could imagine. She wanted to reassure her that everything would be all right. She would tell her the truth, but as the poet of Amherst advised, she would tell it slant.

"My dear, you have stood in the shadow of the pyramids and moved from the extravagant wilds of Texas to the unpleasant chill of Boston. You have stood beside a husband who, I dare say, is not as attuned to your needs as you deserve. And now you have braved Cambridge society in a pretty ensemble when a shield of armor might have been better. I think it's possible that you are every bit as brave as one of Mrs. Swann's heroines. *You* are proof that such women do in fact exist."

Missy's eyes grew bright and her expression satisfied. They bid each other good afternoon. The carriage started to roll away and Victoria fell back into the seat. She yanked off the fine leather gloves and threw them onto the tufted cushions. Artistry could only do so much to knit up the troubles of the world. Closing her eyes, she tried to take solace in the fact that Missy Sturgis had left happy. At least there was that. Victoria didn't dare ask the same question of herself. Happiness remained as distant as the horizon shimmering across imagined desert sands.

EIGHT

Gaustad's assistant peeled off his printer's sleeves and bowed. "Sorry to have kept you waiting, Mrs. Swann. We've had a bit of turmoil here today."

"What's the trouble now? Is Miss Pennypacker causing a disturbance again?"

Before the young clerk could reply, the actual chanteuse herself appeared from the parlor. "Did I hear my name?"

Victoria blanched and wasn't sure what to say, but Miss Pennypacker handled the awkward moment with ease. "I don't like to be kept waiting either," she said. "But what a pleasure to meet you, Mrs. Swann. I heard him welcoming you as if a queen had arrived, which is true in a way, isn't it?"

"The pleasure is all mine, Miss Pennypacker. As a premiere star of the stage, I'd say you are higher royalty than I am."

The two women exchanged kindred smiles, each amused at her own success. Miss Pennypacker was as striking as a peacock on full display, and as self-assured as one too. She wore her jacket so tight at her narrow waist it was a wonder she could breathe, and the mutton-chop sleeves billowed like sails around her. Victoria would have thought a boa more fitting for evening wear, but maybe Miss Pennypacker's sense of night and day was different from everyone else's. She looked lit up as if in the footlights.

"I've enjoyed your books for years. They're better for my dark moods than champagne, which is saying a lot. I take both to the bath with me and emerge from the bubbles with the day bright again."

Victoria had never taken a bath with bubbles, champagne or otherwise. The extravagances of a celebrity of Miss Pennypacker's caliber boggled the mind. But she could tell that the entertainer's enthusiasm was real and regretted her own earlier comment. "I'm sorry I sounded so petulant. I'm in a stir today. I seem to be at a crossroads and don't know which way to turn."

"That sounds promising." Miss Pennypacker's face glowed with optimism.

"I've come to see my new editor to discuss it. I gather you'll be working with Mr. Cartwright too."

"The earnest young fellow?"

"He's awfully smart."

"I don't doubt it. But never forget that we are the talent, Mrs. Swann. We're the ones with the goods. All these gentlemen"—she waved her abundant sleeve and ringed fingers at the publishing house—"they have nothing on us."

Victoria sized her up and spotted the rock-hard foundation beneath the glittering surface. "You're a positive force, aren't you, Miss Pennypacker?"

"I don't see why we'd do it any other way. I mean, why bother?"

"Bother with what?"

"*Living!* We must try for the lives we want."

She was stunning. "You must be mesmerizing on stage."

"You should come see me sometime. I'd love to invite you up. I think the audience would relish the chance to see Mrs. Swann in person."

"I do my best to avoid public appearances."

"That's too bad. I bet your readers have the wrong image of Mrs. Swann. They probably picture a stern schoolmarm."

"A schoolmarm?" Victoria pressed her lace gloves onto her hips. "Why, I hope my books are more entertaining than that."

Miss Pennypacker laughed. "I'm sorry, I wasn't thinking of your wonderful novels, but the advice column. You're always telling young women to mind their manners and behave. Instructing them to do their *duty*. Sometimes, a young lady wants to live a little and have fun!" She made a ripple with her skirts like a flamenco dancer.

"You are something, Miss Pennypacker."

She would have liked to chat longer, but the gangly clerk had returned and announced that the entertainer's carriage was waiting. The two women exchanged farewells and Victoria went off in search of Jonathan Cartwright.

She strode past Gaustad's office and the meeting room, from behind which leaked the boisterous sounds of male voices. Victoria assumed Gaustad was in there, holding forth as usual. But whoever knew that the hidden parts of a publishing house could be arranged in such a labyrinthine way? In dark little rooms, men sat hunched over typewriters. In a large, open loft, reams of blank paper and what appeared to be vats of ink waited to be used. Workmen in aprons tended to an iron printing press, their visors worn low over sweating brows. This must be where Thames, Royall & Quincy churned out her monthly dime novels. But how does a printing press work? It amazed her that in her dozen years as a published author, she had never considered the question.

She came to the threshold of a tiny room, a closet really, where Jonathan sat, feet up on the desk, his chair tipped back. He was reading a manuscript, his face relaxed and happy, angelic. The young editor appeared enthralled by the words before him, his blue editing pencil unused on the desk. A longing rippled through Victoria, and she allowed herself to feel it: if only he might someday respond that way when reading her prose. She said his name, and his chair slammed down on the pine floor boards. He yanked his feet off the desk and stood.

"Why, Mrs. Swann. What a surprise."

The little room barely had space for another person, but Victoria pulled in her skirts, wedged closer, and sat. She took in the cracked walls and the lone window cruelly covered over with a dreadful mustard-colored paint. The plain desk bore the scars of cigarette burns and pen scratchings.

"Wouldn't you want a fresh coat of paint to brighten the place?"

"I don't think I'd notice one way or another. What brings you in today?"

"I read your comments on my latest Mrs. Swann manuscript, and I can't do it."

"Can't do what?"

"Write. At least not as Mrs. Swann and perhaps not at all."

Jonathan sucked in air between his teeth. "I never intended for my comments to lead you to that conclusion. I was trying to be helpful."

"So I assumed, but I've lost the thread. The construction is made out of whole cloth, and it's unraveled in my hands. I can no longer deceive my readers, no matter the consequences."

She had been up much of the night worrying. If she didn't continue as Mrs. Swann, Raymond could so easily make her life more miserable than it already was. Could a woman be arrested for a crime she had committed a decade before? Victoria had tried her best to shake off the question, though it continued to lurk in the recesses of her mind.

"Heavens, what a day this has been. I'm sorry to tell you that Mr. Gaustad was let go earlier. Or he chose to leave. I'm not sure which."

Victoria sat forward in her seat. "He's out after so many years, just like that?"

"Just like that," Jonathan repeated. "Also, I met your husband."

"Oh, him." She leaned back.

"I didn't know he worked in publishing."

"He doesn't. The man hasn't read a book in years."

"I see." Jonathan tucked the pencil behind his ear, so unneeded on someone else's lucky manuscript. "The good thing is that this upheaval buys us time on your revision. I know you feel discouraged, but we really must keep on with the series. Your readers are waiting, as is your new publisher, who, I must remind you, is my employer. I have much at stake in Mrs. Swann, as do my sisters."

Was it possible that there were even more people relying

on her to continue as Mrs. Swann? "How are your sisters involved?" she asked.

"Our father and mother passed away not long ago and they're counting on me."

"I'm so sorry to hear it. That's terrible."

"There are five of them."

"Yes, I know, but that's not what's terrible."

"But it is a burden."

"It doesn't have to be. Do any of them work?"

"Actually, my two middle sisters are now performing at the Boston Music Hall." Jonathan rolled his eyes, which she thought unnecessary, as it was a respectable establishment. He really was a first-class snob. "And my eldest sister Clara has been hired to teach English at the Winsor School for Girls starting in the fall."

"Excellent. It sounds like they're managing all right, given the circumstances. We can relax."

"I can never relax," Jonathan said, but then he seemed to reconsider and added, "except when reading."

He was as nervous as a Yankee hen. And yet, how alike they were, she and her new editor, wanting to stick to a well-charted course and not rock the boat. She knew she should press on as Mrs. Swann to pay her bills and keep her husband at bay, but then she recalled Miss Pennypacker swishing her skirts in her joyous little dance.

"I've come to see about the opening chapter of my new project. I gave it to Mr. Gaustad the other day."

"So I gather."

Victoria sat up again. "Has he read it?"

"I don't think he got around to it. But I read it."

She didn't dare speak for a long moment then whispered, "And?"

"And," Jonathan spoke slowly and seemed to choose his words with utmost care. "I found it a most promising start to what promises to be a promising novel." His tentative nature gave way to a boyish grin.

"What a relief!" Victoria clapped her gloved hands together. "How lovely. Now I must get back to it. I'd like the pages I gave to him, please." She held out an open palm.

Jonathan's moment of confidence seemed to evaporate. "I'm so sorry to say that your pages have gone missing. It could be that Gaustad took them with him. Or," he cleared his throat, "he may have disposed of them."

"No! Why would he do that?"

"He didn't want anything to compromise your reputation as Mrs. Swann."

Victoria let out a groan. "Not that again."

"It is an issue we must consider as we go forward with this new book."

Victoria froze. "You wish to go forward with my new book?"

"That is my intention."

She could see him becoming an editor right there before her eyes.

"But you may want to consider writing this new novel under a pseudonym while also continuing simultaneously as Mrs. Swann."

"But Mrs. Swann is already a pseudonym. Are you suggesting a pseudonym for my pseudonym?"

Jonathan straightened his waistcoat and placed his hands on the desktop. "No need to get ahead of ourselves. Press on and write this fine new novel, while I locate its first chapter. But in exchange for my efforts here, I must insist that you turn in your current Mrs. Swann manuscript for publication. We cannot afford to ruffle feathers."

"I don't care about Mr. Russell's feathers. Why can't I submit my new novel in *place* of the next book in the series, not in addition to it?"

"If you have a contract for a Mrs. Swann novel, you can't offer an altogether different type of book."

"But there is no contract. There's never been a contract. It was arranged with a handshake, ever since I was a girl of eighteen with my first book."

Jonathan rubbed his forehead with ink-stained fingers, streaks of blue appearing on his temples. "That's unusual, but you do understand that if you submit a different style of book your royalties would be affected?"

"Why would that be?"

"Because there's no telling what a different book, even by the same author, would garner. We'll have to make up a new contract and offer you a smaller royalty, say, of only ten percent."

"Ten percent is all I've ever received!" Victoria practically shouted.

"Oh dear, really? All our other authors receive anywhere from fifteen to forty."

"I knew it!" She shot up from her seat. "I knew I was being cheated out of what was due to me. Now I absolutely won't write any more books as Mrs. Swann. Not until I have a fair royalty. I'll speak to Mr. Russell myself." Victoria turned to leave.

But with a tap of his diamond ring on the doorjamb, the man himself leaned into the room. "Tell me what?" he asked.

Jonathan stood and stumbled back a little.

"Madam," Russell said, and gave a bow. "Nice to see you. You gave a fine talk the other evening at the club."

Victoria felt no need to respond. She took note of his heavy watch fob and the Masonic pin shining on his lapel. Russell's tie hung loose, and he wore a smoking jacket, as if at home. On his feet were velvet and gold tasseled slippers, a clear assertion that he could dress any way he pleased now that the publishing house was his.

"What's going on here, Cartwright?" Russell asked.

"We've been having a productive conversation about her latest manuscript, sir. I've read the opening chapter and it's *excellent.*"

Victoria felt her chest expand as she took in a deep breath and held it. People complimented her writing all the time without her feeling dizzy and flustered. Somehow this was different.

"Her next book is somewhat unlike her others," Jonathan

added casually, though clearly on pins and needles for Russell's reaction.

"I don't like the sound of that," Russell said.

The young editor lowered his chin. In a polished Brahmin accent, he continued, "The world is changing and our readers with it. The most successful books of literature"—he enunciated the word with unequivocal flair and expertise—"are written in a realistic vein today, which is what Victoria intends to do. I've studied the market and her new novel will fit right in. It might lead the way."

"Is that so?"

"Mrs. Swann must keep up with the times," Jonathan asserted.

Russell sized up the two of them, but Victoria didn't care. She had floated off, overcome with a surprisingly light and hopeful sensation. Her new editor not only liked her book but was standing up for it. For her. This young man before her, she realized, was what an actual knight in shining armor looked like.

"It's going to be brilliant. Absolutely brilliant." Jonathan gave a toss of his head, the blond streak blown back, adding to his air of insouciance.

Victoria was on the balls of her feet to catch hold of his words before they flitted away.

"If you say so, Cartwright." Russell slapped his palm on the doorframe. "Get to it. Mrs. Swann is our golden goose. I'll leave you to it. Good day, madam." He made a quick bow and strode off down the corridor, smoking jacket flapping and slippers scuffing. Jonathan fell back into his chair and pulled a handkerchief from his pocket.

Victoria held onto the back of her seat and asked softly, "Did you mean what you said?"

He patted the perspiration from his brow. "I did."

A warm feeling erupted in her chest. "I'll be going now. I must write."

"But we haven't decided on your course of action. Are you going to continue to write as Mrs. Swann or not? Stay, and let's discuss it."

He pointed to her chair, exposing the ink stains along the side of his hand where it had skimmed over newly written marks and smudged them. On the soft part of her own palm, dried ink also stained her pale skin. The two hands were mirror images of one another, both streaked blue and shadowed with words.

"Since you've asked me to, Jonathan, I will finish this last Mrs. Swann. But after that I'm done with her. From now on, I intend to write about real people with real and regular lives."

He brought his hands together as if in prayer. "We all have regular lives, Victoria, but when we see them reflected back to us in stories, they become more than that. We are both small and, as our most beloved poet says, 'We contain multitudes.'"

He appeared enraptured, but broke the spell and reached around to gather up a stack of books from the floor. Wiping them off with his elbow, he presented them to her.

"These authors explore the grit of life out there, and the pain in here." Jonathan touched his chest as he whispered, "I give you Balzac, James, Flaubert, and Cambridge's own William Dean Howells."

Apparently, Jonathan Cartwright's most passionate emotions were saved for books.

"Thank you. I know of these authors, and I did make time to read *The Bostonians* when it came out, because, well, everyone here did. But I'm embarrassed to say that with all my writing deadlines, I've had no time to read the others. I look forward to reading them soon, though I hope they're not all drudgery and sorrow."

"No, but they aren't mere romance, either."

"Mere romance," Victoria repeated as she ran her fingers over the spines. "I wonder, Jonathan, if romance doesn't exist in novels, where *can* we find it? Not with any certainty in life— at least not mine."

His own fingers grazed the anonymous manuscript before him, as he replied, every bit as sincerely, "Nor mine either."

The moment stretched on and Victoria waited for a spark to ignite between them, for this was the moment when it should have. If this were one of Mrs. Swann's novels, the handsome young editor and his refined, elegant author would be united after their long quest for love. It might come to them in time, for without question they were growing fond of one another. But what stirred between them wasn't like any romance Victoria had ever written. In place of passion, they shared something like solace and a fondness for one another based on a shared love of books.

"Have you ever fallen in—" she started to ask.

"No." Jonathan shook his head slightly. "Not really."

"Nor I."

"Yet you're married."

"Yes, but things aren't what they seem."

"Ah." He bit his bottom lip. "True."

They gazed at the stack of books in Victoria's hands, as if these volumes might hold the answers to the vexing question of love.

NINE

After his weekly visit to his parents' graves, Jonathan hopped the trolley back to Cambridgeport. The majestic houses down Mount Auburn Street sailed by, with their steep gables and classical columns, widow's walks and cupolas, turrets and wrap-around porches. He assumed Victoria's home on nearby Brattle Street was as grand. Mansions for merchants, sea captains, and other prominent citizens since before the Revolutionary War, these estates suggested not only wealth but refinement and elevated purpose. Now that the trolley line had been completed, there was easy access to the city without having to live cheek by jowl with the riffraff. Even on a future editor-in-chief's salary, Jonathan would never be able to afford to live in this neighborhood, but there was no harm in dreaming.

An elegant couple boarded, and he gave his seat to the matron who wore a fur stole and pheasant-plumed bonnet. Her husband bowed his top hat to Jonathan and stood over her protectively, using his cane to brace himself as the trolley car jostled along. High society returned from supper at one of the finer residences, while students headed back to campus from picnics or other forays in the wilds to the west of Harvard Square. As they reached the turn-around, Jonathan hung onto the strap and ducked his head to see the familiar brick walls and new iron gates of Harvard Yard.

He would have liked to hop off and wander down the familiar campus paths under the springtime canopy that swayed with the evening breeze. A former classmate would let him into one of the houses where they would drink whiskey and toss around ideas late into the night. But he stepped down with everyone else and didn't veer off to that place he loved. He had to be at the office early the next morning. He crossed the tracks embedded in the muddy street and climbed onto a second trolley for the final leg of his journey.

Unlike the first car, this one was crowded with workers heading home after a long day or trudging off to the night shift at one of the factories in East Cambridge. Jonathan made his way to the back and slid into a seat between a woman with bundles of laundry at her feet and a working man in rubber waders which suggested a water trade. The streetcar started up and the riders bumped shoulders, but Jonathan managed to reach into his canvas satchel to pull out a copy of one of Mrs. Swann's most successful novels. According to the ledgers, it had sold more than any other book published by Thames, Royall & Quincy four years before in the year 1895. Jonathan opened the book, though the lurching made for difficult reading. After a moment, he sensed the sewage worker on one side eyeing him curiously, while the washerwoman on the other side pointed at the novel in his hands.

"That there's a good one." She reached across with raw-looking fingers to lightly touch the cover. "Such a dandy tale."

Jonathan could feel the light tweed of his new suit itching his legs and his shirt collar was too tight, but he kept his eyes on the woman. As she recalled the story, she appeared lit up from within and beautiful, even to him, a young man who knew nothing. It was a miraculous transformation brought on by a book. The washerwoman and the man in waders exited at an intersection near Central Square—a nicer neighborhood than his own, Jonathan noted. He opened to the page where he had left off, and, as the car continued toward Cambridgeport, rattling over rough patches and squealing at each bend in the tracks, he began to read.

The novel started quickly and before he knew it, he was caught up in Mrs. Swann's tale. The sentences were overdone, the language lacking in subtlety. The plot, far-fetched. Unbelievable coincidences of fate caused the hapless heroine to hurtle forward unwisely. At the start, she was too perfect, her life too charmed. Her trials and tribulations escalated too abruptly and became too horrible, while the villain of the story was too evil. And yet, despite these predictable elements, Jonathan found himself flipping through the pages, eager to know what came next.

When the handsome hero made his dramatic entrance, Jonathan had to let go and sigh, relieved that the character had arrived in the nick of time. How completely expected. He knew exactly where the story was headed but didn't mind. He wanted to read on anyway. The star-crossed lovers would find one another within a chapter or two. But before being united, they would face seemingly insurmountable obstacles involving a cudgel, a bottle of poison, or a raging storm. It didn't matter which. Perhaps all three. But the outcome was inevitable. Hoodwinked and manipulated, his heart on his sleeve, like every other reader of Mrs. Swann's novels, Jonathan gave himself over to the tale. He longed to be reassured that, against all odds—and the more challenging the better—love would win in the end, as surely as the moon hung in the sky.

He lifted his eyes from the book as the damp evening air rushed in through the windows to caress his cheeks. Only a few passengers remained on board. A chill ran along his arms as he searched past the electrical wires and occasional streetlights to spot the glowing white orb. There it was—unchanged, inexorable, and surprisingly bright. He gazed at the moon for a long time and felt certain he had never seen it so clearly before. How reassuring, how comforting, to be told what we wanted to hear, and to see what we wanted to see. Yes, that was the gift Mrs. Swann gave to her readers after a hard day's work: a happy ending.

A thin veil of clouds passed over the pale surface of the moon and the spell was broken. The trolley had almost reached its final destination in East Cambridge. Jonathan had missed his stop. But rather than exit in agitation and tromp back through the deserted, dangerous streets, he decided to stay put while the car turned around and ride back on the opposite tracks. He opened the novel to read but flushed when he noticed that his finger had kept his place on an interior woodblock plate. The handsome, heroic doctor in a torn shirt gazed out with sultry eyes. Jonathan sneaked one last peek at him before diving into the story. His pulse settled and the trolley rattled on.

In early evening, Victoria strolled the dirt path that followed beside the Charles River. Her boots sank into mud and her satin skirt brushed cat-o-nine-tales and sedge. Low waves sloshed and sighed, and the full moon lay like a coin upon the silver platter of the water. She paused to take in a concert of peepers singing out from the muck and dregs of winter before cutting away toward the higher ground of Brattle Street.

With the breeze at her back, she pulled her green velvet cape tighter around herself and imagined that on a dank night such as this one, her new novel's heroine, Daisy, would have no comfortable home to return to. She would sleep seven to a room in a drafty tenement in the Old West End, a rough burlap blanket pulled to her chin. Her story would be rough too. Victoria herself had only made it out of similar circumstances by the skin of her teeth. It was a miracle she had survived at all. By the last page, the same would be said of Daisy, that is, *if* the story allowed her to survive. For a change, Victoria didn't know her ending in advance, only that it would not be a happy one.

She stopped at the end of a long brick walkway that led up to a grassy terrace bordered by spindly lilac bushes and a low white fence. The yellow clapboard manor house, a few doors down from Victoria's own much more modest address, had been the home of Henry Wadsworth Longfellow for decades. His eldest child, Alice, lived there now. More than a hundred years before, the house had also given shelter to George Washington and his ragtag band of recruits during the Siege of Boston that began in April 1775. The patriots took over the former homes of retreating British Torys and, as was the custom, General Washington's wife had lived with him in the grandest one through a tumultuous nine months of military skirmishes in the towns nearby. Victoria could picture Martha Washington standing at an upstairs window on a moonlit spring evening like this one.

The poor woman would have been sleepless with worry as she scanned the marshy grasslands down to the Charles River, waiting for her husband's return from war. When all was uncertain in our country's future, Martha Washington had surely leaned against the sill, forehead to the glass, and wept—just as Victoria had done when waiting for her new husband at the cracked window of the drafty tenement garret, and as Victoria's latest ingenue, Daisy, would do when faced with her own insurmountable challenges. Each woman's life was precarious in its own way.

Victoria took a last whiff of the old lilacs. Living next door to Longfellow's home, she had wanted to feel inspired by the legacy of the poet and his many respected literary guests. Gaustad often boasted of dinners at the Brattle Street mansion with Thoreau and Emerson and the great authors from England, Dickens and Wilde. But having this intellectual pantheon so close had only made Victoria feel more inconsequential as a writer. The intellectual history of Cambridge could spread as thick as the lilac perfume, smothering and suddenly too much. Victoria knew she must brush it aside and make her own way. Taking her skirts in hand, she did just that. She swept across the lawn to take a shortcut home, gamely trespassing on her neighbors and ignoring the sidewalk altogether, more determined than ever to return to her desk and to Daisy's tale.

TEN

Victoria removed her gloves and feathered bonnet, placed them on the hall table, and was brought up short by the sight of her husband's ratty black Inverness hung haphazardly over the brass coat rack, and his worn Homburg crumpled in the corner. She hadn't seen him since the night at his club a week before, and now here were his muddy tracks on the tiles. All she wanted was to sneak upstairs to avoid him, but if he was inebriated on whatever he sniffed or smoked or stuck in his veins, he would bang on her bedroom door at all hours, demanding attention. An impossible arrangement but there was no way around it.

On the papered walls of the front hall, innumerable pairs of Japanese ladies strolled under pale parasols, their backs bent, and their voices hushed. What did they say to one another as they crossed the arched bridge over the stream where koi circled in the shade of willow trees? Victoria knew now that they whispered of errant husbands and broken hearts. If only she had a friend in whom to confide. She straightened her spine and stepped past the kimonoed ladies and into the parlor.

Colorful Turkish rugs lay scattered under a cut-tin fixture that sent light dancing in all directions. Though she had never traveled, her house gave no hint of New England provincialism or dowdiness. After hours at her desk, nothing made Victoria happier than lounging on Moroccan pillows scattered before a fire or reading with her feet up on a mirrored hassock from India. But the sight of Raymond stretched to full length on the garnet velour sofa, his mud-encrusted boots on the upholstered arm, made her pulse race with irritation though they hadn't yet spoken.

"Where've you been?" he croaked, one arm bent across his face, eyes closed.

Victoria removed the pins from her hair and her wavy locks cascaded down her back. Years before, he used to cup her hair in his hands as if holding a sacred offering. She could barely remember that now and felt only pity and revulsion for him.

"Out for a walk. I might ask the same of you."

Raymond opened his eyes and squinted as if the light pained him. He swung his legs around and slammed his boots on her rug, scattering clods of dirt. She was ready to explode when she noticed how he swayed, his cravat undone and his rumpled jacket hanging loosely from his shoulders. Had he slept on a park bench? The truth was no doubt worse. The brandy in his snifter sloshed as he lifted it to chaffed and trembling lips. With such palsied movements, he resembled someone twice his age. Victoria started to turn away but spotted a folder brimming with papers balanced on his lap.

She stepped closer. "Is that my manuscript?"

Raymond's gaze lifted but remained unfocused.

"I've told you I don't want you going into my room. Give it to me."

Her stern tone seemed to awaken something in him. He set down his glass, tucked the folder to his chest and held it there. "You're behind on your Mrs. Swann schedule. The final galley was due days ago. We can't afford to miss a deadline."

"What we can't afford are your losses at the gaming tables. *I'm* not the problem."

Raymond rose abruptly and brushed past her, his steps loose and unpredictable. "*I'm not the problem*," he mimicked in a high, abrasive voice. "You whine like a girl." He stopped before the fireplace and gripped the mantel. "Though, sadly, that's the only thing about you still a girl."

Victoria ran a palm down her satin skirt, aware of her thicker waistline and sturdy legs. He was right, she wasn't a girl. Not anymore and thank goodness for it. She could stand up to him now. She held out her hand. "My papers."

He turned to her. "I know what I'll do. I'll get Dottie to finish it. She's as good a writer as you and half the trouble."

"Dottie's *my* employee. She wouldn't consider following your instructions."

"You've forgotten how charming I can be. The plump ones rarely resist me."

"You're despicable, you know that? You have no sense of yourself."

She reached for the manuscript, but Raymond careened away to the front window seat where he draped himself over the cushions.

"You reek of that horrible smoke. Are you back on it?"

"Don't hound me, woman. It's most unattractive in a wife." He wiped his lips with the back of his sleeve.

"How can I hound you if I never see you? Please, tell me where you go when you disappear for days at a time."

"That's better. Begging suits you better."

Victoria's gaze fell upon the Japanese statue of a bronze crane that adorned the mantelpiece. One of Mrs. Swann's heroines might use a pretty objects d'art like that to cudgel a n'er-do-well. A real woman's options were so much more limited. Raymond was impossible, beyond impossible, but she made her way back to him and held out her hand.

"My manuscript."

"All right, all right," he slurred. "I was having fun. Don't you ever have fun, Victoria? Alone in your room all the time. You must get lonely up there all by yourself. You must be unhappy. Are you unhappy, darling?"

Her lips formed a thin line, and she crossed her arms over her chest.

"So hard-hearted. You never did know how to love."

Victoria told herself not to take the bait. But his words sank in, and she had to refute them. "I've tried, but you've never made it easy."

"There you go, staging another assault. You thrive on our little battleground." His head lolled against the lush cushions. "You can be quite vicious, you know."

"I'm not the vicious one. I hate how you turn everything around."

"But why don't you admit that you hate me as much as you love yourself."

Victoria stamped her foot. "Stop your mean games."

"It's not a game the way you dismiss me. It hurts *my* feelings." He pouted, his lower lip protruding. "You go about your business. So preoccupied. A husband likes to be noticed from time to time. You're the most self-absorbed woman I've ever known."

"Give me back my book!" Victoria shouted.

"I'll give it to you, darling, once you admit you've written your love stories out of pure hatred for me."

"That's a shameful thing to say." Her voice rose like a child's and a frustrating shiver ran through her. How could he still bring her so close to tears?

Raymond finally gave a contented smile and shut his eyes. Victoria lunged forward and seized the manuscript from his lap.

"You silly thing," he sneered. "I was going to give it back. You never need to worry about me, Victoria. And the good news is, I have a plan for us."

Victoria cradled the manuscript, comforted by its bulk. "I'm not taking part in any plan of yours."

He raised the brandy snifter, his eyes boring into her from over the rim. "You've made plans without consulting me. I really should have had you arrested for what you did. Husbands can do that, you know. The courts rule in our favor, even after many years. I do think you should listen to my plan now."

Though all she wanted to hear was the click of the lock on her bedroom door as she closed it behind her, Victoria's boots stayed glued to the carpet.

"What you did was wrong, and you know it." He stood and loomed over her. "I'm sure the papers would love to hear all about it."

Raymond's hot breath flamed against her face as he lifted her chin with soot-stained fingers.

Victoria yanked her head away. "I should have divorced you years ago."

"You couldn't. Gaustad wouldn't have let you."

"But he's gone now and I'm making up my own mind. I'm finally going to do it. I'm ending our marriage."

Raymond took another sip and studied the amber liquid as he swirled it in the glass. "I wouldn't do that if I were you."

"It's too late. You can expect a letter from my lawyer."

His face contorted, mouth twisting in sudden rage as he hurled the snifter into the fireplace. Shards of crystal scattered over the Portuguese tiles and onto the Turkish carpet. Victoria froze as she had so often, her insides as jagged and broken as the glass. All the times he had frightened her came rushing back and a familiar fear coursed through her limbs. She squeezed the manuscript to her chest to calm her frantic heart. He held sway over her. It wasn't right. Had never been right. But though her heart continued to pound in her chest, she could see it clearly now, as if from a great distance.

"It's over, Raymond. This time, it's really over."

His bloodshot eyes widened, and he seemed to shrink into his oversized coat. Was he going to cry? God, she hoped not. She didn't want to wait to see it if he did. She had made up her mind. Victoria turned and headed for the door.

"Please, darling." He followed close on her heels. "Don't go. I really do need to speak with you."

She hurried into the hall and started to gather up her things. "Clean up that broken glass. I won't have the maid dealing with your mess any longer. I want you out of my house in the morning."

"Please, listen to me. I'm trying to tell you something important. You must be careful. Louis Russell is a dangerous man. A very dangerous man."

Victoria stacked the mail and her manuscript into her arms. "I don't know Mr. Russell, but I have no intention of letting him treat me like a puppet the way Gaustad did."

"Good, good for you." Raymond reached for her hand and

though she tried to yank it away, he held on tight and stroked it with damp fingers. "Please, listen. I promise I won't bother you anymore. But I really do have a plan that will work for us both."

Victoria pulled her hand away. "You're not understanding, Raymond. There is no *us*. Do you hear me?"

"Yes, yes, I do." His head bobbed in agreement, though it was every bit as likely he might explode again. "Please, Victoria, come back in and sit down so we can discuss this." He gestured toward the parlor. "I won't keep you long and then I'll go. I promise."

She let out an exhausted sigh, and despite herself, she followed him back in. Raymond folded himself onto the sofa and she stood over him and studied the chalky white part in his hair, slick with oil and sweat.

"What is it you want, Raymond?" she asked, her voice growing firmer.

Raymond roused himself to sit up straighter. "I want you to be free. I want us both to be free. And we can be if we follow my plan."

She cocked her head to one side.

"Let me explain," he continued. "I want you to turn in your last Mrs. Swann manuscript in exchange for Russell letting me out of my debts. You see? We can both wash our hands of Thames, Royall & Quincy, and go our separate ways."

"That's absurd." Victoria let out a laugh. "Why would Mr. Russell let you out of your debts in exchange for a book that he's already owed? You're not thinking straight."

"Come, sit." He patted the cushion beside him. "I heard Russell yelling at the new editor to keep his mouth shut."

"Mr. Cartwright? What about him?" Victoria perched on the edge of the sofa.

"The nancy-boy."

"Jonathan's not a nancy-boy. He's refined. You wouldn't know the difference. But why was Russell shouting at him?"

"He found out that you don't have a contract."

"I told him myself."

"It means you can walk away whenever you like."

Victoria pressed her back into the upholstery. "How blind I've been," she whispered in stunned realization. "Absolutely dumb and blind."

Raymond tipped in her direction. "It's all right, darling. Don't worry about that now. I've got it all figured out."

Victoria could feel him buzzing beside her, his odor ripe from jangled nerves and whatever poisons he'd been imbibing. She pulled a handkerchief from her sleeve, wiped her nose, and tucked it away. "I highly doubt you've got anything figured out. And besides, my arrangement with my publisher has nothing to do with you."

"But it does. I told him I would get the book from you. He'll let me off if we deliver. I'm sure of it."

Victoria wasn't listening any longer. Her mind had drifted to all the reasons she needed money—for her mortgage and to pay Dottie, but also now to hire a lawyer to start divorce proceedings. Turning in her final Mrs. Swann would cover it. Plus, her new editor had asked her to submit it, too, and she wanted him to be happy with her. She would go ahead and finish it up right away. No more tinkering over Jonathan's unnecessary comments. Victoria knew what her readers expected and could deliver it. Time to submit the last book in the series forthwith.

Victoria turned back to her husband's rheumy eyes, all the bluster and cruelty seeped out of him. Raymond was volatile and difficult, and yet so many times she had relented and let him lead her back into his orbit. So many times, she had helped him in order to keep her reputation intact and her household calm so she might write the next book. Over the course of their marriage, she had tended to him as if he were a sick farm animal, one that her father had diligently cared for until the inevitable moment arrived when he retrieved the rifle from the high shelf and walked with a bowed head to the far pasture. Victoria understood now how he knew it was time.

"What's Mr. Russell got on you?" she asked.

Raymond bent forward and gripped his gut, his weakest organ, and released a low, pained whimper. "A lot."

"You have to stand up to men like him."

"That's what I want us to do together."

"It's a miracle we've kept our marriage going this long," she said.

"Consider this act your parting gift to me. You let me turn in your manuscript to Russell as it is. He doesn't care how it reads. He just wants the book with Mrs. Swann's name on it, and he wants it now. If you let me give it to him, you can have everything else. I don't care about the house or our things. Please grant me this one last request."

The only thing worse than his casual cruelty was his desperation. "All right, we'll talk to Russell in the morning." Victoria stood and brushed off her skirt. "I'm going to bed."

"No, tonight. I need to go there tonight."

"Why?"

"You know why. I don't belong here." His nervous gaze flitted around the lovely room. "You know it, and Russell knows it. He and I are cut from the same cloth. I belong there with him."

"You be careful, Raymond. You said yourself he's a dangerous man."

"Don't worry about me, Victoria. I'll be all right."

He gave a feeble grin, and she tried to remember the young man she had fallen for so long ago. Raymond Byrne had carried himself with ease because he had nothing to lose. And now, he was finally agreeing to leave her. She could wash her hands of him this very evening.

ELEVEN

The carriage let Victoria and Raymond off at the corner of a side street where the sewage ran in open drains and stacks of wooden crates overflowed with rotten produce discarded from the nearby Haymarket. She covered her nose with a gloved hand. The salty air from the harbor misted her skin and caused her fallen curls to stick to her cheeks. Tucked deeper into the hood of her cloak, she stepped over familiar cobblestones. When newly married and with only her first book published, this shadowy place had seeped into her. She had tried to convince herself she was a spy, there to absorb the setting and stories purely for the purposes of research for future novels.

But it was for the sake of her marriage that she had slipped down alleys and entered the unsavory establishments Raymond frequented. Victoria had felt shaken by the low-life characters who kept him in their clutches, always wanting more. They had tried to ensnare her, too, in illicit affairs, and she barely held them off. It wasn't any wonder that when the stirrings of new life began inside her, it brought not joy, but dread. Her marriage, her very life, felt tainted and unstable, fraught with accusation and addiction. Her pittance of a salary as a new author, combined with her sorrow and loneliness—without family to console her and only a degenerate husband at her side—had led her to a most devastating decision. Despite her attempts to leave that dark time behind, heartbreak and self-recrimination followed her. After a long and difficult period of recovery in her Cambridge home, Victoria threw herself back into writing the idealized stories of Mrs. Swann, in which good always triumphed. She had made a silent pledge to never again care about her husband and to remain very much alone. Life, she determined, was more bearable that way.

A tattered awning still hung over the darkened shop window where shelves of laundered packages wrapped in brown paper lay covered in dust. It seemed obvious now that the Chinese laundry was a front for the illegitimate business thriving next door. Down the side of the brick building, a sign read *Deliveries Only*, but men of every sort had come and gone at all hours. More than once, police in brass-buttoned uniforms had sauntered in and Victoria had hoped for a raid. Maybe then Raymond would have come home.

Now, he knocked on the metal door with a secret rhythm and waited in the shadows, shifting from foot to foot and tapping her final Mrs. Swann manuscript against his leg. Anticipation had started to build in him as it used to, as if no time had passed. How often had he come here in the intervening decade without her knowledge?

The door opened a crack and an elderly man in a dingy silk robe took one look at her husband, turned, and led them down a narrow hallway, his braided queue swaying down his back. Victoria hesitated at the beaded curtain, but Raymond put a hand on her elbow and eased her through the sparkling strands. Cloying incense and a haze of cigar smoke hovered over a vast, dimly lit room. From tables at the rear came the clack and clatter of Mahjong tiles. Men in top hats and others in workman's clothing leaned over roulette wheels and craps boxes, their voices rising and falling with the dice. Bare-chested boys carried trays of liquor from the bar, their hips swaying suggestively in silken pajamas and slippers. The same blind musician played his two-stringed bowed instrument, its screech and howl taking Victoria back to her earlier visits. Behind the fronds of potted palms, gentlemen sat on thrones painted in gaudy gold leaf. Young girls pampered them, manicuring their hands, rubbing their shoulders, and combing and oiling their hair. The girls' pert breasts and bony hips were barely hidden beneath their robes as their thin arms reeled in the most eager guests and escorted them to upstairs rooms.

Victoria's heart sank at the sight of the young women.

Were they met as they came off the boat and offered respect-able-sounding jobs but brought here instead? With the Page Act restricting Chinese women from entering the United States, followed by the Chinese Exclusion Act targeting all Chinese workers, these new immigrants were victims of a booming black market that promised safety at the expense of freedom. Many had been kidnapped and kept hungry, friendless, and tainted all too soon. Victoria couldn't blame them for taking to the bottle or the pipe and the needle like their customers.

Lightheaded in the eerie glow of the red lanterns and murky air, Victoria gazed beyond the bar and the gambling tables to the painted chrysanthemum partitions that shielded the line of *kangs*, platform beds with heated bricks beneath. She recalled the stained pillows, fouled by fevered bodies, and the oil lamps and other apparatus laid out on brass trays. Sickly sweet smoke curled out from behind the screens as it had a decade before, thin and blue and treacherous.

She reached for Raymond's arm. In another moment, she would lose him to this place. So many times, she had pleaded for him to give it up and return home. She must have loved him once, a feeling she could barely recall. Yet the sensation of rising desperation began to creep over her—the panic of losing yet another person. She had done all she could to hold on to him, though as she thought of it now, had it been herself she had feared losing? How tempting it would have been to curl up on the *kangs* with Raymond and simply drift away. She had given in only once and under the direst of circumstances. Her knees buckled slightly at the memory and she held his arm tighter.

"I don't want to be here," she whispered.

"We must stick to our plan. Russell gave me an assignment and I intend to complete it."

"I don't know why he's here at all. He's in charge of a gentleman's business now. He shouldn't be involved in a place like this."

"I'm as likely to rub elbows with a fine gentleman here as at

St. Jerome's. Who do you think runs the docks and the police and City Hall in this town? We'll get our business done and you can return to your safe haven in Cambridge."

How sensible Raymond sounded, until he removed her fingers from his coat sleeve and drifted off into the crowd. An elderly Chinese woman in a red satin robe sidled up to Victoria. Despite the intervening years, Mrs. Chang appeared no worse for wear with her jet-black hair pulled tight to her head in a sleek bun. Her ruby-jeweled combs caught the light as she bowed.

"Good evening, Mrs. Byrne. Many years since you pay us a visit."

"Hello, Mrs. Chang."

Up close, Victoria noticed that the left side of her face seemed frozen, and she clutched that arm rigidly to her side. She wanted to feel sympathy for the older woman but couldn't.

"I see business carries on as always. You still run the place with an iron fist, I assume."

"No, I very nice to my girls. I help them, like how I help you."

Victoria felt her cheeks grow warm and she lowered her voice. "It's true, I had no one else to turn to. I suppose I should have thanked you."

Mrs. Chang's hand sliced the air, red nails flashing. "I help many poor ladies. They have no money, but they find me. Mrs. Chang is good to everyone."

She opened her black ivory fan and Victoria recognized those strong fingers. The Chinese matron had held on to her and hadn't let go, even when the doctor told her to clear out. As pain rolled up Victoria's spine, the older woman pressed a pipe to her lips. The smoke burned her lungs, but soon the bucking and writhing slowed until she felt herself rise from the table to float above it. From a great height, she gazed down on the solitary figure seated beside the bed, her head bowed like someone in mourning.

Mrs. Chang gave a nod of farewell and stepped away to oversee her establishment. Victoria went in search of Raymond.

The door that lead down to the cellar was flung open and shouts rose from below. Victoria had visited the rat pits more than once when trying to find her husband and had watched the famished dogs let loose amongst the scurrying rodents. Blood flew from the box as spectators shouted their bets, their crazed voices every bit as wild as the squeals of the panicked animals. On other evenings, the room below was filled with the crowing of roosters, a natural sound Victoria had known in her childhood but here was raised to a more frantic pitch. The blood sport was sometimes dog against dog, which she hoped never to witness again. But not Raymond. He couldn't stop himself from the promise of an easy pay-off that somehow never came.

Victoria stepped past the raised *kangs*, where delirious bodies appeared lost in fitful reverie. Down a narrow hallway, moans of pleasure and pain came from behind closed doors. Thinly clad ladies slipped past, their cheeks vermillion but their skin jaundiced in the subterranean light of the lanterns. Pillowy bosoms protruded above snug corsets, waists cinched with leather belts and copper chains. Victoria glanced into smoke-filled rooms where gentlemen played cards and tossed back whiskey in thick glasses, their voices low and gruff. A disheveled man and a wild-haired woman hovered over an oil lamp, blue smoke rising from a pan. Victoria stared at them too long, mesmerized by their poisonous ritual. A hand pulled her back from the threshold and Raymond greeted her, his voice syrupy and unctuous.

"Where have you been?" she asked. "I was looking for you."

"Tending to business, my dear."

"Couldn't you wait?"

"No, I couldn't. I'm not as brave as you, Victoria."

She wasn't sure if he was mocking her, but it didn't matter now. "Let's get this over with. I want to leave."

Through a tangle of back corridors and up a set of steep, rough wooden stairs, they made their way.

"He goes up here to get away from everything," Raymond said.

They paused on the threadbare carpet of the second floor where the girls plied their trade behind closed doors. Proceeding up one more flight, they stopped before a single door. Raymond arranged his tie and slicked back his hair. Victoria couldn't bear how his vanity magnified his lack of courage. Anxious to leave and worn down by this place, she gripped the doorknob and turned it.

Under steeply sloped eaves, Louis Russell lay on a chaise lounge not unlike the one in her bedroom on Brattle Street, but upholstered in garish crimson satin, with a curved back, the clawed feet painted in the same peeling gold leaf as the gaudy thrones downstairs. His head rested on a gold-fringed pillow and over his eyes was draped a black silk cloth. He appeared to be sleeping, but as Raymond ducked to avoid the rafters, the floorboards squeaked under his boots and Russell woke with a start. He tossed aside the cloth and his eyes flew open. In an instant, he was on his feet, his stance that of a pugilist poised for a fight, jack knife flashing.

"Sorry, sir," Raymond said, his hands up. "Didn't mean to wake you."

Russell tucked away the weapon, swept his silver hair back into place, and buttoned his vest. His shirtsleeves remained rolled to expose a longshoreman's muscular forearms. With his thick neck, firm gut, and square jaw, some women might have found him handsome, but he was far too coarse to be appealing to Victoria.

"I was having a little peace and quiet up here." Russell dabbed his brow with a handkerchief. "Good evening, Mrs. Swann, or would you prefer I call you Mrs. Byrne?"

Victoria didn't feel the need to clarify anything for him. The air in the room felt instantly stifling, and her eyes began to water as she took in the strange setting. The only furnishings in the long, open attic were the chaise that Russell had been resting on and a standing telescope that pointed out toward a closed dormer window. A wood fire blazed in a wide brick fireplace.

"Forgive me, this isn't a proper place to entertain. I only

come up to find relief for my rheumatism. All those years working on the docks have made my bones ache. A roaring fire in a confined space is as effective a solution as any European sauna."

Victoria was surprised by his gentlemanly speech and manner. He seemed almost charming. "It is quite warm up here." Her throat felt dry and her head had started to throb. "I'm not sure how you stand it."

He appeared unfazed by either the heat or her comment. "By the way, I was thinking I might want to send you out on a speaking tour. You and Miss Pennypacker could team up. The crowds would be legendary. I'll call it, *Louis Russell's Ladies*."

Victoria's eyes narrowed.

Raymond stepped forward unsteadily and held up the folder. "Sounds like a good idea, sir. I've got the final version of the manuscript right here, just as you asked. She agrees to let you publish it."

"Well done, Byrne," Russell said, though he kept his gaze on Victoria. "I like a man of action."

But Russell didn't take the book. He had her husband right where he wanted him. Raymond blinked several times, striving to stay focused on winning his employer's favor

"I keep the fire stoked for full effect. Here, take a seat, Mrs. Byrne." He gestured to the chaise. "I don't want you fainting like one of the ladies in your stories."

Woozy and disoriented, Victoria sat on the edge of the chaise, not wanting to appear weak, but feeling strangely so. They needed to get on with this, but Raymond was now swaying under the eaves, and she could tell that he had lost his bearings too.

Victoria swallowed and spoke up. "We've come to discuss a new arrangement with you."

Louis Russell crouched before the fireplace and used an iron poker to prod at the logs, pushing them closer together to consolidate the heat. The flames licked the back of the firebox.

"I'm willing to give you my latest book from Mrs. Swann if you will release Mr. Byrne from his debts."

Russell's broad back and shoulders began to shake. Victoria couldn't see his face but wasn't surprised when his laugh erupted. "You two are an interesting pair. I'd have thought you'd have nothing in common, but I see now that you share the same penchant for wishful delusions."

"I'm finished with writing as Mrs. Swann," Victoria continued, despite the dryness of her throat. "But I'll give you this one last book in exchange for releasing my husband. A real gentleman might have done that anyway, given that I'm one of your most successful authors. At least this way you'd be guaranteed another high seller from me before we end the run."

Russell rose slowly from his crouched position, poker in hand. Victoria could sense the sheer force of the man, his muscular strength so much greater than theirs combined.

"End the run? I don't think so. And, madam, I may be new to publishing, but I'm not new to business. A gentleman must settle his own debts."

Raymond's hands fidgeted with the folder. "But my wife is willing to lend her assistance."

The air was so dry, Victoria felt she might choke. "What if I promised this book now and a final one in the series in six months. Then would you let Raymond off the hook?" she asked.

She didn't want to do it but writing an additional novel would let her say a true farewell to her readers and having Raymond off her back would be worth it.

"Aren't you inclined to write those books anyway, whether I forgive his debt or not?" Russell asked. "You have no choice but to stay at Thames, Royall & Quincy."

Victoria stood, her head spinning. "The only reason I would stay is because I'm working on a new book with Mr. Cartwright. He's my editor now."

"Isn't that nice, you and the handsome young editor working so closely together. How do you feel about that, Mr. Byrne?"

Raymond seemed to have lost the thread of the conversation and stood with his mouth slightly open.

"My relationship with Jonathan is my business. And besides, my husband and I have agreed that our marriage is over."

Russell gave another hard laugh. "My goodness, what a confusing couple. Here I thought you were being a loyal wife. I don't understand why you're doing Mr. Byrne any favors if the marriage is ending. But I assume you enjoy the income from your publications and your popularity, so this can't all be altruism."

He prodded the burning logs with the poker, then lifted it to study the glowing tip. Victoria stepped closer, afraid of the object in Russell's hands but also mesmerized by it.

"My husband isn't to blame for what overcomes him in this disreputable establishment. Aren't you ashamed of this place? I don't see how you consider yourself a legitimate businessman given the trade you're *really* in."

"Please, Victoria," Raymond said.

"It's all right, Byrne. Mrs. Swann must not grasp that my business is perfectly legitimate. I trade in ice from Fresh Pond in Cambridge, cotton from down South, and spices from Turkey. They can't get enough of the stuff over in Asia."

"Spices?" she pressed. "Is that what you call the substance that ruins peoples' lives? I know all about your trade. One of my early novels was set in Old Nanking."

"I suppose you've visited such places in your *so-called* travels."

Victoria nodded tentatively.

"There's no point in keeping up your lies with me, Victoria Meeks. I learned about your deception from Gaustad. You've travelled nowhere and you're a nobody. A provincial woman blessed with a vivid imagination but little else." He returned the poker to its stand. "But your secrets are safe with me, so long as you continue to write as Mrs. Swann for Thames, Royall & Quincy."

Victoria shook her head a little to keep up with him. "You wouldn't reveal my secrets because you want to sell my books."

"But if you choose to stop writing them for me, I'd be forced to unmask you as a liar. People would accuse you of hypocrisy, as your advice column has touted honesty and forthrightness. Your reputation would be badly soiled, and no other publishing house would want to engage with you. Your life as a writer would be over."

His forehead slick from the heat and his tie undone, Russell seemed unflappable. With glossy spats and a flashing diamond ring, he reeked of ill-gotten wealth and a great deal of it. He should have been run out of Boston by now but had somehow convinced the city that he belonged here.

"Mr. Russell," Victoria said, rousing herself, "I find it confounding that your true business isn't known by one and all. How have you managed to hide it?"

He sauntered to the window, opened it, and positioned the telescope. "You know better than anyone that people choose to believe what they want to believe." He bent to gaze into the eyepiece. "There must be clever reporters or astute readers who've caught on years ago that you don't travel, and that you have a duplicitous marriage. But your success has benefitted so many. Your readers like to be fooled. No one wants the truth. We're all complicit in one way or another in the shenanigans that keep us going." He stepped back from the telescope and angled it up toward the stars.

"But my dishonesty," Victoria countered, "if that's what you want to call it, doesn't kill people. The opium trade has been poisoning my husband for years. He wasn't like this before."

She turned to Raymond whose head remained tipped to one side. "Here, darling," she said, and indeed, for a moment, felt some tenderness for him. "I'll take care of everything. Give me the manuscript."

Defeated by the heat and Russell's smart talk, and with the insidious chemicals working in his veins, Raymond relinquished the folder to her.

With book in hand, Victoria could feel her fortitude returning—a welcome, familiar sensation. She had written this novel, and so many others like it, and each had bolstered her and given her strength. She knew how to handle a story—how to conceive of it, build it up, and carry it to its natural conclusion. Her trusted readers would know how this one should come out. With a slight laugh, she untied the folder and withdrew the pages of her final Mrs. Swann manuscript. She hadn't much liked it anyway.

Victoria lifted her arm and flung it into the fire. The pages fanned out, the heat pulling them toward the flames. The fire loved the book, and the book loved the fire. A great roaring began. Raymond, startled out of his stupor, rushed to the fireplace to retrieve what he could, but the paper burned rapidly, blackened and curled at the edges. The smell of scorched ink wafted, sharp and pungent, not unlike the sweet stench of opium smoke from the floors below.

"I intended to give it to you, sir. Really, I did," Raymond blubbered.

"It's all right, Byrne. I'll handle her in my own way."

Victoria ignored Russell's threat, and before leaving that wretched place, gave one last glance at her manuscript as it turned to ash.

PART TWO

TWELVE

From the top of the iron steps, Victoria watched as vacationers streamed onto the platform and commandeered Red Caps to lug their trunks and bulging suitcases. In the last week of June, visitors from Boston and beyond were arriving to Portland in droves, hauling behind them their possessions for the summer season. But not Victoria. Unsure how long she might stay in Maine, she had only two modest bags. With no use for formal clothing, one portmanteau held everyday dresses, a sunbonnet, gardening gloves, a pair of comfortable boots, and an additional pair of sensible shoes. The second, heavier suitcase contained the novels she intended to read and the many blank notebooks she hoped to fill.

From out of the crowd, a tall elderly farmer stepped forward. He tipped his brown felt hat and asked, "Miss Victoria?"

"Yes, hello. Are you Mr. Homer Pearson?"

"I am." No smile. He offered neither a bow nor a handshake, for he wore workman's gloves. "I'll be taking you up to Blaine."

Before she had a chance to thank him, he had picked up her bags and dived into the rush of people exiting the station. He certainly wasn't the high-born husband Edwina had described in her letters from years before. Could this man really be her uncle?

"Watch your step," he said as he wove ahead through the crowd. "Too many people this time of year."

Victoria hurried to keep up as they crossed the marble hall of Union Station and stepped into June sunlight. Homer steered them around a tangle of parked carriages and pedestrians. A policeman pointed and shouted at drays piled high with logs and at flatbed trucks carrying lobster and other seafood to be shipped far and wide. Over it all tolled the bell from the Customs House and the insistent cawing of the gulls. Victoria felt a flush of excitement. This was the farthest she had ever gone from home.

Homer lifted her suitcases into the back of a weather worn buckboard and offered her a hand up to the seat. The old mare and wagon resembled the one her father had driven in the accident years before, right down to the threadbare, faded cushion she suspected had been placed on the bench for her sake. Victoria brushed away the memory, but as they started their journey to Blaine, her uncle continued to remind her of her father. Without a word, he hoisted himself onto the seat beside her, took the reins, and began to steer them through the busy cobblestone streets. As he finessed an especially difficult turn, Victoria clapped a hand over her straw hat and searched for something to hold onto with the other. Homer extended his elbow and she realized he meant for her to take it. She did so with a light touch, not believing that this strong, sturdy, and quiet man was really her uncle.

After a time, they veered off the paved road and began to make their way along the coast. His shoulders relaxed and he glanced at her seated beside him and might have relinquished a slight smile. Though she was wildly curious to ask what was in store for her in Blaine, she knew better than to pester the man. She took in the views of the sea, even more piercingly blue than when she had first sighted it from the train.

From the moment the Boston-Portland local had crossed the Piscataqua River and left Massachusetts and New Hampshire behind, Victoria had leaned toward the glass, taking in the glint of the water and the outline of each schooner, pleasure boat, and working vessel. The seafaring craft resembled children's wooden toys—charming and playful, yet hardly real. The trees of Maine, too, had an innocence when seen from a distance. Rising far above the mountaintops, the pointed tips of the pines strained toward the skies like etchings in a picture book. Both harbor and mountain scenes appeared imagined, as if set in place for the pleasure of a visitor like herself on a summer day like this one.

Unable to contain her enthusiasm any longer, she shouted above the rumble of the wagon wheels, "How do you manage to live in such a beautiful place?" Her lace gloves gestured toward the sparkling water and the grasses littered with wildflowers. "I'd find it immensely distracting. I'd never get anything done."

Homer appeared startled by the question and let out a low humph. "When there's work to be done, you must do it."

Victoria settled her hands in her lap, satisfied with his reply, so like her father's, as if she had returned home rather than to a new destination. She filled her lungs with the seaside air and didn't mind the ruts and rocks as their wagon jolted over the coastal road. Even the washed-out portions charmed her, though her uncle pulled out his red bandana to wipe his brow and cursed the poor condition of the route. Beside them bloomed early phlox and Queen Anne's lace, bachelor buttons and chicory, sweet pea and stalks of Joe Pye weed. The names of the plants came back to Victoria, though she hadn't thought of them since leaving the farm. So much had slipped away from her since then.

Every night of her childhood, her father had dusted off his trouser legs before taking a seat on the edge of her straw mattress and tucking the quilt to her chin. He instructed her to say aloud the good she had done that day and the names of God's creatures whom she had helped. He would kiss her right cheek followed by her left. But one evening, he stayed at the threshold, his oil lamp upraised, as if checking on the livestock before closing the barn door for the night.

"Won't you sit, Papa?" Victoria had asked.

"I believe I'll stand. You're not a little girl anymore."

Her eyes had filled at the thought—for, though she had wanted to be grown up, in that moment, she wished she could be her father's little girl forever. But Victoria had brushed away the thought, consumed by worry for her aunt, whose letters had stopped arriving.

"I'm afraid Auntie Edwina may be lost at sea," she told her father.

Charles's eyes sparkled in the lamplight. "Where do you get such notions, daughter? Is it all the books you read?" Though not a reader himself, he was inordinately proud of her literary inclinations. "Don't you worry about your aunt Edwina. I'm sure she's fine. She does as she pleases in life."

He then left Victoria alone in the dark, flummoxed and awed by his explanation. She wanted to ask what it meant to do as one pleased in life. In novels, heroes did as they pleased, but heroines were seldom so fortunate. All the adults she knew worked hard to get by. No one was free of obligation, toil, and strife. A person might experience joy at the sight of bright green buds in spring, or when downwind of burning leaves in autumn, but was it possible to do as you pleased and find happiness? Victoria had fallen asleep that night tangled in her own unanswered questions and woke with her pantaloons wrapped around her waist and blood on the sheets for the first time, as if she had been wrestling with demons all night. She became a woman with as little understanding of life as before and without her aunt's letters to guide her.

"Will we go straight to Aunt Edwina?" Victoria asked. "I can't wait to see her."

"We'll get you settled first. She's a might busy."

"Oh, I see."

He must have heard the disappointment in her voice. "Have no fear, she'll come 'round—eventually."

Victoria tried to recall her aunt's appearance from when she had last seen her. Edwina was rugged and stout, a woman with strong hands and unruly red hair. But in her letters, she became a mysterious femme fatale who caught the eye of gentlemen when boarding a train or standing on the deck of a ship setting sail from Portland Harbor. Her missives transported Victoria into a world of sea captains, stowaways, and foreign ports. Over the years, Edwina's letters had arrived from Cuba, Caracas, Rio de Janeiro, and Argentina. Victoria admired the exotic stamps, though it seemed odd that the return address was always the same post office box in Blaine.

Caught up in her aunt's tales, she had stopped parsing what was true from what was invented. She would curl up on her window seat overlooking the orchard and relish each divine description. Edwina walked barefoot on sandy shores! She learned the art of basket weaving from local women! She ate mangoes and breadfruit and grew fond of rum! Edwina met cowboys who spoke in rich foreign tongues and wore their shirts unbuttoned to their waists. Victoria had pressed the pages to her budding bosom, not caring if the oil from cargo ships stained her nightdress. Edwina, Edwina, Edwina! Edwina of the vast, wide world!

There was no question in Victoria's mind that her aunt lived at the prow of her life, precisely where Victoria herself wanted to be someday. In her letters, Edwina had one adventure after the next and always wielded a cudgel to defeat any laggards who got in her way. Victoria had created Mrs. Swann's heroines to do the same, although Gaustad insisted that a male hero must arrive to win the day. But from the start, Edwina had gotten it right, at least in her letters. About her actual life, Victoria knew nothing.

At the end of the afternoon's drive, the old mare stopped at the crest of a hill overlooking the sea. Before them sat a clapboard cottage with peeling white paint and dark green shutters that hung askew. Tall weeds had grown over the stone path that led to the front door.

"Last night's storm done some damage, I see." Homer climbed down with stiff legs. "I'll take a quick look 'round and we can head over to the village. There's a room waiting for you above the store."

Though he gestured for her to stay put, Victoria clambered down too. She tipped her head back to follow the trajectory of seagulls hovering on the updrafts. Swallows darted in and out of the eaves of the abandoned cottage.

"What a peaceful place."

Her uncle let out another little humph, and she suspected that was his quiet way of registering a contrary thought. He jangled a set of keys on a brass ring and opened the creaking door. Victoria's skirt brushed aside wildflowers as she made her way up the walk to join him. When he opened the door, a blast of warm air tumbled out of the little house that had heated up under the tin roof, as if it had been holding its breath for some time.

"Wait here," he instructed. "No telling what I might find. Critters and such."

Victoria stood at the doorway and stared into the dusky stillness. Something constricted in her chest as the bright afternoon sun streaked in over her shoulders. The rays caught on cobwebs that tangled in the brass lamp hanging from a beam. More cobwebs connected the stovepipe to the rocking chair, swaying slightly in the breeze let in by the open door. Stepping inside, she took in the wicker furniture with dusty red cushions and a small dining table set for two. Victoria ventured in further and noticed a narrow, orderly kitchen, and a back room where an iron bed lay covered in a faded quilt: a fully decorated home where it seemed no one had lived for some time.

At the table, she touched a finger to the wax tablecloth, tracing a line of dust along the rim of a rose-patterned dinner plate. A blue vase held dried wildflowers, their blooms desiccated and colorless. On the faded cotton rug, lay a child's wooden block, left behind and long forgotten. When Homer noticed her looking at it, he reached down and slipped it into the pocket of his field coat.

"All right, everything's in order. Time to go." He turned and rattled the keys in preparation for locking up.

"Who lived here, Uncle?"

He held open the door, but at her question, the keys drooped in his hand. "Never you mind."

The sea breeze, coming in through the open door, disrupted what had been sealed up for so long. Victoria felt stirred up inside, too, though by what exactly she wasn't sure. Before leaving Cambridge, she had hired a lawyer, Mr. Hector Samuels, to start the divorce proceedings. Brushing aside wisps of hair from her face, Victoria felt the breeze rustle her skirts, as if filling her sails.

"I could help clean up this place," she found herself saying. "I'd like to do that. It's sad to see a pretty home neglected."

"You didn't travel all the way to Blaine to become a deckhand. Edwina would scold me if she knew I put you to work straight away. She's going to be surprised enough that I got you up here in the first place."

The moment he had said it, his hand shot up to cover his mouth.

Victoria sat on the dusty wicker sofa, as if to illustrate her determination to stay put. "Why, doesn't she know of my visit?"

The door shut behind him and he stepped back inside.

"I'm sorry to say, she doesn't. I haven't told her yet. I sent word over to her today."

He started to turn away, but Victoria spoke up. "What do you mean 'sent word'? Doesn't she live here in Blaine?"

Homer took off his hat and held it in his large hands. "I guess I could have made things a little clearer to you. And to her. Suppose that wasn't right."

Victoria placed her own straw sun hat on the sofa beside her and pulled off her gloves, one at a time.

He swayed a little as he seemed to force himself to speak. "When your letter arrived out of the blue, I got to thinking."

What was left of his thinning grey hair stuck out in all directions and his brow was pale above the line left by his hat and shiny from sweat. His lips remained almost closed as he spoke, as he seemed to wince at the sound of his own voice. Victoria recognized his forbearing nature, so like her father's. It would take a lot for a man like him to speak up.

"What did you start to think, Uncle?" she asked more gently.

Homer settled into the wicker chair and bent forward, fingers circling his hat brim. "That you're a lady and you might know a thing or two." His face was as pink as a cooked lobster and Victoria thought she had never seen a more mortified man in her life.

"About what?" she asked.

"About, well, sorting out a problem or two. Customers quote
your advice column. You seem to know a great deal about people and such." His chair released a cloud of dust as he leaned
back and set his hat on his bony knees.

"I'm sorry to disappoint you, but my assistant, Dottie, writes
the replies to the *Letters of the Lovelorn.* The truth is, I'm not
good at dealing with people. In fact, my marriage is a dismal
failure. I'm currently filing for divorce."

His thick grey eyebrows shot together. "Oh no, that's not
right. Wives divorce their husbands nowadays, do they? Must
be a city thing. Or else your situation was dire."

"Yes, most dire."

The faint chatter of the gulls and the buffeting of the wind
beat against the clapboard shingles of the old cottage.

"So Edwina is not here in Blaine?" she asked. "Is that what
you're telling me?"

Homer gazed into the shadowy room as if it might answer
for him. "Ah yup, she's down in Portland. Settled there after
getting back from the Merchant Marines."

Victoria let out a surprised laugh. "My aunt was in the Merchant Marines?"

"Not as a mariner." He scowled. "A galley mate. Saw the
South Seas that way, my Edwina." He gazed across to the dusty
window and the cliffside beyond. "I thought it would end her
roaming, but next she signed up as cook. Made it all the way to
the Indian Ocean that time."

"I've never heard of such a thing."

"Of course, you haven't. Edwina's a remarkable woman.
There aren't others like her." He rubbed his hat with the tips of
his bent fingers. "But I'm an ordinary man. There's the problem. Sad to say, nothing can be done about it."

The wicker arm of his chair crackled as he rose. It was dawn-
ing on Victoria that the far-fetched version of her aunt that she
had imagined from her letters was not so different from the
woman Edwina had become. And for whatever reason, her un-

cle was asking for her help. He put his hat back on and stepped outside. In a corner of the braided rug, Victoria could see that a mouse had burrowed under and left a little nest. A cozy home if you chose it. But her aunt and uncle hadn't chosen to stay here. Why? And where was Edwina now?

THIRTEEN

Early to work, Jonathan slipped into Gaustad's office to search for the first chapter of Victoria's new novel only to find the room had been emptied of everything bookish and wonderful. In place of leather-backed volumes and the many stacks of pages sat a lacquered box, a celadon vase, and a Cantonware tea set displayed neatly on the shelves. The expanse of Gaustad's desk held nothing of substance either—no newspapers, cigars, letter opener, or documents half-written— only a gentleman's silver fountain pen in a marble base, tilted and ready for use. Clearly, the new occupant abhorred clutter, had conventional tastes, and wished to project a well-polished, efficient style of management. Or as likely, Russell took pains to hide any questionable transactions that might lead back to him.

Jonathan let out an injured sound. The manuscripts that had occupied every surface were gone. Not the shadow of a work in progress was anywhere to be seen. He felt an inexplicable sense of loss. While he hadn't read the many unpublished books, just knowing that they were there had given him confidence that Thames, Royall & Quincy was a welcoming home to literature. His heart sank when he noticed that the only remaining piece of furniture was Gaustad's liquor cabinet, newly restocked with fancy bottles.

Worst of all, the promising opening of Victoria's new novel seemed doomed to be lost forever. She might be able to recreate it, but that gave Jonathan little hope. The clearing out of Gaustad's office offered irrefutable evidence that Russell had little regard for books. Jonathan wondered how he could possibly aspire to be editor-in-chief of such a soulless publishing house. It would be impossible to bring important works into the world from this place. Just then, he sensed a presence behind him and turned to make a quick retreat, but it was too late. Russell, who customarily didn't arrive until noon, stood at his office door.

"What are you doing in here?" he asked.

"I'm sorry, sir, I was just—" Jonathan fumbled for an excuse, but having none, fell back on his nature and resorted to the truth. "The opening chapter of the new manuscript from Mrs. Swann is lost. I thought it might be in Mr. Gaustad's old office."

Russell brushed past him to enter. He unwound a white satin scarf from around his thick neck and removed his racing goggles and cap. Peeling off his driving gloves, he handed his leather duster to Jonathan and pointed to the brass coat stand in the corner. The weight of the garment in Jonathan's arms was in marked contrast to his own flimsy summer outerwear. He began to slip out of the room, apologizing and bowing.

"Hold on a minute. I saw Mrs. Byrne burn her latest book with my own eyes. Are you saying Gaustad was clever enough to keep another copy?"

Jonathan gasped. "Victoria burned a manuscript?"

Russell ran a hand over his sleek silver hair. "I saw her do it."

"Are you sure it was her newest effort, the story written in a more realistic vein?"

"How in God's name would I know that?"

"I'm sorry, sir. I'm a bit overwrought."

"Get ahold of yourself. But what is it about this new book of hers that's got you so excited anyway?"

Jonathan stepped closer, taking it as a hopeful sign that his boss was expressing a literary interest. "I've only read the opening chapter, but I believe it's to be a harrowing tale of a woman down on her luck in the worst parts of Boston. Right away, in the first chapter, we learn that she's poor and has lost her family."

Russell settled into his new desk chair and leaned back, lifting his spats onto the table's edge. "Bring me a cigar, would you?"

Jonathan opened the credenza beside the liquor cabinet, using the little brass key that fit snugly in the lock. The cigars were lined up in a handsome teak box, but he felt baffled by which to choose, so brought over the entire case.

Russell took the fattest one and held it to his nose. "Go on."

"Let's see," Jonathan tried, setting the box carefully on the desk. "Her husband's a sorry sop. Not evil exactly, but a weak man. A philanderer and a drunk, and worse. We all know the type."

Russell frowned, either because he didn't know the type, or knew it all too well. He pulled a silver crimper from his vest pocket, nipped the end of the cigar, and struck a match on the sole of his boot. As he lit up, he motioned for Jonathan to continue.

"The story takes place near the docks in Boston Harbor in an area of the North End called The Black Sea, named for a parlor of ill repute, I gather."

"I know the competition, Cartwright. Get on with it."

Jonathan wasn't sure what he meant, but continued. "The opening of the novel quite graphically describes ladies of the night and imbibers of opium." He raised his eyebrows for effect.

Russell put his boots on the floor. "What else?"

"The husband is bedeviled by the nasty substance, and—"

"What about the lady in the story?" Russell leaned his elbows on the desk.

"You mean, does the wife in the story suffer these afflictions as well? I certainly hope not. I have only, as of yet, read the first chapter, and now we've lost the pages."

"Well, find them, man!" Russell let out a cloud of smoke. "We can't let this type of dangerous story circulate about one of our authors. I'll be the one to decide when to reveal questionable things about her."

"Questionable things about who, sir?" Jonathan asked.

"If a Thames, Royall & Quincy author is going to be tied to a disreputable establishment such as an opium den, I want to know about it."

"Interestingly enough, Victoria has imagined it as part of

the bordello. Apparently, it works that way, both at the same location, though of course this is only fiction, so the reality might be quite different."

"Clearly, you don't know what you're talking about."

"True, sir. Very true."

"When you find the manuscript, I want to see it. It could be useful to keep her where I want her."

Jonathan was tempted to ask what he meant by that but thought the better of it.

"Out you go." Russell motioned with the cigar. "I have work to do."

"But, sir, what have you done with all the manuscripts? Where should I search?"

"I don't know, Cartwright. I told the girl to clear it all away. Touchy little thing. Ask around and shut the door on your way out."

FOURTEEN

Victoria slept poorly her first night in the rusty iron bed. When sunlight arrived, drenching the lace curtains in gold, she rose and dressed in a simple frock and sweater. After carting water from the well to wash at the basin, she threw on her sunbonnet and set off along the path. She hoped to find friendly company at her uncle's general store—and perhaps a stack of hot buttered pancakes, or at least a crust of bread. She was famished from the sea air and from her efforts the afternoon before.

It had taken some doing to convince him to let her stay in the cottage, but he had finally relented. He brought over provisions—kerosene for the lamps, logs for the wood stove, a loaf of bread, and a jar of prize-winning succotash made by a fisherman's wife in the village. Victoria had donned an apron over her linen dress and used a broom to bring down the cobwebs and sweep up the rug. Everything was musty with age or damp with mildew. Small vermin had left nests in the cabinets and droppings in the sheets, but she opened the windows and got to work.

Before leaving for the night, Homer had closed the shutters and Victoria felt sealed up tight in the cottage as dusk descended and the wind off the ocean whistled down the metal chimney pipe. She started a fire in the Franklin stove and heard scampering below the floorboards, taking her back to the farmhouse where she grew up, with its country smells and sounds. She hadn't realized how far she had come or how much she had missed her childhood home. As she lay between the chilly sheets, she longed for her father to appear at the bedroom door, checking on her before sleep.

A storm came up in the night, rattling the glass and dragging branches across the tin roof. In half-sleep, Victoria felt as if she were back again at the window of the garret in the North End where she and Raymond had lived as newlyweds. She had filled the gaps in the brick walls with library books to block the winter drafts and crammed old newspapers into the cracks around the windows, though snowflakes still dusted the sill. After hours of waiting, she had spotted her husband striding up the narrow street below, a spring in his step. Had he finally secured a job? And was he bringing them something for supper? Victoria pinched her cheeks and smoothed her skirt, though it hung loosely from her hips.

But just then a man with a hat worn low stepped out of the shadows and called to Raymond. Victoria pressed her fingertips to the cold glass as he turned away and followed the stranger into the city. From then on, he returned only to leave again, alighting long enough to press her for money, or accuse her of unfaithfulness while claiming to love her, though his heart was clearly elsewhere. That night, when Raymond first left her alone in the cold garret, Victoria lit the lamp and sat at the rickety kitchen table where she worked until dawn on her second Mrs. Swann novel. With writing as her sole consolation and sole income, it had saved her in more ways than one.

In Maine, she felt sure it would save her yet again. Victoria filled her lungs with the salty air to dispel the memory. Below was the sea, and the night's storm had made everything fresh and new. Way down on the shore, waves crashed against shale and limestone. Slick black rocks broke the current and created tidal pools that swirled and frothed.

She headed off down the seaside path toward the village of Blaine. The trail arrived at a dirt road with a country store on one side and a one-room post office on the other. The American flag high on its pole snapped in the breeze over a circle of red, white, and blue flowers in a bed of crushed white seashells. With dust on her skirts and a strand of Queen Anne's lace tucked behind her ear, Victoria approached the front porch. Three elderly fishermen in overalls and wader boots sat side by side on a bench with their backs against the peeling clapboard.

One smoked a pipe while another sucked on a wad of chewing tobacco under his bottom lip. They tipped their caps and gave wordless greetings as she came up the wide, creaking steps.

A bell tinkled as she stepped inside and the scent of burning pine from a wood stove surrounded her. On long wooden shelves sat dry goods of every variety: barrels of nails, screwdrivers, hatchets, Mason jars, mangle boards, fishing bait, pancake mix, tins of lard, sacks of flour, baking powder, and bottles of hair tonic. Everything a person might need. Along one side of the store ran a wooden counter crowded with more enticing items: pickled eggs and briny cucumbers in jars, stacks of canned meats, and boxes of graham crackers. Her uncle stood behind a large brass cash register and Victoria greeted him.

"How'd you do last night?" he asked.

"Pretty well." She shifted in her dusty boots. "I'll need another lesson at the stove."

"Didn't think you were paying much attention when I showed you. Have you had breakfast?"

She shook her head.

"Must be hungry. I'll bring you something."

He retreated to the back of the store and Victoria strolled over to a round dining table with several captain's chairs. On the checked oilcloth sat a leather scrapbook. She took a seat and let the book's cover fall open to pages of postal stamps from all around the world. Images of Greek statues, tropical palms, and the British crown filled them. Several sheets in, she noticed that some of the stamps were missing. She bent closer to read the handwriting below the blank spots. A Cuban stamp was missing, as was one from Argentina and the Kingdom of Patagonia.

Homer set before her a warm plate of eggs, bacon, and toast. He took the scrapbook from the table without commenting on it and tucked it behind the counter. Victoria apologized for having taken the liberty of opening it, but he didn't reply. At the Franklin stove, he filled two tin cups with coffee and joined her at the table. His customary stern expression softened as she dug into her breakfast.

"We'd best send you back with more supplies."

Victoria wiped her lips on a red-checked napkin. "You have everything a person might want right here in your store."

He gazed out the door toward the water. "Almost everything."

"And what an impressive stamp collection. Are you the philatelist?"

He nodded over his mug.

"Did you travel to acquire them?"

"Portland's as far as I go."

"How did you get all the stamps?"

"Been collecting since I was a boy. Helped to have a father who ran a post office. He put out the word up and down the coast and other postmasters sent some along."

Victoria placed her elbows on the table and leaned toward him. "Which do you think is your most valuable?"

He cocked his head. "Depends on what you mean by valuable."

"You must know the value of the ones you have?"

"I know their value to me."

She leaned back. "And why are some missing? It appears that you had them once, but now they're gone."

"You city people sure ask a lot questions. Everyone passing through is a reporter. What kind of boats are those, they want to know?" He gestured toward the harbor. "How many lobsters do the men haul each day? And the question that irks me the most—what do you do here all winter? I'll tell you what we do," he said with a snort, "recover from the summer people!"

Homer tugged at his suspenders and stood. The door opened and several tourists came in, their faces flushed under their big hats. They studied the country store, as if it were a museum rather than a working establishment. Shops of this sort were common, but somehow this one seemed especially countryfied and charming.

Her uncle retreated behind the counter. When Victoria finished her breakfast, she brought over the empty plate and thanked him. He had filled a cloth bag with potatoes, a sack of flour, more eggs wrapped in straw, and a bundle of beets.

He pushed it across to her. "This should do you."

Victoria reached for her change purse, but he held up his hand.

"Village of Blaine welcomes you."

"Thank you for the hearty breakfast and the place to stay, Uncle. It's very generous of you."

"What else do you need?"

On Brattle Street, Victoria had become accustomed to her cook making a midday meal which she took alone at the long dining room table. For supper, she ate leftovers in the kitchen or up in her room on a tray. It had been a long time since she had prepared food for herself.

"Remind me, what's the best way to cook beets?"

"Why, you boil them with other root vegetables from the garden."

"A garden! I haven't grown one in years." Victoria tipped toward him over the counter. "Would you be willing to help me start one, uncle?"

"A little late in the season." Homer rubbed his chin. "I'll stop by this afternoon to see what I can do."

She reached across and shook his sleeve. "Thank you, Mr. Pearson. You're a fine gentleman. I'd like to call you the mayor of Blaine."

"Not on your life. I'm no politician."

She gathered the bag of provisions. "Is there any chance I'll see Edwina today?"

"Not likely. She teaches the little ones at the Abyssinian Meeting House on Saturdays."

"My aunt's a teacher as well as a cook on the high seas?"

"Edwina is much loved down there in Portland. She helps with families right off the boats. Don't know what all she does with them, but it keeps her busy."

Victoria got as far as the door and turned back. "Uncle, is it possible that Edwina used your missing stamps for the letters she wrote to me when I was a girl?"

His face didn't change. "A-yup, that's what she done."

Victoria gave a little laugh. "What an elaborate ruse."

"Your father was in on it, but it was all Edwina's idea. She's a natural born writer, can't help writing stories. That's where you get it from. But don't tell her I mentioned it. She's shy about such things."

"I can't tell her if I never see her."

"Patience, patience."

FIFTEEN

Jonathan found Perry in the back office where all the young clerks had their desks, but when he hung up his coat, he noticed that they were the only employees in the office that day. "Where is everyone?" Jonathan asked.

Perry sat hunched over a ledger, pen scratching away and foot tapping nervously. He motioned for Jonathan to shut the door. "Russell's fired them," he whispered.

"What?" Jonathan came to Perry's side. "Why?"

"He's bringing in his own people."

"I wonder why we're still here?"

Perry lowered his voice more. "I assume it's only a matter of time before—" He swiped the pen across his neck.

"Do you know if the young lady who was hired by Gaustad is still employed?"

"Oh no, she's long gone. Russell asked her to rub his stocking feet and she packed her bags and walked out."

"Good for her."

"She handled it better than some of the fellows. You should have heard them pleading for their jobs."

"How terrible."

"I'd rather starve than give that man the satisfaction of my tears," Perry said.

"I couldn't agree more. But do you know what the girl did with all the manuscripts that were in Gaustad's office?"

Perry put his pen into the well and smoothed his moustache. "I helped her myself. We hauled boxes out the back door. I assume they'll be picked up with the trash. Can you imagine?"

"The start of the promising new novel by Mrs. Swann gone out with the trash." Jonathan let out a sigh. "Tragic."

Perry pulled off his sleeve garters and removed his printer's visor. He went to the rack on the wall and began to put on his frock coat and bowler.

"Where are you going?" Jonathan asked. "It's not lunchtime yet."

"I'm going outside to help you find it. And who knows what else we might come across in those discarded papers. If Russell doesn't want them, why not rescue them ourselves?"

"Really?" Jonathan asked. "We can do that?"

"Jon, I've been taking notes on every aspect of the business since starting here. Father says you must think several steps ahead in business, as in chess, and I have been. I have a plan. Come along. We have a business to start."

Jonathan grabbed his coat and slapped on his cap.

"All we need is backing. I'll speak to Father. He knows everyone."

Who was this Perry Bliss? And who was his father?

"Is he—" Jonathan tried to ask. "I mean, does he know about money?"

Perry laughed. "Why, yes, he does."

"Here I thought you were a penniless student like me all those years."

"It may be smoked cod and beans for us for a while, but hopefully not forever."

"Nothing I'm not used to. But are you really saying you have the wherewithal to start a publishing firm?"

"Indeed, that's what I'm saying. You and I are to be partners." Perry held open the door. "If you are willing?"

Jonathan, for once in his life, did not hesitate. "Of course, I am."

"Good. Now, let's go search the trash."

The two young men wove through the labyrinth of Thames, Royall & Quincy for the last time. In the back street, they tipped their faces into sunlight before beginning their search. Like crewmates on a ship without a captain, they were game and giddy. They crouched on the cobblestones and began to go through the many wooden boxes and heaping piles of manuscripts. Seated on the curb all afternoon and deep into the long summer dusk, they picked through the pages. By the end of the day, they had each chosen a thin, discerning stack of promising books.

Their search reminded Jonathan of the times when he and his sisters had scrambled through the South End's back alleys, searching for cast-offs from the better homes. Over the years, they had brought their mother a lamp with a torn shade, mismatched cutlery, a cracked Wedgewood vase, and, Jonathan's favorite, a tin canteen from the Union Army which he wore slung across his chest. Another lucky time, they came upon a hobbyhorse with a broken ear, but perfectly good otherwise. Why, the children had wondered, would anyone discard something so wonderful, though it was made more wonderful for being discarded.

Late in the day as the cobblestones grew cool, Perry called out, "What did you say Victoria's name was before she became Mrs. Swann?"

"Meeks," Jonathan shouted back. "Victoria Meeks."

"Not the best name. Hardly memorable. I see why Gaustad changed it."

Jonathan dropped the manuscript he'd been looking at and hurried over to his friend. "Good going, Perry. You found it!"

Jonathan couldn't help grabbing the pages. He held them high in the air where they caught the last rays of sunlight that slipped between the buildings, then brought the folder to his chest. The overflowing bins of trash and the stench of garbage hadn't bothered him all day, but now, inexplicably, the smell reached his nostrils and made him bend double and retch. His gut flipped inside out, and he felt dizzy, but he could tell he wasn't going to faint. At least he didn't think so.

"What's wrong?" Perry asked. "Aren't you happy?"

"Inordinately so."

"But why so green around the gills?"

"I'm overwrought. That's what Mother called it when I got this way. Nothing to worry about. It'll pass."

His mind was racing ahead. He wanted to tell Victoria right away that the chapter had been found and learn how the rest of the novel was coming along. The future of their new business venture rested on its quick completion. *Their new venture,* he repeated the phrase to himself, each word carrying so much meaning.

"You are a delicate thing, aren't you?" Perry asked in a soothing voice. "It's all going to work out, Jon. You wait and see."

As the two men walked side by side up the cobblestone alley, Jonathan told himself it was Victoria's words in his hands that were giving him a thrill, but he sensed it was more than that.

Sixteen

Homer arrived on the buckboard and brought a scythe, two shovels, a mallet, a stack of wooden stakes, two rolls of chicken wire, and a neighbor boy named Lucas. As Victoria washed the front windows with vinegar and water, she could see her uncle pacing out a rectangle and digging into the rocky soil. She wrung out her rag in a tin bucket, wiped her hands on her apron, gathered up her gardening gloves, and threw on her straw hat. The stiff seaside breeze blew it back from the crown of her head as she stepped outside to join them.

On this sunny, cloudless day, the waves far below crashed in repetition and the gulls drifted and cried. Homer and Lucas worked together to erect the fence and hoe the bed. Victoria knelt and broke up the dirt with her bare hands. The fecund, sweet smell of soil came back to her, familiar and forgotten—it was the scent of her father, when he came in from the fields, as if he had risen from the earth itself. She let it crumble and fall through her fingers. He had erected a writing desk for her in the shed, upon which she would, at not yet eighteen years of age, write her first novel.

On a summer afternoon like this one, when the cows had been milked and the back quarter mown, Charles Meeks had driven his daughter and Miss Ruthann Sullivan on his buckboard over the rutted Concord Turnpike to Boston. Ruthann clutched Victoria's first manuscript to her chest and when they arrived at Thames & Royall, (Quincy having not yet been named as partner), the unassuming librarian spoke with enough authority to get them in the door. As his daughter preened in the gold-framed mirror of the publishing house parlor and waited to meet Mr. Gaustad, her father slid closer to Miss Sullivan on the leather sofa.

"I believe you are a most remarkable woman," he told her. "Most remarkable indeed."

Victoria gazed upon them in the reflecting glass. Only once before had she seen her father appear so rapturously admiring, when he had praised a ewe for her stamina after a breech birth.

His gnarled fingers squeezed Miss Sullivan's tiny hands as she said, "Oh, Charlie."

Oh my! Victoria had thought. Her father and Miss Sullivan were in love. Right there before her eyes, Victoria saw it unfolding. Love had been in their midst all along. She made a commitment that day to recreate it as vividly as possible on the page. And, of course, she had assumed it would be hers in life as well.

Victoria turned back to the forlorn cottage and the old man and the young boy bent over the garden. This place, while beautiful, felt shrouded in sadness. She had brought grief with her, but, she found, it had already staked its claim here. Edwina had fled her home, though Victoria didn't yet know why. She undid her bun and let the wind wreak havoc with her hair. Through that tangle, she felt the too bright, heatless sun, and wanted desperately to be free of her lonely childhood and her many missteps after leaving the farm. The stiff breeze buffeted her ears and the waves crashed in a noisy chorus. All the elements seemed to be telling her something if only she would listen.

She went to the clothesline, undid the wooden pins, and bundled the clean sheets into her arms before heading inside to make the bed. A little while later, her uncle drove off on the buckboard to pick up seeds from the store and seedlings from his garden. Victoria carried a plate with a slice of bread and butter to Lucas. They sat together on a rock above the sea and drank well water from tin cups. Like Homer, the boy didn't say much, and she wondered if that was the case with everyone in Blaine.

"Are there other children in the village for you to play with or are you all alone up here?" she asked.

He finished chewing. "I'm one of six, ma'am. There are the

Bennett boys and the Gazewell sisters and the Baldwin twins. Plenty more children over at the county school."

Victoria's experience of rural life had been so much more isolated. She had had no real friends growing up, only the old mule Oscar, and a slow-witted boy who, like her, stayed home on a farm nearby. She had been alone most days before Ruthann Sullivan and the Town of Lincoln's Public Library entered her life.

Lucas nodded at the cottage. "A child once lived here, you know. A little girl named Ruby."

"What a nice place to grow up."

He leaned over his dusty knees. "That's the thing, ma'am, she didn't grow up." Lucas peered toward the cliff. "She fell to her death, not three years of age."

Victoria's eyes followed his.

"My mum reminds us not to play too close to the edge. Says God brought us, and He can take us anywhere, anytime. We're not to forget it." The boy crossed himself.

Beyond the cliff, the slipstream carried a seagull on outstretched wings. Victoria found her lace handkerchief in her cuff. The clatter of wooden wheels over the rocky drive sounded and they turned to see the buckboard returning.

"Mum says it's no wonder he don't care to talk much."

The boy stood and stretched his lanky arms overhead. He seemed to have grown in their short time together. With a young man's confidence, he donned his cap and strode away, while Victoria remained seated on the rocks. She watched her uncle as he thrust a shovel into the earth, an old man who had lost his daughter and been abandoned by his wife.

And what about Edwina? All these years, she must have carried with her the loss wherever she went, no matter the distance traveled or the time passed. Victoria had kept her losses to herself, quietly hoping they would dissipate on their own. They hadn't. Would the same be true of Edwina? It seemed that she and her aunt were more alike than Victoria had ever realized.

SEVENTEEN

The stench of butchered meat could almost be mistaken for the scent of overripe flowers wilting in a vase. At least that's what Jonathan tried to convince himself as he pressed a handkerchief to his nose while unpacking files and manuscripts in the new offices of Bliss & Cartwright Publishers, Ltd., currently located in two small rooms above Cambridgeport's largest slaughterhouse.

Perry remained oblivious to the ripe odors rising from the first floor. His imperviousness to distraction amazed Jonathan. His friend had shown fierce determination as he pursued their new venture. Since leaving Thames, Royall & Quincy over a month before, Perry had met with a stream of investors and bankers. Jonathan couldn't keep up with all that his business partner had been orchestrating, though he tagged along when asked and spoke on cue about the books they would publish to great success. Perry finessed complex conversations with impeccable manners and diplomatic ease, skills he had no doubt learned from his high-rolling father. He was quite impressive.

His long, lean, exaggerated shape bent over a wooden crate, resembling a blue heron spearing a fish with its beak. While not handsome by conventional standards, he was sleek, his features slim and refined. His large hands as they splayed over the cover of a ledger were a powerful sight. Whatever, or whomever, he chose as the object of his focus might tremble with intensity.

They had been unpacking all afternoon and Jonathan had reached his limit. The lean muscles of his arms ached, and his thirst for a nice, cold ale made him lick his lips. While lugging boxes up the rickety back stairwell, their collars had come unbuttoned, their shirttails untucked, and their suspenders had slipped off their shoulders. Perry's narrow torso wasn't like that of the doctor pictured in Mrs. Swann's novel, yet that image floated to mind.

"Ready to quit for the day?" Jonathan asked. "I could use a pint."

Perry didn't answer, so intent on whatever he was reading. Jonathan pried open the wooden slats of one last crate. The sharp smell of ink and musty paper momentarily displaced the aroma of meat from below. Over the previous weeks, he had sent several letters to Victoria's Brattle Street home but had received no reply. He finally thought to contact Dottie Windsor through her husband Fletcher, and she shared with him a post office box in Blaine, Maine, where apparently Victoria had gone to visit a relative. Jonathan had mailed her the first chapter of her new, realistic novel that he and Perry had rescued from the trash.

In his letter, he had explained about his departure from Thames, Royall & Quincy, and shared the news of the fledgling company of Bliss & Cartwright, which planned to publish several books that first year. In his note to Victoria, Jonathan made it clear that her realistic urban tale was the one that mattered the most to him, and therefore to their company. He hoped, prayed, that she would take a risk and leave Thames, Royall & Quincy to bring out her latest novel with them.

Jonathan set the last few manuscripts on his disorderly desk. Soon it would be a hub of editorial activity. He wasn't sure how he had gotten so lucky. He was an editor at his own publishing house. He had Perry to thank for it all. Jonathan stepped closer and hovered before his friend's tidy desk.

Perry had remarkably long lashes and yellow-brown irises that appeared surprised when he looked up, but to Jonathan's relief, melted in an easy way. "I see," Perry said, a slight question coming into his voice.

What did he see? Jonathan wondered but didn't dare ask. For an instant, his imagination flared. His business partner, who had until now been all business, seemed to be returning his gaze with some interest. Was he leaning closer or was that his perennial forward-tilting stance? Perry shifted. He arched his back, and stretched, and let out a long yawn. This was the awkward, not altogether unappealing young man Jonathan had known since their first year at college. With his moustache and hair so nicely groomed, Perry was becoming downright handsome. Jonathan had begun to imagine—well, he wasn't sure what he had begun to imagine. Nothing, really.

"You know how absorbed I get. Feel free to shake me by the shoulder anytime."

Jonathan buttoned his vest and took his coat from the rack, determined not to imagine too much. The ale would help.

"I believe I'm prepared for tomorrow's meeting at the bank." Perry dropped the ledger he had been reading onto his desk. "If you wait a moment, we can go to the saloon together."

Perry put on his loose coat and oversized hat, his style that of a tradesman who needed many pockets to hold his tools. Jonathan, by comparison, was neat in his conventional attire, though it pained him that his cuffs were worn.

"Everyone needs a pint at the end of the day." Perry gathered up his bulging briefcase. "Maybe we should hop the trolley and celebrate our new location with a couple of those big steaks over at the Porter House Inn."

Jonathan happened to have his hand in his pocket and couldn't help jangling the few bits of change.

"At my expense," Perry clarified.

"You can't always be paying, Perry. You've been doing all the work to make our venture possible. I should be treating you."

"You'll be working hard soon enough. You're the one who's going to make our name. Besides, you carried more boxes than I did today."

"Thank you," Jonathan said softly and waved a hand at the cluttered room, "for all this."

Perry either hadn't heard or chose to ignore him. Such a fine fellow, Jonathan thought, and not one bit highfalutin', though he could have been. They headed down the rickety backstairs and into the summer dusk, escaping just in time. A cattle drive was coming up Cambridge Street in their direction on the way to the slaughterhouse. The muddy road became churned up under all those hooves. The fouled soil and the dirty beasts were enough to make Jonathan bring out his handkerchief to cover his nose.

"I wish we could have found a slightly more civilized address," he said as he followed in Perry's wake.

"Only temporary," Perry replied over his shoulder.

They wove through the congested sidewalk where workmen headed home for the day and shoppers carried baskets full of every variety of goods. With a loud clatter and honking of horns, wagons pulled to the side to make way for the driven animals. A trolley screeched to a halt as the last of the cattle crossed the tracks.

"If you can convince Victoria to let us publish her book by Christmastime, the sales will help us move out of these offices in the new year. Some mention in the press before publication would increase our chances for success."

Jonathan barely kept up with his friend's long strides. "What do you mean?"

"Something to bring her into the public eye. The most obvious thing would be for her to reveal that she is Mrs. Swann. Is there really any harm in that?"

"I think she'd be dead set against it." Jonathan stopped at a street corner. "She's kept her identity hidden for so long."

"But didn't you say she was going to stop writing as Mrs. Swann?"

"Yes, but Victoria doesn't want to alienate her readers. Also, I have hopes about Mrs. Swann. I'd love to keep her alive."

"I had no idea you'd become such a fan. I can't imagine us publishing a romance and adventure novel, can you? I thought we were aiming for a higher, more discerning market."

Higher. Lower. Flummoxed, Jonathan gave up and followed Perry as they dashed across the road, avoiding puddles, and risking their lives in the Cambridge traffic.

"Anyway, it may be a moot point as I gather that she burned

the last Mrs. Swann novel. Such a disservice to her oeuvre."

"Her oeuvre?" Perry shook his head. "Oh my, Jon, you are smitten. Anyway, I heard that Thames, Royall & Quincy is now closed. Not sure if Russell's filed for bankruptcy or what. It's all a mystery."

"I wonder what he's up to."

"I'll ask Father. He has ways of finding out such things."

The extent of Perry's reach continued to amaze.

EIGHTEEN

Weeks passed, the days blending one with the next, and Victoria fell into a routine. She made small improvements to the cottage and tended her garden. At low tide, she collected oysters and mussels from the black mud beneath the cliff. In afternoons, she met the fishing boats at the town dock and brought home haddock, cod, or mackerel for supper. She stopped by the store to chat with her uncle, and on several rainy afternoons, she sat in on a game of cards with his fishermen friends. Every day she took long, solitary walks along the rocky shore where sea wrack swayed, and periwinkles crawled in tidal pools. Further out, grey seals threw themselves onto flat outcroppings to lounge in the sun before slipping below the bright surface of the waves. The long summer days expanded in her open arms.

And in the cool Maine summer evenings, she stoked the wood fire and curled on the wicker sofa with the novels Jonathan had lent to her. She would have liked to discuss them with him. In the bookish quiet, what she wanted most was to sit side by side with someone she loved and read together. That's all she had ever wanted. With her many quiet hours, she reflected on her life. At sixteen, she had stood before Miss Sullivan's desk and announced that she was not only a reader but a writer as well. For years, the bony, wall-eyed, and infinitely kind librarian had been impressed by the self-educated girl. On hearing Victoria's pronouncement, she had used her position to arrange her an introduction to Concord's most esteemed elder statesman of letters.

Wedged between her father and Ruthann on the buckboard and wearing a calico dress that she had sewn herself, and a straw bonnet woven with fresh wildflowers, Victoria had arrived at The Old Manse. She knocked on the plain front door, curtsied, and was led into the somber library. The ancient Mr. Emerson had asked her name several times during their tea together, reiterating that his memory wasn't what it used to be. Mr. Lowell was more congenial but mumbled so badly Victoria had to lean forward to catch his pleasantries. By the end of the tedious visit, she had felt certain she never wanted to grow old and that she didn't much care for overly dense books or those who wrote them. She preferred a good yarn and set out to write one.

Ruthann had despaired that her young charge had missed the opportunity of a lifetime, but eventually, despite her misgivings, the librarian had handed over to Victoria a stack of thin stories that she kept hidden behind her desk. Each was flimsy, but charmingly designed, with intricately drawn covers depicting young women in various settings and attires, surrounded by floral and ivy borders in the decorative style of Art Nouveau. Ruthann had explained that these pamphlets were a newer breed of publication: the dime novel, sold for not more than that and published at a frantic pace to an eager following. She had wanted her young book enthusiast to be well educated in more substantial literature before falling prey to the charms of these easy narratives. Victoria promptly read them all.

The one she liked best was *The Mysterious Key and What It Opens* by none other than Louisa May Alcott. According to Ruthann, the tale had been published the year before *Little Women* when the author was struggling to feed her family. After reading it, Victoria had pressed her father to harness the buckboard again so she might place a posy of pansies on the lady author's unassuming grave. Alcott was buried alongside Emerson, Hawthorne, and Thoreau on Author's Ridge up the hill from the village green in Concord.

Victoria had felt sorry for Miss Alcott because she had never married. But she changed her mind when she saw the mound of bouquets and letters heaped upon the simple white marble stone. She read some of the notes left behind by admirers and her cheeks burned with their passionate words. Miss Alcott's readers were rapturously in love with her.

Victoria had been so sure that if she ever succeeded as a writer, she wouldn't succumb to Miss Alcott's same fate. Yet here she was, alone and unloved in a cottage in Maine, though still adored by Mrs. Swann's fans. With nothing left to lose, she concluded she must risk sacrificing that adulation in order to be true to herself and write something closer to her own honest sentiments and life story.

⁂

On a stormy evening, Victoria went to the desk that her uncle had constructed out of a pine board and lobster crates in the room overlooking the sea. As the wind careened and caroused beyond the window facing the cliff, she began to fill the many notebooks she had brought with her that summer. The story she had begun on Brattle Street unfolded with surprising ease. Her character Daisy would help pierce the heart of what made Victoria feel most alone: her utter helplessness in the face of tragedy.

She wrote on into the night, trying to fill with words the hollow place inside herself. In a crucial chapter, her protagonist returned from the city to the farm where she had grown up. On an outing to the state fair, the girl sat with her legs dangling from the back of her father's buckboard as they drove along a country road. In actuality, Victoria had refused to sit up front with her father after he had forbidden her to see Raymond Byrne ever again. She had given her first reading as an author and was full of herself and didn't see why she needed to heed her father anymore. In Victoria's mind, even now, it was that small rebellion that had led to all her subsequent unhappiness.

In the fictional story, Daisy couldn't wait to get to the fair where she hoped to win a blue ribbon for her blackberry pie. But on the rough dirt track, the wagon hit a rut, and the girl let out a dramatic shriek. Fearing that his daughter had been hurt, her father pulled hard on the reins, causing the mule to take off. The wagon barreled across a field while Daisy, tossed to the ground, sat dumfounded in the dirt, rows of corn looming over her on either side.

Victoria could recall gazing up from the road at the waving tassels, instantly ashamed of having cried out so foolishly. Her father's accident would never have happened if she hadn't let out that caterwaul. Or if she had been a good girl in the first place and obeyed his wishes, instead of petulantly refusing to sit beside him. She had been quietly thrilled with herself for breaking her father's trust and plotting a clandestine visit with Raymond.

But no matter the difference between the novel and Victoria's own life: in both, a tragic crash occurred, followed by a deathly silence. A silence she would never forget. Daisy clambered to her feet and ran as fast as her city boots could carry her. Around the bend, she cried out at the sight of the overturned wagon. Oscar the mule had stood under the boughs of Victoria's favorite willow, lapping water from the muddy pond while her father lay on the hard ground, his lung punctured and his back broken.

In the novel, Daisy's father expired right there by the water's edge. She lost the farm and, penniless, returned to the city alone, vulnerable, and destined for a difficult end. In real life, Victoria stayed at her father's bedside for two long weeks before he passed away. The farm was sold, Gaustad demanded her next book, and Raymond proposed. On a bleak October afternoon, her editor gave her away at City Hall. In mourning, the bride wore black and carried no flowers.

ॐ

Victoria set down her pen as the first rays of morning light crept through the shutters. When she closed her tired eyes, the rectangle of white paper she had been staring at for hours burned itself on to the back of her lids, a white coffin on a black sky. In that moment, she felt a presence at her back on the braided rug but knew better than to turn around. She didn't want to disturb the little girl who she sensed playing there, as they each in their own way constructed worlds out of words and wooden blocks. The loons on a pond nearby exchanged their eerie calls and Victoria and Ruby paused to listen.

The moment faded too fast and never returned with such clarity, but Victoria knew that the little girl was with her, quietly keeping her company. By summer's end, with the help of the mysterious birds and the constant wind and Ruby nearby, Victoria finished her new, realistic novel. She wrapped it in brown paper and mailed it from her uncle's post office to Jonathan Cartwright at his new publishing house.

Summer had come and gone without Edwina. Victoria eventually learned from her uncle that her aunt had left on a fishing voyage the day before Victoria first arrived in Maine. Homer regretted not sending word in advance that their niece was coming for a stay. Despite not seeing her aunt, Victoria was glad to have passed these fruitful months in Blaine. For it was here by the sea that she wrote *The Boston Harbor Girl*.

NINETEEN

The lamp hissed and flickered, and Jonathan worried it might run out before he had finished reading. The house settled around him with its familiar sounds. Rustling came from the straw mattress upstairs where the Roses kicked and played in their dreams. Reaching the final page and the final sentence of Victoria's new novel, Jonathan lifted his eyes and gazed around at the dim parlor. His father's rocker cast a long ghostly shadow across the worn rug. He took off his reading spectacles and rubbed his eyes. He and his sisters were old enough to manage without their parents, but that didn't mean they weren't orphans. The deep sting of loss pierced him as he turned back to the immediate source of his melancholy: the manuscript that had stirred in him a recognition of the preciousness of life and the illusive, fragile nature of happiness, his own in particular.

Starting right after supper that evening, he and Clara had sat side by side on the sofa, reading. Each time Jonathan finished a page, he passed it to her. Close to midnight, she grew too tired to keep her eyes open and gave in and went to bed. But not without first telling him how much she enjoyed the story. Victoria's protagonist's innocence had been taken from her, her hard work had gone unrewarded, and her longing for companionship was thwarted and mocked. When Clara sniffled, Jonathan handed her his handkerchief without looking up from the page. He turned now to one of Daisy's many trials—an incident that pained him more than the loss of the character's father in the wagon accident on the dirt road.

Daisy shut her eyes and let the ether take her into its arms. Twirling and spinning, she was that girl again at the county dance, the hem of her calico dress outstretched.

"Make her stop moving," the doctor snarled, "or I'll strap down her arms, too, the feisty little tart."

"She a good girl," the Chinese lady said, trying to hold Daisy still.

"She's a girl no more," the doctor declared cruelly.

His words seared into Daisy's mind, like the sinewy poison that coursed through her veins. The paddle of the schoolmaster on her backside and the slap of her husband's hand across her cheeks burned in her memory as the disreputable doctor did his job. Hot, flaming pain shot through her womanhood and she let out an unearthly cry. Tears poured forth, but she felt no tenderness for her own tattered soul. As she floated above the filthy table, she looked down with disgust on the ruined woman she had become.

On the window seat, Jonathan hugged his knees to his chest. Peeking around the drawn curtains, he squinted into the first rays of morning light. The lamp at his side sputtered as the last of the oil died out.

In the final pages of the novel, Daisy was beyond saving as she wandered the wharfs of Boston Harbor. Massive ships loomed and heavy cranes lifted goods from around the world. The scene bustled with rough activity, with men shouting to one another. A longshoreman warned the girl to step out of the way, to stop and go no further. But she carried on as if in a trance. Her father and mother were gone, as was her life on the farm. She continued to the end of the pier with unseeing eyes. The tumult of the newly prosperous city rose behind her, but she gazed only at the churning water. The propeller of a mammoth steam ship whirred and frothed as Daisy took one last step over the edge and was sucked down into its hungry maw.

Jonathan stood and shook out his limbs.

Overwritten by literary standards, and somewhat similar in outcome to *Madame Bovary*, yet clearly lacking that novel's sublime subtlety, Victoria's story was no masterpiece. The author couldn't be compared to Tolstoy, or James, or Wharton, for she wore her heart on her sleeve. Restraint was not her style, as anyone knew from reading her romance adventures.

He crossed the room and, without hesitation, sat in his father's rocker, where it began to dawn on him he might have a profitable book on his hands. *The Boston Harbor Girl* would make a name for the fledgling publishing company. It might even make him rich. He let out a stifled laugh, not wanting to wake his sisters upstairs. But if the book catapulted the company into the public eye, there could be a price to pay too. Indecent acts such as the one performed by the disreputable doctor in the fictional back alley were not taken lightly, even on the page. Publishers had been dragged into court for less.

Jonathan held onto the chair's spindly arms and noticed where he had landed. It was the first time that he, or perhaps *anyone*, had ever sat in that seat, besides the reverend. He felt the firmness of the chair beneath him. The thin wooden rails at his back pressed against his spine, making him sit straighter. This was where his father had done his best liturgical thinking. Here in this rocker, he determined the topic for each week's sermon. The uncomfortable chair could not help but remind the sitter that life was not meant to be comfortable or easy. It was hard. And one's response to it must be equally firm.

Jonathan began to pace. He would stand up for this novel. He didn't care that his father would have been scandalized. It was the principle of the thing that mattered. That was the lesson of the sermon he needed to hear in this moment. Yet, high principles aside, he hated that young Daisy had to die in the end. He would have preferred a happy ending. He had somehow become a soft-hearted reader, and, indeed, a soft-hearted man.

Lying down on his favorite window seat, Jonathan pressed his cheek to the wrinkled pages and shut his eyes as the sun was coming up. After a nap, he would consult with his sisters about Daisy's fate, because what did he know about the literary tastes of women, or any literary tastes at all? How, he wondered as he drifted off, had he ever thought he knew so much?

TWENTY

L ight cut through the doorway, illuminating dust motes that swirled in the heat of the Franklin stove. Victoria rubbed her hands together. Though the chill of morning had burned off outside, the empty country store remained cool. She tried to imagine the hush that came over the village in winter when all the visitors had gone home and the fishing vessels were enveloped in ice and fog. Though isolated, her days here had been less blanketed by loneliness than her life on Brattle Street. She wondered if she could ever call Blaine home.

Into this peaceful moment came arguing voices from the back of the store. The kitchen door was flung open and her uncle stormed out. Victoria craned to see up the aisle. Passing baked goods and hardware strode a short, stocky, fierce woman in overalls and men's brogans, her hands jammed into the pockets of a long oilskin duster. She wore a knit cap, from which her frizzy grey hair protruded. Her bottom lip bulged, and as she got nearer, Victoria realized it was crammed with chewing tobacco. When the woman saw her, her eyes widened, and her hands flew up to pull her cap lower over her lined brow.

"Edwina?" Victoria asked.

"Aye," the woman replied in a husky voice. "And you must be little Vicky, all grown up."

The quiet store cradled them. A few paces behind, Homer blinked and waited. All three waited, though for what they weren't sure, unless it was for the past to catch up to the present. So much had happened to each without the other, yet the familial knot pulled taut, and to their surprise, it held.

Victoria inched forward. But it was Edwina who extended a firm hand to pat the side of her niece's arm. She did it once, twice, quickly reassuring the girl, as she had, that everything was going to be all right. But that wasn't enough for either. They came closer and her aunt let out a soft, grumbling sound.

"Let's have it then." She opened her arms all the way.

Victoria fell into them. The scents of wood smoke, tobacco, and salty sea air enveloped her. Edwina's wiry hair poked her cheek. The wooden buttons and stiff husk of her aunt's coat repelled her and the hard pats to Victoria's back alarmed her. It wasn't comfortable, or all that comforting, but Victoria started to cry in absolute relief. First a few tears and then many, which only made Edwina pat harder. "Come now, none of that."

Homer bent closer. "We've upset her. We should have written to her ages ago." He made a sorrowful sigh. "Tell her how we wanted to but didn't want to bother a fine lady like her."

"You tell her yourself," her aunt said as Victoria continued to cry.

Her uncle seemed almost too pained to speak. "Your aunt has all your books. The owner of the Cambridge Bookshop sends them up to her each time a new one comes out. You don't have a more devoted fan than my Edwina."

"Mrs. Swann has lots of fans," Edwina corrected him as Victoria's tears kept coming. "She never could stop blubbering once she got started."

Victoria pulled a handkerchief from her sleeve and blew her nose.

"She doesn't appear to have changed," Homer said.

"But I have." Victoria's voice cracked. "I haven't cried like this in years. I've had no one to cry *with*." Her blubbering embarrassed her, but it was true, and it mattered more than anything to have her aunt and uncle know it.

Homer stroked Victoria's back. "Calm yourself, dear."

Victoria wiped her eyes and tried to compose herself. "Edwina, I want you to know that my father missed you terribly. What happened with my mother's death was lamentable, but he never spoke ill of you. He forgave you. I know he did."

Edwina stuffed her hands deeper into her pockets. "Nothing more to say. Long time ago. We're here now, not there."

They looked down at their creased and dusty boots—Victoria's too dainty and thin-soled for the country paths of Blaine while Edwina's were thick and hardened from travel.

"I would never have gone off to sea this summer if I'd known you were coming." Edwina gave Homer a stern glance. "Sorry to have missed you all these weeks."

"I've been sorry also, but it's wonderful to see you now."

Homer appeared immensely glad to have his wife back too.

"Won't you join me for dinner at the cottage this evening?" Victoria asked.

Edwina tugged her cap lower. "Can't do it. I need to get back to Portland."

"Oh no, you don't," Homer said. "The saloon can manage without you for another day or two."

"You work in a saloon?" Victoria tried not to sound too alarmed.

Homer put an arm around his wife's shoulder. "She's part owner. Edwina likes things lively. The sailors tell her the most interesting tales. Your aunt lives for a great story."

Victoria felt a little breathless. Her aunt was not only a sailor and a cook, but a teacher and a bartender. Was there anything Edwina couldn't do? There was one thing. One thing Victoria wasn't good at either.

"Shouldn't we try to get together as family?" she asked.

"Absolutely," Homer replied. "I speak for Edwina and myself. We thank you kindly for the invitation and would be honored to join you. We'll bring the lobster."

TWENTY-ONE

After supper, the siblings retreated to the parlor where Jonathan stoked the fire, and his sisters found their usual reading spots. Rosalyn and Rosemond lay on a blanket before the hearth and took turns turning the pages of *Rebecca of Sunnybrook Farm*, their heads tipped in unison to one side then the other. From her hours on the piano bench, Philomena didn't mind sitting in a straight-backed parlor chair as she read *Dracula*, her eyes widening periodically, and her foot tapping nervously. Tessa claimed the upholstered wingback where she combed out her long tresses, as if preparing to meet the Shropshire lad, not only read poems about him.

Jonathan took his window seat and prepared to dive back into a stack of manuscripts for Bliss & Cartwright. He leaned into the folds of the faded damask curtains and listened to the fire settle in the grate. The second week of September was early to start the heating season, but in anticipation of Clara's first paycheck from teaching, she had replenished the coal and treated them all to roast chicken for supper, now that their cook had been let go. The leftover bones simmered in a pot for soup, the soothing aroma filling the house. Jonathan's older sister was more well-organized and cleverer than ever, managing the house with an ease that rivalled their mother's. But where was Clara now? Jonathan wondered. He rose and found her by the front door, a linen handkerchief clutched in one hand and her face flushed.

"Are you all right?" he asked.

Without a word, she threw her arms around his neck and knocked him back a step.

"What's all this about, sister?"

The doorbell rang at that moment, and Clara let go. She stared defiantly at the front door. "Go on. Let him in," she said.

"Let who in?"

The two Roses had hopped up and leaned in from the parlor threshold. The others roused themselves, too, at this unusual evening interruption. Jonathan opened the front door and there stood Timothy Maverick, Clara's long-time friend. Before Jonathan could take in the full, handsome sight of him, Tim had said a quick greeting and stepped boldly into the house. He took off his bowler, handed it to the Roses, and made straight for Clara.

"Are you ready?" he asked.

She gave a quick nod and he pulled her to his side. The couple marched into the parlor and Jonathan shooed the twins back inside too. Timothy took up a position before the fireplace. He let go of Clara's hand and thrust out his broad chest, as if tilted into a raging gale.

"Jonathan, may I speak with you?" he asked.

"Me?" Jonathan pointed at his own narrow chest. "You wish to speak to me?"

Clara spoke in a curiously stern voice. "Yes, you, Jon."

Tim ducked his well-groomed head closer and cleared his throat. He was attired formally, with a pearl tie pin and matching cufflinks. Jonathan unobtrusively tucked in his own shirt and straightened his suspenders. He regretted not retrieving his coat from where it lay rumpled on the window seat, as the occasion suddenly seemed quite formal.

"I know that you and Clara are awfully close," Tim said. "As her nearest and dearest, and also, as the *man* of the house, I have come to ask you, Jonathan, for her hand in marriage."

The younger sisters bounced up and down, ready to explode, but managed to keep quiet as they all turned to Jonathan for his reply. Feeling utterly unequal to the task, he did what he always did when flummoxed: he turned to Clara who, he was sorry to see, was inexplicably scowling at him. What did she want him to say? Of course, he would be happy for her to marry Timothy. But shouldn't that decision belong to her and no one else?

Jonathan gathered his wits and spoke. "I say, Tim, I think

Clara's the best judge of her own circumstances. She knows a great deal about, well, absolutely everything." He turned to her. "The question is, dear sister, what do *you* want?"

Her mouth hung open for a moment until she let out a high trill and stood on tiptoes to kiss his cheek. "While it's my decision, as brother dear has said, I want to make sure you'll be all right if I marry. Will you be?"

"Of course, we will," Philomena said. "Don't worry about us. Tessa and I have steady work at the Music Hall and we can mind the Roses in the afternoons when they're not at school."

"The law permits children to work who aren't much older than them," Tessa said and turned to the twins. "You two can tend to yourselves in the evenings, can't you, girls?"

Rosalyn and Rosamond bobbed in agreement.

"Also, I intend to do my best for one and all," Tim interjected. They had momentarily forgotten he was there. "Perhaps I should have mentioned it sooner," he said. "But, as it happens, the house next to ours on Beacon Hill is vacant, and well, Father seems to own it. I don't see why you sisters couldn't move in. That is, if it's agreeable to one and all?"

All six siblings stared at him as if he had ridden in on a white steed.

"I'd say that settles it," Clara said with her usual clarity of mind.

With barely the words out of her mouth, her sisters surrounded her, all talking at once, chattering about weddings and rings. Tim sidestepped the hubbub to speak to Jonathan alone.

"I want you to know, Jon, that you'll be most welcome to visit us anytime."

Jonathan thanked him.

"That is," Timothy said, "you see, Clara and I will have a home of our own and your sisters will have one too. I suspect it will be rather different for you."

It took a moment for Jonathan to grasp what his future brother-in-law was suggesting. The family would no longer live together as they had. His dearest sister wouldn't be here for him. His best friend, his soul mate thus far in life, was moving on. Of course, it was bound to happen someday, but that day was now.

He tried to rally himself. "I'm happy for you both." As he said it, he realized it was true. He wanted happiness for Clara, for each of them, even himself. He lowered his voice. "But I do have a question for you."

"What is it, brother?" Timothy put a heavy hand on Jonathan's shoulder.

Jonathan sagged under the weight of it. "How did you *know*?" he asked.

"Know what?"

"That you had found the right person?"

Tim smiled. "Why, it's simple. A man knows."

"He does?"

"Come now, have you someone in mind?"

"No." Jonathan shook his head quickly. "Not really. I mean, I'm not sure."

Tim let out a hearty laugh. "Be sure, man! I remember how you never could decide anything. That was the cause of our fracas when we were boys, if you recall."

"I remember my bloody nose, but not what made you hit me."

"When you lost at marbles, which was often, you took forever deciding whether to forfeit an aggie or a cat's eye. I got so frustrated waiting for you to make up your mind, I popped you one. Not the best response, I admit. Which is why I can say with confidence that, knowing you, it's time to decide. Probably well past time."

"You may be right, Timothy."

"Look at us, Clara and me. It's not too difficult to be happy. Not difficult at all."

Jonathan sucked in air between his teeth and wanted to say that it was the most difficult thing he could possibly imagine, which is why he hadn't allowed himself to think upon it overmuch—that is, until now.

TWENTY-TWO

Edwina arrived at the cottage and didn't pause to take in the setting sun as it tossed a last ribbon of gold across the ocean. She ignored the cliffside that had stolen so much from her and headed straight into the cottage where she paced the small rooms, restless as a caged bobcat. To distract her, Homer shared improvements he had made to the little home over the years—the tin roof, a rain barrel, an indoor washtub, and a lantern on the path to the outhouse. Victoria, too, had done her part to bring the place back to life and lift the dark shroud of memory.

Over the summer, she had repainted the windowsills and placed Mason jars of fresh wildflowers on them. She had waxed the pine floor, mended the braided carpet, and washed and re-hung the eyelet curtains on their wooden rods. The appliqued flowers on the turquoise bedspread were smooth, thanks to her whipstitch, and the red cushions on the wicker seats were plumper after she had replaced the stuffing stolen by mice. She was pleased with the table she had set for their supper. Now the pink floral plates lay strewn with lobster shells and the skins of baked potatoes. With the meal eaten, the three sat back and listened to the wind rattle the shutters and batter the cottage walls.

After a time, Edwina got up and went to the alcove where Homer had placed Victoria's desk. She pulled aside the curtain and peered into the bruised night outside. It was the first time she had acknowledged the cliff and the sea beyond it. Victoria and her uncle exchanged a glance.

"Nice spot for writing," Edwina said.

Victoria raised her bottle of spruce ale and poured the last drops into her glass. "I've had good luck here." She rarely drank, but this was a celebration of all the summer had given to her.

"Where do you like to write, Edwina?" she asked.

Her aunt let the curtain drop. "What makes you think I write?"

"Something uncle said, though he's hardly shared much."

Edwina sauntered back to the sitting area, her hands deep in the pockets of her overalls.

"I'm curious if you write about your travels?" Victoria asked.

The old wicker creaked as Edwina sat on the sofa beside her husband. "I do."

"And are your settings like those of Mrs. Swann?"

"Heavens no." Edwina gave a derisive snort. "My settings are real. And I don't make the kind of errors you've made."

Victoria should have been offended by Edwina's criticism of Mrs. Swann, but she was already becoming accustomed to her irascible aunt. "And what errors might those be?" she asked and took another sip of lager.

"Oh, every sort." Edwina made herself comfortable, her legs, in thick canvas trousers, crossed with an ankle over a knee. "On Mrs. Swann's last adventure, your Arabian soldier wore a bandolier when a belt slung low at the hips would have been more accurate. It pains me how many times I've wanted to correct you."

"Too late now." Victoria lifted her glass. "I'm done with Mrs. Swann. I won't write another book by her ever again." Victoria liked the sound of that, as if it had been the easiest thing in the world to pry herself loose from her former identity.

"But you can't be done with her. Readers like Edwina would miss her too much."

"Homer's right. You need to improve her, that's all. What you've needed all along is an advisor who's seen something of the world."

"Or to see it myself," Victoria said, the beer giving her courage.

"There's an idea," Homer said. "Could be time for you to have some adventures of your own. You can come back here and tell us all about it."

The wind picked up at that moment. Maybe she would travel, Victoria thought with some giddiness. There was a big world out there and she had been too preoccupied and, in a way, too frightened to explore it. Across from her, Edwina also seemed restless. She was brooding over something, her small, sturdy brogans shifting on the braided rug.

"Here's the problem as I see it," Edwina said. "Mrs. Swann's heroines need to get into worse jams and they need to finagle their own ways out of them. They've been too helpless and not nearly strong enough. You need to let them *truly live.*"

Victoria marveled that her aunt knew what it had taken her so long to grasp. It was time to truly live, on and off the page.

"Sounds like Mrs. Swann is in for some improvements, like our little cottage here." Homer tipped his beer stein toward the tidy room. "It looks mighty good, doesn't it, Edwina?" He reached across and gave a little poke to his wife's ribs through her thick fisherman's sweater.

"He's trying to get me back to Blaine." She swatted him away playfully.

Homer caught hold of her hand and after some tussling, they settled again, fingers entwined. Though they were in their eighth decade, they seemed as smitten as teenagers. Victoria took a final sip and set down her glass. While her aunt and uncle chatted about the cottage, her thoughts lingered on the future of Mrs. Swann. Maybe there was a way for her to carry on?

Homer took a pipe from his jacket pocket and excused himself to have a smoke on the back porch. The wind dodged past him and chilled the room as he stepped outside, the first bite of autumn in the crisp air. Victoria shivered and wrapped the plaid shawl around her shoulders as Edwina retrieved her penknife from her belt to clean her fingernails. They sat with the fire roaring and the loon's lonely call echoing far off. There was so much Victoria wanted to ask of her aunt. The stories Edwina could tell, the places she had been, the people she had met. But Victoria gathered herself to express instead what had been on her mind all summer.

"I was so sorry to learn about your Ruby, Edwina. What a tragic loss."

Edwina's brogans landed on the rug and Victoria feared her aunt might get up and leave too.

"I've sensed her here with me," Victoria said.

Edwina gaze shot up from the carpet. "Is that so?"

"I was writing something new." Victoria pulled the shawl closer. "Something I've never been able to write about before. I think she came to help me with it."

"She was always my little helper." Edwina rose and went to the desk, and after a moment, she picked up Victoria's pen and admired it. "What were you writing about?"

The back of Victoria's neck prickled, and she could feel her cheeks grow warm. She shrugged off the shawl. "I was writing about what happened that day with my father and the wagon. The accident that ended his life." She went to stand beside Edwina at the desk.

"Our family has had more than our share of bad luck." Edwina set down the pen.

"But it wasn't bad luck. On our way home from the county fair, I insisted on riding on the back and when we hit a dip, I let out a shriek and fell off. It surprised the poor mule and he bolted. *That's* why Father lost control. It all happened so fast, but there's no denying it was *my* fault. *I'm* the one who caused the accident."

Victoria's words tumbled out fast and with great urgency. It mattered more than anything that Edwina should understand what Victoria alone had known for years.

"I was a stupid, frivolous, self-involved girl, putting on city airs, as if I didn't know what to expect on a country road. I'd just met Raymond and argued with Father and disobeyed him. My rebellion was the start of so much misery."

Edwina turned to her. "If I remember right, the mule had rabies. Didn't he have to be put down? Wasn't *that* the cause of the accident?"

"Yes, but I'm telling you, *I'm* the one who's responsible. It was my selfishness that killed my dear father."

"You're saying you might as well have put a gun to his head, no different from the mule?"

Victoria hesitated. "No, I'm not saying that."

"It was as if you'd poisoned him with arsenic?" A hint of a smile had started to appear at the edges of Edwina's lips.

"I don't know why you're making light of this."

"Maybe it was the same as plunging a knife into his heart?"

"Don't be ridiculous, Edwina."

"Don't you be ridiculous, either." Edwina pressed a sturdy finger against Victoria's breastbone, sending a seismic tremor through her. "I see what you've done all those years. You've written a version in your mind in which you're the villain, where you're the one to blame."

"But I *am* to blame."

"It was a heartbreaking accident, nothing more. As it was for my Ruby, and your dear mother too. I, of all people, have no right to forgive myself, but I've had to in order to go on with life. The same is true for you. You must put it behind you and forgive yourself."

Urgent, long-held tears burned behind Victoria's eyes.

"Did it ever occur to you that it was fortunate you sat in the back of the wagon that day?" Edwina asked. "If you had been in the front with your father, you, too, might have been injured or killed when it overturned. I couldn't have borne to lose you both. We may not have seen one another all this time, but you've been with me, here in my heart." Edwina tapped a hand to her breast and then reached across to smooth Victoria's lace collar.

Victoria knew that brisk but caring touch. Her aunt had loved her as a child and, it seemed, loved her still. When she dared to look into Edwina's gentle face, there was no holding back. "But I've never known what to *do* about it," she cried.

"Do? There's nothing you can do. You can't make the past go away. You have to let it be. That's all there is to it."

Victoria swiped moisture from her cheeks with her fingers. "But has traveling at least brought you some solace?"

Edwina turned to the desk and leaned against the back of Victoria's chair. "Nothing brings solace but the passage of time. Not voyages, like the ones I've taken, or staying put, like my husband. He's suffered every bit as much as I have." She picked up the last of Victoria's empty notebooks and thumbed through the blank pages, the blue lines blurring as she flipped past. "Writing offers a certain sort of peace in its own way. It helps fill up the hollow place inside." She set down the notebook. "I suspect you know what I mean."

It was true, the shame and the loss receded when Victoria lifted her pen. All the years of churning out stories as Mrs. Swann had felt like a penance. But she was starting a new chapter now. The pages had somehow been turning without her realizing it.

The two stood side by side, shoulders grazing, so unalike in certain ways, they still resembled one another, with their curly auburn hair, bronzed cheeks, and rich brown eyes. With their heads bowed at the same angle over the desktop, an observer might have thought they were praying. But if Edwina was right, absolution was theirs already.

PART THREE

TWENTY-THREE

With the crack of broken glass and the clatter of shards on slate, Victoria entered her house on Brattle Street. She had tried the front and kitchen doors, but the locks wouldn't take her key. The heavy black shutters hadn't budged either. Her only option had been to hurl a stone at one of the small panes of glass in the French doors that faced the side yard. Her gloved hand reached past the jagged edges to turn the handle and step into her home.

The coolness of the conservatory didn't surprise her, as the tile floor kept the room cool year-round. But she sensed something wrong. Through shuttered daylight, she could see that the dining table was missing. The Federal-era antique chairs were gone too. The oak sideboard. The gilt-framed mirror. The crystal chandelier. Even the frosted-glass sconces from the walls—all gone. Victoria hurried deeper into her home, her boots scuffing the hardwood floor, now absent her favorite Kerman rugs.

Robbers had taken everything! They must have seen the house, uninhabited in the summer, as an obvious target. Victoria had made arrangements for property upkeep while away but when the carriage had let her off, she was shocked to see that the place looked abandoned. Shingles from the mansard roof lay scattered in the knee-high grass and the gutters overflowed with debris. No wonder criminals had thought it an easy target.

She steadied herself with a hand on the decorative wallpaper where the Japanese ladies continued their slow and peaceful strolls, unaware of the disaster that had taken place around them. The Persian runner carpet and the hat stand were gone. The front hall table remained, but the silver tray for calling cards, so often empty, was also gone. On the marble tabletop sat a thick pile of mail—mostly bills, Victoria saw at a glance.

Dottie must have brought them in on her last visit. When had the burglary taken place? Had it been done in broad daylight or in the middle of the night? Too affronted to cry, Victoria tossed her straw hat onto the table, grabbed the stack of letters, turned toward the parlor, and braced herself.

Pulling back the pocket doors, she let out a cry. Her favorite room stood empty. A lady's rocking chair covered in a white sheet was all that was left—a solitary ghost surrounded by bare floor and walls. With the shutters closed to dusk, the air felt eerie and still. Her colorful Turkish carpets had been taken away. The grand Chinoiserie urns no longer stood at attention by the windows. The many mirrored and tasseled cushions were no longer strewn before the hearth. Two lonely logs rested on the bricks, the brass andirons stolen out from under them.

Victoria took hold of the mantel with both hands, her breathing fast and jagged. She squeezed her eyes closed but no tears came. When she opened them, she stood face to face with the dejected Japanese crane teetering on thin legs. Who had done this to her? She stumbled to the rocker and fell into it, not bothering to remove the dusty white covering. She wanted to go to her bedroom to lie down but couldn't bear to see it emptied out too. She had nothing left, absolutely nothing.

The mail slipped from Victoria's lap, and when she bent to retrieve it, she spotted a thick envelope from a prominent Boston law firm. Had Thames, Royall & Quincy finally sent her royalties? Or maybe these were the divorce papers. Her hands shook as she unfolded the pages and read the letter with increasing urgency. At the bottom of the last page, she recognized her husband's unsteady signature. Her address on Brattle Street stood out in bold beside an embossed stamp from the Cambridge courthouse.

In trembling fingers, Victoria held a bill of property sales with an extensive addendum listing all her furnishings. Two pages of columns showed the monetary assessment of every precious piece acquired with care and a keen eye over the years. With his signature, Raymond Byrne had transferred the house and all its contents to the South Boston Import-Export Company, Ltd. in lieu of debts owed. Victoria let out a scream that died in the hushed air.

Her husband alone couldn't have done this to her. He wasn't capable of a crime as thorough and cruel. He might have stolen a thing or two, but not everything. Victoria bolted from the rocker but didn't know where to go. Could a home be sold by someone other than its owner? Women in Massachusetts had long since gained the right to own property and she had bought the address with her own money, earned and saved from the revenue of Mrs. Swann's books. The house was hers. Her lawyer would fight it. She would fight it.

The crisp autumn evening air came rushing in, carrying wood smoke from her neighbors' homes. Victoria loved the house and had wanted to find peace here, but rarely had. She filled her lungs to give herself strength and took the stairs two at a time. Ignoring Raymond's bedroom, she went straight into her chambers. The charming floral carpet was gone, as was the four-poster bed and the bookshelves. Only the pink chaise lounge sat like a lonely island in the center of the empty room.

The mirror was gone, and the dresser had been removed, too, and with it, her jewelry and the many perfume bottles, powder puffs, and atomizers that she had fussed over like a silly girl. The handsome chiffonier cabinet no longer occupied the corner. Gone with it were the hatboxes for her plumed and decorated chapeaus. No hangers sagged under the weight of her fine clothing. All her possessions, her many ways of filling her solitary days, were gone, all gone.

But what about her precious keepsake box that had held her childhood things? She dropped onto the chaise and let out a sob. Her mother's comb. Her youthful journals. The scraps left of her life. They, too, were gone. She had nothing from the past. A sob came from deep within as she pictured the wooden crate tossed out with the trash. Her eyes overflowed, and she hugged her knees to her chest.

Saddest of all, the alcove sat empty where her little writing desk had faced the window overlooking the back garden. She had loved the petite *cheveret* with its fine inlaid wood, brass knobs, and jaunty tapered legs. But had she really been so lonesome as to consider an inanimate object as her closest companion? A sorry admission, though it did not make her miss it less. Victoria rocked from side to side as a hollowness spread through her and the metallic taste of fear filled her mouth. The empty room in the empty house echoed with solitude and loneliness. Who had she been in these rooms? A young woman far, far too alone in the world.

TWENTY-FOUR

I'm terribly sorry," Mr. Hector Samuels said. "The owner-ship cannot be contested, as the transfer of the property appears to be completely legal, though I wouldn't be sur-prised if the assessment of the furnishings was done by an associate of Mr. Russell's and drawn in his favor."

Russell. There was no question the man had the city in his pocket.

"But I don't understand, the house is *mine*."

"Apparently not. I see your signature here allowing your husband joint ownership, which permits him to sell it."

Victoria reached across the desk and grabbed the papers. "It can't be!" she exclaimed. "I would never have authorized such a thing."

But there was what appeared to be her own signature, dated one month earlier, at a time when she was in Maine with her uncle. Victoria began to sputter with fury at the sheer audacity of her husband's crime.

She fell into the chair. "Raymond's not clever enough to orchestrate something like this on his own. It must be Louis Russell."

"Mr. Russell is in with the top brass at the banks. It's quite possible he bribed someone who was willing to look the other way."

"We must fight it."

"We can try, but it won't be easy. Many judges are of the opinion that a wife is lucky to be co-owner of a property in the first place."

"But it's *my* house. I can't lose it," Victoria repeated and let the papers drop onto her lap. "I have nothing and no money. I'm owed royalties for these past months too. They've stopped all payments."

"I've written to the publishing house several times but received no reply. I gather a number of authors have suits pending. It's terribly sad to see a respected company run aground."

"I refuse to shed tears for Thames, Royall & Quincy. They deceived me for years. I'm not only owed recent royalties, but I deserved a larger percentage all along."

Victoria felt faint from lack of food and had a crick in her neck from sleeping on the chaise lounge. She hadn't even been able to wash, with the water turned off in her house on Brattle Street. But none of that mattered.

"We must do something, Mr. Samuels."

"Yes, yes, of course." His hands were as flighty as birds. "But there's another unpleasant matter to contend with as well."

"What other matter? What else could possibly go wrong?"

"I'm afraid you've been served with a suit. Your husband has issued a counter claim."

Victoria's insides sank and she held onto the leather arms to steady herself. "But he agreed to an amicable divorce. On what grounds is he coming after me?"

Through his reading spectacles, Hector Samuels studied the second legal document. "I see here an accusation of abandonment. He claims that you left him for your writing."

Victoria let out a groan. "At least he's not accusing me of mental infirmity."

Over the glasses that wobbled on his nose her lawyer gave a pained expression.

"Russell again. May I see those papers?"

Mr. Samuels gave them to her. "Your husband is demanding fifty percent of your earnings on all future books by Mrs. Swann and a percentage of those currently published."

She tossed the documents onto the desk and rose to her feet. "All right, I agree to the divorce. But he won't receive a penny on any future books by Mrs. Swann because I don't intend to write any."

"No more Mrs. Swann?" Hector Samuels asked as he stumbled to his feet. "My wife will be most upset."

"What matters now is that you extract my recent payments from my publisher. That is of the utmost urgency, do you understand?"

"Absolutely, madam."

"We have no choice, we must sue Thames, Royall & Quincy for my back royalties. We will petition for damages against Mr. Louis Russell, the current owner." She gathered up her carpetbag. "Now, do you need further instruction from me, Mr. Samuels?"

He dipped his head and hesitated before speaking. "There is the issue of payment."

"Ah." Victoria hadn't thought of that. "I'll see what I can do. In any case, please get me in the queue of those suing Russell." She started for the door when her lawyer spoke up with greater confidence.

"An arbitration would be faster and more efficient. Shall I pursue that avenue? I do recommend it." The little man stood with his splayed fingers asserting his authority on the desktop.

"Whatever you think best, Mr. Samuels. I'm in your capable hands."

Across the Square at the First National Bank of Cambridge, Victoria marched straight into the banker's offices sealed off behind an impressive brass cage. She asked to speak to the manager and after a few moments a spry young man with peach fuzz on his chin came out from the back. He was only an assistant manager, he explained, and new to the position, but eager to be of help. Victoria informed him of the many years she had entrusted her income to this establishment, but he reminded her that the withdrawal of funds by a wife required her husband's signature. She tested the waters and when the young man brightened at the mention of Mrs. Swann and burbled that a young lady of whom he was inordinately fond was a great fan, Victoria whispered her pen name. She next pounced on the antiquated, inconvenient rule regarding a woman's right to her own money, explaining that her husband was away on business, and she needed the funds immediately. She only wanted what was hers.

The young fellow hesitated, confusion on his face. Victoria sprang again, asserting the obvious. Women today made earnings of their own. Their mothers and grandmothers had hidden cash under their mattresses or stuffed bills into cookie jars, but today's women needed banking to keep up with the times. She would be happy to lend Mrs. Swann's name to such an effort. Also, she would autograph one of her books for his lady friend. The young banker's brow remained furrowed, but he went to retrieve her money. But, as it turned out, Raymond had siphoned off the accounts, leaving little in Victoria's purse when she left the bank.

In need of clothing, she next made her way to the Radcliffe Ladies Dress Shop, where she purchased two plain dresses right off the rack. Her days of elegant bespoke costumes were over. She had enjoyed choosing every detail of her outfits, obsessing over color schemes and textures, with accessories to match. The store-bought frocks were perfunctory and lacking in charm, though she had come to appreciate reduced bustles, far better for gardening and traipsing through the countryside in Maine or the sidewalks of Cambridge.

At least her new winter coat was less voluminous than those she had worn in the past. The velvet cloak she had loved wearing was more suited to one of Mrs. Swann's heroines, an exaggerated costume that evoked mystery and romance in the minds of her readers, but highly impractical. Her new dull brown overcoat, lacking contrasting silk trim or satin piping, would keep her snug while riding the trolley, though where she would be heading while wearing it remained unclear.

The muddy streets of Harvard Square bustled around her with every type of vehicle: hansom carriages, horse and buggies, bicycles, carts, shiny new electric streetcars, and an eccentric, steam-powered automobile designed by an engineering professor from Boston Tech. The world was moving faster by the minute, but Victoria remained stock-still. Harvard boys cut through the busy intersection, as preoccupied as ever, their minds on their studies or on some bright horizon they moved toward, confident that their futures waited for them outside the gates of Harvard Yard.

Lacking their self-assurance, Victoria tried to envision what came next for her. It was one thing to act boldly at a bank or decisively in a dress shop but seeking an altogether new direction in life left her stunned on the street corner, her heart pounding, and her head dizzy. She placed a gloved hand on a lamppost, bowed her forehead to touch it, and tried to think.

TWENTY-FIVE

Their desks faced one another across the narrow office, a lone window at Perry's back. Jonathan's task that morning was editing a manuscript on recent improvements to New England agriculture. A volume not exactly primed to be a big seller, though deserving of his best effort. But he couldn't concentrate and kept gazing across to where the late afternoon light streamed in over his business partner's shoulders. Bathed in gold, Perry's hand rested on a ledger, decisive as he made his checkmarks, the opposite of Jonathan as he dallied with his corrections.

The minutes ticked by in the tall-case pendulum clock that had belonged to Perry's grandfather, the founder of the family fortune that had made possible their enterprise. Perry felt it carried within its dark burled wood the luck they needed to succeed in publishing. In its new habitat, the silver hands, winking blue moon, and smiling yellow sun continued at their effortless pace. There was no escaping the passage of time. At twenty-eight, Jonathan was practically middle-aged. *Carpe diem! Carpe diem, man!*

Perry glanced up and gazed across at him. Was he lost in thought about the numbers on the page, or rehearsing a pitch for investors? *What* was Perry thinking as he continued to stare directly across, as if seeing Jonathan for the first time? Jonathan wanted to say something but didn't dare break the spell. Perry pushed back his chair with a scraping sound on the pine floorboards and stood. He really was a giant of a man or would become one when he aged and filled out more. He was a Bliss. A descendent of one of the great American families and he wore it well. Not handsome, but he would become distinguished in time.

And now, here he came, stepping with long, confident

strides, coming closer, but veering toward the brass coat stand. He threw on his canvas tradesman's jacket and looped his scarf around his long neck. Perry smoothed his moustache and pulled his gloves onto his thin fingers and up his narrow wrists. Jonathan sat stunned and unmoving as he watched the man.

Perry turned and came back slowly. Jonathan wondered if he'd somehow willed it. But, no, his friend moved of his own accord and slipped around the side of the desk and stopped behind Jonathan's chair. It was an alarming moment. He tried to surreptitiously glance over his shoulder to see if Perry might simply be adjusting the framed Hogarth engraving that he had borrowed from his parent's home to grace their office wall.

Yet, Perry didn't stand behind him for that purpose. He hovered close enough for Jonathan to hear his breathing, until all of sudden, his gloved hands were on his shoulders. One hand on each. Jonathan let out a quiet, ecstatic release of breath. Perry squeezed the bone and the muscle beneath the frock coat, and Jonathan felt everything at once.

"Keep it up. I'll be back shortly."

"Yes," Jonathan managed to say, hoping his breathy voice didn't reveal too much.

Perry let go. In his usual distracted way, but with a purposeful step, he left the office. Jonathan flopped back against his seat where he remained for the rest of the morning, replaying the moment in his mind until he thought he might have imagined it.

TWENTY-SIX

As the trolley pulled east from Harvard Square and slowed through the bustling streets of Central Square, the plain three-story buildings pressed closer together and grew shabbier by the block. Fewer trees or shrubs softened the austere architectural outlines. Cambridgeport was a world away from the countryside in Blaine and felt at least that far from the refined air of Victoria's neighborhood to the west. How had Dottie managed to cross the vast distance from her home to Brattle Street all those years? As Victoria had stood with her forehead against the lamppost, it had come to her that what she needed was her assistant's sage advice. Everyone turned to Mrs. Swann at some point. It was Victoria's turn now.

She exited at Central Square where carts pulled by work-horses trundled past, some piled with iron rods and flagstones, others stacked with planks and pipes. They were steered by surly drivers in workman's clothing, caps low and shoulders hunched. One hod carrier, his cart sagging under the weight of freshly baked bricks, touched his cap to Victoria. She was reminded of her reticent uncle and nodded in return.

After a number of blocks down River Street, she took a left, then a right, followed by another, and another, until each three-story clapboard building became indistinguishable from the next. Victoria entered at the correct address and climbed a dingy staircase. Voices murmured from behind closed doors, foreign words spoken at a fast clip. She stopped on a landing to absorb the melodic singsong of what she guessed might be Italian or Portuguese. The cooking smells made her stomach rumble, and she tried to picture the hearty meal being set before a worker on his midday break. She had heard of garlic root and wondered if it was the cause of the enticing aroma that made her wobbly with hunger. On her way across town, she had felt a rising sense of urgency about her untenable situation and neglected to stop for a bite to eat. She needed to see Dottie. Dottie would know what she should do. Dottie always knew what to do.

At the apartment door, Victoria knocked once, twice, and was about to leave, when she heard a muffled voice inviting her to enter. She opened the door cautiously and stepped into a kitchen where clothing hung on a makeshift rack over a tin tub. Beside it stood a cold coal stove, a basin for water, and a cabinet that appeared to hold not food items, but books. On a tiny eating table pushed into the corner sat more volumes and papers and a pair of gold-rimmed glasses teetering on a stack.

"Hello? Dottie?" She stepped deeper into the apartment. "It's me, Victoria."

Dottie let out a little gasp at the sight of her on the threshold of the narrow, windowless parlor. She patted down her hair and straightened her housedress and apron. "Oh my, what a surprise." She swooped to pick up a sofa pillow from the worn carpet and began straightening other items littered about. "If I'd known you were coming... What a mess I am!" She wiped her sleeve across her face, her cheeks damp and slick with tears.

"Please, please, don't make a fuss." Victoria felt alarmed to see her secretary in such a state. "I'm so sorry, I should have sent a note before coming unannounced."

"No, it's grand you're here. When did you get back into town?"

"Yesterday."

"And you've come straight away to see me? I'm so glad, but I never wanted you to visit my shabby dwelling. You can see why I liked coming to your house on Brattle Street."

It was true that the faded floral wallpaper, threadbare sofa, and overstuffed chair, covered in crocheted blankets and lace antimacassars, were far from cheerful.

"Your place is nice and homey." Victoria stepped closer. "But are you all right?"

Dottie sat heavily on the sofa and wrung a handkerchief

between anxious fingers on her lap. Victoria joined her, their knees practically touching and a metal spring poking her back.

"Have you had some bad news, Dottie?"

"No, we've had nothing but good news." Dottie gave a sigh. "The truth is, I'm expecting."

Victoria let out a joyous shout and reached for Dottie's hands with her gloved ones. "How wonderful! I'm so happy for you and Fletcher. What lovely news."

Dottie's head bobbed as she thanked Victoria, but she wasn't smiling. "The problem is, I'm confined for the duration. Doctor's orders. And I'm already starting to go mad being cooped up here and it hasn't been that long."

"But now you'll have time to write your lovely poems."

"Plenty of time but only so much a person can imagine from within these walls."

The grim wallpaper did seem to close in on one.

"I haven't even offered you a cup of tea."

"Don't worry about that. I want to help you for a change." Victoria hesitated before adding, "Though I'm at a bit of a disadvantage myself at the moment."

Dottie's forehead creased. "I hope Mr. Byrne hasn't gone missing again. I hate to think of you managing all on your own. I wish I could come help you." She looked as if she might start to cry.

"No, no, nothing to concern yourself with."

"And don't forget, winter's coming. You must batten down your beautiful house and order more coal delivered to the cellar. You know how cold drafts distract you at your desk."

"Thank you, that's so thoughtful of you to remember."

"And how is the writing coming along? Was it productive in Maine? You must be into a new Mrs. Swann by now." This thought seemed to perk Dottie up.

"Yes, my writing is coming along splendidly." Victoria squeezed Dottie's fingers for emphasis before letting go. "I can at least say that."

"Excellent. Then nothing else matters."

"Exactly. Nothing else," Victoria echoed, and for a moment, believed it. "Now, we must figure out how you can pass your time productively if you can't go about your usual business."

"Fletcher doesn't want me straining. He insists on doing all the household chores, which explains why our home is in such disarray."

"What a good fellow he is."

"I desperately need to do *something*. I'll go nutty without work of my own."

Not knowing how else to help, Victoria offered to make them tea. In the kitchen, as she filled the kettle and searched for a cookie or cake to serve, she decided not to share the loss of her home on Brattle Street. Dottie had loved and cared for it, and Victoria didn't want to burden her further in her precarious state. She poured hot water into a plain teapot and found biscuits in a tin that Fletcher had stored between books on the windowsill. Back in the narrow parlor, she explained what Hector Samuels had told her about Thames, Royall & Quincy and how she had instructed him to start a lawsuit against the company, not only for recent missed royalties, but for the decidedly low rate she had received all along, especially compared to their other authors.

"Glad to hear it," Dottie said. "I have some papers of yours here. The juvenilia. I was cataloging them for you. Also, many of your ledgers. They could be useful in determining what you're properly owed. I never felt it was right."

Victoria took in the tattered furnishings and suspected that Fletcher's salary as a young professor couldn't be much. Dottie's income must have made all the difference to the couple, and she hadn't been paid for months. That wasn't right either.

"I'd like to ask for your help as I make my case, but I want to pay you for it, though I won't be able to until after it's settled."

"You don't have to pay me now or later. I *want* to take them on." Dottie's eyes sparkled with determination. "And by the way, Jonathan Cartwright came by the other evening, and asked after you. He wondered when you might return from Maine.

He's read your new novel and wants to speak with you about it."

"Oh?" Victoria sat forward, her pulse making itself known. "I'd like to pay him a visit at his new publishing house. Do you happen to know the address?"

"They've started out down the street from here, where the rents are low. Quite pragmatic of them."

"My publisher is in *Cambridgeport*?" Victoria's surprise tumbled out, but not meaning to be rude, she added, "I suppose that makes sense, with the Riverside Press nearby."

"Riverside is the best printer in the country, some say. They do a beautiful job on every book they put out. But mostly, Bliss & Cartwright isn't on Beacon Hill because they can't afford it. Maybe someday."

Victoria gathered her carpetbag that held her new clothing and little else. She had left her two suitcases in the empty house that was no longer hers. For a short time while visiting Dottie she had forgotten her own problems, but the afternoon was getting on and she needed to figure out where to sleep that night. Not on the chaise lounge again in the hollow shell of her house. And she must find something to eat besides a single dry biscuit.

Before leaving, she asked for the address of the offices of Bliss & Cartwright. As Dottie wrote it down for her, Victoria took their dirty tea dishes into the kitchen and pulled out the bulk of the cash she had gotten from the bank. She stuffed a handful of bills into the small ceramic pot hidden behind a stack of books in the larder. Dottie's money jar had held only coins before, but not anymore.

TWENTY-SEVEN

I f it were possible to come upon a less attractive street in Cambridgeport, Victoria couldn't imagine it. By contrast, the leafy boulevards and charming side streets west of Harvard Square seemed out of a fairytale. The massive beech in her own front yard, the lindens at the Longfellow manse, and the spreading chestnut tree at the blacksmith's house, made famous by the poet, all flitted through Victoria's mind as she walked past looming tenements and stepped around puddles of slop that had been tossed into the street.

She stopped before a butcher shop where Bliss & Cartwright was supposed to be located. Removing the linen handkerchief from her nose, her stomach churned. Huge sides of beef on enormous metal hooks hung in the window alongside wide accordion lengths of ribs, the bodies of rabbits with their coats on, several pigs' heads, and innumerable ropes of pink sausages in tight casings. She had never seen such an array of freshly cut meats, and in such variety. It almost made her wonder if the Hindus had it right.

Inside the slaughterhouse, a butcher with a massive beard put down his cleaver, wiped his hands on a bloody cloth, and shouted across to her. "Sorry, ma'am, we don't sell to the public. Only wholesale."

Victoria explained that she'd been given this address for a publishing house, clearly incorrectly.

The man lifted his sizable knife and pointed down the hall. "Back stairs, second floor."

Victoria slipped sideways between hanging carcasses and climbed the back staircase. Any secret hope of being greeted with the fanfare she had once enjoyed at her former publisher was dispelled with each step. Profiteroles and tea were clearly out of the question here. Her belly rumbled and, with another waft of scent from below, it flipped, as a headache bloomed. Victoria hesitated before knocking but could think of nowhere else to turn.

She wasn't sure what she was going to ask Jonathan Cartwright. All summer she had imagined chatting with him about books and the wildflowers she passed on the trails and the quality of the light on the sea. Would he be as handsome and solicitous as he had appeared in her imagination? Would he rise to the occasion and save her in her moment of need? Victoria chided herself for that hackneyed hope. Hadn't she learned that knights in shining armor existed only in books, and not very good ones at that?

She knocked and the door swung open. Before she could say a word, Gaustad's gangly former assistant, Mr. Bliss, barked a greeting without looking up from the manuscript he held in his hand. "What now?" he asked.

Jonathan had explained in a letter that his business partner in the new venture was, in fact, the young professional, Perry Bliss—a name, Victoria conceded, that could indeed work for a leading man. He was as spectral and rangy as ever, though his reading glasses and the premature silver starting at his temples added maturity to his narrow face. Upon lifting his eyes from the pages, he seemed shocked at the sight of her.

"Oh, Mrs. Swann. I mean, Mrs. Bryne. I'd thought you were the repairman back to fix the water leak. I'm terribly sorry. Won't you come in?"

"Thank you, Mr. Bliss. Please, call me Miss Meeks. I am in the process of obtaining a divorce and will be reverting to my maiden name."

"We never intended to have visitors here. You can see why."

He gestured to the charmless space, clearly embarrassed to be running a publishing house out of a slaughterhouse. The thought of it struck Victoria as funny and she let out an unsteady laugh.

"Who's there?" Jonathan's voice came from an inner office. "Is everything all right?"

Before Perry could answer, Victoria called out, "Hello, Jonathan, it's me, Victoria."

She listened for the thud of his chair slamming down. Of course, he'd been reading with his seat tipped back. A moment later, he appeared in the doorway, this man she had dreamed of all summer. Dressed like every other young editor, with a white shirt and black sleeve garters and rolled cuffs, he kept a pencil behind one ear and a distracted expression on his face. He quickly put on his waistcoat and patted down his disheveled hair, the blond streak finding its habitual place across his brow. She wasn't surprised to see him brush aside breadcrumbs from lunch eaten at his desk.

"Victoria." He stepped forward and took her hands in his. "What an unexpected pleasure. Come in. Let me take your coat."

"I've got it, Jon," Perry said, and proceeded to help her off with her things. "Please, have a seat. You don't look well, Miss Meeks. Are you feeling all right?"

Victoria didn't answer but let them lead her into the office where two desks faced one another across an unadorned room. Jonathan pulled out a chair and she sat, dazed, and feeling quite poorly now.

"I'll get you a glass of water," Perry said.

Victoria's vision was starting to grow fuzzy around the edges as heat rose up her neck and the headache came on full force.

"I've been trying to reach you for weeks," Jonathan said. "I read your manuscript and have so much to discuss with you. How perfect that you've found us."

He seemed far too bright and energetic. In her mind these past months, Jonathan had seemed slower paced and patrician, even wise. It was as if she had seen into his future, glimpsing the man he would become decades hence. But for now, he was shorter and slighter than she had remembered, diminished overall, and far too young. Perhaps it was that she had aged while away. She did feel more mature somehow.

"Perry and I are going great guns here. I want to tell you all about it."

Victoria wished to give an encouraging reply, but nausea was creeping up from her belly and it made her tongue thick and her mouth coated with saliva. She eked out an approving whimper. Perry handed her a glass of water and she took a cautious sip.

"We were so excited when your novel arrived," Jonathan said. "It's a gripping story. A truly winning tale. We think it could be an important book." He looked to his business partner for corroboration and Perry nodded. "And I'm honored to say," Jonathan continued, "on behalf of Bliss & Cartwright, that we would be greatly honored if you would give us the honor of publishing it."

"Oh?" Victoria stayed unmoving in order not to jostle her innards, which seemed to feel she was on a storm-tossed deck of a ship.

"We're prepared to stand by it in the face of controversy," Jonathan explained. "Given the scene with the illegal course of action taken by the main character, the novel may become a sensation."

"We've consulted our lawyer," Perry clarified. "Because of the contentious aspects of the tale, we've been advised that you should consider putting it out under a pseudonym."

"Though certainly not as Mrs. Swann. This is definitely not her type of story."

The two men shared a gentle laugh. Victoria did her best to control her quivering hands as she took another sip. The stench of the butchered meat swirled around her. She gulped, shut her eyes, and tried to will it away.

"I'm sorry," Jonathan said. "We've been rude to spring this on you. But we've been conceiving of it since reading your novel and, well, you see, here you are. We will offer a written contract with a generous royalty. We'll also agree to allow you to keep the copyright of your own work. Too often, authors are denied it and lose out on future opportunities for continued revenue. Our intention as a publishing house is to be genuinely supportive in order to enjoy a long and fruitful partnership to our mutual benefit. What do you think, Victoria? Can we do this together? Will you allow Bliss & Cartwright to publish *The Boston Harbor Girl?*"

With eyes closed, she whispered, "No pseudonym."

Jonathan leaned closer. "Pardon?"

"Victoria Meeks, or nothing at all."

She promptly fainted, her vision black and her mind blank.

The two men in the little publishing office bustled around her with care and concern not unlike the treatment she had received at Thames, Royall & Quincy. She was, once again, a star author.

TWENTY-EIGHT

"D on't wake her, girls," Jonathan said. "She's not well."
The two Roses ignored their brother as they knelt
beside the window seat where Victoria lay curled
under a tartan throw. Perry hovered nearby, assessing a dour
oil portrait of one of the Cartwright ancestors that hung over
the mantel.

"Do you think she needs another pillow?" Jonathan asked
Clara, as she stood beside him in the parlor.

"I think she's fine," Clara replied. "The doctor said all she
needed was sleep. We should have taken her upstairs while she
was awake. And you," she lowered her voice, "need to calm
down, or you'll be the next one to faint. You know how you
are."

Jonathan's eyes returned to his friend across the room. Perry
bent over the Cartwright family Bible on the carved mahogany
bookstand, the only ornate piece of furniture in the house, and
the only other piece, besides his wooden rocking chair, that had
mattered to the reverend.

"What an interesting lineage," Perry said as he browsed the
family tree on the frontispiece. "The Cartwrights came over not
too long after the *Mayflower*, I see. Not as early as the Blisses,
but no matter. My people were never engaged in ministering,
though it might have suited me well."

"What's occupied your people through the generations, Mr.
Bliss?" Clara asked.

Perry gave a sad shake of his head and replied, "Money."

"Ah," she said politely.

"A terrible scourge," he said.

Jonathan would have liked to remind him that money made
possible many things, including Bliss & Cartwright and the surprising future they had embarked upon together.

"Our father would have agreed with that," Clara said. "I'm sorry you never met him. He would have liked you."

Jonathan saw Victoria stir on the window seat. She was an attractive, petite woman, not much older than he, but somehow infinitely more mature. Once her new novel was published, her life would be pried open, like the thick Bible that Perry peered into with his reading glasses perched on his nose. Such a bookish man, in any setting he managed to find a volume to entertain himself. Jonathan let out an audible sigh.

"Maybe you should sit down," Clara said.

Jonathan pulled his father's rocker over to sit beside Tessa and Philomena. Lost in concentration, they used charcoal pencils to draw Victoria's sleeping profile in their sketchbooks. Into this peaceful scene, the doorbell sounded, and Clara hurried off to see who was there. Since announcing her betrothal, she bustled about more than ever before. As Victoria sat up and straightened her skirts, Jonathan peered into the front hall where Clara greeted her fiancée and a handsome grey-haired gentleman whom Jonathan didn't recognize. No doubt someone from Tim's society church where Clara had consented to be married next month.

Timothy was well dressed in his usual crisp business attire, which Jonathan inordinately admired. The distinguished older man beside him was equally well turned out in a tweed sporting outfit with knickers, a belt cinched snugly, and mountaineering boots. The minute Bliss & Cartwright turned a profit, Jonathan intended to purchase an elegant pair of boots made of fine Italian leather, like Perry's. In the hall, the younger sisters took the gentlemen's overcoats as Clara welcomed them. Jonathan shifted to sit shoulder to shoulder beside Victoria on the parlor window seat.

"Are you feeling any better?" he asked. "Did the soup agree with you?"

"It stayed down. I'm mortified that I was sick on your front doorstep. I wonder if your sisters will ever forgive me."

"They certainly won't forget you."

"Thank you for taking such good care of me, Jonathan."

"I'm glad you're feeling better. Simple nervous exhaustion, the doctor said. It's happened to me too. I've fainted more than once myself."

Her eyebrows rose, and Jonathan wished he hadn't volunteered that bit of information.

"I suppose," Victoria said, "there's no reason why it shouldn't happen to men, though I've only ever heard of ladies being overcome, and mostly in books."

"Especially Mrs. Swann's."

They shared a smile.

"If you want to stay over, we could set you up right here in the window seat. Not exactly luxurious accommodations, but I've fallen asleep here many times when reading late into the night."

"This is the corner where you like to read?" Victoria admired the shabby cushions and ratty blanket. "It reminds me of my reading nook overlooking my father's apple orchard."

"I was so sorry to learn about your house."

"You mean the farm? We lost it years ago."

"No, I mean your home on Brattle Street. You spoke of it in your fever."

Victoria squeezed her hands together. "I wasn't going to tell anyone, though I suppose it would have come out sometime."

"How terrible to lose the home you worked so hard for."

"I have to figure out what to do next," she murmured.

"Don't worry. We'll help," Jonathan offered without hesitation. "Perry and I."

Timothy and the grey-haired man ducked their heads below the low lintel as they followed Clara into the parlor. Perry greeted them warmly, as if he knew them, no doubt from Boston circles that went back several generations. Imagine all the grand doors that opened to Perry simply because he was a Bliss of Boston. It was both thrilling and maddening—all the good fortune and opportunity given to these men because they happened to be born into the right families. And think of all the fascinating, attractive men that Perry was acquainted with as a result of his background. Jonathan barely withheld an anxious groan.

"It seems you two are a team."

"I suppose we are," Jonathan said, "in a way."

His voice may have revealed more than he intended, but he was too worn out to care. Victoria cocked her head and her gaze travelled to Perry and back to Jonathan. Later he would replay the moment when she reached out to touch his hand that frittered anxiously on his lap. She stilled it with a kind pat that frightened him as much as it relieved him.

The gathering shifted toward Jonathan and Victoria. She quickly tidied her hair and surreptitiously tweaked her cheeks, an odd gesture that he had noticed his sisters doing before answering the door to callers. Victoria stood and accepted a bow from the elegant older gentleman who, as it turned out, was Timothy's older brother, Lance Maverick.

"An honor to meet you, Mrs. Swann. My late wife was a fan of your books and I've enjoyed them as well. I took several with me to the Amazon but unfortunately had to abandon them in a village where they didn't speak a word of English. Last I saw, they were using the pages to line their lean-tos."

"Why, that's the best use for my tales yet."

"I've wondered about the woman who writes such adventurous tales."

All the color that had drained from Victoria's cheeks with her nausea and fatigue came rushing back. She resembled a girl, an ingenue with eyes cast down at her boots, until she let out a guttural laugh, not one bit girlish.

"You're a brave man, Mr. Maverick, to admit that you've read Mrs. Swann's books. Not many would say so in public."

Tim stepped forward. "My big brother's unlike many men. He takes after the Texas side of the family. He's an explorer. Recently back from the Arctic or was it the Antarctic? I can never keep up with him. His journeys are legendary, but he's planning to move back to Boston later this year, aren't you, Lance? Mother says it's time for him to settle down."

"I've had enough adventure for several lifetimes. I'm going to pick up the mantle of the family business."

"What business is your family engaged in, Mr. Maverick?" Victoria asked.

Perry answered for him, "The Mavericks staked their claim in Boston long ago, much like the Blisses. What they don't have a piece of, we do. Isn't that right, fellows?"

Tim's brother touched his mustache with a finger that bore a signet ring from a secret society Jonathan would never be asked to join. He didn't want to want to belong, but he did. Not for the money or the fine old possessions and furnishings and homes, but for the sense of optimism it fostered in such gentlemen. Surety made Jonathan weak in the knees. Things came so easily to men like Lance Maverick, which may be why they had to go to the ends of the earth to challenge themselves.

"I'd love to hear about your travels, Mrs. Swann, and please, call me Lance."

"And you mustn't call me Mrs. Swann. I use my original name now: Victoria Meeks. And the truth is, despite Mrs. Swann's adventures, I've never travelled farther than Maine."

"How remarkable!" Lance gave a genuine laugh.

"Why is it remarkable?" she asked.

Jonathan would never have guessed Victoria was capable of such flirtatious behavior. She was charming when not trying to impress or lord her success over others. He liked her better with all the stuffing knocked out of her, though of course he didn't wish her ill health or lack of success. But she did seem different now that she wasn't Mrs. Swann.

"Because," Lance said, "you write so convincingly about other lands. You must tell me how you've done it."

"And you must tell me about your travels."

"So you can steal them for your books?"

"No, simply for my own entertainment."

"I'd be happy to. I hope you'll permit me to call on you when I return to Boston?"

"I'd be delighted."

Philomena and Tessa had moved closer and absorbed the interaction with eager, discerning eyes. Jonathan knew that the minute the guests had left, his sisters would share their interpretations of this exchange and all that it suggested. They were already imagining nuptials, not that love was ever simple, though for his sisters' sakes, he wished it would be. For himself, Jonathan had given up.

He tossed one final, hopeless glance across the vast distance of the small, crowded room. But to his surprise, his business partner was staring right back at him. For once, Perry did not turn away and neither did Jonathan.

TWENTY-NINE

Mrs. McAlister ran a strict boarding house for up-and-coming young ladies. She accepted shop assistants, stenographers, typists, clerks, bookkeepers, and private secretaries, but no factory girls. She served breakfast at seven a.m. sharp after the young women had stood for inspection. The boarding house matron put a premium on hygiene. If a girl had dirt under her fingernails or soot behind her ears, back upstairs she went for another wash. Young ladies unable to meet her standards with proper coaching, by being either too flashy or too shabby, were shown the door.

Philomena's best friend, an Irish redhead named Emma Sinclair, had been the one to suggest Mrs. McAlister's as a suitable accommodation for Victoria. Emma vouched for the boarding house's respectability and considered herself one of Mrs. McAlister's most successful turnaround cases. She had been a puny, sallow-cheeked ragamuffin when she first arrived, but had come to look right nice under the boarding house matron's strict guidance. The oldest of four, Emma had grown up not far from where she now lived, a bone of contention with her parents who didn't approve of her spending a whole dollar a week on lodging when she could as easily commute to her bookstore job from home. Emma justified the expense by using the rest of her salary to purchase medicines for her mother, who was quite ill, without retaining any pennies for herself for sundries. Working at the Cambridge Bookshop took care of her other major expense—books.

"I would miss it here so much if I had to move," she said. "I love being out on my own and could just pinch myself, I've been so lucky living at Mrs. McAlister's."

A sign by the door read, "Ladies not home by 9 p.m. will

find the door locked and property seized." Not so lucky for those young ladies, Victoria thought.

Before ringing the doorbell, Emma patted down her thick red curls. "How do I look? Mrs. McAlister will take a hot iron to my mane if it isn't under control."

Emma had spent several stops describing all the clever ways the matron instructed her young ladies on the latest bouffant, chignon, and pompadours made famous by the Gibson Girls. Victoria reassured her, and she rang the bell. After a few moments, a stout, heavily perfumed woman with a high nest of hair invited them inside. Emma mumbled something and Mrs. McAlister replied in a piercing voice. "A new boarder for me? Well done, Miss Sinclair. You might work out after all."

Her nerves jangled, Emma fell apart on the introductions, but regained her tongue to explain that Victoria was Mrs. Swann, the renowned author.

Mrs. McAlister's painted eyebrows pinched together. "Is she now?" She pulled a monocle from a chain entangled with several beaded necklaces that plunged off the precipice of her bodice. "I haven't time to read books, but I've seen portraits of Mrs. Swann in the broadsides. This woman looks nothing like her. You must be careful, Emma. The world is full of disreputable people."

"No, really," Emma said, panic growing in her eyes, "she's the *real* Mrs. Swann."

"It's all right," Victoria said. "It doesn't matter."

Mrs. McAlister had the audacity to reach across and finger the brown wool of Victoria's coat sleeve. If only she was wearing one of her fine ermine cuffs and not this rough material to show the crass woman who she was dealing with.

"Whoever you are, you've got a practical style, appropriate to your age, though you should take it in at the waist to get yourself up to snuff."

"Mrs. McAlister knows all about fashion."

Victoria couldn't imagine how Emma could be so fooled by this woman.

Mrs. McAlister pointed at Victoria's small diamond engagement ring that she intended to pawn soon. "I don't usually allow married ladies to stay in my establishment. The husbands show up and haul them back before settling the bill."

Victoria had intended to keep her business to herself, but said, "My husband won't be coming. I am getting a divorce."

The matron staggered back dramatically. "I never." She thrust out her ample bosom. "I run a respectable boarding house. I can't court scandal by allowing a divorcee to stay here."

And yet, the lady had escorted them into the parlor and positioned them before a chalkboard that listed the prices for lodging, food, laundry, and every other conceivable expense. She didn't turn away from the list as she lifted a lace fan attached by a string at her waist and fanned herself vigorously.

Emma rose onto her toes and summoned her courage to say, "Mrs. Swann has been a fine example to young ladies. The other girls and I follow her advice all the time. She's clever at solving every sort of problem."

Victoria reached into her carpetbag for her purse, pried open the matron's lace-gloved hand, and pressed a stack of coins into the pudgy palm. "This should cover the first week." She turned to Emma and asked her to show her to the room they would be sharing.

❧

But the next morning, when Victoria tried to rouse the girl for breakfast, Emma lay curled on her side and was weeping.

"Perhaps you should go home and tend to your mother, dear, since you're so worried about her."

"I'd like to be at her bedside all the time, but I have to go to work. Mr. Roebuck is expecting me. And Mrs. McAlister won't serve me breakfast if I'm not presentable."

"What a ghastly harridan."

"Mrs. McAlister's not a harridan. She's a lady with high standards. I hate to disappoint her."

Victoria didn't want to argue with her young friend. Instead, she stayed with her as she dressed and offered to do her hair. Shortly before the strike of seven, the boarders stood behind their chairs at the breakfast table as the matron entered. Each girl greeted Mrs. McAlister in turn and underwent inspection. But this morning, the tea grew cold in the pot and the stack of toast hardened as Mrs. McAllister refused to allow anyone to sit. She was waiting for Emma to, in her words, stop sniveling. The girl tried her best, but Mrs. McAlister's harsh tone only made her cry harder. The more Mrs. McAllister's glare bore into her flushed cheeks, the less Emma was able to control herself.

"Life isn't meant to be easy," the matron said. "We must be strong in the face of it." With a forced smile, she continued. "Chirpy and chipper are we. That's how gentlemen prefer us. Isn't that right, ladies?"

The other girls nodded with various levels of enthusiasm.

"We must never," the matron continued, "abandon the quest for perfection and beauty, even in the face of tragedy. If some of us are too weak to rise out of the feeble stock into which they were born, we must blaze ahead without them. Onward, I say. Onward!"

"That's taking things too far," Victoria spoke up. "Emma's a fine girl and of perfectly good stock. But she's in the midst of a family crisis. Her mother is ill. We should be consoling her and offering her our love, not berating her. A *true* lady," Victoria turned to the young, impressionable women, "is sympathetic to the pain of others. Her *heart* matters more than her *hairstyle*." She liked the sound of that phrase and wished she could use it in one of Dottie's advice columns.

But Mrs. McAllister didn't appear impressed. She lifted her monocle and spoke sternly. "The world is a cruel place, Mrs. Swann, though you may not know that, living as you have—" she paused for effect, "on *Brattle Street*."

"How do you know where I've lived?"

"I asked around. You were married to a gentleman, a member of all the right clubs, and you lived at an elegant address. You can't fool me that you choose to be here at my boarding house. It's clear you've been dismissed by society. You're on the decline, while my young ladies here are on the rise. Aren't you, ladies?"

The girls tried to smile.

"I had hoped to bypass your unfortunate affairs when I learned you were a divorcee," Mrs. McAlister said, "but I see this will be a useful lesson to my girls. You can serve as an example of how *not* to conduct oneself as a lady. Miss Sinclair might not be able to discern such distinctions, given her background, but there's hope for the others." The matron tugged at her lace cuffs.

"I don't care how you treat me, but don't speak cruelly of Emma." Victoria snatched a folded napkin from beside her plate and threw it onto the table. She wanted to topple the stack of toast or pour tea over the lace tablecloth.

"It's all right," Emma said. "I need to move back home, anyway. Mother needs me."

"You're a good girl, Emma. Don't ever let anyone tell you otherwise."

"You see," Mrs. McAlister spoke to the girls assembled at the table, "not everyone can come up to scratch. Some go back to where they came from with their tail between their legs. Go on, return home. You weren't meant to make it in the big city."

"That's quite enough, madam." Victoria stood. "We're leaving. I will expect a full refund for the rest of my week."

"No refunds. House policy."

"I'll be back to collect. Emma, I'll walk you to work, and we can find breakfast along the way." She recalled that her purse was empty and grabbed several pieces of toast on the way out. Victoria turned back from the threshold. "Good luck to you, New Women. The world is waiting for you, but so are people like this one." She pointed with the toast at Mrs. McAlister. "They will exploit your new-found freedom for personal gain. But you must not let them!"

The young ladies barely heard Victoria's advice. They were too eager to tell the other girls at work about the morning's fracas. That same evening, they would carefully compose letters to their mothers back home, sharing the sad fate of Mrs. Swann as a way to bolster their own chances for success, though her plight could as easily confirm that these were dangerous, unpredictable times for young ladies alone in the city.

THIRTY

After seeing Emma off to join her family, Victoria walked into Harvard Square. She wasn't sure what she was going to do next or where she would sleep that night. She raised the collar of her brown coat and tried to hide under her simple hat. What would she say if she crossed paths with high society acquaintances, such as the ladies of the Book and Travel Club? Running into Lance Maverick would brighten things considerably, but he had no doubt set sail already. With no plan in mind and confidence flagging, Victoria stepped into the Cambridge Bookshop. The tinkling of the bell and the chatter of customers immediately helped settle her nerves. The activity was heartening and even before she had a chance to peruse the books, her spirits began to lift.

As she looked around for Mr. Roebuck to tell him that Emma wouldn't be coming in, a young assistant behind the counter threw up her hands and left the store in a huff. The little bell chimed angrily behind her. The shop proprietor hurried to take her place at the brass cash register, his muttonchops twitching in agitation.

Victoria slipped unnoticed past the carved cherrywood bookshelves. Conscious of her vanity, she couldn't help going in search of her own books. Her pulse quickened as she stopped before a glass-fronted case dedicated exclusively to Mrs. Swann's nineteen novels, plus a decent selection of her flimsier dime stories as well. Her tales of Egypt and the Yukon, Paris and the Amazon sat lined up and ready to transport the reader to distant and far better worlds.

"Why, Mrs. Swann, to what do we owe the honor?"

The portly, red-vested owner of the shop beamed at her. He wore a newsboy's cap indoors, his plump cheeks sporting fluffy sideburns and his pipe optimistically poking from his vest pocket, though she had never seen it lit. He was always bustling about the store and unable to rest.

"Busy in here today, but never too busy for you, Mrs. Swann."

Victoria noticed him taking in her simple attire, wondering, no doubt, why she wasn't outfitted in her customary stylish clothing.

"May I introduce you to some of our customers? They would be delighted to meet Mrs. Swann."

Victoria raised a conspiratorial eyebrow. "I'm incognito, Mr. Roebuck. I don't want to be recognized."

"Is that so?" He tilted toward her. "How exciting!"

"It's for a novel I'm writing. But it's so good to be here in your bookshop. It's been far too long." She let out a surprisingly contented sigh.

"Your readers have missed you. A young lady was in this morning asking if there's a new one in your series."

Victoria's heart sank at the thought of her jettisoned readers. But she brushed aside her regrets. "I should mention that I bring a message from your employee Emma Sinclair. She had to go home but will be in as soon as she's able. Her mother is ill."

"Yes, I know, poor girl." His concern was genuine, but he glanced over at the line forming at the front counter. "I'm not sure what I'm going to do today. I'm short-handed. One of my assistants decided to leave right at the busiest time of year. I must get back to it." He tipped his cap and gave his apologies again before stepping away.

"Mr. Roebuck," Victoria called as she caught up to him. "I wonder if you might consider hiring me for the recently vacated position. Or I could at least fill in for Emma until she returns? What do you say?"

Several young Harvard scholars jostled past, their black robes swishing, stacks of books held high in their arms.

"Why, that's not right. A lady author like you working as a shopgirl? I can't imagine it."

"It's not as bad as all that. This is for research. My new novel is not set overseas, but right here in our hometown."

His face fell a little. "A Mrs. Swann not set in exotic lands?"

"No, I'm afraid not. But, you see, I've never worked in a store before and have no experience with customers and books. I'd like to give it a try."

"No experience with books?" he exclaimed. "How can that be? But wouldn't you prefer to visit us from time to time? I could introduce you to the business myself on a less harried day."

"Actually, it would be better if you treated me like any other employee, even in terms of—" Victoria paused, and made herself continue, "payment. That way I can have the full authentic experience."

Mr. Roebuck wiped a thick hand over his mouth. "I wish I could offer you better wages, but you must know we exist on a shoestring. Nothing like what you've been accustomed to, living over on Brattle Street."

"As it happens, I'm in need of new lodgings too."

His muttonchops stilled. "Is that part of your research as well?"

"Exactly! Though also, to be honest, I'm at a juncture. I have a new editor and am making other arrangements."

Comprehension seemed to dawn. "I heard that Frederick Gaustad had retired. That explains why we haven't received a Mrs. Swann in a while."

"Precisely. I do appreciate your help as I embark on this new chapter of my career."

"Why this is like something out of one of your novels, isn't it? Next thing you'll tell me you're a lady detective or a spy in disguise."

Victoria raised an eyebrow.

"Oh my, you're up to something!"

He helped her off with her coat and hung it on the brass stand behind the counter. With little fanfare, he handed her a forest green apron with the Cambridge Bookshop insignia

embroidered on the front pocket. Victoria thanked him a little
too much and got to work.

࿇

At the end of her first day and every day thereafter for several
weeks, Victoria closed up shop so that Mr. Roebuck could leave
early and enjoy his pipe in peace at his home nearby. The bell
tinkled softly behind the last customers, and Victoria turned
around the wooden sign and locked the door. She switched off
the lights over the cherrywood counter and used the little brass
key to secure the register. Wandering up and down the aisles and
running a finger along the spines, she paused at Mrs. Swann's
special shelf to bid goodnight to *Kidnapped in Far Cathay*, *Mistaken Marriage to a Russian Prince*, and one of her favorites, *Stolen
in the Swiss Alps*.

Since working here, her books had come to seem no better
and no worse than any others. They all sat patiently waiting to
be read. She imagined the authors laboring over the course of
innumerable days, spending hours at a desk with pen in hand,
or with fingers tapping on typewriter keys, their dreams unfurling over the platen. Victoria knew the stamina and heart that
went into each effort. The books, and their authors, were all
equal in that way.

In their brief time working together, she had come to respect Emma's literary knowledge. Emma placed the books she
read in a hierarchy of merit, while Victoria was less discerning.
She didn't mind striving to appreciate what an author had intended while recognizing they hadn't quite achieved it. She was
forgiving, probably because she counted on books to be there
for her like family. They were as imperfect as family, but she
loved them just the same.

Victoria hadn't sought out another boarding house, because,
with some convincing, Mr. Roebuck had agreed to let her sleep
on the narrow cot in the bookstore's stockroom. In return, she
had recommended Dottie Windsor as a top-notch accountant
for the store. The shop owner had been more than happy to
relinquish the bookkeeping to such a competent soul. From her

home, the new business manager was already reorganizing the financial dealings of the company. Dottie was grateful to Victoria for helping her relieve the boredom of her confinement, and of course, to be receiving a paycheck again.

A neat stack of blank notebooks and a pen had been left on the table beside her cot. Days earlier, she had confided to Mr. Roebuck that she hadn't written a word since leaving Maine.

"That won't do," he replied. "You must keep writing! We all stand to benefit, especially if your next book takes place in a bookshop like ours. I can picture Mrs. Swann's fans lining up to see the setting that inspired your bookstore tale. We might have to issue tickets to keep them from breaking down the door."

The man was determined to sell books any way he could. Victoria picked up the pen and twiddled it familiarly between her fingers. Her latest protagonist existed in her mind and not yet on the page, but she felt she was coming to know her better since working as a shopgirl. In her last days in Maine, she had started a new novel about a character named Theresa Olivera of the North End. Theresa lived in a boarding house and, in a case of life imitating art, worked in a dress shop, though it could just as easily be a bookshop such as this one. Victoria had eked out a promising first chapter but had lost the thread of the story in the chaos of finding herself both homeless and destitute. But in the quiet store this evening, Theresa flickered and shimmered once again in her mind, as if recalled from a dream. Impressions, feelings, and details of setting and character all swirled and seethed, demanding to be explored in written prose.

Victoria sat at the desk, opened an empty notebook, and placed the nib of the pen on the first blue line. The cottage in Blaine came back to her, with the fire burning in the Franklin stove and the sea raging below. There was no window in the storage room through which to see dusk descend. From beyond the store aisles, she could hear the rattle of carriages passing by on Harvard Street. For once she didn't long to be part of Cambridge's finer set as they headed off to Memorial Hall to enjoy a performance under the soaring wooden ceiling. Victoria didn't hear that music or the symphony of the shore. Instead, she shut the stockroom door and listened only to her own inner voice as her hand began its progression across the page.

Sentences flowed and time passed quickly—first minutes, then an hour, then several, until soon it was past midnight. Scheduled to open the shop the next morning, she would be tired, but she couldn't stop now. Her imagination discovered a setting that had been growing brick by brick since her return to Cambridge. She had a long way to go, but the wide-open ocean of possibilities made her laugh out loud at the joy of creating— the sheer pleasure of forming a new world out of this one.

Her latest heroine wouldn't succumb to misery and misfortune like Daisy in *The Boston Harbor Girl*. Nor would Theresa end her quest with a requisite march down the aisle like the heroines of all of Mrs. Swann's novels. She would stake her claim in the city alongside the many other young women finding their way. She would be a *real* woman.

As the hours passed, Victoria had no interest in the dawn light as it crept along the spines of books. When it slipped under the door of the storage room, she released a long, furious sigh, set down her pen and stared, dumbfounded, at the page. Her hand shook from the effort, exhilarated by this new story that she held firmly in her grasp. The towering storage shelves offered no applause, but Victoria didn't mind. She shook her head in amazement at what she had accomplished on a wearisome night in November in the back room of the Cambridge Bookshop.

At that moment, Mr. Roebuck flung open the door. He let out a startled yelp and apologized but didn't step away. His eyes had fallen on the full notebook.

"My dear lady, forgive my intrusion. I'll leave you to compose." He gave a formal bow.

As he backed away, Victoria spoke up. "It's all right, Mr. Roebuck, you're not interrupting me. I was writing."

"A new book, is it?" he asked with a high tremor of hope in his voice.

"I believe so."

"What wonderful news!" He let out a laugh. "Bless you, Mrs. Swann. Bless you."

Victoria took in the crowded stock room. "No, bless you, Mr. Roebuck, for this inspiring setting."

THIRTY-ONE

At half past six, Jonathan was glad to find the Cambridge Bookshop open. He brushed the rain off the sleeves of his plaid McIntosh and stamped his wet boots. When he looked up, Victoria was coming toward him from the back of the store, a feather duster in hand.

"Sorry, we're closed," she called out before seeing that it was him.

She appeared full of gumption, and healthier than when he'd last seen her.

"That's a fine welcome," he said.

"Oh, Jonathan, I'm so sorry, I didn't see it was you. Come in, come in."

"You look well, Victoria."

He leaned to kiss the air near her cheek but fumbled and smacked her ear instead. He never knew how to greet women. A handshake was too formal, but clearly, he'd missed the mark with the continental approach. He needed to ask Perry's advice. Perry knew such things.

"I was about to close up shop."

"How remarkable that you're working here. I was a little surprised when I heard."

"Who told you?"

"I tried to find you at the boarding house that Philomena's friend had recommended, but the matron explained you'd left weeks ago. She's a scary sort."

"She is, isn't she?" Victoria removed her apron and hung it on a hook behind the counter. "I didn't last long there."

"She said as much. You might have ruined her reputation had you stayed a moment longer. I've tracked you down because we're about to go to press with *The Boston Harbor Girl.* Payment will be ready as soon as we complete the first orders."

"That's good to hear. Things have been a bit tight." Victoria put on her wool coat.

"You should have told me. Perry would have helped."

"I'm managing perfectly well."

She lifted her chin and threw a scarf around her neck. She certainly seemed perfectly well. Somehow more substantial and stronger.

"Let's go for a stroll," she suggested. "You can tell me about the press."

"I'd be happy to, but only if you promise to be in better touch going forward. I shouldn't have to search every neighborhood in Cambridge to find you."

"So sorry. I've been terribly busy with my new position here." Victoria locked up behind them, and they headed out onto the crowded sidewalk.

Jonathan hurried as she picked up her pace.

"By the way, over the summer, I read the novels you gave me."

"Excellent! Did you enjoy them?"

"Mostly."

Taken aback, he slowed, but Victoria kept on toward Harvard Yard.

"Weren't you at all impressed?" he asked, catching up.

"Impressed? Yes. Though Mrs. Swann's readers would have thrown one of her books across the room if it took her as long as it takes Henry James to stoke up the engine of his story. My steamboat would have stirred the waters and left the harbor while Mr. James stood on the dock, studying the contours of the pilings and the mood of the sea gulls as they strutted and cawed."

"But don't you admire his characters for their complexity?" Jonathan asked as they entered the new iron gates of the Yard.

"I do, but I also sense that American colonial simplicity is being usurped by European excess. Mr. James's writing resembles the intricate designs of William Morris whose tendrils have crept across the Atlantic from England to paper the walls of the best Beacon Hill homes."

"Why, Victoria, I believe you're a scholar of aesthetics."

"Not at all." She waved away the compliment and continued up the brick paths.

Where was she taking him? Did she know?

"I imagine you would encourage me to write more like James and delve into that most popular and baroque subject of the day?"

"And what subject might that be?" he asked, no longer merely tickled by her musings, but intrigued.

"The infinite, knotted morass of the human psyche and soul."

"Why, yes!" Jonathan found himself exclaiming. "That is most worthy of exploration."

Victoria had brought them to the low, wide steps of Appleton Chapel, its white spire piercing the brooding sky. She scurried up the stairs and stood under a brownstone arch. The leaves on the ivy vines had fallen, except for one or two bright red ones that managed to hold on. Victoria appeared quite pleased with herself, as if she had ascended a great mountain, not a dozen granite steps.

"But it irritates me that Mr. James and Mr. Flaubert seem to think they've discovered something no one else has ever realized before," she called down.

"What might that be?" he asked as he climbed the steps after her.

"That women are crushed under the weight of the world's disregard. All my life, I've known I wasn't much. Every girl knows it in her own way. But those gentleman authors seem to believe they're the first to have discovered the absolute torment of being an intelligent woman in this day and age, or any other. To be unseen and unheard is a tragedy of the first order, yet women routinely endure it."

Splendidly framed by the dark columns, she had, somehow,

in her cavalier way, put her finger on Jonathan's own deepest concerns.

"That's a sad commentary, but I must confess I believe I know exactly what you mean."

"You do?" She frowned down at him. "How is that possible. You're a gentleman."

"True, but some gentlemen suffer a similar fate. We, too, can feel, as you say, unseen."

He felt heat flame over his cheeks. He wanted to say more, a great deal more. Victoria was right, it was absolutely maddening to be a man like him in this day and age, or any other.

He could picture them together years from now, a tough old editor and his feisty, outspoken lady author putting out one important book after the next. It was thrilling to be a team with Victoria Meeks, thrilling to be on the cusp of something—though of what he wasn't exactly sure. But she was thinking in an altogether new way, and he would do all he could to encourage her.

"We're so pleased," he said, setting a calmer tone, "that the orders for *The Boston Harbor Girl* are better than we had anticipated."

"Excellent!" She spun around one of the brownstone columns like a schoolgirl. "That's good news."

"And yet," Jonathan deepened his voice, "we must brace ourselves. This book may not receive a quiet welcome. I want to help prepare you for what we must assume will be inevitable criticism."

Victoria stopped spinning and seemed to consider the question. "Critics have never bothered with me before. Mrs. Swann wasn't worthy of their attention. The truth is, I rather look forward to reading their assessment of my writing."

Jonathan could see that she had her head in the clouds, and it was his job to bring her back down to earth. "Of course, we hope for a good literary response, but we're also concerned that some readers are going to focus exclusively on the controversial aspects of your tale. Perry suggests that you write a letter to the editor of one of the broadsides to accompany the publication, to frame the issue and beat your detractors to it. We must take the reins on this most difficult subject."

"But the novel frames the issue. I don't see why I must elaborate on what it shows."

"Ideally that would be enough. But we think you'll want to defend your position."

"You mean my position regarding abortion?" she asked loudly.

He lowered his voice. "Victoria, please."

"Jonathan, you need to become comfortable with the subject. We can't have a conversation if we can't say the word."

"And you must face that you will most likely be attacked. You won't have a pseudonym to hide behind. You must be prepared."

Victoria let out a little huff. "I'll consider writing a letter to the editor. I would argue in it that a young lady deserves to live her life freely and make her own decisions. That's what I care about. That she have her own say. But honestly, I think criticism is apt to come no matter what. Reviewers are bound to notice that I could have done better."

"What do you mean by *better*?" he asked.

"*The Boston Harbor Girl* is a bit overdone, don't you think?" she asked, but didn't wait for his reply. "The tragic ending feels forced and unrealistic."

"I had concerns about the ending too. I had thought to ask if you could make it, I don't know, rosier?"

"Daisy's ending rosier?" Victoria's voice rose. "Why, that would have changed the book entirely. What on earth were you thinking, Jonathan?"

"Perry dissuaded me from suggesting it."

"I should think so," she scoffed. "You of all people should have noticed that the final chapters are too broadly drawn, similar to my romances which are completely exaggerated."

She let out a carefree laugh that Jonathan didn't care for.

"I don't see any need to criticize your romances. They're appealing," he protested. "There's nothing wrong with that."

"Since when do you like them?"

"I've read them all, some twice. I enjoy them a great deal."

"Enjoy, but not admire?"

He hesitated. "Perhaps admire. They are precisely what they are."

"I don't admire them." She threw her scarf over her shoulder and started back down the steps. "Not anymore. I think they come dangerously close to melodrama."

"And what's wrong with melodrama?" he asked as she passed him on her way down.

At the bottom, Victoria turned to him. "What's gotten into you? I thought you were a literary scholar. Isn't discernment what they taught you here at Harvard?"

"I've come to appreciate the hope that your books offer to the heart. Mrs. Swann's novels are set in imagined lands because no one would believe that happiness of the romantic kind could be found right here, right now. But it should be attainable everywhere and by everyone. There's no shame in wanting that to be true."

Her irritated expression lifted, and she let out a contemplative sigh. Together, they studied the geometry of brick paths that cut across the muddy lawns. There were so many paths in life that a person might take, yet none led with any certainty to happiness. The two of them, of all people, knew that to be true.

After a long moment, she said, "I think I may have a way for Mrs. Swann to continue."

"Really?"

"Her name is Edwina. She's my aunt and a wonderful writer of romance and adventure tales."

"Oh, now, I don't know."

"Of course, you don't know, but you must trust me about this if we're going to work together on the next book." Then, as if she had read his mind, she asked, "You would like to work together on the next book?"

Jonathan couldn't help the smile that broke over his face. "Yes, very much so."

"Good! That settles it." She straightened her hat. "You'll be pleased to hear that last evening I made progress on it. I'm going to title it *The Boston Shopgirl*, and I think it will be by far my best effort yet."

"How clever of you to inaugurate a new series!" he exclaimed.

"No." She held up a hand. "Not a series. I'll decide what I write next. It might be altogether different, if I so choose."

His head bobbed in agreement. "Of course, of course, you decide, Victoria."

"But for now, there's more work to be done on it. I must run an errand to make that possible. So, if you'll forgive me, I'll take my leave. I shall be in touch!"

Before Jonathan had a chance to object, Victoria had started down the path, the clatter of her heels echoing off the bricks.

THIRTY-TWO

B efore ringing the bell, she read the sign: "Ladies not home by 9 p.m. will find the door locked and property seized." Victoria braced for a fight as she had come to retrieve the suitcase that held the opening of the novel she had started in her last days in Maine. After storming from the breakfast table in such a flurry, not even thinking to march upstairs for her things, she hadn't had a moment to return to the boarding house until now. The future of *The Boston Shopgirl* lay in the clutches of the unpleasant battle-ax. The front door swung open and the stout, highly rouged woman greeted her not with a scowl, or by shutting the door in her face, but with a painfully ingratiating smile.

"Mrs. Swann, what a nice surprise to see you." She gave an awkward curtsy, her many beaded necklaces swinging, and the keys, monocle, and other attachments clanking. "You must know that Miss Pennypacker is here looking for you."

Victoria stepped inside. "No, I had no idea. What a happy coincidence."

The matron waved her black lace fan in the direction of the parlor. "I wasn't aware you two were such dear friends."

Seated in an overstuffed armchair, with her flamboyant skirts spread extravagantly around her, Miss Pennypacker was more regal than ever. One corner of her ruby red lips rose, along with a single eyebrow.

"My dear Mrs. Swann," she emoted from across the room. "Mrs. McAlister was expressing her concern that you had ended your time here so abruptly. She hoped she hadn't offended you and feels chagrined that you left without receiving a proper refund."

"Is that so? How kind of her."

The matron fanned herself. "I'm sorry I didn't recognize

you before, Mrs. Swann. My girls fall for outlandish stories. I thought they were just carrying on, putting on airs that they knew you. But now I see the truth, I can't wait to tell the neighbors that you ladies were here in my humble establishment. Won't you stay for tea?"

Miss Pennypacker politely declined on their behalf and made a great show of crossing the room to kiss Victoria on both cheeks in the continental fashion. The boarding house matron registered their exchange with a shiver of excitement and didn't blink for fear of missing a moment between the two stars—one of the written word, and the other, more glorious, of the stage.

"We have much to catch up on, Mrs. Swann," Miss Pennypacker said. "Would you care to join me for supper at my home?"

At the mention of Miss Pennypacker's famous Back Bay mansion, Mrs. McAlister clasped her hands together. From the society pages, everyone knew of the spectacular parties that the chanteuse threw there.

"Thank you for the invitation. I'd be delighted. But first I must retrieve the things I left behind. That's why I came by."

Miss Pennypacker and Victoria turned to the matron who flushed in the glow of their attention.

"Mrs. McAlister, would you mind retrieving Mrs. Swann's things for her? We do so appreciate your help."

"Yes, Miss Pennypacker. I'm more than happy to oblige."

She waddled off and Victoria spoke to Miss Pennypacker. "Lovely to see you again, but how did you find me?"

"We share the same lawyer. He told me where you had been staying. Hopefully he's not giving away our secrets so easily to the other side."

"Which other side?"

"We're both suing Louis Russell. That's what I've come to discuss with you. I think we should join forces."

A great clamor came from the rear of the boarding house. Was Mrs. McAlister dragging in a dead body from the back yard? Victoria craned to see. She couldn't relax until the valise that held her latest manuscript appeared.

"Russell's cheated us both," Miss Pennypacker continued. "I know all about your house sale."

This caught Victoria's attention. "What do you know?"

"I know that your husband signed over the Brattle Street address in an attempt to pay off his debts to Russell."

"I suspected as much. It was a despicable thing to do, and I intend to get my house back, but I assume that Raymond's free of him now."

"Not according to my sleuth."

"Oh dear, I was afraid of that."

"Mr. Byrne remains in bad straights. Russell continues to supply him with what he craves."

Victoria let out a long breath. "Poor man."

"You sound sympathetic. Aren't you done with him?"

"I am, but somehow the divorce allows me to feel more for him than I could before. He was a domineering, treacherous husband when in the throes of his addiction, but I was never entirely convinced he was evil, just weak. Terribly weak."

"I've had several husbands of that ilk myself."

Victoria would have been curious to ask more about her numerous marriages, but they were interrupted by Mrs. McAlister as she brought Victoria's luggage into the parlor.

"Let's put our heads together over supper. Russell has no idea what he's up against."

"He wanted us to perform as a team. He was going to call us *Louis Russell's Ladies*. Can you imagine?"

Miss Pennypacker let out a laugh. "He'll rue the day we met. Feel free to call me Penny, by the way."

"Victoria."

They shook hands, as modern women did, and the matron noted it for her girls. She turned over the valise that held the pages of Victoria's latest novel and an envelope containing a refund. When the two women left her on the boarding house front porch, she continued to call out, inviting them to come back anytime, anytime at all.

THIRTY-THREE

In summer, the grand elms and oaks of Harvard Yard offered cooling shade, and in autumn, they provided a canopy of riotous color. But now, in winter, the silhouettes of bare limbs etched the steel-grey sky. The Yard was a lonely place with its stern brick facades looming in judgment over the dormant lawns. Jonathan felt a chill and stuffed his hands deeper into the pockets of his McIntosh as he headed for the gate.

He hadn't taken ten steps when he noticed a former colleague, George Santayana, coming toward him. Though in the prime of life, Jonathan's old drinking companion walked with a silver cane, not because of any infirmity, but to enhance his impressive swagger. Under the billowing folds of his scholar's robe, he wore a three-piece lounge suit with a high stiff collar. Shoulders thrust back and chest forward, he strolled up the paths with proprietary pleasure.

Santayana was known for his jaunty aphorisms and clever asides delivered on all occasions, most especially late at night at the Hasty Pudding Club. Jonathan had often felt tongue-tied when in his orbit, but in this moment, he was hungry for any pearls of wisdom the philosopher might let fall. If he could tolerate his former colleague's high self-regard, he might get some useful advice out of him.

"Hark!" Santayana called. "Can it be Odysseus back from the wars? I believe it is." He bowed deeply, as was his custom.

Jonathan bowed, too, though minus the dramatic flourish of the hat swept low.

"What brings you back to our happy Eden?" Santayana asked.

"I was meeting with one of my authors. You probably passed her going out the gate."

"I believe I did. A fine-looking woman."

"I suppose so," Jonathan said in a tender, appreciative tone.

"Don't tell me you hadn't noticed?"

"I guess I—"

"What's the matter, Cartwright?" Santayana's mustache quivered with barely contained mirth. "The lady giving you trouble? Look at you—" He used the silver tip of his cane to point at Jonathan. "I've never seen you in such a dither."

"I'm all right. Perfectly all right."

"Son of a New England minister, aren't you? No wonder you don't understand the finer things in life."

"I do," Jonathan answered reflexively, and added, "such as?"

"Women!"

"Right, of course, women."

"My dear Cartwright, I believe you're caught."

Jonathan's attempt at composure crumbled. "What do you mean by caught?"

"I prefer the Spanish *encantar.* Sanskrit's better on this sort of thing with its *kama,* a highly erotic definition," the philosopher clarified. "You seem to be learning that life is neither a spectacle, nor a feast, but a predicament."

"How true. But what do I *do* about it?"

"*Do?*" Santayana repeated. "Why, many things. As I often say, knowledge of the possible is the beginning of happiness. You're on the cusp of knowing. Enjoy it, my friend. Take it in. Look around you! What do you see?"

Jonathan did as he was told and noticed the other young men hurrying past. Each walked alone and anxious, fraught with doubts about their futures. He saw trees, shadowed and glum. Beyond the gate, he saw the town's citizens, worn down by work, slogging home to lives that contained little joy.

"Notice the little buds forming up there." Santayana jabbed his cane at the sky.

Jonathan tipped his head back.

"Springtime, my boy, springtime is in the works already. You can see it if you look closely. But the real question is, can you *feel* it?"

Jonathan didn't see or feel anything remotely like spring, as it was late November, but said, "Thank you. That is most helpful."

"You must open yourself to hope, to portent, to possibility. The possible exists. Never forget it." The philosopher brought down his cane and thrust his hand into his waistcoat pocket.

"The possible exists," Jonathan echoed softly.

"Also," Santayana said with a laugh, "a lady likes to be taken seriously, but not too seriously, if you know what I mean."

Jonathan had forgotten they were speaking of Victoria.

"She's a fine writer," he offered, "and I'm honored to be her editor."

Santayana shook his head. "You Americans do amuse me so. You're a simple people."

He tipped his hat in farewell. "I recommend wine and lots of it. For it's the wine that leads us on!"

THIRTY-FOUR

Victoria slept on satin sheets, the smoothness of which she had never felt before, in Penny's guest room with its gilded trim and aubergine-colored walls. Exotic bird feathers rose from Egyptian-inspired vases on either side of a Portuguese-tiled fireplace. A jewel-encrusted chandelier hung over thick Persian carpeting and the four-poster bed was curtained by heavy Renaissance brocade. From under a down quilt and surrounded by imperial décor, Victoria began to grasp her new friend's ease with opulence. Penny Pennypacker's home in Back Bay made Victoria's house on Brattle Street seem positively modest.

She had slept deeply not only because of the comfortable accommodations, but because the two women had worked together the night before to form a plan to take on Louis Russell. Penny was a hard worker, diligent and pragmatic in her approach to tasks. Victoria was sorry that in the morning when she came downstairs to the elegant dining room, her host had already left the house on business. At the long, carved oak table under the pretty lights of a different chandelier—crystal this time—and surrounded by the heady aromas of a massive floral centerpiece, a butler shook out her napkin, placed it before her and filled her coffee cup. The eggs, sausage, and biscuits served from silver trays was the best breakfast Victoria had ever eaten. Sated and well rested for a change, she headed out into the pale Boston sunshine, sad to leave behind all that delicious, distracting luxury.

She strolled along the promenade down the center of Commonwealth Avenue on her way to the Public Garden and then cut across the open field of the Commons where several sheep trimmed the grass as part of a quaint country festival. Wandering up Park Street, she passed the State House and the

Boston Athenaeum. Soon, Victoria wended her way through the narrow cobblestone streets of the North End. She hadn't known where she was going on this peaceful Saturday morning, but the closer she grew to the harbor, the more she sensed her destination.

The usual congestion of carts, carriages, and omnibuses thinned out on the weekends with the remaining activity at the wharf and the nearby Italian Haymarket. In wooden stalls, purveyors spread an array of foods. They sold cheeses from the western counties, elongated purple tubers, mounds of green beans and legumes, and smoked meats. Every variety of fish, straight off the boats, lay on blocks of ice—one-eyed rays, ruby red snapper, and of course cod, both dried and fresh. In their leather aprons, the merchants shouted to one another, exchanging quips while snapping their suspenders. Victoria walked with a lift in her step as she took in the city around her. "'Just as any of you is one of a living crowd, I was one of a crowd,'" she recited Whitman's words under her breath. Victoria could now say the same of herself.

The neighborhood was much changed from when she had last visited with Raymond and had tossed her manuscript into Louis Russell's fire, and even more so since she had first lived here as a young wife. She was here now, she realized, to say goodbye to that past with growing confidence in her future. Crowded clotheslines blocked the sun and fetid refuse lined the gutters. At the darkened door under the torn awning, she rapped once, then twice. The elderly Chinese man, whose name she had never learned, opened it.

"Closed. Come back later."

"Is my husband here?"

It took a moment, but he seemed to recognize her. He turned and disappeared down the lightless hall. Victoria caught the door and ventured in after him. Past the veils of beaded curtains, the inner den was dark and still. The many red lanterns hung dully, their lights extinguished.

"Is Mrs. Chang here?"

"Boarding house across the way. She and girls sleep in day-time." The old man placed his round cap on his head and used his hands to form a pillow, indicating that he was leaving now to get his rest too.

"And Mr. Byrne?" she asked again.

The old man's eyes shifted toward the chrysanthemum screen before he left. Victoria stepped deeper into the low-ceilinged, shabby room. Dim sunshine streaked through the half windows and she ran a hand along the sticky surface of the bar. No light illuminated the bottles that lined the mirrored shelves, their allure lost in daylight. A black stocking hung haphazardly over a stool and several chairs by the Mahjong tables lay toppled on the stained carpet. Otherwise, there was little evidence of the careless acts of the night before or the many nights before that. A dismal place, a trap for poor girls and weak-willed, self-deceiving men.

A sound came from behind the faded screen and the heavy bite of opium encircled her, infusing the air with its sickly sweetness. Victoria stepped past the partition and into the area of raised *kangs*. She made her way down the line where a grimy mattress and tattered pillow covered each yellow-brick bed. Brass trays displaying pipes and needles sat waiting. On the last bed in the narrow room, a man lay curled on his side, knees to his chest, and facing a cracked and peeling wall. She could see his shoulders tremble, the thin grey blanket doing little to warm him. She knew that long, lean body. A weak flame sputtered in the oil lamp on the table beside him, but he remained in shadow. Soiled sheets lay scattered on the floor all around the bedside.

"Raymond," she said.

He opened his eyes slowly and his lips curled into what was meant to be a smile, though he had lost more teeth. With some difficulty, he turned toward her, long legs stretching. His bare feet protruded from under the cover, bony and dotted with constellations of red scars. Giving a deep groan, he wrenched an arm free from under the blanket and let it fall onto the mattress. Shirt sleeves rolled high on sinewy arms exposed more scars. His skin shone translucent, blue veins protruding. Raymond squinted, and Victoria wondered if he thought she was a mirage. He lifted a thin hand and flailed it toward her. In the flickering light, he appeared ghoulish and frightening. A specter, a demon, or merely a destitute soul.

"I knew you'd come."

His forehead was slick with soot and sweat, and the black wave of hair he had worn so vainly had lost its shine and fell lifelessly over his brow. Victoria crouched beside the bed and, with a gentle touch, pushed his lank hair back into place.

"You poor man, let's get you out of here."

He extended a single finger, clearly too exhausted to do much more.

"You'll never get better if you don't leave."

"I'm all right, Victoria. You go ahead without me. I'll be along soon."

He let out a soft moan, shut his eyes, and turned his head away. Her hand hovered over him, but what could she do? What was the point if he was unwilling to change? It was too late. After a long moment, her shadow climbed the cracked wall in the lantern light as she stood. One last time, she gazed down on her husband before leaving him behind in that deadly, desolate place.

THIRTY-FIVE

Jonathan turned away from Harvard Yard and set out walking. He didn't care where he was going as he wove past workers trudging home. They may have felt a great weariness, but at least they had homes to return to where someone waited for them. If he couldn't have that, others should. He left behind the busier streets and wandered the dirt cattle path toward Cambridgeport. Like the animals that were prodded and steered in that same direction, he followed an unavoidable destiny that took him to the office above the slaughterhouse, which was, if not an actual home, at least a place he could call theirs. That was all he could hope for.

Inside the butcher's building, his nose twitched with the bite of ammonia as he moved through the chilly, scrubbed-down warehouse. For such a messy trade, they left it spotless every evening before starting the next day. It made Jonathan weak to consider how much blood was lost here, so much life extinguished, if only that of beasts. At the top of the rickety steps, he stopped before the door of Bliss & Cartwright. A thin band of golden light streamed out from under it. Jonathan's heart began to beat faster as his hand fumbled to fit the key into the lock. He opened the door and stepped cautiously inside.

Perry sat with his feet up on his desk, his glasses low on his nose, and a manuscript held before him. He was reading, the room quiet except for the purr of the grate. Jonathan watched him for a long moment and felt what had been growing inside. It was time, past time, to speak up, but he could not make himself do it. Would he go through his entire life like this, stalled on the threshold?

"Perry," he made himself say.

His friend looked across and didn't seem a bit surprised to see him standing there. He gave an imperceptible smile, at least that's what Jonathan hoped he saw in the low, gentle light of the lamp. Perry stayed tipped back in his chair, his feet up on the desk. He wore no coat, and his vest was partly unbuttoned, his shirtsleeves rolled, his collar undone. The room's warmth made his cheeks pink, and in the soft illumination his pale brow appeared glossy. Beneath his pronounced beak, his moustache quivered, and his lips were moist.

Jonathan stepped closer and his heart skipped a beat as Perry tossed the manuscript onto his cluttered desktop. It was a startlingly free gesture, as if he were ready to throw away everything as Jonathan made his way to him. In Jonathan's mind, he knew how the moment should unfurl, like those pages born aloft for an instant on the air. If he was the author of the story, a gesture like that would set them both free. He stopped beside Perry's desk and stood over him.

Perry removed his reading glasses. Could he see the question on Jonathan's lips? There was no way to know. Jonathan had to screw up his courage and make himself speak.

"Your boots," he said in a high, anxious voice. "Your beautiful boots."

Then Jonathan did the bravest thing he had ever done in his short and sheltered life. He placed a hand over the top of the fine Italian leather. He could sense Perry studying him closely. A slight twitch of his ankle or leg, a tip of his head to one side, or the slightest sound, and Jonathan would have yanked his hand back as if burned by a flame. But Perry remained unmoving, his boots still up on the desk. Jonathan gripped tighter, his palm pressing down on the thin, elegant shoelaces.

"My boots?" Perry asked, his voice not offended or teasing, but curious, relaxed, and even a bit encouraging. "What about them, Jon?"

"I love them," he blurted out.

"Is that so?"

Jonathan's gaze dared to shift up to Perry's face. He felt a wash of relief that his friend did not appear frightened or even all that surprised by the declaration.

"Why don't we buy you a pair of your own when we go to Venice?"

Jonathan couldn't help the panic and the hope and the incredible confusion in his voice. "Venice?"

Perry lifted his feet and set them down evenly on the floorboards. "We'll go next summer so the Italian sun can burn away the chill of our New England winter. Would you like that?"

Jonathan moved his head ever so slightly.

"Men like us need to get out of Boston from time to time."

"Men like us?"

"Yes, Jon, men like us."

Perry stood and the great, tall, lanky height of him struck Jonathan as magnificent. He couldn't believe that the story he had wanted for so long was the story that was actually taking place. All the novels he had ever read and all the scenes he had ever imagined paled in comparison to this one in which Perry dipped his head and Jonathan lifted his. He shut the book of his mind and let himself feel it.

PART FOUR

THIRTY-SIX

When Victoria arrived at the shop on Monday morning, Mr. Roebuck had already cranked open the awning and turned around the wooden sign. He seemed more jovial than ever since he'd employed Dottie to do his finances. Emma had continued to work part time and had taken over ordering stock. His three female assistants, he readily confessed, had steered his little enterprise back from the brink. For the moment, Victoria was alone in the bookshop, as Emma was off tending to her mother.

Victoria made her way past the bookshelves to the storage room where she hung up her tired scarf and bedraggled coat. Refraining from buying new clothing was worth it if she could have a hook in a place of her own before long. By staying as a guest at Penny's and taking on Emma's extra hours, in addition to any forthcoming royalties from Bliss & Cartwright, an apartment might not be too far in her future. On her way back to the counter, she joined her boss at a table where he was unloading a box of newly printed books.

"This one's causing quite a stir already." He lifted a copy.

In his hands, he held *The Boston Harbor Girl*, by one Victoria Meeks. She felt her face grow hot as she took it in her hands. The heft of it! The smoothness of the leather cover! The embossed spine! Her fingers danced over and around it, and into the interior, which was beautiful too. Bliss & Cartwright had done a masterful job. She hadn't felt this proud of one of her novels since her first. This book didn't belong to Gaustad, or to Mrs. Swann, or even to Jonathan, just to her.

Mr. Roebuck continued to unload copies onto the table. "Thanks to my connections, we received ours early. Everyone's going to be talking about it. Apparently, a sordid tale, a little too realistic for some."

"What do you mean?" Victoria asked as she helped him display the books.

"Certain people will have their hackles up. Take a look at the editorial in this morning's *Boston Herald* from the New England Society for the Prevention of Vice. That contemptible man Comstock is badgering us again, even after getting his indecency law passed. He wants to tighten strictures in the realm of the novel too. Soon he'll censor our dreams!"

Mr. Roebuck was usually too busy for conversation, and she couldn't recall ever hearing him string together so many sentences at once. His muttonchops shook in irritation, and he clearly had a lot to say.

"I'm glad I ordered many copies. Nothing like the threat of censorship to help a book sell like hotcakes. It's our duty, Victoria, our absolute duty, to sell as many as we can. I refuse to allow our government to tell authors what they can and cannot write."

"I'll do my best to share that perspective with our customers."

"But you must be prepared that some will find the book highly offensive. We must insist that the freedom of the press is essential to our democracy. It makes my blood boil what evil is taking place in our fair land."

Victoria agreed but was ashamed to admit that she hadn't thought much on the matter. For now, she retreated behind the counter and braced herself to read the critical editorial. But after spreading out the newspaper on the polished wood, she became sidetracked by an image above the fold. It showed a shadowy street with the crumbled remains of a brick building. The headline jumped out at her:

FIRE DESTROYS NOTORIOUS BOSTON BROTHEL

She leaned against the counter and read.

> Midmorning on Saturday, the brothel at 118 Priestly burned to the ground, taking with it the laundry shop next door and an empty warehouse on the opposite side.

Captain Thaddeus Seamus of the Harbor Fire Brigade reported that Engine #6 was too wide for the narrow passage and water hoses were not long enough to reach the structure. With no other options, the firemen executed a bucket drive brigade up from the wharf. Their heroic efforts and a shift in the wind kept the blaze from taking the entire block.

The residents of a boarding house across the way remained unharmed. A dozen young ladies were roused from sleep to watch the fire consume their place of employment. Luckily at that hour, the notorious brothel was empty, with the exception of one man, Mr. Raymond Byrne, who was dragged from the fire, but succumbed at the scene to smoke inhalation.

Victoria let out a gasp. Her knees caved, but luckily Mr. Roebuck was at her side and caught her elbow to steady her.

"What's wrong?" he asked.

She lifted the paper. *Oh, Raymond!* She had had no illusions he would ever escape the clutches of his addiction, but his death came as a shock, nonetheless. Victoria pictured the flickering oil lamp and the bedding on the floor. Had he knocked it over in fitful sleep and ignited the nest of sheets and pillows? Or did the fire start elsewhere in the tinderbox of a building? She bent over the newspaper and continued to read.

The wooden tenement structure housed an infamous brothel and a den of gambling and the imbibing of illicit substances. The deed on the property belongs to the South Boston Import-Export Company owned by Mr. Louis Russell. He is also in possession of numerous other companies, including Russell Shipping, which recently filed for bankruptcy, and Thames, Royall & Quincy, Ltd., the once esteemed publishing house. He is currently named in no fewer than twenty-seven lawsuits against his various entities, including litigation involving his best-known authors, Mrs. Swann, lady scribbler of

romance novels and a popular advice column, and Miss
Pennypacker, dancehall singer and public persona.

Victoria sank onto the stool beside the register. Angry tears
hovered in her eyes but refused fall. She had cried for Raymond
too many times. He was a weak and undisciplined man, but he
didn't deserve to die in such a squalid way. He and the young
ladies who worked at the brothel were victims of a greedy man
and a system of exploitation that trapped them and used them,
ruining any hope for a better life.

Mr. Roebuck hovered nearby. "Has something troubled you,
my dear? May I bring you a cup of tea?"

She pointed at the newspaper.

He shook his head sadly. "Terrible, that fire down at the harbor. There ought to be a public outcry, but knowing this paper,
they'll use it to beat the drums of intolerance. People should
be charitable after a tragedy like this, but more likely they'll say
good riddance to bad rubbish and call for a police crackdown
on poor neighborhoods. There'll be a renewed effort to wipe
out immoral behavior. They'll blame the girls."

"But that's not fair." Victoria's voice rose. "Those young
women have no other options."

"I agree, a tragedy of this sort should *help* their cause not
harm them more. But I'm afraid, it'll send them into worse
situations."

"What could be worse?" Victoria asked.

Mr. Roebuck gazed down at the stacks of new books. "I
gather there are things depicted in this novel that should never
take place in a civilized society. A poor girl with no options but
to risk her life in a back alley. It makes me weep to think of it."

"But you haven't read it yet."

"No, but I shall straight away. I recommend that you do too."

Victoria realized that her boss was no mere bookseller, but a
true humanitarian. A principled man, he didn't deserve her lack
of forthrightness. She had fooled him for months, but it was
time to reveal the truth.

"Mr. Roebuck, forgive me, but I need to tell you that I've been deceiving you."

He pursed his lips. "How so, Mrs. Swann?"

"I'm not Mrs. Swann. I mean, of course, I'm the author of her books, but also the author of that novel." She pointed across to *The Boston Harbor Girl*. "My real name is Victoria Meeks."

He turned from her to the books and back again and, after a moment, let out a high titter. "*You* are the author of this highly anticipated novel?"

"And the new one that I'm currently writing in your stockroom is in the same realistic vein. I'm no longer writing as Mrs. Swann but as Victoria Meeks."

He pulled both palms down his muttonchops in a moment of comprehension. "That is big news. We've had a good run with Mrs. Swann. But I suppose that you, as the author, are entitled to create what you please. That's the freedom we must accord our artists and writers."

Victoria could see him rallying his good spirits.

"Indeed, you should write whatever you like!" He patted the counter for emphasis. "And whatever you write, I'm sure to like!"

"That's good of you, Mr. Roebuck. Thank you for understanding."

Victoria turned back to the newspaper. Russell's name caught her eye, and she could feel agitation rising. The young women had stood shivering in their thin robes as their world went up in smoke before their eyes. Who would help them now?

"Something really must be done for the victims of that fire. Those poor girls, what is to become of them?"

"They'll probably be sent back to where they came from, deported under the Chinese Exclusion Act, or put in jail here. As new immigrants, they have no rights and no country to defend them. Politicians will use them for their own purposes and toss them away."

"How reprehensible to treat people like refuse."

Mr. Roebuck came closer. "You know, if you wanted to

share your opinion on the mistreatment of young ladies—whether those employed at a brothel or ones who've been given no choice like your fictional Boston harbor girl, I'm sure your readers would like to hear what you have to say."

"You think so?"

"I think everyone is going to be curious to learn the identity of the author of such a controversial tale. A rebuttal editorial from you would garner a great deal of interest. Someone needs to speak up against intolerance and cruelty."

"My publisher suggested the same idea, but I thought I might be able to stay hidden behind the scenes, as I always have."

"I'm afraid that won't be likely for you anymore. Your privacy is going to be disrupted no matter what with this new book. You might as well take the bull by the horns and state your case forthrightly." He reached under the counter and brought out a blank notebook and pen and held them out to her. "Also, it will help with sales."

"You're a clever man, Mr. Roebuck."

"I do know a thing or two about selling books."

She took the pen and paper. "I don't know what good it will do, but I have a strong urge to write about this dire situation. It really isn't right."

"That's the spirit! Go to it. I'll handle the shop this morning."

Victoria retreated to the stockroom, uncapped the pen, and opened the cover of the notebook to the first blank page. Pressing her hand to the scarred wood, she considered the young working girls staying at Mrs. McAlister's boarding house, and those who wrote desperate letters seeking advice from Mrs. Swann, their lives limited by circumstance and dependent on the whims of men. Like them, she had been vulnerable to bad influences and forced to make a most difficult choice that had pushed her to the limits of her health and sanity. Victoria wanted all young women to have greater autonomy and independence with ample opportunity to support themselves and live as they chose. And perhaps someday, they might even gain the right to vote.

For years, Mrs. Swann and her readers had escaped to imagined, far-off countries. But now, Victoria was ready to return to this imperfect one, her voice stronger and more determined than ever. Her editorial essay would appear the following day under the name of Victoria Meeks and would reveal her former identity as Mrs. Swann. Her treatise would end with the following forceful words:

> For too long, the lives of women have been kept narrow and constrained. It is time to take our rightful place at work and as equals in the home. We New Women must stake our claim in the vast, wide world.

THIRTY-SEVEN

Jonathan and Perry stood side by side on the loading dock of the Riverside Press as workmen in heavy boots and leather aprons carried box after box to the delivery wagons. The first snow of winter fell on their shoulders and Jonathan clapped his bare hands together to help blood circulate to his icy fingertips. He had forgotten his gloves on the front hall table at Perry's Back Bay mansion that morning but had hardly felt the cold as they made their way on foot across the Harvard Bridge. The wind had whipped up the Charles and bit into his cheeks, and a dusting of snow swirled around them. They were in the thick of things now—the place where Jonathan had always wanted to be but had never believed possible.

A foreman approached with papers on a clipboard for Perry to sign. A tremor came over Jonathan, more from excitement than cold, as his partner placed his John Hancock on the dotted line with a flourish.

"You and your team have done a fine job," Perry said to the man.

"As Mr. Houghton used to say, '*Tout bien ou rien*,'" the foreman said. "Your books will be in the stores from Maine to Maryland by the end of the week, sir." He tipped his cap and took back the papers.

Perry addressed the workmen who stood nearby. "May we offer you fellows a pint as reward for working on a Saturday?"

The men declined but mumbled their thanks. Perry discretely slipped each an extravagant two-dollar bill. They took off their hats and bobbed their heads in appreciation. Jonathan wanted to question him about the overly large tip but realized that was the man Perry was—generous and, well, rich. As they turned away, one of the crew mumbled, "There's a gentleman for you."

Jonathan felt a hum inside that could only be described as

happiness. They watched the final freight wagon laden with Victoria's newly printed books pull away. The other men returned to the warehouse and Perry slapped his gloved hands together and rocked on the balls of his feet.

"Now all we do is wait for the revenue to start streaming in."

"And the reviews."

"Ah, right. We may have a *succès de scandale* on our hands. But luckily, the only thing worse than being talked about is not being talked about, as Oscar says."

"Don't tell me you know Oscar Wilde."

One corner of Perry's lips lifted slightly under his moustache

"Why haven't you ever mentioned it?" Jonathan asked.

"Need I remind you there's much we never mentioned to one another?" Jonathan squeezed Perry's arm through his thick fur coat. "Besides, I'd be disowned if I were as audacious as Wilde. But in no way does he deserve the persecution he's endured."

"It scared me so. I followed the trial in the papers. Something like that could happen so easily here."

"With the Comstock Law expanding the very definition of vice, there's no question we're in a backward nation. All the more reason to be forward thinking."

Jonathan worried what that might mean for them but understood there was no turning back now. Perry would help him to be courageous. They would be brave together. The two stared into the grey day as the snow began to fill the hard-packed dirt road. In the distance, the horses pulling the last delivery wagons turned at the corner and were off. Despite all that seemed impossible, the white clouds of their breaths steamed before their faces and washed the air anew. How could it be that in a time so bent on stealing all hope from unsuspecting souls, he could still feel it? He had no business being happy in such a difficult world, and yet he was.

Perry's voice cut into Jonathan's thoughts. "You know, Victoria may become a *cause célèbre* like Oscar."

"She wouldn't like that."

"It all depends on the reviews. If they respect the book enough, salacious gossip about the author's past will matter less. But I'll go ahead and make out a check for you to take to her. That should help with the sting."

"Who are you? How do you know such things?"

"Oh, Jonny." Perry shrugged. "I just do."

Jonathan shivered, but this time not from fear or excitement but from cold. Perry reached for his hands and rubbed them between his own gloved ones. Jonathan glanced around to see if anyone was nearby. But they stood alone at the back of the printing press with the ice on the Charles River forming for the first time and the faint lowing of cattle in their pens behind the slaughterhouse not far away. The city was settling into itself for the winter. A hush fell as the snow drifted and lofted before landing peacefully on the frozen ground.

"Let's get you home," Perry said.

THIRTY-EIGHT

The response to Victoria's newspaper editorial was swift. In the days after it appeared, Mr. Roebuck had to swim through a sea of people to enter his shop. The more who gathered carrying placards calling for the novel to be banned, the more customers arrived to buy it. Cambridge was a notoriously fair-minded city. Readers insisted they were above lowbrow judgments of the author and were only interested in assessing the book on its own merits. And yet, Mr. Roebuck was having a hard time keeping in stock not only enough copies of *The Boston Harbor Girl*, but of the gossip pages as well.

When it became public knowledge that the controversial author was an employee of the Cambridge Bookshop, a reporter from *The Boston Herald* showed up, begging for an interview, followed by others from national papers. Mr. Roebuck could not remember such a fuss since Dickens stayed at the Parker House and read to sold-out audiences at the Old North Church. Miraculously, the press hadn't caught on that Victoria was a guest at Miss Pennypacker's in Back Bay. Penny's own devoted fans always lurked about outside, so it was only a matter of time before someone spotted the two women together.

On this morning, Penny had sent Victoria off to Cambridge in one of her carriages, hidden behind an elaborate hat with birds on the crown and a violet-toned veil over her face. Victoria hoped she might be able to travel on the trolley someday again without attracting attention. She could not imagine being the permanent focus of such tiresome gossipmongering and was eager for the newspapers to get bored with her and move on.

She sneaked in the back door of the shop and unburdened herself in the stockroom of her brown coat, the frivolous hat, and her carpetbag. She had enough money now to buy new clothing, but that was the last thing she had time for. Since the publication of her editorial, she had spoken at several women's clubs, marched with a local chapter of the suffragettes to the State House, and visited the Cambridge Neighborhood House, a good works establishment that offered uplifting programs of every sort for new immigrants. Realizing that her new commitments would not let up any time soon, Victoria had reluctantly given notice at the bookstore. She was happy to see Emma's cloak on the hook this day and went in search of her.

"My dear girl," Victoria said as Emma rose from dusting books on a bottom shelf. "How is your mother?"

"Better, thank you. We've managed to nurse her back to health."

"By we, I suspect you mean you."

Emma gave a modest smile.

"I'm so glad to hear it, but we've missed you here."

"I missed being here, but I managed to read like a fiend while at home. I'm up to date on all the latest."

"How marvelous. With my many distractions, I haven't had a moment."

"But you must stop everything and pick up a new novel called *The Awakening* by Mrs. Kate Chopin of New Orleans. I don't want to give away too much, but the ending is remarkably similar to yours in *The Boston Harbor Girl*. You both managed to put your finger on the plight of women today."

"How interesting."

The little bell tinkled, and Victoria stepped back to avoid being seen by customers. She spied a handsomely dressed Cambridge matron followed by a slight, well-dressed man, who, even before he took off his fedora, she recognized as Jonathan.

"This will be fun," she said to Emma. "My editor's here. I want you to meet him."

Together they peered around the bookshelves.

"That stylish young gent? Aren't you the lucky one?" Emma smoothed her recalcitrant hair as she followed Victoria to the front of the store.

"Hello, Mr. Cartwright." Victoria gave him her hand.

He really was quite a dandy these days and deserved to be addressed by his surname.

Jonathan shook her fingers and gave an awkward bow but recovered well enough and made a show of introducing Victoria to the matron who wore an impeccably chosen Regency hat, which harmonized perfectly with the deep maroon of her coat. Her fine Italian gloves matched her elegant purse in the style preferred by women who spent a part of each year on the continent.

Before Jonathan had a chance to introduce the older woman, she turned to Victoria and said, "I believe our paths have crossed before."

The woman was right—they had passed any number of times on Brattle Street but had never spoken. Victoria had been too intimidated to initiate conversation and had assumed the woman hadn't noticed her.

"You are my neighbor on Brattle Street," the woman said.

"I was, but not anymore."

"I always wanted to meet the lady author who lived so close by."

Victoria almost lost her voice, but managed, "And I, you."

They had lived only a few doors apart, but Victoria had assumed the woman, like all her neighbors, were too far above her to be interested in getting to know her.

"And where are you now?" the woman asked. "Closer to Harvard Square? Many of my Radcliffe girls live on the side streets. I would find it too congested."

"Understandably. You must be accustomed to your expansive lawn, and the massive trees, and your lovely lilac bushes. Your home is the *most* beautiful in all of Cambridge."

The woman's expression softened. "Thank you. And I, over the years, have enjoyed your entertaining books."

Victoria let out a surprised little laugh. "I can't imagine Mrs. Swann's novels in your distinguished household."

The woman's plumed hat quivered as she chuckled too. "Father would never have approved, though as I think of it now, he admired a well-told yarn, so he might have enjoyed Mrs. Swann."

Victoria thanked her, but the thought of her romance and adventure tales being read by Henry Wadsworth Longfellow made her heart do a little flip.

"Lovely to meet you, Miss Longfellow."

"Call me Alice. I'm an old friend of Perry's father and am delighted to help these young fellows get their business off the ground."

"How wonderful," Victoria said, then turned to Emma and introduced her.

"An honor, Miss Longfellow. I read your reports on the rights of women and also your travel logs. I wouldn't miss a single installment."

"Thank you, my dear."

Jonathan spoke up. "How are you managing, Victoria, with all the public interest?"

"I'm far too busy."

"You'll be happy to know that *The Boston Harbor Girl* is in its second printing already. I have the latest accounting statement and a check for you." He passed her an envelope. "I wasn't sure where to send it."

"For the time being, sending any correspondence to the bookshop should be fine. I won't be working here much longer, but Mr. Roebuck is happy to receive my mail until I find a new residence. And you'll be glad to know I have something for you, Jonathan. Something *you've* been waiting for."

He broke into a broad smile, his boyishness returning. For a moment, the other women receded, and it was only the two of them.

"With everything else going on, you had time to work on it?" he asked.

"It's been keeping me sane. I finished the first half last night."

"How exciting. May I see it?"

"Of course! I wouldn't let anyone else read it but you."

The others listened to this exchange until Alice interrupted. "Are you two speaking in code, or may you share some hint of what you're chattering about?"

Jonathan apologized and said, "We're discussing a new novel that I hope Bliss & Cartwright will have the great pleasure of publishing, with your help, of course, Miss Longfellow."

"I may receive a return on my investment sooner than I thought," Alice said.

"Miss Longfellow is our most generous patron," Jonathan explained.

Victoria turned to Jonathan. "I think you'll be interested to know that Miss Pennypacker wants to bring her advice book over to Bliss & Cartwright. I wouldn't be surprised if you end up with other women writers too."

"The one thing missing from this promising equation are females on your staff," Alice said. "Don't you feel remiss at not having any in your employment, Mr. Cartwright?"

Jonathan cleared his throat. "I suppose we should."

"Sounds sensible to me," Victoria said.

"If I may suggest," Emma spoke up, pink blooming under her freckles. "You may want to hire someone who knows the tastes of younger ladies, as they are the fastest-growing readership. At least that's what we've noticed here at the shop."

"Excellent idea," Alice said.

"And I feel confident to suggest," Victoria said, "that Emma herself is the perfect candidate. She comes from a well-read family. Her father taught English in the old country and is now president of the Tool and Die Mechanics Literary Association of Boston. Her mother taught Latin, and when unable to find employment of that sort here, initiated the Cambridge Laundry Ladies Reading Brigade."

"My, how impressive," Alice said. "What true dedication to the book."

A slight smile hovered over the girl's lips, but she contained it. "I'd be honored to be considered for the position but could only accept it once Mr. Roebuck finds new help. But that shouldn't be too difficult, given how popular the store has become, thanks to Victoria."

"Perhaps Emma can bring you my new chapters, Jonathan, and you two can have a chat about her future? That way, all things will be accomplished at once."

"Whatever you ladies wish."

"We don't hear that often enough from gentlemen, do we, ladies?" Alice asked.

Jonathan explained that while his mission to find Victoria had been accomplished, he was also curious about the latest books from Joseph Conrad and Rudyard Kipling. Emma escorted him to the correct shelf but encouraged him to consider Mrs. Chopin too.

Alice turned to Victoria and asked, "Why on earth are you working in a bookshop?"

It was such a blunt question that Victoria felt compelled to answer just as bluntly. "I need the money."

"A successful author like Mrs. Swann shouldn't need a second income."

"I agree, but I was cheated out of my proper royalties for years and my publisher stopped payment altogether these past six months. Also, there's the issue of ownership of my property. My former husband sold it without my consent. I'm trying to get back on my feet."

"A highly published author working as a shopgirl." Alice shook her head. "I must bring you over to Radcliffe to speak to my young ladies about your difficult journey. And where are you living now?"

"With Miss Pennypacker in Back Bay, but I hope to find an apartment soon in North Cambridge."

"Not far from where you used to live, yet a world away." Alice let out a disconcerted sigh. "I'm worried about Brattle Street. It's changing, and not for the better. I try to get along with my new neighbors, but they're remarkably dull. They stick to their own kind, and it makes them tedious. They are constantly making improvements to their compounds and hardly ever venture outside of them. Worst of all, they do not *read*."

"I'm sorry to hear it."

Alice inched closer and Victoria could sense that, though impeccably dressed and strongly built, Miss Longfellow seemed strangely vulnerable.

"Victoria," she asked, "do you think you might consider returning to Brattle Street, if the right opportunity were to arise?"

"I can't imagine what that might be. With housing prices so high, I can't afford to buy at such a fine address any longer."

"But you care for it?"

"For Brattle Street?" Victoria let out a surprised laugh. "I will always love that street."

"That is most fortunate. You see, I am searching for the perfect tenant for the carriage house on my property. I believe that a writer should live there in an honorary residency supported by the estate." Alice lifted her chin and announced, "I see now that you are the woman of letters who should carry on the legacy of my father and his home and all that it stands for. It's a perfect match. Don't you agree?"

It took Victoria a moment to reply, for a strange lightness had come over her, a sensation she recognized from long before, from when she had climbed into her father's apple trees to read. The feeling traveled down her limbs all the way to the tips of her fingers and toes. She knew the satisfaction of working with determination in both writing and in life. But this was different. This, she suspected, must be what it felt like to be genuinely, deeply happy.

THIRTY-NINE

The steps to the Boston Courthouse rose so steeply a lady had to lift her skirts high to avoid tripping as she forged her way up. Considered one of Boston's most assertive structures, the building projected the grand stature the city aspired to as it expanded. In the shadows of massive Greek columns, lawyers milled about in long, elegant waistcoats and top hats, as if ready to dash off at any moment to the opera. Were a woman attorney ever to practice here, she would be forced to wear a full-length gown and tiara to compete in formality with the gentlemen. Victoria caught her breath under the heavy pediment that hung like the furrowed brow of a vengeful god, cowing citizens on the wrong side of the law and warning them of the stern justice they would face inside. That is, if they had the strength to open the mighty doors, as Victoria struggled to do now.

She heard her name and turned to see Penny gliding effortlessly up the steps. Under a billowing black velvet cape, Victoria's friend wore the striking ruby red ensemble she had worn months before when Victoria first laid eyes on her down the hall in the offices of Thames, Royall & Quincy. In contrast, Victoria wore her dull brown wool coat over a plain shopgirl dress, having turned down her friend's offer to borrow clothing, though most of the famed Pennypacker outfits were too outlandish for anyone else. Penny took Victoria by the arm and led her away from the clusters of lawyers in their black robes.

"Are you ready?" she asked.

Victoria patted her carpetbag. "I've got the diary and the ledgers from Dottie, also the testimonials gathered by Alice. I'm grateful for their help."

Penny jabbed the air with her ringed fingers. "We're going to hit him with a one-two punch. By the time I bring him into court next month, the public uproar will be deafening. Have you considered how you're going to deal with the press?"

Before Victoria could answer, she and Penny were set upon by newspapermen, their notebooks held high, and their caps tipped back. They cornered the two women and vied for their attention with questions shouted over one another.

"Mrs. Swann—or should I say Miss Meeks?—can you verify that you are indeed suing your former publisher?"

"What do you hope to get out of Mr. Russell?"

"Is it proper for a lady to appear in court unaccompanied by her husband?"

"Sing a ditty for us, will you, Miss Pennypacker?"

The two women glared at this last reporter.

"I've lodged a serious complaint against Thames, Royall & Quincy," Victoria answered. "On the advice of my lawyer, I cannot share more at this time."

Penny squeezed her elbow in solidarity at that forceful reply.

"Miss Pennypacker, are you involved in the suit as well?"

"I'll be bringing Mr. Russell to court on a different matter. Today, I'm here to support my friend and colleague as she fights for fairness for every lady author, not only herself. Make no mistake, Victoria Meeks is an inspiration to *all* women."

Penny wished the cluster of reporters a good day and helped Victoria escape through the substantial doors into the court-house. Inside the bustling marble hall more lawyers and judges met in small clusters to barter and boast, their chatter not al-together different from that of the fishmongers down by the wharf. Mr. Hector Samuels managed to slip through the throng. He bowed quickly and held open a set of leather-backed doors for the two women and followed them into a courtroom. The din of voices receded, and Victoria released a breath.

She removed her simple hat, and her lawyer helped her off with her coat. While not as rotund as Mr. Roebuck, Hector Samuels was of the same short stature and seemed to run on a similar current of nervous energy. His gestures were unsteady and quick as he situated her in the front row facing a raised desk behind which she assumed a judge would soon preside. Penny kept on her showy cape and spread out her satin skirts on the bench directly behind Victoria. From her carpetbag, Victoria took several thick files and placed them on her lap and waited for the proceedings to begin.

"As this is an arbitration, Miss Meeks," Mr. Samuels said as he sat beside her, "and not a case before a jury, an informal magistrate will be an advisor to both parties. After hearing all the testimony, he will offer a non-binding ruling. Most likely, he'll suggest a resolution on the spot, though if the issues are complex enough, he will follow up with a written recommendation in a timely fashion. The trusted party will serve with the wisdom of a judge to assure that the results are equitable."

"But he isn't a judge?"

"Not technically."

"And either side can disregard his ruling?"

Mr. Samuels waggled his head. "I suppose so, though that would be most unusual."

Victoria didn't like the sound of that. Despite all the bad press against Russell, and the evidence that she and her team had gathered, she still feared that her former publisher held all the cards. He would do as he liked, unless forced by law.

"Have no fear, madam." Her lawyer gave a pat to her hand. "Arbitration is the gold standard in a gentleman's business, such as publishing."

Victoria removed her hand. "Publishing hasn't behaved in a gentlemanly fashion toward me, Mr. Samuels, so why should I believe it will do so now?"

"The fact that your agreements were done by word of honor is how gentlemen prefer it, though it does make our task more difficult today."

"It was Gaustad's way. For a man devoted to print, he didn't like to put things in writing."

Her lawyer frowned. "I'm sure he never imagined it would come to this. But since we have nothing set in stone, so to speak, it is harder to pin down our opponent."

"Not to worry, I have the situation under control." She lifted the folders from her lap.

"What are those?" He pointed at the stack.

"Evidence of my publisher's perfidy."

"But I haven't been informed of what you have there."

"Have no fear." She patted his hand. "Our cause is blessed with many good friends."

Hector Samuels cleared his throat. "I'm not sure what you have in mind, but I shall do my best on your behalf."

"I do appreciate you arranging this arbitration, but I'll take it from here. I'm going to present my own case today."

"What? That isn't done."

"I intend to speak on my own behalf," Victoria reiterated.

"Ladies rarely appear in court, unless on the witness stand, and I don't believe I've heard of one representing herself in Boston."

Her lawyer was about to object further when the opposing side entered with a bustle of activity and raised voices.

"I'm a busy man," shouted Louis Russell as he made his way past the newspapermen on the other side of the swinging leather doors.

He strode up the aisle between the rows of wooden benches and stopped at the front of the room. He wore a conservative morning suit, without flash or flare, which was a departure for him. Victoria assumed it had been chosen to benefit his case, though anyone who had read the broadsides in recent weeks knew that the businessman had ties to gambling, black market trade, and, of course, the infamous former bordello.

"There she is, the blasted scribbler," he grumbled to his lawyer who came along at his heels.

Victoria's eyes met his with unflappable calm.

"Do you have any idea how much you've cost me already?" he demanded. He spotted Miss Pennypacker and offered a perfunctory bow.

"Why, Mr. Russell," Penny said, "you appear ready to pop."

He growled in irritation. "Ladies."

"Good day to you, too, sir," Victoria said.

Russell stepped closer and lowered his voice. "Your poor husband, whom you heartlessly abandoned, revealed everything to me. I know things about you, Mrs. Byrne. Sordid things. *Illegal things.*"

The half-smile faded from Victoria's lips.

"Call it off," Russell said through clenched jaw, "before I ruin what's left of your reputation."

Mr. Samuels jittered beside her, but Victoria remained stock-still. "Unfounded rumors about me abound, but my readers trust me. That's what matters."

"Do they now? They won't mind, then, hearing from someone who knows you intimately."

Russell turned to the back of the room. Seated in the furthest corner, with a modest purse on her lap and a black veil partly covering her face, sat Mrs. Mei-ling Chang. She wore a subdued grey suit and matching suede shoes. Her shiny black hair was swept up in its usual tight bun minus the flashing, sparkling combs.

As Russell sauntered to his seat beside his lawyers, Victoria tried to think, her fingers tapping the files. She had no doubt that he would stop at nothing to win. What if the arbitrator wanted to make an example of her? Raymond had threatened that a husband could report his wife to the police at any time for what she had done. Victoria shuddered as she pictured a bailiff marching her away in handcuffs.

She swiveled to speak to Penny, but her friend was busy signing autographs. Victoria found herself searching for Dottie, who had agreed to make a rare trip out of her home to help her case. Or was Emma here, or Mr. Roebuck? And where on earth was Jonathan? She needed her friends as ballast in the hold. But the thought of them gave her the confidence she needed to be the captain of her own ship.

Victoria knew that her friends would stick by her side, but she worried about the rest of the spectators who were filling the court room to capacity. Some were well-wishers, but some had come to witness the downfall of Mrs. Swann. Her loyal readers were already reeling from the news that the creator of their beloved romance and adventure tales was in fact a writer named Victoria Meeks who had written a controversial newspaper editorial and a new realistic novel. They might turn on her completely if they learned she had more in common with the unlucky character of Daisy than with one of Mrs. Swann's heroines.

The crowd hummed behind her. Mr. Russell sat surrounded by a bevy of well-dressed, slick-haired lawyers tending to him, offering reassurances and flattery. Victoria sat alone with Hector Samuels, who seemed insubstantial and unsure compared to her opponent's robust and high-priced team.

At that moment, the red leather doors swung open simultaneously like those of a saloon, and in stepped a bear of a man. Buckley Johnson, the young author who Victoria had met months before in the lobby of the St. Jerome's gentlemen's club, came striding in, his ten-gallon cowboy hat on his head and his heavy canvas coat sweeping the floor. His Western-style boots clacked on the marble. Being Miss Pennypacker's biggest admirer, he had responded immediately to her request to assist Victoria with her case. Since his arrival from out West, the society pages had reported that the two had been seen at some of Boston's finer establishments.

Victoria was grateful for his help but wished someone had coached him on the appropriate attire for a Boston courtroom. He was the spitting image of a rugged cowboy on the cover of a boy's dime novel as he strode back to his seat. And Penny was the spitting image of a heroine of a girl's dime novel as she welcomed him with her eyelashes fluttering. Taking hold of her hand, he kissed it for a prolonged moment. The report in tomorrow's gossip columns would make the City of Boston swoon.

That's when Victoria noticed the publishing types seated in the gallery—the bookish older gentlemen in tweed with leather patches on their elbows, and the younger gents in scruffy suits.

Jonathan stood amongst them, leaning against the paneled back wall of the crowded room. She wondered how long he had been watching her, for even from a distance, she could sense his gaze. He looked older somehow in his stylish new suit and perfectly chosen cravat. He gave a funny little wave, wiggling a few fingers of his gloved hand, as if conveying a secret signal. With his other hand, he held a top hat that she couldn't imagine he had much use for, though now that he and Perry were such a team, perhaps he would find opportunity to wear it again—given that Perry lived a more gilded life than anyone had suspected.

Jonathan tipped the hat toward her in encouragement. His eyes were bright and hopeful as he wished her good luck across the distance. Perry leaned in beside him and bowed respectfully her way too. The two conferred, their heads close together. Victoria didn't know what they were saying to one another, but something about their interaction struck her. In an instant, she realized what it was—Jonathan was in love. To the discerning eye, there was no mistaking it.

At that moment, a side door at the front of the room opened, and Victoria turned back to see an elderly gentleman shuffling forward. He wore a tweed hunting outfit, jodhpurs, and high sporting boots, another surprising costume for the conservative Bostonian setting. His white hair ruffled wildly like her uncle's after a morning on the windy field beside the sea. The octogenarian hunter leaned on an ivory cane with a silver tip, the handle in the shape of a lion's head. The gentleman himself had leonine features, for in addition to his pale halo and tawny beard, his chest was broad, and his legs scrawny.

Mr. Samuels whispered, "The Honorable James Prescott Abernathy, Dean Emeritus of Harvard Law School."

"I thought you said he wasn't a judge."

"He's not. Not really, though everyone refers to him that way."

The ancient man walked not to the high bench that rose above the room, but to a small table off to the side, one clearly meant for a court stenographer or sketch artist. He folded himself into the chair and set his cane crosswise before him on the table. Facing the two sets of lawyers and their clients, he spoke.

"Welcome, everyone. Mr. Russell, I see that you grace my courtroom yet again. Let's hear what you have to say this time. Defense, the proceedings will begin with you."

Victoria felt surprised by the informality, but also grateful for it. That the arbiter was already familiar with Mr. Russell seemed to suggest he wouldn't be impressed by the bluster and pomposity of the man and his team. Russell's lawyer started by asserting his client's lack of culpability due to his recent arrival at the helm of Thames, Royall & Quincy. Her opponent's line of defense wasn't that she had been given the correct percentage on her royalties all those years, but that Russell himself was not responsible for any errors. Also, other gibberish about how he was selling the company anyway and was already in arrears, his other enterprises in bankruptcy, and he'd recently been the victim of arson, so couldn't possibly pay. This last comment caused Victoria to grip her folders tighter, infuriated by Russell's overarching guilt.

All the while, Hector Samuels took notes on a pad. Victoria could feel a bead of sweat roll down her side under her wool dress and longed for the linen smock she had worn in summer when the wind came off the ocean to tangle her hair. She thought of Edwina, who had lost so much but went on to forge a daring and unusual life, one that made little sense to anyone else but had a logic and purpose all its own. Victoria needed her aunt's courage in this moment.

"And therefore, esteemed sir," Mr. Russell's lawyer concluded, "since there is no written record, no legal document, we ask that all accusations be dropped, so that Mr. Russell's reputation may be restored. He does not deserve to be dragged through the mud by a divorcee with nothing better to do than make life difficult for an important man of business."

Russell shouted out, "Hear, hear," and whipped back his head, nostrils flaring and chest straining against his too-tight suit. With his overall size and strength, he could have snapped Mr. Abernathy like a twig, but the old gentleman seemed unfazed.

The door at the back of the room opened at that moment, and the general hubbub from the marble hall poured inside, along with a wheelchair pushed by a grey-haired woman. A rotund, bald-headed figure slumped under a plaid wool throw in the wicker seat. The elderly man's jowls shook, and his cheeks were every bit as rosy as ever, though his eyes didn't sparkle with joviality, but with something Victoria suspected might be called revenge. As the wheelchair proceeded down the aisle, Frederick Gaustad kept his gaze pinned on Louis Russell.

Mr. Abernathy spoke from his seat at the small table. "Good of you to join us, Frederick."

"I've come to say my piece," Gaustad announced.

"We didn't authorize additional witnesses," Russell said. "This isn't allowed."

"Both sides may present their cases any way they wish," the arbitrator clarified.

Gaustad headed straight for the front of the room, apparently intending to shake hands with the arbitrator. But Mr. Abernathy gestured for him to stop where he was.

"Sorry, Bunny, no preferential treatment for old friends in my court. Everything is above board here." He addressed the room. "While Frederick Gaustad and I have known each other for decades, this personal relationship will have no bearing whatsoever on my decision in this case. Understood?"

Everyone mumbled in agreement, then Gaustad patted his chest several times with an open palm and tapped his wrist with two fingers. These special gestures registered some meaning that only he and the arbitrator knew. Victoria marveled at the mysteries of men, particularly those of an older generation bound together in secret societies the knowledge of which they would carry with them to their graves.

"I've come with crucial testimony to contribute in this unfortunate case."

"All right," Mr. Abernathy said. "Mr. Russell's side concluded. Unless Mr. Samuels objects, we might as well hear from you next."

Victoria's lawyer appeared shocked to be called on but nodded agreeably. "No objection, sir."

Gaustad turned to face the room, and when he spotted Victoria his expression melted.

"My dear girl," he said, "you take me back to the best years of my life. We were such a marvelous team."

"Address the whole court, please," Mr. Abernathy said. "And kindly save your fond remembrances with Miss Meeks for after the proceedings are completed."

"*If* she will speak with me," Gaustad muttered.

Victoria didn't answer, her expression cool and reserved. She intended, after all, to unmask a deceit perpetrated by her former editor. And yet, to see him now, he appeared so weak as to be ineffectual, incapable of any evil. Gaustad lifted his chin and began to speak, his voice far less booming than she remembered. He suffered from palsy and didn't look well. But he had come to offer his opinion and she realized with some surprise that he was here to help her case.

Gaustad carried forth, so accustomed, as he was, to being listened to. "As many of you know, I had the honor of serving as editor-in-chief of Thames, Royall & Quincy Publishers for more than four decades. I'm here now to assert that a publishing house is more than a mere business. It is a noble enterprise whose value is as significant today as it was when Benjamin Franklin extolled the uses of the printing press. Publishing is woven into the fabric of our democracy and protected by our sacrosanct First Amendment."

The arbitrator lifted a liver-spotted hand. "Yes, yes, but get on with it, Bunny."

"So, it is with great regret and utmost sorrow that I have witnessed the esteemed house of Thames, Royall & Quincy fall into the hands of someone who does not grasp its profound and preeminent role in our society."

"Here comes the hot air," Russell said. "This has nothing to do with the case."

Gaustad glowered at him. "But it has everything to do with you, sir. You are not a publisher, but a parasite on the community in which you live. You have no business being in the business of letters. You should go back to the corrupt shipyards and failed countries where your form of trade is acceptable. You do not belong in Boston!"

The crowd leaned forward on the benches while others pressed back against the walls. The most daring shouted aloud their approval, proud of this dinosaur of their kind. The arbitrator appeared sympathetic to his old friend's speech but banged his cane on the desktop anyway and asked for silence.

"That's enough. May I remind you that we're here to settle the conflict between Miss Meeks and Thames, Royall & Quincy. What have you to say about that, Mr. Gaustad?"

Victoria's old editor turned his wicker wheelchair toward her. "My dear." His voice rumbled with affection. "You have grown into the accomplished author that I knew you would become from the first day we met and I discovered your talent."

Victoria's teeth hurt from her tightened jaw.

"Bunny," Mr. Abernathy said with growing impatience, "could you please address the question at hand: was Mrs. Swann, nee Miss Meeks, robbed of her correct royalties or not?"

Gaustad's chin plummeted to his chest. His wrinkled, bald head bobbed up and down in the affirmative. Victoria bit her bottom lip and experienced two conflicting impulses at once: she wanted to hurry over to her former mentor's side and console him and thank him for his honesty. But she also wanted to berate him and demand an explanation. Though what she really wanted was the money owed to her.

"I never studied the ledgers, so I didn't realize our error until near the end of my tenure," Gaustad explained. "I tried to raise the problem with Mr. Russell, who was by then asserting his will as principal owner, but I couldn't get his attention. It seems we hadn't been paying Victoria her proper royalty for some time.

You see, the early Mrs. Swann books were published for one dollar apiece and she received a ten percent royalty, so ten cents per copy sold. But as the price of the novels rose, she continued to receive only ten cents per copy. Her actual payment was no longer ten percent of the net revenue, but a lesser amount. She remained at that flat, unchanging figure, her income never properly reflecting her success. When I discovered the mistake, I should have insisted more vociferously on her behalf, but I didn't, fearing for my job. I am sorry to say, I lacked backbone."

"You admit there were errors made in what the company owed the lady?" Mr. Abernathy pressed.

"I do, and it is regrettable."

"Hold on now." Mr. Russell brushed aside his lawyers. "You can't prove that. No contract exists. There's no telling if she was promised five percent or fifty. She got what she got and that's all there is to it."

"I'm afraid he's right," Gaustad said. "We have no proof of our arrangement. We did it all with a handshake, didn't we? How good we were to one another, so very good."

Victoria's long-time editor's words galled her, but she bit her tongue. There was so much she wanted to say to him about his condescension and lack of respect over the years. How he had belittled her and stripped her of her innate confidence. How he had robbed her of her voice by insisting that she didn't have one without his guidance. But seeing the dampness in his eyes, her heart softened. Gaustad was a man of his time, that is, the past.

"It was how business was done in my day. I wish it could be that way forever at Thames, Royall & Quincy."

"What romantic nonsense." Russell leaned back in his chair, shiny boots stretching forward. "Business is business, though publishers don't accept that fact. How did I ever get myself caught up with such namby-pamby people?"

Victoria could stand it no longer. She lifted the thick folders from her lap. "Excuse me, Mr. Abernathy, sir, may I bring something to your attention?"

The arbitrator's bushy eyebrows rose "I suppose, Miss Meeks, if your lawyer agrees?"

Mr. Samuels let out a nervous titter. "I believe it's not up to me. The lady does as she pleases."

Victoria liked the familiar ring of that phrase and, with her aunt in mind, stood and smiled down at her lawyer. "Thank you, Mr. Samuels." She opened the first folder and brought out a stack of mismatched pages and slips of paper, all in a jumble. "Here are a number of items you may find interesting."

"Come forward, please."

Victoria sensed all eyes on her as she made her way to the small table at the front of the room. She lifted the first page, which appeared to be torn from a notebook.

"This," she began, "is from my diary, dating back to when I was a girl of eighteen. I'm most grateful to my assistant, Dottie Windsor, for preserving some of my early writing. On this page, I describe the financial arrangements promised to me by Mr. Gaustad on behalf of Thames, Royall & Quincy Publishers."

She handed it to Mr. Abernathy who gazed over the rim of his thin gold-rimmed glasses and gave a hum of acknowledgment. She held up a second page, this one lavender in color and, like the previous one, also written in a girl's penmanship, all loops and generous curves.

"And this is a letter I wrote to my aunt Edwina. In it, I boast of the terms promised to me. I mention how kindly Gaustad was, like a trusted uncle."

She spoke pointedly, so the courtroom might register the irony. Her former editor slipped lower in his wheelchair, as if struck by the arrow of her words.

"And finally," she continued, "in this note, written some years later, Mr. Gaustad himself confirms those percentages by saying, and I quote: 'We are honored to continue our relationship with you according to our long-standing agreement of ten percent.'"

The court erupted and Mr. Abernathy slapped his cane on the desk until they settled down.

"Well, that's significant. I'd say it concludes the case. You weren't paid the ten percent royalty you were owed. I'll make a ruling after studying the ledgers. Thank you, madam."

But Victoria spoke again. "That's not all. I have more to say. Much more."

FORTY

Victoria held up another folder thick with papers. After a moment, the audience took notice and grew quiet. "May I continue?" she asked.

"What's this, more charming diary entries?" Mr. Abernathy's abundant sandy beard shook with amusement. "I believe you made your point, and in time for lunch. Well done."

"But I'd like you to consider an additional aspect of our case," Victoria pressed, her smile evaporating.

"More?" The old arbitrator fell back in his seat. "All right, if you must. Please, continue."

"This is a letter dated six months ago from Mr. Louis Russell to the Henry Wadsworth Longfellow Trust promising them an exorbitant sum of two thousand dollars for the esteemed poet's final work. Mr. Russell purchased it and intended for Thames, Royall & Quincy to publish it, but never did."

Russell sat forward, his legs no longer splayed confidently. "How the devil did you get that?"

"Alice Longfellow, the poet's daughter and executrix, wishes for this to be entered into the public record as proof that Mr. Russell did not act in good faith when he agreed to purchase the poem. He gave her a deposit, but never paid the full amount. He owes her that money. She intends to seek it in court."

"That's no business of yours," Russell said.

"What interests me," Victoria continued, "is that he made his arrangement with the Longfellow Trust when he anticipated Mrs. Swann's next book. When I withdrew that novel, he couldn't afford the price he had negotiated for the poem. Thames, Royall & Quincy couldn't pay other authors as well without my books. I think the court would benefit by hearing from a successful young writer, Mr. Buckley Johnson, on the subject."

"Is Mr. Johnson here?" the arbitrator asked.

"You bet I am." Buck rose from his seat and swaggered to the front of the room.

"This fellow here? You're sure he isn't an actor of some sort? Or a rodeo hand?" The octogenarian chuckled to himself.

"No, sir, I'm a writer." Buck removed his large cowboy hat. "Nice to meet you, Judge."

"Hello, young man. Would you like to take a seat?"

Buck waved his hat at the elderly arbitrator. "I prefer to stretch my legs, if you don't mind."

"Certainly. Now, Mr. Johnson, Miss Meeks and her lawyer seem to think you can shed light on her arrangements with Thames, Royall & Quincy. Tell us what you know."

"Honestly, I'm no businessman, but I do know a few things about books."

Victoria, who had moved to the side, interjected, "It should be noted that Mr. Buckley Johnson is a much-respected author. *He* is the voice of America today."

On the far side of the room, the short grey-haired Theodore Upchurch smiled to himself, not grasping the irony in Victoria's tone. Mr. Abernathy seemed impressed by the introduction and gestured for the strapping young author to continue.

"Everyone published by Thames, Royall & Quincy knew that Mrs. Swann's big sales made possible the publication of less popular novels like mine. That's not news. It bolstered the house's reputation, and Gaustad's own I might add, to publish more literary works, but hers were their bread and butter."

Gaustad made a sound in agreement and wiped his chin.

Buck continued, "My own next novel is a casualty of her departure from the house. Mr. Russell couldn't pay me without her. So, you see, I have a stake in this."

"I see that you do. Anything else?"

"What's less obvious," Buck said as he continued to shift his hat from hand to hand, warming to his subject, "is that Gaustad knew he was underpaying her, though she was making the house rich. I distinctly remember one time," Buck used his hat to point at the crumpled figure in the wheelchair, "when he had one too many schnapps and boasted that Stephen Crane's best book, or the one readers like the best—personally, I prefer *The Little Regiment*—was being published because they were taking advantage of Mrs. Swann's profits. He *liked* the arrangement. We all did. But now that I know she was being paid only ten percent and a newcomer like me was getting fifteen, well, that's plain not right."

"Thank you, Mr. Johnson." Mr. Abernathy ran a quaking hand through his leonine hair.

Buck made his way back to Penny, who greeted him with her gloved hands clapping softly. Victoria stepped forward.

"Mr. Abernathy, as Mr. Gaustad has admitted, my payment per book remained stuck at a mere ten cents per copy. But I also wish to draw your attention to the letters that my friend Alice Longfellow has obtained from the widows and daughters of respected gentlemen authors. You'll see that they show that those men routinely received a much higher royalty than my ten percent. They were given anywhere from fifteen to forty."

"Why, Victoria, I'm shocked," Gaustad said. "You know such matters are private in a gentleman's business."

"It worked in my editor's favor that our arrangement was private too." She turned to Mr. Abernathy, whose eyes had widened on hearing her argument. "As you consider the written testimony I submit here, I think you'll see the unfair nature of such business practices. They were far from gentlemanly."

Victoria let the heavy stack of folders drop onto the small table with a thud. The old magistrate didn't pick them up or examine them, but gently ran the tips of his arthritic fingers over them, as if they were sticks of dynamite. To a man, the courtroom frowned at her, with the exception of Jonathan and Perry, who were beaming with pride at their most modern author.

"What a preposterous claim," Gaustad said. "We paid what we felt the esteemed gentleman authors deserved. It was a mutual agreement. Man to man. Perfectly acceptable. Not one bit out of the ordinary." He turned to Mr. Abernathy. "The authors I published are of profound importance in the American canon. I believe I speak for all educated people when I say that the literary significance of those men of letters are unparalleled in our country's history. Thames, Royall & Quincy would have done anything to see their works published."

"Including cheating your other authors?" Victoria rummaged in her folders and brought out a ledger written in Dottie's best hand. "Ah, here it is," she said, ignoring the arbitrator's sigh. "May I call one more witness crucial to my case, sir?" Mr. Abernathy agreed wearily. "I believe my former secretary Mrs. Dottie Windsor is here?"

Everyone waited for this important person to identify herself. With a gasp, the crowd watched the woman push herself up to standing, her hand on her back and her enormous belly protruding. Gentlemen averted their eyes—an expectant mother simply did not go into society in such a florid state. Several nearby offered her a hand, but she made her own way, waddling and puffing, but with a determined expression, clearly intent on being of service to Victoria.

"Are you all right, madam? Please take my seat," Mr. Abernathy offered.

Dottie thanked him, but instead settled into a chair that Victoria had pulled out for her.

"Hello, Dottie. Thank you for coming."

"You're welcome, Victoria. I wouldn't miss it for the world."

"Can we get you anything?"

"No, I'm fine. Happy to be out and about, though getting up those front steps was a chore."

"Indeed," Victoria said.

The spectators let out a breath, relieved that the woman wasn't going to burst like a ripe melon right there in the courtroom.

"Now, will you please take a look at the ledgers you're so familiar with and also the summary of accounts that you compiled for this case and tell us what they convey?"

Dottie took the legers and gave them a glance. "Anyone can see that the sum totals of the books sold by Mrs. Swann, plus the dime novel pamphlets, and the advice columns are staggering. Absolutely staggering."

"Excellent. And how much did I receive for them?"

"Far less than you deserved!"

The room exploded at that declaration Victoria spoke over the noise. "And why do you say that?"

Dottie's already ruddy face grew redder. "Anyone can see that the percentages are, as Mr. Gaustad suggested, paltry. And now we know he did nothing to correct it. Makes me hopping mad to think of it."

Mr. Abernathy banged his cane on the table once again to control the room.

"I'm corroborating Mr. Buck," Dottie continued. "But I also want to make it perfectly clear that when a style of dress is in demand, the price for it rises, because people are willing to pay more for it. You should have been paid more because your books were loved more than others. I have the numbers here to prove it."

Russell, who had sat uncharacteristically quiet as he watched with intense curiosity, slapped his boots on the marble and stood. "I'll be damned." He tucked his jeweled fingers into his vest pockets. "Finally, someone who understands business. Supply and demand. I told you that books are no different from sacks of flour or bottles of ale. If you have a bestseller like Mrs. Swann, you pay her more." He shook his head at Gaustad. "Ridiculous to treat the worst sellers in such high regard and ignore the most successful ones. It makes no sense."

His lawyer tried to pull him back to his seat and whispered, "You're not on the lady's side, you know."

"But these people," Russell said, waving at the old editor and the room of publishing professionals, "they're the ones talking like ladies. They whisper about private agreements and a business based on sentiment and flimsy notions of posterity. What matters is the marketplace right now, right here in Boston and all across America. Miss Meeks and her assistant have got it right. Why, they sound more like men than these nancy fellows. Good for you, ladies. Good for you!"

Russell's lawyer succeeded in making him sit down and he pulled out his pocket watch, as if he had elsewhere to be and didn't care how it all came out. Victoria imagined that he was already onto the next enterprise he would ransack with a clear conscience. Yet, she also worried he had more up his sleeve. Was he pretending to rally on her behalf so he might attack her when she least expected it? Mrs. Chang remained in the back of the court room. Why was she here? Victoria shook her head to dismiss the thought and thanked Dottie. Her husband Fletcher came forward to escort her to her seat.

Mr. Abernathy patted the stack of folders. "I must admit, you make an interesting argument, Miss Meeks. It seems you were treated unfairly in several different ways." He asked his long-time friend if had any further reply for the lady.

"I remain shocked at this accusation. I had thought she was rather grateful to me."

"But is it true what she says?" the old arbiter asked. "Thames, Royall & Quincy underpaid her in order to finance higher royalties for your gentlemen authors?"

"I suppose *technically*, but you can't compare her efforts to those books."

Victoria was about to counter this argument, when a high, clear voice came from the third row behind her. The courtroom turned to see an exceedingly pretty young woman stand and speak. Victoria beamed on seeing her familiar face. There was no mistaking the quality of the lady's deep rose-colored shirtwaist with impeccable detailing in velvet and pearl, worn over a slim gored skirt in peppermint stripes, and accented by a jaunty hat covered in tulle and feathers. She was the picture of a romantic. And while Victoria wasn't that way herself any longer, she felt wistful at the sight of a woman so pleased with herself and her many lovely things, especially knowing that she was a devoted friend of Mrs. Swann.

"Excuse me, I'd like to introduce myself," the pretty young woman spoke up. "I'm Mrs. Harrison Sturgis and I am the president of the local chapter of the Mrs. Swann Appreciation Society, one of fifty-seven chapters all across the country."

"Is that so?" Mr. Abernathy asked.

"Yes, and I brought my ladies with me."

She extended a pink-gloved hand toward the rows of women seated on all sides. Victoria had never seen such a bevy of beautiful outfits, the hats cascading with finery, the matching fans, the silk scarfs, all of it worn by ladies who lifted their chins and widened their eyes, eager to offer their support. On the edge of their seats, they resembled a sporting team hungry to take the field.

"Impressive," the arbitrator said.

"We are, actually, and we're here to vouch for Mrs. Swann, who is every bit as important to the education of young women as any writer who's ever written. Plus, she's a lot more fun than most. There's no reason why she shouldn't be paid as well as other authors. We, like so many readers, love her stories a great deal."

Gaustad appeared both pleased and alarmed at this outpouring and gripped his blanket tighter. Mrs. Sturgis turned to him, her brow knitted. "Did you really pay all your women authors less?" she asked.

"To our credit," he replied, trying to rally some confidence, "I believe Margaret Fuller and several other serious lady authors were paid respectable percentages equal to their male peers."

"Oh, her," Missy said. "I'd take Mrs. Swann over her any day."

The crowd erupted, everyone with his or her own opinion. The most vocal of all were the ladies who waved their copies of Mrs. Swann's books in the air. When the courtroom quieted down, Mr. Abernathy put his head in his hands, elbows on the table, and rubbed his temples.

"This has evolved into a most unusual conversation. In fact, I don't recall ever having this conversation before. Never has a woman spoken up so forcefully, backed by evidence, and with such a grave complaint. I believe that Mr. Gaustad and the house of Thames, Royall & Quincy thought they were doing you a favor all those years by publishing you, madam. It may be time for them to repay you for the favor that you, in fact, were doing for them."

Hearing this, Russell shot up from his chair, too quick for his lawyers to grab him. "Hold on." He strode forward. "There is no way you're blaming this on me. It's not my fault there was a discrepancy all those years."

"Take a seat, Mr. Russell," Mr. Abernathy said.

But he didn't sit. He faced off against Victoria, the two mismatched opponents practically toe to toe before the quiet courtroom. Spectators teetered forward on their seats and others pulled in air through open mouths. No one could miss the fact that she was so much smaller than he—her petite, thin-boned frame contrasting with the powerful hulk of the man.

Victoria looked up at him with her piercing dark eyes. "Mr. Russell, you're the owner of Thames, Royall & Quincy, are you not?"

"I am, but we're in bankruptcy. You can't touch me."

"But you also own 127 Brattle Street, I believe. I propose we exchange my back royalties for that charming home that you've let go to wrack and ruin, and which," she paused for effect, "was once *mine*."

People gasped and more mumbling ensued, but the arbitrator held up his hand for quiet.

"What's this? Are you two coming to an agreement? That's perfectly all right if you are, but you must inform me."

Neither Victoria nor Russell acknowledged him. Their eyes stayed locked on one another.

"I don't barter, Miss Meeks. And I don't lose. I want to call one more witness."

"Now?" Mr. Abernathy asked plaintively. "I thought we were finished."

"Mrs. Chang," Russell bellowed, "it's time!"

Victoria felt her pulse careen as she and the rest of the crowd turned to the elegant woman who sat unmoving in the back row. That's when Victoria noticed that Dottie had seated herself right next to Mrs. Chang and was quietly speaking with her. Victoria thought she saw Mrs. Chang move her head in reply. Some agreement had been made between them, though she had no idea what it might be. Several seats away, Emma practically bounced in place. She made the strangest faces, and it took a moment for Victoria to grasp that the girl was mouthing something, though what or why, she couldn't say.

"Mrs. Chang!" Russell bellowed again.

But the elderly woman continued to sit motionless as the courtroom leaned in her direction and waited.

From her seat, Dottie spoke up. "Mr. Abernathy, sir, this nice lady has told me she had a stroke not long ago. Given her infirmity, she would rather not testify."

"Totally understandable," the arbitrator said. "Thank you, Mrs. Windsor." He turned to Russell. "Enough of this nonsense. Your side had plenty of time. We're not a court and you have no right to subpoena anyone. Also, I don't like you harassing elderly people. We must be treated with respect." Mr. Abernathy made an effort to raise his voice, though it warbled with age as he spoke across the room to Mrs. Chang, "Forgive us, madam. No need to trouble you."

"But I was going to prove that this woman here," Russell shouted, pointing at Victoria with his diamond ringed fingers, "did disreputable things. *Criminal things.* Her latest novel centers around a crime that she herself committed." He faced her. "You, madam, are no lady!"

Victoria did not raise her voice. "Mr. Russell, don't you think this crowd of publishing professionals knows the difference between fact and fiction? I'm flattered that you were so fooled by my craft, but you really mustn't believe what you read in books."

"But you're lying. I know the truth about you. Like your

character, you visited a back alley and underwent an illegal procedure!"

The room grew instantly quiet. All eyes turned from him to her. Victoria swallowed and prepared to answer. This was the moment she had most anticipated and feared. The time had come for her to share the truth, the whole truth. Her career of creating heroines would come to an abrupt halt as everyone understood that she was no heroine herself. They had all but pieced it together. Her editorial to the newspaper arguing for the general rights of women, and specifically the downtrodden and mistreated young immigrants, had convinced many that Victoria's life was every bit as sordid as those she advocated for. But now, she would be forced to reveal how very true that was. A fine lady living on Brattle Street was as without options in life or recourse under the law as a waif living on the wharf. Victoria opened her mouth to finally tell fact from fiction.

But Mr. Abernathy leaned over the little table and pushed himself to stand. He lifted his cane and pointed it at Louis Russell. "You, sir," he shouted as forcefully as he could, "have gone too far. I've never heard such vile words spoken in a civilized setting. You have no business accusing this woman of something so heinous and unrelated to the current case. It isn't our right to meddle in her affairs, whatever they may be. She is a creator of fictions, and I gather, rather good ones at that. Gaustad was correct about you. You, sir, are no gentleman!"

Louis Russell stumbled back a few steps. For an instant, he seemed to shrink, as if the sharp silver tip of Abernathy's cane had burst the shiny balloon of his ego. He pulled out a handkerchief and swiped at his brow.

The ancient arbitrator turned to Victoria. "Miss Meeks, I offer you a public apology on behalf of these proceedings. I let things get out of hand. Your reputation remains intact as the lies spoken by this man are clearly spewed out of desperation. I believe that you are an artist, and as such, you may write whatever you like. You have succeeded at it so spectacularly that your readers, including Mr. Russell, have been fooled into believing the worlds you create are real. Bully for you, madam. Bully for you."

Voices from the crowd shouted, "Hear, hear."

"I encourage you to continue to do so, as I gather you bring pleasure and insight to those who enjoy your books. Reality, as the great bard himself said, is but a thin veil and all this," he waved his cane randomly at the room, "is the stuff of dreams. We count on writers like you to illuminate for us the difference. Now, if you'll excuse me, it's time for lunch."

Victoria bowed her head. "Thank you, sir."

He gathered up the folders and clutched them to his side. "I will send my opinion via post. Thank you, Miss Meeks, Mr. Russell, Mr. Gaustad, Mrs. Windsor, Mr. Buckley, Mrs. Sturgis, and lawyers. Good day to you all."

With some effort, he hobbled off in the direction of the side door, leaning more heavily on his cane than when he first arrived. Gaustad rolled his wheelchair forward, but Abernathy waved him away.

"No, Bunny, don't offer to buy me a drink at the club. This is a serious matter and I intend to take it seriously."

In that moment, the esteemed gentleman in the sporting outfit reminded Victoria of her plainspoken uncle Homer, who, though sometimes aloof, was always decent and fair. Mr. Russell loomed over his lawyers at their table, throwing up his hands and berating them. He brushed off their protestations and strode through the crowd and out of the courtroom. Reporters latched on to him in the hallway and Victoria could hear him shouting for them to leave him alone.

She realized that she, too, would be accosted by well-wishers or detractors, but first, she went to greet Gaustad, who had sunk lower in his seat and watched her with sorrowful eyes. She approached and held out her hands so that he might feebly shake them.

"Miss Meeks." He winced, as if pained to say her original name.

"Mr. Gaustad. I hope you're well."

"I am. And you?"

"Quite well, thank you."

Victoria smiled but had nothing more to say. They wanted to care for one another, but the possibility of that had passed. Mrs. Gaustad appeared and took hold of his wheelchair. She explained that Bunny had had enough for one day. It was time to get him home.

After they were gone, Victoria's lawyer approached and, for once, he didn't seem nervous.

"Fine job, Victoria. Highly unorthodox, but I think you made a case for yourself."

"Thank you, Mr. Samuels."

"If you think it appropriate, I'll follow up with Mr. Abernathy about 127 Brattle. I can let him know the background on the property and how Mr. Russell came to own it. Given the bankruptcy issues with Russell's various entities, a barter of the house is exactly the sort of arrangement an arbitrator might consider an agreeable compromise."

"Wonderful." Victoria thanked him before he headed out of the room.

She would soon brave the crowd herself but first took in the sight of Penny and Buck engaged in banter with Jonathan and Perry. As the crowd continued to stream out of the courtroom, Mrs. Sturgis and the other well-dressed ladies lined up along the side wall and waited patiently for Mrs. Swann to sign their copies of her books. Victoria spotted Mrs. Chang slipping out the doors, her back hunched and her palsied arm held close to her side with one leg dragging. Emma came up the aisle and Dottie pulled in like an ocean liner returning to port.

"Congratulations," Emma said, "you were terrific."

"I couldn't have done it without Dottie."

"I think we put him to shame," Dottie said. "But unfortunate the mention of that other business. The arbitrator did right, though, thank goodness."

Victoria made herself look her former assistant in the eye but was relieved to see that Dottie didn't appear perturbed or angry. Did she know it was true? Something in her expression seemed to suggest it didn't matter one way or another. She was, undeniably, a friend.

"Mr. Abernathy was our most unlikely knight in shining armor yet," Victoria said.

"Oh, I don't know, they were all pretty unlikely, weren't they?" Dottie said and the two shared a smile.

"And Mrs. Chang did her part too," Emma said.

"I expected the worst," Victoria said.

"We introduced ourselves while waiting for the proceedings to begin and were about to appeal to her sense of fairness," Emma said, "but it turned out we didn't need to. Mr. Russell had made off with her insurance money after the fire. She intends to bring him to court soon too."

"The man has a great deal of enemies."

Emma stepped away to catch up with her new bosses as they left the courtroom with everyone else. Jonathan paused at the door and turned back to bow in Victoria's direction. The top hat in his hand swept the floor as he made an elaborate show of congratulating her. Victoria waved goodbye and knew they'd see each other soon to go over her latest manuscript.

She stood alone at the front of the room for a moment before diving in and greeting the line of ladies who had been waiting for her. Taking the seat vacated by Mr. Abernathy, she motioned for Missy Sturgis to come forward.

"How wonderful to see you," Victoria said and took Missy's kid gloves into her own and gave her hands a vigorous shake. "I'm so grateful to you and your ladies."

"We're the grateful ones. When I first met you, I didn't know a soul in this town, but thanks to Mrs. Swann I've made many fine friends. Without her, or rather you, we might never have found one another." She glanced over her shoulder at her companions.

"Friends do make all the difference." Victoria finished her autograph on Missy's copy of her book with a flourish.

The next lady stepped forward and the one after that and the one after that. Victoria chatted with each one, thanking them for coming to support her. She wrote the name of Mrs. Swann repeatedly, and with each signature she sensed how finished she was with this chapter of her life. If the Brattle Street house was gone for good, she might move up to Blaine. There was no telling what would come next for her. The one thing for certain was that there would be visions and revisions in her life and on the page.

Closing the last of the Mrs. Swann books, she put the cap back on her pen. It was then that a shadow crossed the desk and she looked up to see Lance Maverick standing before her. He had made his way steadily from the back of the room, and before that, from across the seas on his return to Boston.

"Brilliantly done. You were magnificent."

She rose and thanked him for coming.

"But what a great deal you've been through." He dipped his handsome silver head closer. "But really, what I want to know is, *how are you*, my dear lady?"

Such a simple question opened so much between two people. His clear grey eyes took her in with interest, inviting her to reply in any way that she liked. What a pleasure it would be to tell her own true story to such a sympathetic ear. She took his arm and they ventured out into the city together.

FORTY-ONE

Snow fell on Christmas to the delight of the children of Cambridge and Boston, a thought that warmed Victoria more than the paltry heat in her rooms on the second floor of the Longfellow carriage house. All day, it had cascaded out her window and covered the ground below. Alice's father had planned the garden in an Italian Renaissance style, with a central rose window-shaped flowerbed and a labyrinth of low boxwoods lining the paths. In spring and summer, the beds overflowed with irises, peonies, dahlias, and roses. Fragrant fruit trees and wisteria vines draped along the trellises. There could hardly be a more inspiring setting for writing than this one.

Victoria's desk in the carriage house had the best view, a different landscape from the vast Atlantic Ocean off Maine, but no less stirring. But knowing that America's most renowned gentlemen of letters had once strolled these paths, engaged in conversation or solitary contemplation, had been enough to make her stop writing altogether. Since moving in, she had put down her pen and been good for nothing. All she could do was gaze out the window and let the heavy weight of literary history smother her like the snow blanketing everything now.

At dusk, a light turned on across the way in the Longfellow manse and a fan of gold spread over the snowy yard. Alice was expecting Victoria soon for sherry and conversation. Her landlady had been more than generous, extending invitations and folding her into her extended flock of friends who constituted the literary and progressive heart of Cambridge. These were the people Victoria had longed to know and yet had been afraid to know. As it turned out, they weren't so terribly intimidating. The gentlemen were respected scholars in their fields, though, truth be told, they tended to go on a bit long. Their wives were also exceedingly clever and weren't afraid to show it, which could be a little wearying too. But in general, Victoria liked them and they, to her surprise, seemed to like her. The night before, she and Lance had been welcomed into the neighborhood's grand holiday tradition: the Longfellow Christmas Eve supper.

Victoria leaned back in her chair and recalled the long table covered in an elegant jacquard cloth with silver place settings and cut-crystal wine glasses. Guests of all ages enjoyed a feast of oyster stew, halibut, mutton, ham, yams, turnips, and English plum pudding, seasoned with quince, rosemary, or sage; and not to mention the steaming baked beans that could only be loved in Boston. The sweet taste of Belgian chocolates lingered on her tongue even now at the memory. Never in her life had Victoria enjoyed such a delicious meal or such fine company, Lance's in particular.

He was not only worldly, but charming. Late in the evening, he had pulled her under the mistletoe that hung from the parlor threshold, popped a peppermint into his mouth, and brought his lips to hers, right there in front of everyone, though by then the other guests were too sated and lubricated to care. The mint startled her with its sweetness and his hand on the small of her back anchored her in just the right way. What a man! Almost too good to be true.

Victoria turned back to the blank page before her and fiddled with the cap of her pen. The fire had died in the grate, and she wanted to hop up to add more coal but made herself stay in her seat. It was time to write. Past time to write. But she doodled in the margins of her notebook instead, making crossed lines that led nowhere. It bothered her inordinately that she hadn't heard from Jonathan about *The Boston Shopgirl*. He must have read it by now, despite the holiday. If so, why hadn't he told her his impressions? The only explanation was that he hadn't liked it.

Victoria reached across the desk and yanked the curtains closed. Noting the time, she rose and hurried to dress. Alice was always impeccably attired, though she never commented on anything so frivolous as lady's fashion, which only made Victoria more nervous about what to wear. Her host preferred purposeful topics and determined initiatives. Alice would inform Victoria about the expanded programs at the Cambridge Neighborhood House, where new immigrants took free classes in the fine arts, domestic science, cooking, woodworking, dressmaking, and, of course, literacy. Victoria was interested in volunteering in their library, but not if she couldn't get herself properly dressed and out the door. She threw down not one, but two, and finally three ensembles, none of which were right. Letting out an irritated cry, she felt as vain as a schoolgirl, though not nearly as clever.

How had she composed so happily in Mr. Roebuck's storage room, while here on the hallowed grounds of America's greatest poet, her pen went dry and her thoughts withered? It made her wonder if the good owner of the Cambridge Bookshop might allow her to return to his closet from time to time so she could eke out another book.

Victoria adjusted her emerald silk turban, a rare, recent indulgence, pulled on her heavy boots, and started down the carriage house steps on her way to the Longfellow manor. The nighttime storm buffeted and shocked her with its fury. She considered turning back, but kicked on through the falling snow, down the long driveway, and up the formal front walk. At the top of the short set of stairs between dormant lilac bushes, their delicate limbs bent low with their burden, she paused, noticing the light streaming down from a second-story window.

Not many months before, she had imagined Martha Washington weeping there at the sill. Lonely and alone, as Victoria had been all her years on Brattle Street, the future First Lady had longed for company and a positive outcome. Though as easily, Victoria thought now, she might have been laughing or singing a tune, for Martha Washington and her husband must have been optimists. They believed they could overcome any obstacle in pursuit of a goal of their own choosing. Following their dreams guaranteed them happiness of a sort no matter the outcome. For happiness was in the striving. A simple truth Victoria knew now for herself.

She tipped back her head and watched singular, wet flakes tossed about on the wind. Caught in a maelstrom, the cold encircled her and wrapped her in its embrace. She had last felt the surge of nature's power when living by the sea. The ecstatic air filled her lungs as something high in the night sky called down to her, urging her to lift herself up to meet it. She rose in her soggy boots and balanced on her tiptoes, as if teetering on the brink of a precipice. She longed to let go and fall into that peaceful deluge that would catch her and carry her and bring her to safety.

As the snowfall gusted around her, she considered her imperfect life, the one created over many years and undone in a matter of months. If there was a cliff from which to fall, she supposed it had already happened. The windblown snow flecked her cheeks and burned cold, as the storm brought her back to the farm on nights like this one, when the windowpanes rattled and the rising drifts pressed against the door. Many times, she had pushed it open anyway and trudged to check on the animals in the barn. Were they warm enough, were they hungry, were they frightened? No wind, or cold, or icy storms could stop that small heroine as she cared for the ones she loved. It was nothing special to be fearless and intrepid, nothing at all. Every woman knew it to be true of herself. Every woman was valiant in her own way.

Victoria began her trek again through the snow. After her visit with Alice, she would return to her new lodgings and to her desk, ready to use paper and pen to tell just such a story.

Swags of holiday greens framed the wide front door and hung over the fluted crown cornice. Victoria lifted the brass knocker in the shape of a hand and banged it. Alice flung open the door and welcomed her in, the maid and butler having been given the day off after the party the night before.

"Merry Christmas! But you must use the side entrance from now on. It'll be more convenient, especially in bad weather. Come and go as you please. Everyone does."

Victoria thanked Alice and wished her a merry Christmas too. In the front hall, she brushed snow from her coat and her new hat, which Alice took from her and placed over the heating grate to dry.

"Come, warm yourself by the fire. We'll take our sherry in Father's study. The flue in the parlor is stuck again and would smoke up the place. This blasted old house." She gave a shake of her head.

Alice often complained about her home, though it was clear that she loved it. In all seasons, the Longfellow house was uniquely grand, but especially at Christmastime when holly swags and ropes of pine hung above the doorways and over the windows in all the main rooms. A mammoth Christmas tree infused the air with the scent of New England's out-of-doors, bringing Victoria back to the Maine countryside. Small white candles in brass holders dotted the boughs. They had been lit for the party and had spread a warm glow over the tinsel and stringed cranberries. The effect was nothing short of magical.

Victoria followed her host into the study where dark green interior shutters and maroon velvet drapes remained closed against the storm. When Alice left to retrieve the sherry, Victoria took in the writing room of Henry Wadsworth Longfellow. She ran her hand over his heavy walnut desk and peered into its many cubbyholes. Behind the blown glass of the floor-to-ceiling bookcases his leather-backed volumes lined the shelves, many in German, French, and Italian.

Three white plaster busts looked down from high pedestals at the blotter where Longfellow wrote, assessing his every word. Imagine that—having Shakespeare, Dante, and Goethe leering at you as you tried to compose. Would it inspire a writer, or intimidate her? If Longfellow could write in such company, Victoria decided she could manage with the literary ghosts in the garden below her window. Besides, at least in the carriage house, she could pull the curtains closed.

Alice returned with sherry glasses and a crystal carafe on a silver tray. She set them down on the round cherry wood table at the center of the room.

"Several letters have arrived for you in recent days. I meant to give them to you last night, but with all the activity and children dashing about, I'm afraid I forgot." Alice handed over the envelopes and began to pour.

Victoria noticed that the return address on one was from her lawyer. "Do you mind?" she asked, holding it up.

"Please, go ahead. I'm all talked out from last night. Help yourself to Father's letter opener there on the desk."

Victoria reached for the thin ivory-handled knife and tried not to feel too overwhelmed by its import. Longfellow may have used it to open letters from Dickens, Tennyson, and Queen Victoria herself. The sharp side of the blade cut the first envelope and she scanned Hector Samuels' handwritten note. He explained that the arbitrator's decision was as he had anticipated, but she shouldn't lose heart, as the battle over the ownership of her Brattle Street home appeared promising. With some complex legal pressure, aided by Mr. Abernathy himself, Hector Samuels felt confident of a positive outcome in the new year.

Lifted by this news, Victoria was eager to learn how the arbitrator had ruled on the principles of the case. Had she been vindicated or not? After several pages of legal terms, the mention of rights and responsibilities, fault and ownership, she got to what Louis Russell might have called the bottom line: five hundred dollars. Thames, Royall & Quincy Publishers, Ltd., would pay her five hundred dollars and that was all. Victoria slapped the letter against her skirt.

"What is it?" Alice asked.

"The judgment from the arbitrator is that I will be paid far, far less than what I'm owed. It's an outrage. I should have received many times more. Damn them!" Victoria rose and started to pace. "I'm sorry for my language, but truly, damn them!"

"I speak that way myself when circumstances require it."

"All those years, they made off with what was mine. How do they get away with it?"

"*They*," Alice said as she sat in her father's favorite reading chair, "do it all the time. Is it really such a shock? Come, sit. Drink your sherry." She gestured to the seat opposite hers before the fire.

Victoria sat and took a sip but could barely keep still.

"You've laid the groundwork for future women." Alice tipped her delicate glass in a ladylike salute. "Consider that a victory and not a small one."

"I don't consider any part of this a victory." Victoria set down her sherry.

"Nonetheless, you'll be an inspiration to the young ladies in the offices and factories and sweatshops."

"I've never thought of myself as an inspiration to anyone."

"None of us thinks of ourselves that way, but we can be to one another."

Alice rose and went in search of the holiday cookies, saying she hoped Victoria would help her finish them off, otherwise she'd become stouter than she already was. Alone in Longfellow's study for the second time, Victoria lifted the second envelope and was happy to see Edwina's familiar penmanship. How perfect to hear in this moment from her strong and seemingly invincible aunt, who had managed to hold her own in the world of men on both land and sea. Victoria tore it open, dispensing with the bothersome letter opener.

Since moving back to Blaine, Edwina had written often about her life at the general store. She filled her letters with entertaining anecdotes about the eccentric fishermen and her husband, who was the endless brunt of her good-natured teasing. Homer usually provided a contradictory and friendly postscript. He never wrote more than a sentence or two, but his additions made Victoria miss her aunt and uncle even more.

She unfolded the letter and filled her lungs with the piney scent of the Christmas tree from the next room, helping to transport her back to the Maine seaside. But on reading the first sentence, Victoria's heart clenched up and her eyes began to well. She let out a cry, followed by a sob, and pressed the page to her chest.

Alice hurried back into the room. "What is it, my dear?"

Victoria shook the letter high in the air and released the word, "*No!*" into the room. It swept through the quiet study, twisting in the heavy drapes, sliding over the deeply hued carpet, slipping around each leather-backed volume, and grazing the busts that gazed down impassively on her sorrow. She had mistaken this house for one that knew only high literary sentiments and joyful family occasions. But this was also the home, and perhaps the very room, in which Longfellow's wife had accidentally set herself on fire. Sealing wax had dripped onto Fanny's dress and the flames had ignited and taken hold. The poet awoke from a nap and raced to try to rescue his beloved by wrapping her in a small antique rug, like the one that lay by the door to the dining room. He had risked his life trying to save hers. Yet despite his heroism, his efforts weren't enough. Two days later, after hours of tortuous pain, she succumbed, leaving the poet to raise their five children alone. Longfellow grew a long grey beard to cover the burn scars on his neck and torso. He never shaved it off but kept it as a constant reminder of the grief he could not escape in his lifetime.

"My uncle," Victoria spoke in a croaking whisper, "has gone on to a better world. His heart gave out while he was lifting a sack of potatoes onto a shelf."

"I'm so sorry." Alice came and rested a gentle hand on her shoulder. "What a terrible loss."

"My poor aunt." Victoria's tears began to flow. "She had only recently moved into the apartment above the store. He was so happy to have her home after her years at sea."

Alice appeared a little puzzled at this explanation of the family's arrangements but continued to stand beside Victoria and handed her a fresh handkerchief.

"But I imagine he wasn't a young man?" she asked.

"No, not young."

"He had a good, long life?"

"Yes, good and long. He was such a decent man."

"I'm sure he was."

The two stared dejectedly into the fire that crackled and burned.

"Take to heart what Father once wrote," Alice offered. "'The grave itself is but a covered bridge, leading from light to light, through a brief darkness.'"

Victoria thanked her but sat stunned. Her uncle's kindness and generosity had saved her when she was most in need of saving. And now he was gone from her.

The doorbell rang at that moment.

"Who could that be on Christmas evening? I'm not expecting anyone, are you?" Alice asked.

Victoria continued to stroke the letter and gave no reply.

"I'll go see who it is. Try a bite of those cookies. They may bring some comfort."

But Victoria didn't want another sip of sherry or to taste anything sweet, her sadness beginning to register in her bones. Poor Edwina must be feeling it too. She would visit her as soon as possible. Would her aunt stay in the little village of Blaine and run the store in her uncle's memory? Or would she return to her lonely, though busy, days in Portland and on the sea? Edwina had loved her child and her husband, and now both were gone.

Victoria blew her nose into the handkerchief and when she lifted her eyes Jonathan Cartwright was standing before her, dripping slow puddles on to the carpet. His cheeks were chafed and raw from the cold, and his sandy hair wet from thawing snow. His brow knotted and she wondered if there was trouble with him or his business—had a sudden illness provoked him to visit on Christmas Day? Was Perry all right? Was Emma?

But then she understood that the concern on his face was not for himself, but for her. When inviting him in, Alice must have told him of her uncle's unexpected passing. Victoria wiped her nose, somewhat more aware of her appearance. But before she could say hello, Jonathan had rushed to her side and knelt down at her feet before the fire.

"I'm so terribly sorry, Victoria." He reached for her hand with frigid fingers. "What tragic news to receive on Christmas Day. You poor, dear, excellent woman."

Victoria looked down at her hand in his. Alice entered the study at that moment but seeing the young man on bended knee, she promptly turned back around, mumbled something about needing more cookies from the kitchen, and left them alone. Victoria and Jonathan noticed their entwined fingers, and both seemed aware of the awkwardness of his position. He gathered his wits and stood.

From the heat of the fire and the sherry and her sadness, Victoria felt light-headed. She brought her handkerchief to her brow, but realized that gesture, too, was too much like one of Mrs. Swann's characters. She tossed the linen cloth to her lap and shut her eyes.

"You've been through so much." Jonathan shifted to the armchair opposite hers. "Enduring the worst mistreatment by your husband and your publisher too. You are heroic in your capacity to manage it all. I find you to be—" He paused, searching for the words.

Victoria peeked out and through her lashes, his blazing blue eyes caught the firelight and she shut them again.

"Remarkable! You are a remarkable woman."

"Thank you." Victoria recalled that was how her father had described Ruthann when first pledging his love.

"I don't think you grasp my meaning," Jonathan continued. "I mean to say, it goes without saying that you're a remarkable writer."

Her eyes opened a little more to see him point to the round table in the center of the room where he had placed her manuscript.

"Your newest book is brilliant."

This news might have meant a great deal to her on any other

day. But beneath the layers of sadness, she could only dip her head lower and retreat into the encompassing leather chair. A puff of hidden pipe smoke from the cushions reached her and she thought of her uncle and started to cry.

"I mean it," Jonathan said, as if she had argued the point. "This is going to be a truly fine book. If you will allow us, Perry and I will see that many people read it. We will make it our absolute mission."

Victoria barely moved.

"Also, I genuinely appreciate your earlier efforts as well." He stood and began to circle the rug before the fire. "I look forward to working with your aunt, after her period of mourning, of course. And our intention is to carry on in the style Mrs. Swann has made famous, because it is so worthwhile, albeit with a more modern approach."

Victoria raised an eyebrow because this, too, might have brought her joy on any other day.

"You have a knack, Victoria, an absolute knack." Jonathan gripped his hands behind his back, like a professor lecturing a class. "A talent, I say, for telling a keen story, but with actual sentiments that reach the reader in most piercing ways."

She watched as he strode, his head bobbing for emphasis, the lock of blond hair falling across his brow.

"Your earlier novels are clever, but they also get to the heart of the matter."

"The heart?" she repeated.

"Yes, I believe you are an expert on the heart," he insisted. "Don't you think so? You seem to know the business of the heart extremely well."

"I suppose that makes sense, given that I was a romance writer for years."

"Oh no!" he practically shouted as he stepped closer and abruptly knelt down before her again. "You mustn't think of yourself as merely a romance writer. You are far, far more than that."

Victoria inched back in her seat and Edwina's letter fell to the carpet, but she did not retrieve it. Jonathan took her hand and squeezed it harder this time.

"You are an exceptional writer, no matter the category. But also, and here is my point—"

He paused, and they both became aware that he was in the same awkward pose. How had Jonathan done it not once, but twice?

"Heavens. I'm terrible at this."

What was he trying to say?

"What I'm trying to say is that you're not only a fine writer, but a fine person. A fine human being. A very fine human being indeed." He pumped her hand up and down.

"That's kind of you to say, Jonathan." She tried to retract her hand, but he wouldn't let go.

He lowered his voice to not more than a whisper. "Victoria, I'm no master of words like you. I can help you with yours, but I cannot seem to generate my own with any grace. And yet, I feel that together we can create something of great significance."

"You mean," she asked—with some hesitation, for who knew what a man on bended knee might mean?—"as editor and author?"

"Yes!" he shouted and gripped her fingers painfully. "And," he added, tipping toward her, "also as devoted, life-long friends. I would like that. Would you like that too?"

His question took her back to the window seat overlooking her father's farm where she had longed for someone to join her but had only the book in her lap for company. She was that same girl now, and the writer that girl had become. All the versions of herself both on the page and off came together to answer Jonathan Cartwright in the study of Henry Wadsworth Longfellow.

"Why, yes, of course, I'd like that. Now stand up, you silly man. You're making me nervous."

But the truth of it was, she had a dear friend.

Jonathan studied his pose and laughed. "I do so love a romantic trope."

"Don't we all."

Alice came into the room with cookies on a tray. "Pardon me. I don't mean to intrude."

"Not at all." Jonathan stood and brushed off his knees. "We were exchanging vows."

Alice stopped, her brow creased.

"Vows of friendship," Victoria clarified.

"Ah, that makes more sense. I wouldn't want the gentleman to go off course. We all know who *he's* fond of."

Jonathan tried to mumble a reply.

"It's all right," Victoria said. "Love is love, and we'd be fools not to accept it."

"You seem to know how," Alice said. "I saw you last night under the mistletoe."

Heat warmed Victoria's collar, but not unpleasantly. If Alice had seen it, it hadn't been a dream.

Jonathan scooped a cookie from the tray and pointed it at her. "I was saying that Victoria here is an expert on the heart. She knows all about love."

Victoria sank back into the leather cushions and realized he might be right.

FORTY-TWO

Spring blooms spread a gaudy profusion over the Boston Public Garden for which the weather-worn citizens were nothing but grateful. In the first week of June, the bursting cherry and plum trees attracted attention. The willows dipped their light green strands into the Lagoon, the copper beeches shimmered in the dappled late-afternoon light, and the mild air stirred the emerald grass. Oh, Boston, so miserable so much of the year, and yet so ready to forget it for the rest.

Victoria waved down from the iron-railed walking bridge to Dottie and Fletcher as they boarded a swan boat at the edge of the pond. Once seated on a bench, Dottie turned her baby daughter around on her lap and made her pudgy little hand wave up at her auntie. The water soon began to churn at the stern as the driver peddled out from shore. At the start of the summer season, the wooden bird's feathers were freshly painted white with a bright red beak and shining black eyes. The frivolous conveyance appeared stately as it glided over the dark waters.

Victoria called out, "Bon voyage!" and headed along the path through the Boston Common. Crossing to the other side, she passed Joy Street at the base of Beacon Hill with its window boxes overflowing, brass knockers and doorknobs recently shined. Late as usual, she didn't stop to admire the State House with its extravagant gold dome, so out of keeping with Boston's puritanical tastes, yet the pride of the city, nonetheless. The new statue of General Shaw and his honorable regiment caught the last rays of light coming over the capital, its patina appropriately as black as onyx.

A little out of breath from the climb, she arrived at the venerable Boston Athenaeum. As if at the entrance to a pharaoh's tomb, the thick bronze doors had been propped open, and Victoria needed only a little muscle to part the red leather-fronted interior ones. The Athenaeum, being a private library, was usually quiet and somber. But as she stepped inside, she was greeted by the voices of partygoers. On this early summer evening, Boston's most select book aficionados gathered to celebrate the annual awards hosted by the Boston Literary Society.

From behind a linen-covered table, a young assistant welcomed her and on learning her name, she clapped her gloved hands together in delight. "Oh, Miss Meeks, we've been waiting to meet you. We're all rooting for you, ma'am."

Another young lady stepped forward and stuttered words of encouragement as others materialized from all sides—the serving girls and kitchen helpers and young librarians. Victoria thanked them all. One took her linen duster and held it in open arms, as if it were made of golden thread, while another curtsied and presented her with the evening's program. They pointed her in the direction of the crystal punch bowl and Victoria stepped away.

She was proud to be here but had no illusions that she would win an award. Although her novel had received favorable reviews in *The Boston Daily Globe* and *The New York Herald*—the first of her books to warrant a response in a serious publication—no one had called it a masterpiece. And thanks to Alice, she had given readings for the ladies of Cambridge and Boston and Perry had arranged a program in the private dining room of the St. Jerome's Club. She was only the second woman ever to set foot on the upper floors, the first being Mrs. Ida Saxton McKinley, the invalid wife of the president, who rarely left his side.

Victoria accepted a punch cup. The pink bubbly, with an extravagant strawberry floating in it for added panache, went down smoothly. She was about to take a second sip when Jonathan and Perry appeared at her side.

Raising their own crystal cups, Perry said, "To your good luck."

"And to yours," she replied, taking another tasty swallow.

"We worried you might not make it in time. They're about to start the program," Jonathan said.

"Sorry, I got waylaid by baby Vicky."

"Totally understandable. She's quite adorable," he said.

Dressed in surprising satin, Emma came swishing in and gave Victoria a kiss on the cheek. "I brought my lucky hare's foot. Mother says we're bound to win with it."

"My father had a lucky horseshoe over the barn door. It often did the trick for us at the county fair," Victoria said.

Jonathan emptied his cup. "I believe good luck has already befallen us."

"But a win wouldn't hurt," Perry added.

At the front of the room, the master of ceremonies was calling everyone to attention. In a practical Boston way, folding chairs had been set out for elders or the infirm, but everyone else would stand while the brief proceedings took place in the sunlit library. High above them in pristine, half-dome alcoves sat white marble busts of literary greats dating back to Roman times, their long noses and prominent foreheads suggesting patrician sagacity and power. The shelves of books on all sides towered over the crowd, while the prize-nominated volumes were passed amongst the guests for visual review, receiving *ooh*s and *aah*s, for they knew a good book when they saw one.

Victoria felt supremely at home here with these book people. She had wanted to know them all her life, ever since Miss Sullivan had first welcomed her into the Town of Lincoln's Public Library. Perhaps it was the punch, but she relished the opening words from the speaker at the podium and admired the dowdy audience who no doubt would have been happier at home in their slippers and robes reading in comfortable chairs.

The categories of awards were many, though when else would the author of a study of shore birds be properly honored for his passion for his subject? Or an historian of the maritime battles of 1812? Or a botanist who not only catalogued, but drew, the fungi of New England? The winners, one after the next, made their way to the podium to thank the Literary Society. Though often their eyes remained on their notes or their feet, Victoria admired them.

She and her friends moved closer to stand before the tall, arched windows overlooking Granary Burial Ground. No one gave a thought to those who lay buried there or to the past that they had inhabited. This was a moment for the future. Reputations were being made and new voices amplified to be heard far and wide.

When the moment came for the announcement of Best Work of Fiction, Victoria felt Emma's gloved hand slip into hers. On her other side, she could feel nervous energy coursing through Jonathan. They exchanged a firm, reassuring glance, as if to say that no matter the outcome, they were a team. But then she heard another author's name and felt Emma's hand go limp.

"It's all right, my dear," Victoria said to her. "We'll try with the next one."

But as the crowd applauded for the winning author, Victoria could hardly make herself pay attention. She gazed up at the shelves of books and blinked back mortifying tears that mercifully did not fall. But in that moist blur, the volumes seemed to rise on clouds up to the heavens. The busts at the top seemed shrouded in white rain and she was far below. It was never to be.

The other author returned to his seat and the master of ceremonies took back the lectern. Victoria put on a smile and waited for him to invite everyone to stay for refreshments. She pulled up her gloves and prepared for the stroll back across the Commons. It would be her reward.

But as she started toward the exit, Emma snatched her hand and Victoria turned to the front of the room where the gentleman was speaking. Before she could catch on, he had removed his pince nez, and was saying her name.

"We've won!" Emma squealed.

Jonathan patted Victoria vigorously on the shoulder and Perry pumped her hand.

"Best Book of the Year. Congratulations!"

The applause rolled toward her and Victoria froze in place until she felt Jonathan push her forward. As she made her way up the aisle, some members of the audience smiled confidently as if to show they'd known it all along. Victoria certainly hadn't known it, but here she was, making her way to the podium. The master of ceremonies stepped forward and greeted her with a formal bow. A young lady with stars in her eyes held up a thin gold medallion on a tasteful black ribbon for everyone to see. With trembling hands, she tied it around Victoria's neck.

With the medal on her chest, Victoria was transported back to the county fairs of her childhood. She had received the first of her ribbons for the best children's apple pie, followed in subsequent years by awards for peach preserves, and, the most meaningful of all, a blue ribbon for her first story. Each award had mattered equally to her in its moment of glory, and this was no different. She stepped forward and the audience gazed up at her, ready to listen. But Victoria was afraid she had nothing left to say. Hadn't she said it all already in her books?

She cleared her throat and pulled herself together to thank the esteemed Boston Literary Society for this honor and the audience for their kind attention. What she really wanted to say wasn't for them, as friendly as they seemed. She would have liked to thank Dottie, absorbed in her new life as a mother, and Edwina, too busy manning the store up in Blaine to get away. She would thank her father and her uncle, both gone, yet here with her just the same. Victoria wanted to mention these dear people, living and departed, who had helped her become the writer and woman she was today. Instead, she turned to the side of the room where her friends stood beaming.

"I'm grateful to my publisher, Perry Bliss, whose generosity has made this possible. And to my editor, Jonathan Cartwright, who challenged me to write better and so I did."

While this sounded like an easy prescription for success, the writers, editors, and publishing professionals in the crowd understood it was anything but. They continued to gaze at her, clearly wanting more. Victoria gripped the lectern with both

hands and would have liked to give them more but remained at
a loss for words.

It was then that she noticed the young ladies who had
appeared from every corner of the Athenaeum. Several wore
aprons or uniforms. One balanced in her strong arms a full tray
of dirty dishes she must have been clearing from the reception
room. Even the cook in her white hat had come out from the
kitchen to stand at attention in her sensible shoes. They formed
a line at the rear of the room, and some held hands in girlish
excitement. Several pressed handkerchiefs to their eyes and
appeared to be weeping.

"What a wonderful surprise for me, but also for my readers."
She turned in their direction. "As you may know, for many years
I was the author of romance and adventure novels. I set my
characters in distant lands and took my readers far away from
our present place and time. I believe that my readers and I enjoyed our fictional journeys together."

"That we did!" the cook called out, brandishing a ladle in
the air.

The audience turned, shocked at the outburst but interested,
too, because they could sense something different afoot with
this author.

"But over time," Victoria continued, "I realized that my readers deserved more. They deserved stories that reflected their
lives in the here and now. Stories in which *they* are the true heroines. In recent months, I've come to see that so many women
have stories to tell, but few have the privilege or opportunity to
tell them. I am profoundly grateful to be able to use my voice to
share my version of their stories as best as I can."

The older ladies in the audience nodded crisply at this sensible idea, while their husbands fiddled with the programs on
their laps.

"And," Victoria continued, building up some steam, "while
rewarding adventures once took place only in fictional landscapes like those of Mrs. Swann, in today's world, at the start
of a new century, we women are freer to go in search of more

fulfilling lives. We have created for ourselves a new and different reality. These young ladies," she gestured to the back of the room, "right here in our midst are the inspiration for my novel that you have so graciously awarded a prize to today. I could not have done it without them. For *they* are the brave ones. *They* are the ones deserving of our applause."

Victoria started the clapping this time and the patrons turned in their seats to study these heroic women more closely. They were surprised to notice the coat check girl, waitresses, maids, and the meek librarians who they routinely spoke to without ever really seeing. Why, they thought, these women were nothing special, but at the encouragement of the lady author, they gamely applauded, because they gathered that was the point.

Victoria thanked the Boston Literary Society again and started to move away from the podium. But after taking a few steps, she noticed a rickety cane wheelchair tucked into one of the alcoves. Out of the way and unseen, in it sat a shriveled old woman. Though she was bent double, the lady squinted up at Victoria with unbounded pride. Peering down at her, Victoria could see emerging from the ancient features, a person whom she had loved dearly many years before. For here, before her, was the wise and patient wall-eyed librarian of her youth.

"Miss Sullivan? Can it really be you?"

Victoria knelt before her and caught the attention of her one good eye. She wanted to fall upon the old woman's breast in a long embrace but instead let out a cry and returned to the podium.

"Excuse me, excuse me, everyone," she called out to the audience that had begun to gather up their things. "Please, stay another moment. I want to share something important with you."

The audience turned back to her. Who was this bold woman author demanding their attention? Weren't cakes and tea being served in the next room? But they did as she asked and sat.

"I'd like you to meet Miss Ruthann Sullivan," Victoria announced. "This wonderful woman seated here. Do you see her?"

The audience craned their necks to spy the tiny lady in the wheelchair.

"This fine woman here was the first person to introduce me to the world of books when I was a child. Though she spoke to me in a whisper, as librarians must, her instruction and insight, like that of *all* librarians, speaks loudly to who we are as a nation. The wisdom of librarians shapes future generations and our democracy hinges on their softly spoken words."

"Hear, hear," came voices from the crowd, for they all loved a good librarian.

The young librarians at the back of the room clenched their fists in rapturous agreement, though of course they didn't shout out loud. Victoria continued, her message gaining in strength.

"I encourage everyone here today to venture outside this venerable private library and explore the grandest public library in the country that has been built down the street in Copley Square. It's magnificent and not called the 'Palace of the People' for nothing!"

Several gentlemen frowned at the comparison to their beloved Athenaeum, though those who had visited the new library had to agree, and the more generous in the audience already supported both institutions.

"My dear aunt Edwina," Victoria continued, "helps to educate children at the Abyssinian Meeting House in Portland, Maine. Closer to home, our esteemed friend Alice Longfellow offers support to the Cambridge Neighborhood House, among other charities. We, as the educated sector of society have an absolute obligation to give of our time and resources to those less fortunate, and to those less literate. Librarians and teachers do this routinely, and so they can be our guides."

The audience turned to the young librarians who could no longer control themselves and were making a great deal of racket.

"In these changing times, we must open our minds and our hearts to learn from a general populous that is growing and changing by the day. These young ladies and those of all stripes new to our shores are exerting a positive influence on society and helping to make our cities more vibrant. It's high time that their strong, clear voices be added to our national conversation."

"Brava!" Emma called out, her voice surprisingly strong and clear.

"Our country is a magnificent tapestry. We must do all that we can to encourage new strands be woven into it. Let's go out and get to know one another, not stay hidden behind our books, though that may be our preference."

The audience's hands remained stuck to their laps at this suggestion.

"Of course," she continued with a conspiratorial smile, "we readers and writers know the profound way that books help us to understand one another. In the pages of a story, we enter into the lives of people we might not otherwise meet, and we grow only the wiser for it."

Her fellow authors mumbled approval of this point and the many readers leaned back, reassured of the superior value of their favorite pastime.

"Stories, as we all know, are woven into the fabric of our lives. Each book we have read and those that some of us have written, create a thicket of recollections and emotions too tangled to unravel in our minds. It is a challenge to parse what was read from what is real in our lives, which only makes our experience of life the richer."

The audience let out a little gasp of recognition, for this they deeply understood.

"A life in books is a joyful swirl of invention, my friends. Life and books, books and life—woven together forever!" Her voice echoed off the many volumes in the literary sanctuary.

The audience burst into applause. They had wanted to hear something uplifting from a gentleman of letters, but a woman of letters would do. This Miss Meeks was all right. They might even buy her book.

Victoria left the podium for the last time and hurried over

to Miss Sullivan. She took the brittle fingers into her own and kissed the parchment of the old woman's cheeks. The perfume of apple blossoms and the warm, familiar scent of old books surrounded the librarian. Victoria's love of them had begun long before. She was that girl reading at the window and this brave, new woman here. Her books and her life were of her own invention, and she was the author of both.

ACKNOWLEDGEMENTS

This novel is wholly fictional although a real woman writer inspired it. Her pen name was Gail Hamilton and in 1867 she sued her Boston publisher, Ticknor and Fields, for deliberately underpaying her compared to her male counterparts. She didn't succeed in court, but her case exposed inequities in the publishing world at that time. After reading a brief description of Hamilton's case, I began to wonder what it must have been like to be a women writer in a renowned bastion of literary men of letters, especially if what she wrote wasn't high literature. Victoria Swann's challenges began to take shape in my mind.

Cambridge, Massachusetts, where Victoria's story takes place and I live, is still a bookish town where it's not unusual for drivers to read at red lights or people to stroll the sidewalks with a paperback held up before their eyes. Our excellent bookstores fuel our reading habit and serve as vibrant and essential community centers. I'm grateful to Dina Mardell and David Sandberg of Porter Square Books and Linda Seamonson of Harvard Bookstore for taking the time to read my manuscript and encourage me with this project.

Cambridge also excels at preserving its own stories. I'm thankful to the following research institutions who helped me properly locate Victoria here in the nineteenth century: the Schlesinger Library at Radcliffe College; Cambridge Room at the Cambridge Public Library; Cambridge Historical Commission; History Cambridge; and the Longfellow House-Washington Headquarters, where down in the basement I was thrilled to hold in my white gloved hands a letter written by Dickens. Nearby, Brandeis University Archives & Special Collections has a trove of original dime novels that helped me understand the popular tastes of that earlier time.

It's been wonderful working with Jaynie Royal, my publisher

and editor at Regal House, and I so appreciate her talented team for expertly bringing this novel to readers. My agent Gail Hochman was generous and wise as ever through the process of finding a publisher. And Megan Beatie's expertise as publicist was also essential to helping Victoria Swann find her way. The authors who endorsed this novel in advance of publication are gems of the literary community and I'm honored and lucky to have their support: Jennifer Finney Boylan, Christopher Castellani, Elizabeth Graver, Marjan Kamali, Margot Livesey, Kerry Maher, Roxana Robinson, Whitney Scharer, Katherine A. Sherbrooke, and Laura Zigman.

Encouragement and insight from fellow writers and dear friends make all the difference, and I'm grateful to those who helped me over the past five years with this book: Jane Rosenman, Caroline Leavitt, Lindsay Hatton, Julie Brown, Margaret Grant, Nicholas Kilmer, Katrin Schumann, Crystal King, Pamela Painter, Anne Bernays, Lynn Waskelis, Margaret Buchanan, Rebecca Ravenal, Julie Heffernan, Lyndy Pye, Valentine Talland, Sandra Chinoporos, Mollie Sherry, Ann Goethals, Kate Davis, and others I'm afraid I may be forgetting.

Editorial acumen and love were once again provided by my husband, John Ravenal, without whom I wouldn't have such a fulfilling literary life. My son Daniel was unfailingly supportive and smart throughout; and with this novel, my daughter, Eva, proved an excellent editor, helping me feel I've done my job as both writer and mother. Nothing is more satisfying than that.

VIRGINIA PYE is an award-winning author of novels and short stories. Her short story collection, *Shelf Life of Happiness*, won the 2019 Independent Publisher Gold Medal for Short Fiction, and one of its stories was nominated for a Pushcart Prize. Her two historical novels set in China, *Dreams of the Red Phoenix* and *River of Dust*, also received literary awards. Virginia's essays have appeared in *The New York Times*, Literary Hub, *The Rumpus*, *Huffington Post*, and the *Cleveland Plain-Dealer*, as well as numerous literary magazines. A graduate of Wesleyan University, with an MFA from Sarah Lawrence College, Virginia moved back to her hometown of Cambridge, MA after thirty-five years living up and down the East Coast. Upon returning, she was struck by how Boston, and specifically Cambridge, is noticeably more bookish than all the other cities where she had lived. www.virginiapye.com